TILLER'S WATCH

Joe Pilgrim was a gun-artiste and troubleshooter who would go anywhere. But the trip to the town with the strange-sounding name was a mystery, and at first he couldn't find the man who'd sent for him. Then there was the legend of the old gold strike and a prospector who'd died as he watched the lake that held many secrets. Soon, Pilgrim was caught in the long brewing, bloody aftermath of an unsolved past crime.

JAY HILL POTTER

TILLER'S WATCH

Complete and Unabridged

LINFORD
Leicester

First published in Great Britain in 1997 by
Robert Hale Limited
London

First Linford Edition
published 1998
by arrangement with
Robert Hale Limited
London

The right of Jay Hill Potter to be identified
as the author of this work has been asserted
by him in accordance with the
Copyright, Designs and Patents Act, 1988

British Library CIP Data

Potter, Jay Hill
    Tiller's watch.—Large print ed.—
Linford western library
    1. Western stories
    2. Large type books
    I. Title
    823.9'14 [F]

ISBN 0–7089–5368–9

Published by
F. A. Thorpe (Publishing) Ltd.
Anstey, Leicestershire
Set by Words & Graphics Ltd.
Anstey, Leicestershire
Printed and bound in Great Britain by
T. J. International Ltd., Padstow, Cornwall

This book is printed on acid-free paper

Part One

Message for Murder

1

The town was in a valley at the edge of a small lake and had been hard to find. Pilgrim had never heard of it before. It had a telegraph office, though, and from there a message had reached him at Fort Worth where he'd been sojourning for a while.

However, how had the correspondent, Creegan, known Pilgrim was at Fort Worth?

He'd never heard of anybody called Tim Creegan. Nobody he'd discreetly questioned at Fort Worth seemed to have heard of Creegan either. But when he was nearer to his destination, the town with the strange name of Tiller's Watch, he heard the name Creegan mentioned, though not numerously or helpfully.

He viewed the place from the other side of the lake and next to a rocky hump that at a distance looked like a great dead buffalo.

Then it was a huge shadow as the sun shone in his eyes and he had to shade them with one hand under the brim of his Stetson.

He skirted the lake by a narrow well-used trail which widened as it curved its way into the main street. Smaller streets and passages led off this in a higgledy-piggledy way as was often the case with smaller Western settlements. Bits had been added on piecemeal over the years, all sorts and shapes and sizes.

Folks moved about. Animals. Vehicles. Pilgrim gentled his horse towards a building that seemed to have the most horses racked at its hitching posts.

The local saloon. Maybe folks imbibed early here. Maybe the place did a good breakfast.

There was a long trough at one end of the rack and he looped his horse there, said, 'I'll get you some oats, boy.' The neat paint stallion flicked

4

one ear, already had his nose in the brackish water.

Pilgrim was still on the sidewalk, the saloon batwings ahead of him, when they swung and two men came out, shoulder to shoulder.

Both of them laughed in the newcomer's face. One of them said, 'Here he is I guess.' Pilgrim didn't think he'd seen either of them before.

He went to step around them. One of them hooked a foot, tripping him up. He lurched forward and hit the log wall between the batwings and a grimy window.

The tripping had obviously been deliberate. But a mite misjudged.

Pilgrim might have gone headfirst through the doors; but he'd missed them and the wall held him up, hands against it as he regained his balance.

The wall did him no harm at all. He swung half-around.

He hadn't reached for his gun. But he saw that one of the men had his hand on the butt of his own weapon.

5

Pilgrim raised his elbow, drove it. The hard bone struck the man just above his belly, between his ribs, propelling him backwards. He hit his companion broadside and they both spun across the boardwalk.

One of them landed on his ass on the chewed wooden edge and a tethered horse took umbrage and began to skitter.

The feller was too involved in scrambling away from iron-shod hooves to worry about the stranger by the batwings. But his partner, beginning to rise, had his gun half-out of its holster.

He went grey under his tan when he saw that Pilgrim had him well and truly covered.

Speaking then, though, was the big man who came through the batwings with a bulky, shiny carbine in his fists.

'Why don't you boys shuck your hardware an' do this right?'

'This ain't your put-in, Dacey,' said

the man who faced Pilgrim.

Having evaded the fractious cayuse, the second feller stood in a safer position and stared blankly at the little scene before him.

The big man with the elevated shooter said, 'You're creating a disturbance in front of my place an' I sort of take hurt at that.'

Half-turned now, gun levelled, eyes as watchful as a cougar's, Pilgrim said, 'I'm willing to do what you suggest, my friend, and I thank you for your put-in.'

'I do what I gotta do.' The big man called Dacey looked half-Indian. His jet eyes surveyed the two hardcases, both youngish like the newcomer, both hardbitten like the newcomer. 'You heard what the man said.'

The one directly in front of Pilgrim grinned and unbuckled his gunbelt, handed it to Dacey who took one hand off the carbine. The second man followed his partner's example but wasn't grinning, looked mean.

7

Pilgrim pouched his gun. A rotund individual came through the batwings and Dacey said, 'Hold these for me, Hank, will yuh?'

'Sure will, Dacey,' said the fat man and took the three belts with their armoury.

More folks started to come out of the saloon as the three contestants moved past the hitching rack and the now browsing horseflesh and out on to the rough-terrained street.

Pilgrim was a little in front of the other two. He stopped dead, turned. Maybe the partners had figured to close in on him. But they were both a mite too late. There was something tigerishly swift about the newcomer's attack.

It certainly took the meaner, dumber of the two other fellers by surprise. He was stopped dead by a fist like a hammer.

It was as if, like Pilgrim before him, he had run into a wall.

Then he toppled. All the way. His

head hit the sun-baked ground with a thud and he lay still.

Like a corpse stretched out for burying.

His partner had quicker reflexes, flung up his fists to protect himself. He half-crouched too, and though Pilgrim's pile-driving blow smashed through his guard it only hit his temple, glanced off.

He was spun around however. But he didn't go down. As he was swaying, regaining his balance, he managed to drive the toe of his heavy riding boot into his opponent's knee.

Pilgrim's one leg gave way beneath him, the pain shooting up to his groin. He fell sideways. The other man was still dazed. His second blow only buffeted his opponent's shoulder, spinning him, not dropping him. And the two fighters were momentarily apart.

Pilgrim had all the tricks of a street fighter. He let himself sag. The other man's fist came at him again (this feller was no slouch himself), grazed the top of his head.

All three had doffed their hats, hung them on the end of the horse-rack. The fallen man was still unconscious on his back, the sun in his eyes . . .

Pilgrim let himself fall. Not hard. He rolled away from his man. Then he leapt to his feet, went for his man head-on, taking him by surprise with this tactic, favouring his own bruised knee at the same time.

Hoppity. Amid delighted shouts from the crowd as the two men clashed. And now the attacker's fists worked like pistons.

His opponent was driven back, fell over the unconscious man on the sod.

Pilgrim's momentum carried him on.

For a few moments it seemed that the two fighters were squabbling like animals over some prey. Then they were away from that, the man on the ground in no peril now but groaning, beginning to come round.

The two other men crouched low,

facing each other. The crowd screamed them on. Big Dacey held over-excitable onlookers at bay, yelling, 'Let 'em finish it.'

Both men hurled themselves forward. They clashed. Dust rose, half-clouding them. They were both down. It was the newcomer who rose first. Awkwardly, painfully, and when upright moving again, hoppity.

His two opponents lay at his feet, the second one unconscious now, the first one groaning, trying to sit up.

Pilgrim, swaying, said, 'Goddamnit, that's a fine way to welcome a feller to a new town.'

2

Dacey said, 'C'mon inside an' get yourself fixed up.'

Pilgrim said, 'I want some oats for my nag.'

Evidently a somewhat singleminded young man. 'That can be done.' Dacey turned as folks clustered around them. 'Give those two their gear and get them on their horses. Tell 'em I don't want to see 'em again until they learn to behave themselves.'

He led Pilgrim into the saloon which wasn't enormous but appeared well appointed. 'Do you know those two?'

'Never saw 'em before in my life.'

'Well, they weren't drunk. I've never seen either of them really drunk.'

'Maybe they took exception to my face, me being a stranger an' all.'

Pilgrim went on to introduce himself. Dacey did the same. But Pilgrim, of

12

course, already knew the big feller's name and that he owned the saloon and, judging by his actions, was a force to be reckoned with in the curiously named town of Tiller's Watch.

'Pilgrim. I think I heard the name someplace.'

'It's likely. How about those other two jaspers?'

'Dill Rickles. That isn't his real name o' course. He's the smart one. And his regular pard, Knocky Dowson, who ain't so smart. But they both seem to get along all right.'

'Doing what?'

'This an' that.' Not a forthright answer now from this forthright man.

And they had gone right through and were in a spacious, shining kitchen. A lady came through a door and asked, 'Trouble again, Obe?'

'Nothing we couldn't handle, honey.' Dacey introduced the lovely, elegant Mexican lady as his wife, Reba. Her hand was cool and firm and she appraised the newcomer with bright brown eyes and smiled and said, 'You look like you walked into a wall.'

Dacey spluttered with laughter, a deep explosive sound. 'He did. An' a couple of moving walls also.'

'Sit down, Mr Pilgrim.'

'Folks call me Joe, ma'am.'

'All right, Joe.' She had a pure American accent. 'I'll go get my stuff.' She left the room.

Dacey said softly, 'Pilgrim. A hired gun.'

'I prefer to call myself a range detective.' It was a new thing with him.

'Here on business, huh?'

'Likely.'

The quiet session of questions — and ambiguous answers — was at an end then as Reba came back.

She had everything that was needed and was very gentle.

Pilgrim felt as good as new again and was sipping hot coffee, Dacey opposite him doing the same, Reba about her household chores when the crackle of gunfire came from outside.

Both men shot to their feet.

'Stay here, honey.'

'All right.'

The two men went through the back door and round, up an alley to Main Street, Dacey leading the way, saying then, 'The livery stables.' Some folks were already trotting down that way.

A man came running back, said, 'It was Dill an' Knocky. Young Pete was sassy with them, joshin' about them lookin' beat up. They hung him up in the roof.'

'Who did the shooting?'

'That was ol' Cracker. Don't think he hit anything. He see'd them two riding out, just as he was comin' back from yur place, Dacey. Young Pete was screaming and sort of chokin'.'

They had the fifteen-year-old boy down on the floor. His face was red and he was still choking a bit, tears rolling down his cheeks.

Somebody said, 'The sheriff's coming.'

15

'He must be back from his trip then,' said Dacey.

'Pete's gonna be all right,' said the old hostler, Cracker.

A stout man came in out of the sun, a silver star shining on his checkered chest. He was out of breath. But he was smart, got the gist quickly, said, 'No matter what the boy said they shouldn't have served him like that. Hell, they could've throttled him to death. I'm goin' after them two. Where's Jules? Anybody seen Jules?'

Nobody had seen Sheriff Salliwell's deputy lately. 'I'll go with you,' said Dacey.

'So will I,' said the lean, dark man called Pilgrim.

The sheriff looked at him hard. 'I'll vouch for him,' said Dacey, surprisingly.

There were other volunteers. 'These two'll do,' said the plump sheriff, brusquely. 'Rest of you go on about your business.'

The trio rode out. Round the lake.

Past the outcrop that looked like a dead buffalo. No signs of riders ahead of them. A few cattle. What looked like a dog in the distance, disappearing in the growing, heat-haze, could've been a coyote.

They veered off the trail away from the direction that Pilgrim had taken when he made for Tiller's Watch. Small hills appeared like waiting puppies.

Dacey began, 'Do you think they . . . ?'

Sheriff Salliwell made a sound like 'Ug' and swayed in the saddle. The whiplash crack of a rifle echoed. 'Spread out,' yelled Salliwell thickly, then he fell from the horse.

Pilgrim was first down. 'I'll be all right,' grunted the fat lawman. He'd been hit in the shoulder. His eyes rolled and he passed out.

Pilgrim vaulted into the saddle. Dacey, figuring that the lawman was going to live, was galloping his horse on a slanting way. Pilgrim made a sort of quarter-circle, keeping abreast of

17

Dacey, a sizeable gap between them.

They both took out their hand-guns. Another rifle-bullet zipped over Dacey's head. They saw the white puff of smoke in the sunlight and they opened up, figuring to at least pin the marksman down, curb his enthusiasm: whoever he was, he was no slouch.

They hit the rocks, left the horses, took cover. Looking back Pilgrim saw that the fat sheriff was on his feet, was sheltering behind his standing horse. The rifleman had lost interest in him and Salliwell was doubtless trying to fix himself up best he could.

There was silence above in the bigger rocks.

The two men were closer to each other. The horses browsed below, taking their chances. The sniper didn't show himself. Not even dust pattered now.

Pilgrim made a signal to Dacey, mouthed silently, 'Cover me.'

Dacey nodded and, circuitously, Pilgrim began to crawl. Nothing happened. He paused. Dust whispered. He picked up a stone and threw it to the side of him, away from Dacey.

The rifle sponged, the slug not near either of them. Pilgrim fanned the hammer of his cunningly modified, heavy Starr pistol, sending a stream of lead up at the rocks where, again, he thought he had detected a puff of smoke.

There was no answering fire. Just rolling echoes. Dying. And then silence.

Out of the corner of his eye Pilgrim saw that Dacey had begun to move, not coming too close, just climbing. Crawling on his belly, keeping his ass down, his bulk.

Pilgrim did the same, lean like a snake.

Dust pattered. Small stones left them. Small stones went past them, as if there was movement up above them also. But there was no more sign. No more shooting.

But then a voice. Calling. As if for help.

3

There was another sound. The clattering of hooves, an echo. Fading quickly, the echo too. But still the voice calling plaintively. Words: sounded like 'Help me.'

'Watch yourself,' said Dacey to Pilgrim. But, keeping their heads down, they both climbed.

When they reached the lone man in the rocks he had passed out. Like the sheriff down below he'd been hit in the shoulder. There was no rifle beside him and his hand-gun was in is holster.

Dacey said, 'Knocky Dowson. Dill Rickles' sidekick. I guess Dill's long gone now. And we have to get back to our horses anyway. Better take this jasper, and the sheriff, back to town.'

'Sure,' said Pilgrim. 'I'll help yuh. But I ain't stoppin'.'

Dacey said, 'I guess Dill was more

drunk than I thought.' He had said previously that the two men could hold their liquor: words to that effect. Pilgrim wasn't buying much of anything now.

Sheriff Salliwell had fixed himself a tourniquet, was fully conscious, cussing a blue streak, the obscenities thickening when he spotted Dowson who was whimpering like a sick calf. They'd found his horse in a dip in the hills and piled him on it.

Not accepting help from anybody the fat lawman climbed up on to his own mount. He watched impatiently as Dacey gave Knocky Dowson the kind of help with his shoulder that he (the sheriff) had earlier done for his ownself. Then, not going too fast, they turned back for town.

A lone rider came to meet them round the edge of the lake. It was Jules, Salliwell's deputy, a lean young man with a black pencil moustache and a dandy appearance. Dacey said in an undertone that Jules had probably been off sparking a filly someplace. He'd been pinch-hitting for Salliwell while the latter went up country visiting. The town had been quiet, though.

Until Pilgrim turned up . . .

Knocky was conscious and talking in agonized bursts. That bastard Dill shouldn't have left him. Dill had only meant to scare off the pursuers, hadn't aimed to hit anybody. Said his foot had slipped or something as he fired a shot. Even while reviling Dill, Knocky seemed to be giving his partner an alibi.

Pilgrim asked why the two men had attacked him. Knocky said he didn't know why, Dill never told him anything.

Pilgrim snarled, 'Goddamn stupid.' Seeming to dismiss the whole business out of hand. But Dacey knew he didn't.

After helping Dacey at the doc's, Pilgrim went riding. He didn't ask Dacey to accompany him and Dacey didn't make the offer.

* * *

As he rode a name went round and round in his head.

He had almost forgotten it.

It had been knocked out of his head, he thought, by the violent encounter with Dill Rickles and Knocky Dowson. And so much had happened since then.

Things often happened to him. More times than most he himself made them happen.

Well, now Dowson was laid up. And Rickles was on the hoof.

Come to think of it Pilgrim still bore his lumps from the violent altercation with Dill and Knocky. He still owed Dill for a bruised and aching knee. But first things first. Or back to the beginning square on the checkerboard.

The name: *Tim Creegan*. That was the moniker of the man who had invited him to Tiller's Watch in the first place. And in that town, what with all that had happened, Pilgrim hadn't asked about Creegan, hadn't mentioned the name to anybody.

Hell, he could be as cagey as the rest of 'em! And after the fight outside the saloon . . .

He remembered noticing that the saloon sign, lopsided and hardly swinging, had had the name obliterated by weather and what looked like bullet holes.

He had heard it being called merely Dacey's Place, which seemed appropriate anyway.

That gink Dacey played his cards close to his chest all right. But he'd been a good man to have as a sidekick in a pinch. Certainly as good as a fat lawman who'd gotten himself shot-up by a sniper.

Riding into Tiller's Watch in the first place Pilgrim hadn't spotted much sign of habitation till he came to the lake and saw the town on the other side of the gleaming water. So now he'd decided to go out the other side.

And, eventually, and not too far

from town he hit what might have been called pay-dirt.

It was in the shape of a sprawling smallholding beside the thin ribbon of a creek. Little more than a conglomeration of hutments as it was, it would have been difficult to pick out which was the main house and which was shelter for the lone mule, the few scuttling chickens, the raggy dog that began to bark but did not attack and, as the rider got nearer, shut up and began to wag a raggy tail.

A woman came out of a low middle building. She had long black hair, not raggy but flowing, and no tail, just a rifle and a threatening expression.

'Hold hard, stranger,' she said.

He saw that she was beautiful, even in a shirtwaist, a floppy brown linsey skirt and riding boots. Her waist was slim, her breasts high and plumply round. He heard that her voice, sweetly contralto, and feminine, had a quiver to it.

He said, 'I come in peace, ma'am.'

She was the second lovely woman he'd seen since he hit this territory. The other one was Reba Dacey. But she was as old as her husband Obe, or almost. This one, though, was of about Pilgrim's own age, maybe somewhat younger.

Unspeaking now, she seemed to be weighing him up. But she didn't lower the rifle.

I suppose it is time I showed a hand or two, he thought. And he said, 'I am a sort of lost traveller looking for a man called Tim Creegan.'

Then he was looking past the woman as the man in a wheelchair came round the side of the house, pushing with hands at the rims of the wheels, pushing powerfully, coming fast.

Rifle still ready, the woman only slightly turned her head. Pilgrim didn't move, patiently sitting on the paint stallion, the intelligent beast taking his cue from his master and only flicking his ears as he often did.

The woman said, 'This is my

husband, Jabez,' as the man drew his equipage up beside her.

He, too, was of about Pilgrim's age. Dark, sturdy, fit-looking. Except for the motionless legs which appeared strangely lifeless.

'He's looking for Tim Creegan,' she said.

The man had a shrewd look. He was almost as handsome as his wife. He said, 'Tim's place is 'bout two miles ahead. But if you're just moseying, come in for a cup o' coffee.'

'That's handsome of you,' Pilgrim said. 'I can bide just a while.' He got down from the saddle.

In the small cluttered kitchen, sipping coffee that was good, he learned that the Clandells were Debbie and Jabez. And he learned something about Tim Creegan, though not much.

It seemed that he was something of a recluse and the Clandells saw him but rarely. He didn't visit town much either and they had figured that maybe he got things he wanted delivered from elsewhere, even from Tombstone which was in the far distance. Maybe Creegan went to Tombstone. Jabez didn't think much of Tombstone.

Pilgrim wondered how this virile young man had come to such a pass, a shadow of pain across his face from time to time as he talked with a sort of cynical intelligence.

About his condition Jabez had no information for the good-looking but hard-bitten young stranger who called himself Pilgrim. All in all, the Clandells weren't too forthcoming about Tim Creegan either.

The couple invited him to call again if he passed that way and he bade them 'so long' and continued on his shortish journey.

Two miles or so. And no other habitation between the Clandell place and the Creegan one, and not much difference between them. Did Creegan have a wife? The Clandells hadn't mentioned a wife, family.

Even if Creegan had a spouse she

was no better housewife than was the beautiful Debbie Clandell.

Pilgrim wondered whether somehow he'd gone astray. He remembered the gist of Creegan's message. 'Urgent — pay highest rates'.

Certainly Pilgrim didn't sell his talents cheaply: he had a rep to consider.

There was nothing wealthy-looking about this conglomeration. Far, far from it. He reined in his horse. Nothing moved. There was a brooding silence.

He called, 'Halloah the house', then wondered if he'd been premature, was looking to get his head blown off.

But still there was no sound, no movement. 'C'mon, boy.' A pressure of his knees. The paint moved.

Nobody came out to meet them. There looked to be a main house, a bit larger than the gimcrack buildings that surrounded it. With a narrow veranda too, and a newer-looking extra bit tagged on the side.

But Pilgrim, wary, bloody-minded,

didn't make for this edifice. He skirted it. Maybe there was somebody out back.

There were open plains and a soft, soughing breeze which did little to break the silence.

Pilgrim dismounted, said 'Stay, boy' and approached the back door of the main house making very little noise on the hard ground, the patches of stunted grass, the occasional debris, the dust. Certainly not awakening the silence.

4

In the house, windows and doors were closed. At one of the outhouses — Pilgrim couldn't identify which — a door thudded gently in the small breeze. There was no other sound but the searching man's boot-heels clattering on wood floors, sibilantly passing over rush and woven mats.

A two-storey edifice, but with short stairs and two upper rooms little more than attics, ceilings so low that he had to bend a little to pass beneath them.

There was one unmade bed, a lot of junk in the neighbouring upper room. The whole place was clean, but untidy. Signs of human habitation: unwashed crockery in the tiny kitchen, a few garments thrown about, a rifle in a corner, a gunbelt with a pouched Colt over the back of a chair.

Pilgrim stood at the kitchen window

and looked out at the flatness of the plains, no other habitation in sight, nothing moving. Usually if a man was outside his spread for any length of time he at least toted his long gun in case of prowling varmints, animal or human.

The adobe of Tim Creegan — and surely this was it — didn't tell a prosperous story. How could a man who seemed to own so little expect to pay the rates expected by a top gun and investigator like Joe Pilgrim?

On the way in he had seen a few steers. There was one horse in the small corral. But out back here there was nothing. Plumb nothing.

The back door was not locked or bolted. He opened it on creaking hinges and he passed through, leaving it slightly ajar. He skirted the building then moved in and out of the outhouses.

Hay, oats, bundles of straw, bailing wire (he had seen no fences), a privy that stank as privies do in the hot sun. From the corral a brown horse eyed him curiously. Getting nearer, Pilgrim said, 'Where's the old man then, honey?'

The mare chewed stolidly, gave him a look, no more. A big docile beast, probably a workhorse. Had Tim Creegan gone a-riding on another steed?

Whether or not, Pilgrim decided to sojourn no further. 'C'mon, pizen,' he said to his own steed and they moseyed on, the man setting the paint to a steady trot the way they both liked it.

Maybe they were going in the wrong direction. Maybe Creegan had gone to Tiller's Watch and they'd missed each other. Maybe Pilgrim had been taking coffee with the Clandells when Creegan passed that way.

Maybe Creegan had learned that Pilgrim was in Tiller's Watch and had gone to meet him there. But how had Creegan learned that, who could've told him? Who else had ridden out this way? Dill maybe. But Dill could've gone the other way.

Pilgrim hadn't forgotten Dill. He owed Dill, but had figured that the business with Creegan was more important. Now he was back with Dill; and with Dill's partner, the injured Knocky who hadn't been able to tell anybody anything.

Were Dill and Knocky somehow in league with Tim Creegan?

But it had seemed that these two had been aiming to prevent Pilgrim from going anyplace for a while, preventing him from seeing Creegan. Maybe! Such a hell of a lot of maybes.

Dill Rickles and Knocky Dowson were sort of hired hands — Obe Dacey had said that — hardcases and pickers-up of unconsidered trifles. Had they been hired by somebody to get in Pilgrim's way? Or had they picked on Pilgrim because he was a stranger, a saddle tramp, and they'd felt like having some rough fun? Obe Dacey had sort of implied that.

Or had he?

I've called myself a range detective, Pilgrim thought, but I sure as hell ain't doing much detecting right now.

The shimmering plains were ahead of him, but then he saw the hills. Have I been wandering in my mind as well, he thought? Those surely were the hills that he'd seen before, where he and Obe and Sheriff Lou Salliwell had been bushwhacked and the lawman had caught a pill in the shoulder.

Like a bunch of squatting puppies, a few upstanding taller dogs hazy behind them in the sun. Waiting for him. Here we go again, he thought. And he kept going.

I'll go that far and look for sign, he determined. And, if I don't find anything, I'll turn back.

He saw the vultures wheeling in the sky. He hadn't seen vultures there before. Some of them were plummeting down into the rocks. He set his horse at a gallop and the obscene birds whirled away with plaintive cries.

He slowed the horse, climbing, the

paint picking his way daintily, snorting his soft contempt of the birds flapping in the blue skies above.

They found where the birds had been. Pilgrim reached for his gun, but then took his hand away from the warm, serrated butt. There was a man sitting against a boulder. Two vultures rose, squawking, and flapped away. The man was undeniably dead.

Pilgrim dismounted. 'Take it easy, son.' The horse blew at him, stayed put. His master approached the corpse.

Red, bloated face, the eyes gone. Some of the clothing too, and some of the flesh it had covered. Mutilated; torn; red gouts.

A grotesque sight. But recognition suddenly flared in Pilgrim's eyes. He was looking at what was left of hardcase Dill Rickles.

He got down on one knee before the corpse, which wasn't smelling yet. How had Dill, who had seemed plumb full of piss and vinegar, come to so suddenly die?

There didn't seem to be any bullet holes. Unless the predators had destroyed any evidence of them, gobbled it.

Dill had a sort of bloated look. Pilgrim thought, a rattler: a rattler got him! Sunning against the rocks, or sleeping beneath. Disturbed, striking in swift fury as a rattler would.

Pilgrim rose, looking warily about him. He didn't see any signs of sidewinders, whether a big diamondback or a little 'un like a coiled speckled ribbon.

He spotted the mouth of the cave a few yards ahead almost directly behind the big boulder where Dill had met his strange come-uppance.

Pilgrim went to the cave. Drawing his gun, he moved slowly into its darkness.

He heard a sound that made the hair prickle at the back of his neck. It sounded like the plaintive whimper of a small, wounded animal.

Pilgrim took out a box of lucifers, shook one out, ignited it with his thumbnail while he kept his gun levelled.

Yellow light blossomed and, in the glow, he saw the second man back there against the curved wall of the cave. The whimper had changed to a mumble.

The man mumbled at him, imploringly. And he went forward, bent, struck another lucifer. The man was naked to the waist. His ankles were lashed with rawhide and, likewise, his hands had been fastened behind his back.

He had been beaten badly, maybe tortured. He was in a bad way, and his rescuer had never seen him before.

There was no other horse except Pilgrim's paint patiently waiting. The vultures were waiting too, hovering above, making plaintive scolding noises.

With his jack-knife Pilgrim cut the captive's bonds.

The man made his loudest sound yet, a sobbing cry of agony as his rescuer lifted him. Then he passed out and Pilgrim was glad of that, carrying him out to the horse.

He figured that Dill's mount had probably made his way back to town.

That was the rescuer's destination now.

5

The shoulder-wound that Knocky Dowson had received was considered by the local doctor to be a particularly bad one. Far worse it seemed than the similar bullet-hole that Sheriff Lou Salliwell had sustained during the same go-down in the hills. The wounded Knocky had been left high and dry there while his partner, Dill Rickles lit out.

Knocky's bones and muscles in his shoulder had been smashed, hideously torn. The big man was scared of the wound, the pain. He whimpered like a sick baby and kept passing out while the doc ministered to him.

The doc, a small irascible Scotsman called McTreen, had finally given the hardcase, who wasn't so very hard, a sedative, putting him out for good and a fair while. The sheriff had said that, under the circumstances, Knocky could remain in bed in the little room behind the surgery in McTreen's place instead of cluttering up the jail.

Anyway, Salliwell's deputy, Jules, would be pinch-hitting for his chief while the wounded fat man rested up, scorning bed though, preferring to prop himself against cushions in his favourite armchair, dozing, his busted fin in his sling, propped on another cushion.

* * *

It was dark in the little back room where Knocky lay, opening his eyes, hurt, scared, not knowing where he was, looking around him slowly, apprehensively. Not so dark outside, folks moving around, talking. Town life. And Knocky remembering then.

At least he wasn't behind bars. But he didn't feel like trying anything. His arm throbbed. *Later*, he told himself, and he snuggled down in the narrow cot like a big infant.

When he awoke again the darkness was absolute. There was somebody in the room with him. Obviously it was that presence that had awakened him.

'That you, Doc?'

There was no reply. But the presence was nearer.

Grunting with pain, Knocky hauled himself up in the bed, not knowing that was the worst thing he could do.

The steel loop went over his head and down and around his throat and was tightened immediately.

He tried to cry out, but he couldn't. He was whimpering again. And then gurgling. Choking. Involuntarily, his one hand went up to his throat. And then clasped the wrist, one of the hands that gripped the steel noose that was choking the life out of him.

There was a blackness shot with a terrible red like an explosion that took him with it, took him down to nothingness.

* * *

It was dark when Pilgrim hit Tiller's Watch. With the battered man still unconscious over the front of the saddle, he'd had to go easily.

There was nothing he could do for the victim except get him to a doctor as soon as possible. At least the man was still alive, if breathing somewhat raggedly.

Pilgrim took him straight to Doc McTreen's place. He'd only met McTreen briefly but had him figured as the genuine article. He met the little man almost on his doorstep, just returned from a birthing on the edge of town, the opposite side to the way Pilgrim had come in: he'd picked the quickest route he could from the hills, missing the Clandell place, and the Greegan place also.

As he rode he'd been doing some cogitating. He wasn't too damn' surprised to learn that the brutalised man he'd hauled back to town was none other than the person he'd been seeking: one Tim Creegan.

'I found a dead one back there as well,' he said. 'I left him for the buzzards.'

Called from the surgery doorstep, a young helper came forward and he and Pilgrim carried the prone form of Tim Creegan inside, laid him on a not very comfortable horsehair couch.

The doc said, 'I've got another one in bed out back. Knocky Dowson. He'll have to be shifted. I guess he's rested. Whether that fin of his is going to be any good to him after all is in the lap of the gods now I guess. I've done the best I can.'

The little Scotsman bustled away. Out of their sight the youth and the lean gunfighter heard McTreen's shocked exclamation. There was a glow from back there. McTreen had lit the lamp. The youth at his heels, Pilgrim went through into the glow, the small room, the sight that had met the doctor's in the yellow glow.

Knocky Dowson, redder-faced than ever, eyes bulging from skull, tongue

44

protruding between teeth and mouth stretched in a rictus of violent death. Stout bailing wire, or something similar, almost hidden, cutting into mutilated flesh, a near decapitation.

A powerful hand had done this, had done it thoroughly and without mercy.

'Great day in the morning,' said the youth, white-faced, open-mouthed, sick.

McTreen turned on him. 'Get back in there, boy.' He retreated. He went out on the stoop and they could hear him puking. But then he began to yell.

The doctor said, 'Stop 'im!' Pilgrim went out. Come back in here an' set, boy.' The youth followed him meekly. But already folk were coming forward, among them Deputy Jules, dark, handsome, self-important.

Pilgrim left them to the sight of Knocky and went into the passage, the surgery one way, the kitchen the other.

The kitchen door was unlocked. Anybody could have come in from outside. Doc McTreen didn't guard himself in any way — why would he? His forthright thoughts were for the hurt and sick.

Pilgrim went out back. A mundane sight lit fitfully by light from other back doors and windows. With many patches of darkness also, and rubble, and privies, and dug-outs and odd outhouses.

The mundane backs of a Western township, no better and no worse than hundreds more. And places like this growing all the time. Pilgrim could have been in Ellsworth, Tombstone, even back in Fort Worth. Sun-baked ground hard beneath his feet: he didn't expect to find any tracks.

A murder set-up as neat and clever as a card-slick's double flush.

Pilgrim paced, gazed, bent, retraced his steps.

Way out to the town or the prairie, to the saloon or anyplace, or to a horse and a wide-open getaway, if the killer had even planned a getaway; he could be supping a cathouse filly in a bordello right now for all Pilgrim knew.

Deputy Jules was suddenly at his elbow, asked, 'Anything?'

Damnfool question!

'Nothing.'

Somebody called, 'The sheriff's here.'

'He should be resting up,' said Jules petulantly.

Folks were already stealing his thunder. The boss-man back. And gunfighter Joe Pilgrim, whom Jules had heard about. A man who moved like a cat in the night and seemed just as quiet and unpredictable, tickling the dark hairs at the back of Jules's neck as if a ghost was breathing on them.

Jules and Pilgrim went back indoors where they were met by Sheriff Salliwell who had questions to ask about two men, one already dead, the other, mutilated, still fighting off the grim spectre. At least Doc McTreen hoped so: Tim Creegan was unconscious

47

again, and breathing hard.

The fat sheriff ignored Deputy Jules's petulant comments on his health, his busted shoulder. Neither Jules nor Pilgrim could tell him anything about the horrific murder of Knocky Dowson. More clues would have to be sought, questions asked around town.

The consensus was that Knocky was no great loss anyway. Pilgrim told his own tales about the other thing, how he had found the beaten and tortured Creegan, a deed done by Knocky and his partner, Dill Rickles — and maybe by others even, identities as yet unknown.

But Dill was gone now also, Pilgrim explained. Dill, taking a rest from his labours, had gotten his come-uppance from a startled sidewinder.

Doc McTreen said, 'Get that body out of the bed. There are fresh bedclothes. Tim can be put in there, so I can see to him better.'

'I want to hear him talk,' said Pilgrim bluntly.

'You have some talkin' to do yourself, bucko,' said the sheriff.

'Leave us be,' said the little doctor, already bending again over his patient. 'I hope I can pull this man through. I'll tell you if and when you'll be able to talk to him. Don't push me.'

'All right, Doc,' said Lou Salliwell.

Pilgrim said, 'I'll go with you, Sheriff.'

The fat man, stepping lightly for all his bulk, led the way. Pilgrim followed him. Jules brought up the rear.

They ranged the town, asked questions. Salliwell, arm in sling, seemed to be ignoring his bad place. He was like an old hound dog on the scent. But it led nowhere. They went to the law office.

Jules made coffee. Pilgrim talked. But he didn't now say a hell of a lot.

6

The sheriff decided they should ride, take a look up in the hills. Pilgrim agreed. Jules made more remarks about his chief's 'condition' but was over-ruled. On their way out they ran into Obe Dacey. It was almost, as if having heard the name, he'd been waiting for them. He volunteered to come along. Previously he'd seemed to be acting as a sort of honorary deputy. 'All right,' said the sheriff.

They took the same route that Pilgrim had used when bringing in the injured Tim Creegan. Eventually, the vultures in the hills guided their way.

Dill Rickles was even an uglier sight than when Pilgrim had last seen him. The squawling birds rose in a cloud.

'Cover him,' said the sheriff who, with foresight, had made Jules tote a digging shovel.

The deputy and Pilgrim did the job, not wasting too much time about it. Dacey and Salliwell went into the cave after the former improvised a torch out of twigs and dried grass.

Joining the two older men, Jules and Pilgrim learned that not much had been found.

The remains of a fire, the smoke being expelled through a convenient slit above (probably being dissipated before it reached the open air), a sort of twisted wrought-iron poker that had obviously been used on the victim strapped against the wall. Near the wall there was a chewed rag that had been used as a gag. It lay among the rope that Pilgrim had earlier cut away from the victim, and he hadn't noticed it then. There were splashes of blood and some cigarette butts.

The cave wasn't all that big, and it didn't lead anywhere. It told a grim story but not a long or particularly understandable one.

'They wanted him to talk,' said

Pilgrim. 'They tortured him to make him talk.'

'Looks that way,' said Obe Dacey. 'But what could Tim talk about that would interest two greedy jackals like Dill and Knocky? Tim didn't own much, didn't cotton to much as far as I know.'

'Sure,' said Lou Salliwell. 'Only Tim can give us some answers. I guess we'd best get back to town an' see how he's coming along.'

They rode back. The night was long now.

There was plenty of light in Tiller's Watch, blobs like swollen stars glittered in the waters of the lake.

The quiet waters that seemed to lie very deep.

Pilgrim asked, 'Why do they call this place Tiller's Watch?'

Dacey said, 'Comes from a kind of a legend I guess. To do with the lake . . . '

'I've always thought there was somep'n kinda funny about that lake,' put in Deputy Jules.

Dacey gave him a hard sidelong look, said, 'I'll tell it.'

And he did.

His voice soft but sonorous.

He had a way with him. Like an old travelling pedlar of potions and elixirs, who told ghastly tales about bringing bodies up from the dead.

But the one Dacey talked about was *brought* up, delivered by waters that afterwards ceased to ripple and stayed quiet and deep as if still hiding some secret beneath them . . .

★ ★ ★

An old feller you might think, a half-crazy wandering prospector who found gold in the hills and got himself bad sunstroke with overwork, digging deeper, and went plumb loco.

And wandered down to the shores of the lonely lake — no settlements then for miles around — and fell in. And then he came to his senses, threshed, saved himself. But his precious bundle had floated away.

There was some talk of a burro, but no burro was ever found. 'Loco' Tiller — if that was his real name — had left his prospecting gear in the hills and it was found much later.

Tiller's body was also found. What was left of it. It was on the edge of the lake, little more than a skeleton after all kinds of predators had been at it. But, strangely, grotesquely, still in a sitting position, the skull, with shreds of dried flesh adhering to it, pointing out at the gleaming, mocking waters of the lake.

It was said that Tiller had gone out into the lake, which wasn't very deep and he wouldn't have to swim much, seeking his riches. And he hadn't found them. And he had sat beside the lake and watched as if he thought in his craziness that eventually the waters would give up the booty to him.

'But then again,' said Obe Dacey, 'mebbe somebody just killed Tiller and took his booty an' just left him there.

Lots of folks went out in the lake afterwards and didn't find anything, prospected in the hills and found a bit of pay-dirt and nothing else. That's how the town began, though and got its name. For all we know mebbe Tiller's spirit is still down there watching on the edge of the lake. *Waitin'.*'

'Creepy,' said Deputy Jules.

'Horse-shit,' said Sheriff Salliwell.

Joe Pilgrim didn't say anything at all.

★ ★ ★

Tim Creegan was back in the land of the living, and Doc said to Pilgrim, 'We told him how you found him. He seems to have some dim recollection of that. He wants to talk to you. He's fighting, but don't tire him. Those bastards treated him mighty badly.' The little man, though notoriously irascible, didn't look or talk like a person given to profanity but his embellishments now were colourful.

Pilgrim went into the bedroom, which was quiet and neat. Knocky Dowson's corpse had been toted to the undertaker's. Creegan was half-propped in the bed, strapped and slinged and white looking like a freshly prepared Eastern mummy. He managed a crooked smile and said, 'Mr Pilgrim.'

'Hello, Tim. Call me Joe.'

'All right, Joe. I've seen you before, y'know. Once in Fort Worth. You were with your father, another Joe, the one they called Marshal Joe — who was pointed out to me.'

'Yeh, my dad did stay there awhile. He's back at his ranch now on the Pecos.'

'I discovered you were still there and I got in touch with you.'

'Well, I'm here.'

'You heard about the legend?' asked Creegan. 'The one about how Tiller's Watch got its name?'

Pilgrim said, 'Well, there's a coincidence! I did just hear about that.'

Creegan talked haltingly but talked a lot. When Doc horned in he was told to leave them be. But the sick man took a breather and Pilgrim sat on a hard chair near the bed and had a smoke: Tim said that didn't bother him none. But soon the story was continued. A strange one. Like something out of an Eastern dime novel.

Jeremiah Tiller, prospector. Had a wife, but away from her a lot. No family until they took in a nephew called Tim, son of Mrs Tiller's sister and her husband, Matt Creegan. Their only son and just a sprig when both his parents were killed in a raging prairie fire. The boy, put in the root cellar, had escaped.

While prospecting in the hills beyond the lake old Jeremiah had had a partner, one Caleb Tripp. Caleb was nowhere around when the skeletal body of Jeremiah was found on the shores of the lake.

'After she found out about Jeremiah, Aunt Sukey died. Grief I guess.' Tim gave a little painful spurt of laughter. 'It's right that absence makes the heart grow fonder, huh?'

Pilgrim had no comment to make.

Caleb Tripp was on the drink, met a friend called Dollar Crane, who shot Jeremiah. But the old man must have suspected drunken Caleb and his drunken friend Dollar. He had his gear and a small stash of coin, but no gold. He must have hidden it. Caleb and Dollar didn't find it.

Grown up, the Tiller nephew, Tim Creegan, went looking for the two men. He found Caleb Tripp, who was dying from alcoholism combined with lung disease. It was Tripp who told Tim about Dollar Crane but didn't know where he could be found: they'd split up long since after an express office job they'd tried to pull. Dollar had killed a guard. They hadn't got away with much.

There was a price on Dollar's head. He'd probably changed his name — even if the moniker Caleb had known him by had been his real one: who the hell would christen a kid 'Dollar'?

Tim Creegan had worn himself out trailing. He figured he'd go to Tiller's Watch territory, the hills, look for the hidden stash — why not? He took over the old smallholding which had been falling in on itself. It was his base.

'Anybody else know you were searching?' Pilgrim asked.

'Not at first I don't think. I didn't pass near town or any other place on my way here. I even worked by night in hidden places. I didn't find a thing. Those are good hills. Except for a few rattlers . . . '

'Dill Rickles found out about the rattlers.'

'He sure did. What I mean is, folks use the hills by day.'

'Who else?'

'Nobody in partic'ler I guess . . . But then, recently I began to get the idea I was being followed, being watched all the while . . . '

'So you sent for me.' Bit of a lame reason, Pilgrim thought, went on, 'I don't come cheap. Where would you find the money?'

Creegan's face twisted grotesquely. 'I didn't tell you. I'll tell you now. I had a communication from a lawyer. They'd been trying to find me. Aunt Sukey had left me some stuff. Jewellery. The lawyer found a sale for me, delivered the cash. Not a hell of a lot, but enough I thought.'

'Did you know your aunt had that jewellery?'

'I don't remember it.'

'Could your Uncle Jeremiah have gotten his boodle to his missus somehow and she got it converted to jewellery for safe-keeping?'

'I dunno . . . ' Creegan gave a deep breath. Then before Pilgrim could speak went on a new tack. 'Dollar Crane'd be getting on in years now. He could be anybody. Maybe he's here. Maybe he hired Dill an' Knocky.'

'They ain't about to tell us anything

now.' But, Pilgrim reflected, maybe that was why Knocky Dowson had been killed, to keep his mouth shut. What other reason could there be?

Doc McTreen came in again. But Creegan was all talked out. Pilgrim left them.

Questions and possibilities chased around in his head like playful squirrels in a cage. Most wandering prospectors were considered by folks to be kind of crazy. Or they got that way. Had Tim Creegan got that way? Or had he still a driving inner fury to arrange his uncle's death, the brutal murder of a man who had been like a father to him, his wife a mother to the orphaned boy, her life brought to a finish too by the tragedy?

Or was Creegan, though he now had a base, still going around in circles in his mind? He wasn't suffering delusions: what had happened formed a negation of that theory.

But Creegan could still be sort of *paranoid*. It was a word that Pilgrim had come across recently. He had more spare time now and, like his father, had become a reader. Alone in hotel rooms or dens in strange places, smoking, having a drink, waiting . . .

7

He had a room at a small hotel. They didn't serve food. He went to Dacey's place. Dacey was behind the bar. 'Chow?' Pilgrim queried and the big, dark man handed him a scribbled menu. Three set meals for the evening — or permutations thereof.

Pilgrim chose turkey with a spicy sauce of powerful ingredients he savoured but couldn't rightly identify, this with bread and sweet onions stuffing, string beans that weren't a bit stringy, baked potatoes and peas. It was followed by a nut and fruit pudding with hot custard; and of course lashings of sweet, strong coffee and a couple of quirlies.

It was served to him by Dacey's handsome spouse Reba. Pilgrim asked her to compliment the cook on his behalf. She gave him a flashing white smile and a warm glance from her huge dark eyes and said she would do as he asked. He didn't learn till later, from her husband Obe, that Reba did most of the cooking herself, though not all the serving, this she saved for favourite customers.

'She's taken a shine to you I guess,' said the big dark man without any trace of spleen.

After the meal Pilgrim bellied up to the bar and had a couple of shots from a raggedy-moustached barman. Right then there was no trace of big Obe.

Pilgrim left, got his horse, rode. It was a good night, the sky full of stars.

However, as he moseyed along, not pushing the paint horse, the rider began to feel as if he were on a carousel at a county fair, going round and round. On one of those huge swingboats that go to and fro, and up and down.

Still, he knew where he was going this time, no swings and roundabouts (he remembered suddenly a colourful fair he'd seen in Kansas City), so that was something. He saw the lights of the little spread of Debbie and Jabez Clandell in the distance but skirted it widely, hearing no sound.

No sound either when he reached Tim Creegan's place.

He had passed a few strolling beeves, heard them, heard no human sounds.

The lone horse was still in the small corral. The same docile mare that only turned her head slowly as he rode past, then went back to munching. Didn't she ever sleep? She had a small trough, the water glinting in the starlight. She had plenty of hay.

As he approached the house he could still hear her munching behind him. The breeze made sighing noises; there was nothing else.

He dismounted, left the horse with reins dangling. The beast cropped at sparse grass around him, wouldn't move far.

His hand on the butt of his big Starr pistol, Pilgrim made for the main house, stepping lightly, his boot-heels making only small thudding sounds on the hard ground.

The door was shut but not locked or bolted. He opened it.

Darkness. He sensed a movement in the darkness and began to draw his gun. He was a fast draw. But he wasn't fast enough. There was a swishing noise.

A noise? No, more like just a sibilance.

Something that felt like a huge hammer hit him on the side of the head. There *was* a noise then. A sort of *clang*.

Then nothing. A blackness that was like a huge bag enveloping him.

If he fell he didn't even feel that.

But he must have fallen; for when he came to it was to find himself flat on his back on the hard wood floor. And he was very hot. There was a grinding, thudding pain in his head, but even that wasn't as intense as the heat. He didn't think he'd ever felt such heat, even in the flat middle of the unshaded desert with the sun at its zenith.

The house was on fire!

There was redness all around him and a *searing*. But he didn't think he was actually burned. The pain in his head goaded him. Through the smoke he saw the rectangle of the door lit by the starlight from outside.

He didn't attempt to rise, didn't want to lose his balance, maybe fall backwards. He could see the flames: they threatened to engulf him: they were ravenously hot at his back, reaching for him. He crawled. He scuttled like a frantic crab evading the chop, the boiling-hot water.

The fresh air, though it was already somewhat polluted by smoke, hit his temples, his smarting eyes. He raised those eyes towards the stars. His head spun and he lowered it again. He remained still, on all fours, motionless, fighting his weakness with his mind.

He didn't feel in any danger. Had his assailant wanted to kill him he could've finished the job by now. Maybe he'd figured the fire would do it for him. And it nearly had . . .

He hauled himself to his feet and only then did he raise his hand to his wounded head.

There was a swelling there, and it was sticky with blood. The wound, such as it was, didn't seem too deep, but he probably had concussion or somep'n he figured.

He lurched away from the heat of the fire and made for the small corral, knowing there was a horse through there. Moving away from the smoke, he looked back. The house was a mass of flame, the black smoke now reaching for the stars. Some of the outhouses were alight too. There was plenty of timber, plenty of fodder which the flames devoured.

He looked about him, couldn't see his paint stallion anyplace. His head began to thud, spin. He lurched. Then he went straight ahead again, reached the corral fence and draped himself over it, panting.

The quiet mare was not in the corral.

He wormed his way along the fence, it creaking at his weight. He opened the gate, lurched toward the small trough, made it, went down on his knees. He drank deeply but slowly, then laved his face and his head.

The water wasn't clean. Could get blood poisoning, he thought wryly. He took the bandanna from around his neck and wiped himself gently.

He reached out and grasped a rail of the fence and hauled himself into an upright position once more, if a sort of topheavy one: just now his head felt like a small sack of badly packed oatmeal.

He couldn't believe his tricky eyesight when he saw his horse approaching him, as if without a care.

But Pilgrim's eyes weren't after all playing him tricks. 'C'mon, you tricky ol' jasper,' he said softly. The horse seemed to hear him all right, though, and quickened pace a little but with his usual hint of cussedness, a cussedness

69

that served him well. But then he came closer more quickly, hung his head over the top bar of the fence and looked at the man reproachfully as if it were all his fault.

Still holding on to the fence for support, Pilgrim moved along to the gate and passed through, and the horse joined him, even nuzzled him.

'Oh my,' the man said. 'What's got into you all of a sudden, pizen?'

He hauled himself up into the saddle. His Starr handgun was gone, but he saw with relief that his Winchester was still in its saddle scabbard. He'd had a second weapon, a double-barrelled derringer in the back of his belt. That had gone too.

It was the Starr he missed most of all, very much so, remembering now how and when his father, Marshal Joe, had given that big hogleg to him.

Would he ever see that prime weapon again, that specially modified tool of fast action and accuracy?

Well, maybe he would: if he caught

up with the bastard who slugged him and set the fire and left him to burn to death. You had two extra guns, brother, he reflected sardonically, whyn't you use one of 'em — even the derringer would've blown a hole right through my head? Hell, you should've finished me off, should've made sure . . .

Becoming lightheaded, brains swimming in pea soup. Had to get help, a doctor. Maybe Tiller's Watch. If he could make it without pitching out of the saddle. Maybe . . .

Maybe what?

He rode instinctively gentling the horse. A mischievous beast, but intelligent, trotting smoothly. Understanding maybe.

The man couldn't bear to look back, couldn't risk it.

The horse carried him.

Until another horseman reined his mount in their path and there was the glint of a lifted rifle — not Pilgrim's! — and a gruff voice said, 'Stop right there, stranger.'

8

A man in the starlight. A big man on a big horse. An older man than Pilgrim, obviously. Purposeful. Levelled rifle in steady hands.

'Who are you?' the man asked.

Pilgrim told him.

And the man said, 'Debbie and Jabez Clandell told me about you. Jabez's my younger brother. I'm Trace, that's what folks call me.'

Trace Clandell. The name sounded an echo in Pilgrim's mind, but that was all. The Clandells, when he saw them hadn't mentioned a brother, brother-in-law. Where had Trace been then? And the big man was going on, changing tack abruptly. 'What do you know about that fire?'

'Somebody slugged me an' tried to burn me in it,' said Pilgrim caustically.

'Do tell!'

They both heard the sound of wheels. Trace Clandell swung his horse half-around but didn't lower his rifle. His brother Jabez was coming along on a one-horse gig. Obviously he could somehow get from his wheelchair on to something like that: maybe it had been specially made for him.

He was on his own. He shouldn't have left his missus back there on her lonesome, Pilgrim thought. Still, maybe they'd thought the fire was some kind of accident; and Trace had come out to investigate and then, not to be outdone, his younger brother had come after him.

Pilgrim was taken to the spread. It wasn't the first time that place had been a port in the storm where he was concerned. It wasn't the first time he'd felt the gentle hands of the delectable Debbie, Mrs Clandell. He remembered how the dog, who was called Tricks, had barked at him the first time. But now the little mongrel fussed around him as if he were a long-time friend.

The coffee was hot and the treacle cakes were sweet. The makings were good too, and the three men sat and smoked while the woman clattered around in the kitchen.

Pilgrim had a light bandage around his head, a soft pad, salve. He still had a worrying headache and wasn't completely prime again. But he didn't feel too bad. And he listened.

Brother Trace had been a-roaming, was returning to the house when he saw the fire at the Creegan place. He had told Jabez, advised him to stay put. But Jabez hadn't taken that advice. Neither of them had seen anything. Trace hadn't heard hoofbeats until Pilgrim was approaching.

Trace Clandell. Pilgrim now had his head right, or almost.

Anyway — he was remembering. Trace. A man who'd been a Texas Ranger and, as Pilgrim had heard, was now a freelance hired gun. Hell, who wasn't?

Not showing his full hand, he asked

74

about the Ranger part, mentioned his father who'd been a well-known lawman. Trace said, Yeh, he remembered Marshal Joe, had run into him a couple of times on law business.

Trace admitted that he wasn't Rangering now. But then it was Jabez who took up the tale, not seeming to be outdone by his big brother.

Jabez had been a Ranger too, though not for a long while.

'I was bushwhacked, shot in the back, bottom of my spine someplace, took the use from my legs.'

'Was the backshooter caught?'

'No. And I don't even know who he was. But I'll find out eventually . . . '

'Or I will,' put in Trace.

Pilgrim asked, 'How about your legs?'

'I do special exercises Doc McTreen of Tiller's Watch laid out for me. He's a little cracker that man. Sometimes I wonder why he buried himself in that one-horse town.'

'We all have our reasons for doing

things I guess,' said Trace Clandell cyptically. He and Pilgrim exchanged glances. But they didn't seem to mean much.

The brothers asked about Tim Creegan, and Pilgrim said he figured Tim would be all right. But certainly the news of what had happened to his little spread wouldn't be any tonic to him.

'I guess we ought to go there and see if we can find anything,' Jabez said.

'I guess,' said Pilgrim.

Jabez said, 'Can you . . . ?

Pilgrim said, 'I can.'

He was mighty interested to see how Jabez got into the little gig behind the trotting pony, using his wide shoulders, his clenching fists and his strong arms, gasping and grunting and heaving and not asking any help from anybody.

Trace had said haltingly that maybe Debbie shouldn't be left on her own. She said she'd come along herself but she had a whole heap of chores to do and, with the men out of the way, could get at 'em.

Anyway, she had a rifle (and a derringer she'd toted for years) and she could shoot as good as any of the men — *well, almost*. But straight anyway.

Her husband said if she spotted anything, or even heard anything that sounded kind of strange, she should fire off a couple of single shots. She agreed to do this. And the men went on their way.

★ ★ ★

When Doc McTreen reached the door of the law office he was gasping for breath. Must get my weight down, he thought. But it was a minor detail: his main thoughts were not for himself but for somebody else. Near-panic had driven him to this spot and he wasn't usually a panicky man, far from it in fact.

He had ignored folks he had passed on the street, although a couple of them at least had asked him what was going on, what was his hurry?

It was gratifying to him that folks cared so much, but it didn't stop him. He knew that a few folks were still gazing at his back. But he didn't turn. He hammered on the closed of lice door.

It was opened immediately. Maybe they'd heard his clattering heels. A little while ago he'd been at a local birthing and had kept his boots on.

The door opened. Deputy Jules stood there, asked, 'What's botherin' you, Doc?'

McTreen didn't like this fancypants, moustached young man very much.

The plump medico got his breath back and barked, 'Let me see Lou.'

'I'm right behind you, *amigo*.' Lou Salliwell, on his night rounds, had caught up with the doctor. He went on, 'Somebody told me you were running down the street like your pants were on fire.'

Jules stepped aside and the two older

men went past him into the lamplit office. The deputy shut the door on staring folks who weren't used to seeing their local sawbones in such a state.

The doc said, 'Tim's gone.'

The sheriff was suddenly open-mouthed, and that was unusual for him. 'What? Tim? Tim Creegan?'

'Yes.'

'But how?'

'Don't ask me how.' McTreen was still not quite himself. 'I thought he was too ill to move. I'd been to deliver Molly O'Dealey's latest. I'd left Tim in bed, sleeping I thought. When I got back the bed was empty. The bedroom window was open. The back door was still locked.'

Lou Salliwell had gotten himself together. He asked, 'Was the window forced?'

'Didn't look like it. I went out back, didn't see anything.' Then McTreen voiced what was on all their minds. 'First Knocky Dowson, now Tim Creegan.'

'You think Tim was took?'

'I don't know. How would I know?'

'Jules, you stay here. C'mon, Doc.'

Jules began, 'I think I . . . '

'Do as you're told, goddamn it.' The sheriff marched to the door, the doctor at his heels. The door closed behind them.

Outside at a discreet distance, some townsfolk followed them. Something else had happened. This was a restless town. What was this? They didn't know, but they wanted to find out.

The sheriff surprised them by turning and asking, 'Anybody seen Tim Creegan out on the street?'

A surprising query. Wasn't Tim laid up? At death's door somebody had said.

A few of them had visited him at Doc's discretion. But Tim had never been much of a townie, had kept himself pretty much to himself. Nobody had seen him on the street tonight. What the hell . . . ?

The doctor and the lawman searched,

the townsfolk, wisely now, keeping out of their way. The two town elders didn't find Tim, dead or alive. They didn't find anything that Salliwell might have called a clue either.

'Maybe he fooled us,' the sheriff said. 'Maybe he lit out.'

'He didn't have a horse. Maybe he was picked up. Or maybe he stole a horse.'

Nobody had complained. Salliwell and McTreen went to the livery stables. Cracker the old hostler was at Dacey's Place and the younker called Pete was on duty, had a worried look. Yes, a horse had been stolen, or had drifted. Pete had looked for it, without success. He hadn't yet gotten around to telling Cracker, who had a cantankerous temper, particularly when he was in his cups.

The sheriff said, 'We'll go look.'

The doctor said, 'I'll have my carriage and pair, Pete. Lou, maybe Creegan's gone off his head. Maybe he's roaming and we can pick him up.'

9

The Creegan place was just a smoking ruin, the flames having died after eating away at everything, doing a thorough job. The task the three men had set themselves was ticklish and messy.

There wasn't much Jabez could do, so he stayed in the gig and kept lookout.

The other two, stepping carefully, stooping, rummaging with gloved hands — maybe the gloves would be useless afterwards — were finding the task arduous, time-wasting. They began to wonder about Jabez, restless in his seat, turning to watch them from time to time.

Maybe Jabez was beginning to worry about his pretty wife. Should they have left her alone? Time was passing. The men had found nothing of interest.

What did they expect to find? They didn't know.

Jabez drew the gig nearer, asked, 'Anything?'

'Nothing,' said his brother Trace.

Pilgrim, bent in the darkness, a prowling form, didn't say anything.

Trace said, 'We can manage, Jabe. I think you oughta get back to Debbie, don't you?'

'Yes, I guess so. I'll go right on back.' Jabez turned the gig around.

Pilgrim straightened, turned around to say 'So-long'. They watched Jabez go. He didn't turn. He handled his equipage very well, and the trotting horse was a cracker.

★ ★ ★

Debbie heard hoofbeats. But they seemed to be coming in a different direction from the one the three men had taken when they left, from the direction of town even and Jabe, Trace and Pilgrim certainly hadn't gone that way: Tim Creegan's place, the scene of the fire, was in the opposite direction entirely. There was no glow over there now.

The dog began to bark and from the lighted window Debbie saw him tugging at his lead. He should be free, she thought, like he usually is.

When she went out, the rifle in her hands, he turned towards her and stopped his clamour. Then she could hear the hoofbeats more clearly, and what sounded like carriage-wheels bumping over the sun-baked land.

The equipage came in sight under the stars and she raised the rifle and, at the top of her lungs, shouted, 'Pull in there! Hold it!'

The two horses were pulled back. The carriage, two men on its seat, ground to a halt.

A voice shouted back at her, calling her name, identifying its owner as Sheriff Lou Salliwell of Tiller's Watch, who had Doc McTreen of the same township right there beside him.

She recognised the voice, the men, lowered the rifle, told them to come ahead.

They wanted to know where Jabez was.

Why was she alone at night with only the dog to keep her company, the latter sniffing at their heels, wagging his tail now in frenzied friendliness?

She told them about the fire.

'Stay with Debbie, Doc,' Salliwell said. 'I'll go on.' He climbed back into the carriage, clicked his tongue at the horse who moved. Tricks began to follow but returned when Debbie called him, ran to where she stood, her rifle-butt grounded, Doc McTreen's arm around her shoulders: they were old friends.

* * *

'God, what's this?' said Trace Clandell and he squatted on his haunches in the black dust.

Pilgrim joined him, dust rising, bent,

said, 'That ain't no animal.' It certainly wasn't. It had two arms and two legs but, past that, didn't resemble anything human, anything that had once been living. It was a black, charred effigy.

'We can't lift him,' Trace said. 'It — it might fall to pieces. We'll have to drag . . . '

'Yeh.' Pilgrim bent further.

'I just lifted that lump o' wood, scraped a pile of ash . . . ' Trace let the sentence run off. He sneezed. When he was ready Pilgrim and he got a leg apiece.

The dust rose. They should've covered their mouths. But they didn't stop, until something came away in Trace's fist. Fragments of black stuff, parts of a shoe. And a black lump that had once been a human foot, that Trace threw away from him with an exclamation of disgust.

The two men straightened up and Pilgrim said, 'Trace, we need a tarp, somep'n like that.'

'Christ,' snorted the other man. 'Jabe

has a tarp on his gig. But he's gone.'

'I have a big saddle blanket,' said Pilgrim and he went to get it.

They still had to struggle, gingerly though, and it took them a long time.

They finally had their burden — what was left of it — on flat ground. And it was then that they heard hoofbeats, and the sound of wheels.

It was Jabez returning, easier in his mind now he knew that Doc McTreen was with Debbie. And with Jabez now was Sheriff Salliwell in the doctor's two-horse carriage. They had met as the lawman was crossing the flat, long space between the Clandell spread and what was left of the Creegan one; and Jabez had turned about.

He was as surprised and shocked as the sheriff was at the new, terrible news which met them both as Trace and Joe waited with the gruesome bundle at their feet.

More covering was available now, however, both from Jabez and from Lou Salliwell, and the charred body, swathed and hidden, was placed in the back of the doctor's carriage, much the bigger of the two.

Jabez said, 'We mustn't let Debbie see this.'

The sheriff said, 'Of course not. The doc'll have to have a look at it. We'll call him out and him and me and Joe here will go back to Tiller's Watch. We've got to find out . . . '

He let his voice tail off. The hooves beat; the wheels whirred.

★ ★ ★

Returning to the town with their grim fourth passenger, Pilgrim, Salliwell and the doctor learned that the horse that had been taken from the livery stables had returned of its own accord. It wore only a saddle blanket, didn't even have a hackamore. So whoever had ridden it maybe hadn't had a saddle, no reins, could have been clinging to the beast's mane or neck, a friendly, rawboned stallion with an eye for home and sustenance. He was still clean, not sweaty or blowing at all, evidently hadn't been ridden hard or long.

There was no means of knowing how long he'd been gone: the hostler kid Pete hadn't a notion. There was no sign of Tim Creegan or anybody else who might have been missing. Even the doc, thinking Tim was sleeping had no means of knowing just how long Tim had been missing. Maybe it was longer than at first had been figured.

McTreen asked the boys to leave him alone with his new 'patient' the black 'effigy' laid out now on a trestle table.

There wasn't much sleeping night-time left. Pilgrim got his head down.

He hadn't locked his door. He was awake like a cat as he heard the sounds in the passage. He was reaching for his gun on the little table beside the bed when the door opened.

'Keep your hands still, Joe,' said Sheriff Salliwell and he had a levelled shooter in his fist, the perpetual lamplight from the passage raising wicked glints from the blue steel.

Reeling in beside his chief, Deputy Jules had a levelled gun also.

Pilgrim, his hands supine on top of the bedclothes, asked, 'Godamighty, Lou, what's bitin' you?'

The sheriff didn't answer the question right off. His eyes were direct, his gaze unvarying as he said, 'Get 'is gear, Jules.'

Jules got a big Colt, one that Pilgrim had borrowed from Jabez Clandell, after having his own big Starr stolen in the fire at Tim Creegan's place.

There wasn't much else. Pilgrim's rifle wasn't in the room. The deputy rejoined his chief, who said, 'The doc has discovered the identity of the burned corpse.'

'How did he do that?' asked the man in the bed.

'Teeth, Joe. Teeth. The only way. Tim Creegan got kicked in the face by a pony months back and lost a couple teeth on the left-hand side of his mouth. Doc fixed his face, his mouth.'

'So it was Creegan we found.'

'That's for sure. And I'll tell you somep'n else, bucko. That corpse was in a hell of a terrible state, you know that. But the doc was still able to tell that Creegan had been shot in the back o' the head. Maybe you wasn't slugged as hard as you pretended at the Clandell place. You could've set the fire at Tim's place. It was a good one. But it wasn't good enough . . . '

'I didn't shoot Creegan, Lou, and I didn't set no fire. I reckon I was supposed to burn up with Creegan. Why was Tim Creegan there anyway? Why'd he take those chances with his well-being? What was he after there in his own home?'

'You tell me. Why were you there?'

Pilgrim, propped up in bed, smiled thinly, without humour. 'I'm supposed to be a range detective. I was investigating. Hell, Lou, you don't believe all that horse-shit you've been givin' me.'

Salliwell had no comment on this, only said, 'I've gotta take you in, Joe. Get outa bed, an' let's move.'

10

The news was around town of the terrible thing that had happened to Tim Creegan. By this time the 'black corpse' — and this was what it became known as — was in the undertaking parlour, though the two experts there wouldn't be able to do much more with it than bury it.

And the way things were happening around the territory now there would have to be more than one funeral arranged, and the sooner the better.

The other surprising news was, of course, that of the incarceration of Joe Pilgrim who, since his arrival in town, had become the friend of Obediah Dacey and a sort of deputy of Sheriff Lou Salliwell's, the man now responsible for his capture and imprisonment — though deputy Jules had helped and was now bragging about his part in the capture.

He had never trusted Pilgrim anyway, he said, the man was a notorious paid killer.

Some of the townsfolk who didn't know Pilgrim very well didn't know what to think. But the barflies and hardcases who had thought of this young stranger as a friend of the sheriff's and of that outspoken and forthright 'senior citizen' Dacey, were pleased with the news. They felt that the sheriff had made a fool of himself in picking Pilgrim as a virtual sidekick and now it was time both of them got their come-uppance.

If the town was split into two factions it was hard to figure where one started and the other left off: maybe they sort of dovetailed.

Deputy Jules began to run around as if his ass was on fire and then Lou Salliwell came out and got him, wanted him to join the jailer, a part-timer called Gully, while the sheriff himself went off to do some investigating.

He didn't say where he was going and, by now, Jules appeared too nervous to be asking.

* * *

By the time the funerals were fixed the sheriff was back and wasn't saying much to anybody.

There had been three fatalities in recent times. Dill Rickles, Knocky Dowson and Tim Creegan. Dill's body had been buried almost on the spot where an irate sidewinder had struck him down. His partner, Knocky, was to be put to rest in the boothill of Tiller's Watch, which was more than some folks thought he deserved.

But the local preacher was a tolerant man and this was what he decreed. He was also a popular man so folks went along with him, particularly the barflies and hardcases who'd been friends of Knocky and his late and murderous partner, Dill.

Although the townsfolk hadn't seen

a helluva lot of Tim Creegan he had always been kind of offhandedly friendly with them and they turned out in force.

Strangely, pretty much the same could be said for Knocky's contingent. They weren't so numerous, but they were rowdy and rough. And a few cathouse girls who had been special favourites of the two partners egged the men on and wailed on the sidelines like they had lost loving relatives.

Tim Creegan had a better show, however.

He had a hearse drawn by four ponies, two mostly black, one piebald, one dark grey, a stallion a few hands taller than the other three. A handsome feller, he acted as if he were demeaning himself and, being one of the lead two (his companion was the piebald), kept shooting ahead impatiently, causing a sort of sidetracking that threatened to turn the tall, glass-sided hearse over, coffin, corpse, wreaths, the lot.

A small elderly drunk called Dougal

had insisted on marching ahead of the cortège banging a drum that he said he'd captured at Bull Run. But he gave up after the grey stallion, with a sudden wild gallop, almost kicked his head in: then Dougal went back to the saloon to steady his nerves.

Spitefully, the stallion destroyed the drum. And the cortege began to climb the hill toward the sky and this seemed to please the temperamental beast and he began to behave himself.

Knocky and his lot only had a flatboard wagon and two ponies. But now Dougal and his drum were gone and Creegan's mourners were dutifully sorrowful and silent. There was only the whisper of dust under their feet. And Knocky's lot were making the most of things.

They were led by a broad six-foot-odd brawler known as Saratoga Jack who had once been a rough-rider. He had a badly crooked arm, but it was his left one and he was a right-handed man. No other brawler in town had been able to beat him in a fight. He had a right hand like a hammer and a left elbow like a scythe.

He said the words over Knocky, whose grave had been prepared by two of Saratoga's brawling sidekicks — he'd beaten 'em both — and his voice was like a showboat foghorn.

The town's favourite preacher, Lane Deakes, wasn't to be outdone, however, and he had a clear tenor with great carrying power, swooping and echoing over the hills until, during a pause, Jack was heard to say, 'Oh, hell, fill 'im in an' let's go back to Dacey's Place.'

Obe Dacey himself wasn't at the burying place: he indeed had a saloon to run and, knowing that there was usually a lot of imbibing and hurrawing after a funeral, was getting primed for such.

He was also, right now a very, very thoughtful man.

The buryings hadn't been in the morning times as was often the case, there had been too many things happening beforehand. And now, as the sun was going down, the mourners were returning, and a goodly number of the menfolk entered Dacey's Place.

Saratoga Jack and his cronies were already there and Jack, hail-feller-well-met but with a wicked glint in his eyes, called expansively for drinks all round.

Dacey attended bar, his dark face impassive. He'd never had a run-in with Jack. In some strange way these two seemed to respect each other.

As things got noisier a barman joined the boss, and Dacey's missus came out from time to time to look things over. Her beautiful face was expressionless but Dacey, who knew her so well and loved her so much, could detect the worry deep in her dark eyes.

As was natural, as the liquor flowed, the conversation getting louder by the minute, the subject of most speculation — and more — was the murder of Tim Creegan and whether the stranger in the jail was responsible for that.

Saratoga Jack and his minions who were growing in number, figured that Pilgrim was the killer all right.

And Jack asked them, all right, what did they aim to do about it?

Dacey had disappeared. The barman was doing the attending on his lonesome, but he had a shotgun under the bar. He was reluctant to use it, however, as the boys began to march, for they then had their backs to him. He couldn't have got big Jack anyway as Jack was in front of the mob.

Jack, going through the batwings, was the first to come face to face with Obe Dacey and Dacey had a big Navy Colt in each hand.

'Where you goin' Jack?' he asked.

'You know where we're goin', Obe. Get out of our way.'

'I'm liable to shoot you, Jack.'

'You won't do that.' But Jack came to a puzzled stop and the men behind jostled into him.

He was forced nearer to the man with the two guns, a man almost as big and brawny as he was himself. For a moment things seemed to balance on a knife's edge.

Then Jack said, 'You put them guns away, Obe, an' I'll take you. I don't need any help.'

'Horse-shit.' Dacey was goading him now.

Saratoga Jack turned and shouted, 'Spread out, all o' you, along the wall. Clear the doors, let the folks come out. Me an' Obe Dacey are gonna have a little conflict between us, just me an' him, an' I'll personally have his 'ead, I'll guarantee that.'

There was a moving and a scuttling, a jockeying and a shouting — and more folks were appearing. The news was spreading like prairie fire.

Obe Dacey put his two guns away.

11

'Shuck 'em right off,' said Saratoga Jack harshly.

Dacey took off his gunbelt, the full load, handed it over to a friend behind him. Saratoga's regular sidekick, a squint-eyed wiry man known as Snuff, collected Jack's gear, backed off.

The two men strode to the middle of the street and faced each other, went in immediately. Jack was bigger, but Obe seemed a mite faster.

Jack was a seasoned brawler, would fight anybody at the drop of a hat. He had never been bested — not in Tiller's Watch anyway. There were rumours that he'd once fought in the bareknuckle ring, but nobody knew the rights of that, not even Snuff: maybe he, an inveterate chatterer, had started the rumour in the first place.

He had been putting out the tale

lately that he had an Eastern author rather interested in doing a book about Saratoga Jack, 'Wild West hero' — but there'd been no such fancypants in town lately, not even a drifter, except of course Joe Pilgrim (jailbait now!) and he was a Westerner through and through. If he got hanged maybe somebody would do a book about him!

The two big men were almost obscured by dust — and the jostling populace was yelling at the dust.

But suddenly Jack staggered out of that dust as if he'd been back-kicked by a furious horse. And there'd been no horse in that cloud, that was for sure.

Jack's face streamed with blood. His nose was at an odd angle and his eyes were blind.

Nobody had ever seen Obe Dacey in a street free-for-all before. He had put folks down, was fast with a hand-gun and adept with a long one. Brawling in the street had never been his style.

But Saratoga Jack was going backwards. Pure instinct it seemed.

Blindly. And Obe was coming out of the dust after him. And the dust was settling.

Jack had had the surprise of his life. He didn't like it. Who would? He was completely disorganized. As if Obe's mighty blows had scrambled his brains and, rubbery-legged, only instinct was keeping him up.

He didn't like it!

But his pard Snuff liked it even less. His idol was being toppled before his eyes. He screamed 'Jack!' and he tossed one of Jack's guns towards the big man.

Whether Jack saw it arcing in the sunshine or whether he didn't would have been hard to figure. But who was figuring? Instinct was all now. Snuff's rage: his furious instinct. Jack's instinct.

Obe's instinct. And the crowd screaming like banshees.

With his good arm Jack reached for the gun and missed it. It thudded to the ground. Both he and Obe bent and reached for it, blindly it seemed. But Obe was, of course, the fastest, and he got it.

He swung it upwards and sideways and the steel barrel hit Jack across the temple and he fell forward on his battered, bloody face.

Obe whirled, the gun in his hand. His own face was bleeding. His eyes blazed.

Snuff was trying to lift his own gun — but he hadn't a hope in hell. He was almost at Hell's gate. But Obe didn't shoot him, only strode forward, long-legged, his eyes like balls of fire.

Snuff tried to back but the crowd held him. He went sideways. Then Obe Dacey was upon him, the gun swinging in a shining arc. The crowd wasn't shouting now. There was silence — and the thud of the gun barrel against Snuff's head was a cruel sound. Snuff's battered Stetson fell off and he fell upon it. The crowd ringed him. A few more ringed Saratoga Jack, who was moaning, beginning to come round.

Dacey, carrying his gunbelt, went back into his place where his barman and his wife questioned him anxiously. The barman had watched the fight through a window; Reba hadn't.

'I'll live,' said Dacey and went through to the back, Reba following him.

★ ★ ★

In his cell Pilgrim heard the shouting from down the street. He did some shouting himself and Jules came into the cell-block. There was no sign of the sheriff.

'What's going on?'

'None o' your business,' said the deputy nastily. 'A fight 'tween your friend Dacey an' a big ox called Saratoga Jack. He'll cut Dacey down to size, you mark my words . . . But, don't worry, I don't guess the mob'll be coming for you just yet.'

'Get outa my sight, yuh — now!' said Pilgrim.

106

Jules's eyes got nasty and it seemed as if he would come to the bars. But he didn't; turned on his heels and marched out of the prisoner's sight.

The clamour was dying down outside. Pilgrim went across to the barred window and looked out, as he'd been doing a lot lately. This wasn't the first time he'd been in a jail-cell, but he was restless. Like a big cat in a cage.

The window looked out on to a walled yard with a tall privy in good condition and a small tumbledown outhouse that didn't look useable. The wall was of thick adobe. It was high and festooned at the top with wicked-looking barbed wire, thickly stapled, the pernicious stuff that was proliferating on what used to be open ranges, the stuff that the cowboys called 'bobwire'. Neither the privy nor the outhouse were near to the wall and Pilgrim didn't know what was on the other side of it.

There was a pile of rubbish near the wall, but it didn't look very high.

Even if a man got to the top of that and jumped he wouldn't be able to reach the top of the wall unless he had wings.

To Pilgrim's surprise Jules came out into the yard and went over to the rubbish pile. He delved among it as if searching for something. He still wore his side arm.

There was now no sound from down the street. Above the hush Pilgrim could hear the deputy burrowing like a squirrel.

With Pilgrim watching, whether Jules had spotted him or not, the deputy gathered battered cans and a couple of bottles and placed them on top of the pile which he seemed to have spread out with his fingers so that it was flatter and longer.

Pilgrim saw that the man wore old range gloves, the sort you'd keep for stringing wire and other dirty, scratchy chores. Jules placed the cans and bottles along the top of the elongated pile of rubbish. Then he stepped back and he turned and grinned at Pilgrim as if he'd been aware all the time that the prisoner was watching him.

Jules stamped his foot, faced around, drew. He was fast. And he was accurate. He fired three rapid shots. A bottle was smashed, and two cans jumped.

Jules turned again, grinning. 'Big gunfighter,' he said. 'I'm better'n you.'

Pilgrim said, 'Let me outa here and I'll prove to you that you ain't.'

Kid stuff, he thought, but maybe I could goad him.

But where in hell was Sheriff Lou Salliwell, why wasn't he out here? Did Jules do this sort of thing regularly, practising in the backyard? Most folks practised in the lonely open, that was the way. But this Jules was a goddamn show-off anyway.

Show-off or not, he wasn't it seemed about to be goaded. He turned again and fired off more shots and Pilgrim had to admit he was pretty good, must have practised a lot; wherever.

He was reloaded, was raising his

gun again when Obe Dacey appeared, must have gone right through the office and out of the back door. Jules must have been mighty careless to leave everything open like that. Had he done it purposely?

Dacey had a bandage on his face and his hat didn't sit right on his head. He looked as mad as a turkey in a thunderstorm.

Jules turned, gun still lifted.

'Don't point that at me,' Dacey stormed.

Jules holstered the gun. 'I didn't know it was you. What . . . ?'

'What do you think you're doin'? You're scaring the town.'

'I thought Saratoga Jack had put you down,' said Jules weakly.

'Well, he ain't. I'm here, ain't I?'

'I was just showing this big gunfighter that I'm as good as he is.'

'Now I've heard all the horse-shit I can stand. Where in hell is Lou Salliwell anyway?'

'He's gone to Tombstone.'

'Why would he go to Tombstone? At a time like this an' all!'

'I dunno. I guess he must have pressin' business there.'

Dacey had his gunbelt on. He drew. Jules started. His right hand was near his belt but he raised it. The watching Pilgrim figured that, though Jules was faster than Pilgrim had expected, Dacey was faster.

'Move back here, boy,' said the big man.

'What do you . . . ?'

'Do as I say. Move!'

Dacey jerked the gun. Jules moved. They both passed out of Pilgrim's sight.

When Pilgrim saw them again they were in the cell-block and Dacey still had the gun on Jules, had taken the deputy's own gear from him as well, had it looped over his free arm.

He told the deputy to let the prisoner out, and the bemused Jules did as he was told. Then he was locked in the cell himself, trussed and gagged with rope that Dacey hadn't found hard to discover.

Moments later, the two men were traversing the backs of town, both horsed, Pilgrim on his own paint which Dacey had thoughtfully gotten beforehand.

Like Jules before him, Pilgrim was somewhat bemused. Dacey had said, 'Come with me, Joe, I want to show you somep'n.' So Joe dutifully went along.

12

The shooting awoke Saratoga Jack fully from his doze and reawakened his headache also.

Hell, couldn't a man get no rest and quiet?

He didn't say the words aloud. To do so would've made his badly swollen jaw ache. He had a thick ear too, so right now wasn't hearing so good either.

Doc McTreen had told him that he was lucky his jaw didn't have to be wired, that he must keep it still anyway.

Jack wanted to call the doc, but he didn't dare. Instead he hammered on the wall with his big fist. Even that made him wince with bruised knuckles. However, persevering, cursing soundlessly, he knocked three times, with breaks in between.

No doc appeared. In fact, Jack didn't hear any sound at all from the direction of the surgery.

Maybe somebody had been shot, hurt bad, and the doc was needed. Jack lay back in his bed, his head thumping like a hundred midget Indians were doing a war dance right in there, complete with drums.

This bed! The two patients who had been its occupants before Jack had both come to a nasty end. Knocky Dowson. Tim Creegan.

That ain't gonna happen to me, Jack vowed, and he kept awake, listened to his thumping head and cursed monotonously under his breath.

★ ★ ★

Jules worked at his gag with his teeth, and at his bonds too, wriggling.

Dacey and Pilgrim didn't seem to have made a particularly careful job in either place. Maybe that had been on purpose and they just wanted to give themselves a start to where they were going, and they must be going someplace.

What had Dacey been playing at for Godsakes?

Jules got his gag off, spitting cloth from his teeth, cotton from his tongue. His bonds were a tougher proposition but, though he wouldn't have expected it, he had more success with those at his ankles than at his wrists. In the jail he wore moccasins. He wriggled these off and kept wriggling until the rawhide became untied.

He hopped over to the window and began to yell.

* * *

Despite his resolve not to do so, Saratoga Jack had dozed off again.

The yelling brought him fully awake with a start. He jerked involuntarily upward in the bed and let out a curse. Red-hot wires went through his jaws. Tom-toms beat in his head.

115

The yelling didn't quit, seemed to get louder. And there were other noises in the street.

To hell with it, thought Jack petulantly and he again went a little lower in the bed, watched the room through slit eyes and tried to ignore the continued yelling — as if somebody was calling for help. Now the drums in his head served to shut other sounds out anyway, though the drums weren't exactly for the better.

He didn't know how long he'd been in that half-lying position. But the yelling ceased. There were other noises though, and Doc McTreen came into the bedroom.

'What's goin' on?' Jack complained.

Doc said, 'Pilgrim's escaped from jail helped by Obe Dacey. They locked Jules in the cell, left the keys on the floor outside. Jules has taken a posse out. Your friend Snuff has gone along, says he wants Dacey's head.'

'He's an idiot,' said Jack. 'Anyway, where's the sheriff?'

'He's out of town it seems.'

'I'm getting out of bed, Doc.' Like a whale Jack moved. Doc didn't try and stop him.

Jack sat on the edge of the bed. Despite his pain he talked, but haltingly, softly.

'Anyway — Snuff's hurt, ain't he?'

'He's hurt all right. I put a bandage on his head. But he's going.'

'That business with Dacey, Doc, I didn't want it that way, didn't want the gun when that loco little bastard threw it. I — I just grabbed it sort of instinctive like. Dacey beat me fair an' square an' there ain't no blame for him in that.'

Jack stopped, gasping. He'd run his string, couldn't get any more words out. He still had his shirt, long-johns socks on. At loss for a time, Doc McTreen just stood looking down at him.

Struggling into his pants, Jack managed to get more words out. 'I don't know what Dacey's playin' at.

But I guess, lying here an' thinking, I'm not sure at all now that Pilgrim was responsible for Tim Creegan's death. I'm goin' after them.'

He was gasping again, shaggy head nodding.

The doc said, 'You shouldn't . . . '

'I'm goin', and you ain't gonna stop me.' His strength, and his words, seemed to come in spurts.

McTreen knew that he would be no match for the giant, halfway weakly though he still was. He did not get in the way, watched Jack lumber down the street to the livery stables. Doc didn't know what was behind anything any more. He was here to succour the sick and that was what he'd do and to hell with the rest of it, including huge, pigheaded Saratoga Jack, a man of many parts and strange visions.

★ ★ ★

Doc had only got things half-right. The first posse to go out after Pilgrim and Dacey wasn't led by the law in the shape of Deputy Jules but by Saratoga Jack's sidekick, small, squint-eyed Snuff.

In that part the fugitives had been unlucky, through the window of a canting where Snuff was drinking coffee and nursing his aching, bandaged hand, Snuff had, his squint eyes goggling for once, watched the two men leave town and, pronto, had got friends — and friends of Jack's — together and followed them. He'd thought that that was what Jack would have wanted him to do. When he'd seen Jack a while back the big feller had been out to the wide and hadn't been able to tell his little sidekick anything.

Dacey had done a job on Jack all right. And on Snuff too — though Snuff had surely asked for it. But Snuff, a murderous-minded, vengeful, little half-pint with a well-developed mean streak wanted his druthers, and then some.

The mob was a mob again, and they

were right on the heels of Pilgrim and Dacey, who hadn't expected pursuit nearly as soon as this.

A second posse set out somewhat later under the leadership of Jules, brought out of incarceration, untied, not quite as vengeful as Snuff, but almost.

'We'll have to make for the hills,' said Obe Dacey, looking back. 'That wasn't my first plan, but I hadn't figured on anybody coming after us so soon. We've got to shake this lot off, an' I know them hills.'

Pilgrim began, 'Why . . . ?'

Dacey interrupted him. 'Hell, I know you didn't kill Tim Creegan. I suppose Lou Salliwell, being the law, did what he figured was right. I still can't think why he moseyed off and left Jules in charge. Then Jules got my goat with his goddamn target practice, his goddamn showing-off, and things went on from there. Maybe I acted hastily but done is done an' here we are.'

He shut up, as if that was the

end of it and, for now, it was and Pilgrim, certainly not the gabbiest of individuals himself, said nothing. They both leaned over the necks of their galloping steeds.

Somebody fired a shot.

But they figured they were still out of range. And the foothills were before them, the craggy higher reaches going up to the sun.

The sun was in their eyes. But it would be in the eyes of their pursuers too, making shooting difficult.

They figured on four or five men. They had spotted that nasty little Snuff was at the head of them. They wondered if Deputy Jules had been let loose, but neither of them said so.

When they got into the hills they could get the sun at their backs and the pursuers, out there in the light, would be prime targets.

They made it, hunkered down in some rocks after stashing their horses further back out of harm's way, got set with their long guns. Dacey had sidearms too, but Pilgrim didn't. If only he had that trusty hogleg, the big Starr. But he hadn't. And probably he'd never see that well-modified big weapon, a gift from Marshal Joe, ever again.

His brain was making wheels now. He couldn't help that.

. . . Dacey had suggested that his letting Pilgrim out of the jail-cell after bracing noisy, show-off Jules had been on the spur of the moment. But, as Pilgrim recalled, Dacey had already had Pilgrim's paint pony ready and waiting for him beforehand. Had he? Well . . .

A bullet spanged off a rock not too far from his head, the snap of the rifles, the thin echoes rolling. He ducked, a pure reflex action.

'Let's not let 'em get in cover in the rocks,' said Dacey. 'Let's keep 'em horsed an' restless an' out in the open.'

They were both good with the Winchesters and the range now was just prime. They didn't really want to kill anybody if they could help it. Just nick 'em a bit, make 'em look at Old Man Death sideways and back away from him before he clawed them good.

Part Two

Revelations

13

The roughride to the hills was like a wild pilgrimage.

Snuff and his friends like rodeo riders on spooked horses. Snuff had already lost his hat, which had been perched perilously atop his bandage. Although he didn't know it, he could have had a hole in his head; but the marksman who'd been responsible for the sharpshooting hadn't wanted it that way.

Rifleshots snapping; horses skittering. And, at back, coming closer in the sun, Jules and his party, half a dozen in all.

And, bringing up the far rear, where nobody had spotted him yet, Saratoga Jack, a huge figure on his own big horse — and he certainly needed a big 'un — striving valiantly to catch up.

The men in the rocks were two

shootin' fools. But Snuff recklessly waved his men on. They weren't taking so much notice of him now, however.

He moved in a sidelong way himself, his horse skittish because of the gunfire. Dacey took a shot at him, the slug buzzing over the little man's shoulder. He wasn't a good target. His horse carried him backwards towards the others.

They were spread out. Nobody was doing much shooting then.

Dacey said between gritted teeth, 'If that little bastard comes that near again I'm liable to kill 'im.'

Pilgrim didn't know whether he meant it or not. He obviously hated Snuff, which was not surprising after the way the little skunk had tried to get Saratoga Jack to bushwhack the opponent who was fighting that big brawler fairly.

In his jail-cell, hearing the commotion, Pilgrim had heard about the fight from a jeering Deputy Jules.

Jules didn't have much to jeer about now. But there he was, in the distance, leading his men; and Snuff and his boys turning towards them and a bit of shouting on both sides.

'We can't fight an army,' Dacey said. 'Let's get further back.' He rose and, half-crouching, led the way. He flung orders over his shoulder. There was no shooting to blanket his voice now.

His grandmother was a Yaqui Indian, he said. She married an Irishman called Coolihan. They had three daughters, one of whom married a Yankee called Dacey, who came West to ranch. His son Obediah Dacey didn't remember much about him, he'd died of fever when the boy was just a kid.

The boy had visited his grandmother and her people in the hills on the Arizona borderlands. He had been an honorary brave among these people who, though not pillaging whites like the more numerous and warlike Apaches and Comanches did, mainly kept themselves apart from Anglos and the like and even native Mexicans.

'I've spent much of my life in places like this,' Dacey said, climbing. A supremely fit man, he didn't seem at all short of breath. He bore marks of his battle with Saratoga Jack but they didn't seem to faze him. It had been a short fight, mainly due to little Snuff's treachery. But Snuff and all the rest were way below now, though, glancing back, Pilgrim had seen some of them climbing, out of gun-range, he hoped, soon out of sight.

He could imagine Dacey as an Injun boy. He moved like an Indian now, like a prowling cat as one with this craggy environment, picking his way unerringly as if all the time he'd known where he was going.

Had they been making for here in the first place, Pilgrim wondered? Dacey had said it was because of the pursuers coming sooner than had been expected. Dacey had promised to show Pilgrim 'something'. Would that be soon, or later?

Weaving and sliding, panting a little, Pilgrim followed the big man. Big for an Injun, Yaqui or not. But some Yaquis were handsome people; proud people too with their own culture and traditions.

Hell, Dacey was only part Yaqui, and married to a Mexican lady. An enigmatic man. What was he up to now? Where was he going?

Dacey paused on flatter ground and, suddenly, Pilgrim knew where he was.

The jumble of boulders where he'd found the rattler-bitten body of Dill Rickles. And beyond that, and in his sight now, the cave where Tim Creegan had been tortured by Dill and his partner, Knocky. And all three of them now to their happy hunting grounds.

Dacey was making for the cave, and Pilgrim followed him. Like the tail of a goddamned kite, he thought, *what am I doing*?

Swinging his Winchester; Dacey ahead of him swinging his too. Pilgrim not wanting to lose sight of the big man in the thickening darkness, getting closer, trying to step lightly, but awakening ghostly echoings which seemed to go on, and on, *and on*.

The cave seemed to bend at the top. That had been the end of it, Pilgrim had thought last time he saw the place. But he had been in a hurry to get the battered Tim Creegan out of there. He hadn't explored. He hadn't been back there since.

Dacey suddenly halted. Pilgrim almost cannoned into the shadowy bulk. Not much light penetrated in here from outside. Looking back, Pilgrim couldn't see the entrance, just a faint glow, and a spear of sun through the thin fissure in the vaulted roof. But the sun didn't reach back here.

'Step back, Joe,' said Dacey. 'There's a queer-shaped boulder here blockin' the way. You'd think it was part of a wall. There's a knack in shiftin' it, but I can do that.'

Pilgrim didn't feel like being obedient. But he did as he'd been told anyway.

There was a rumbling noise. Momentarily, Dacey looked as if he'd become part of the wall. The wall seemed to move. Then Dacey was out of sight.

'Step right forward, Joe,' the voice said, sounding strangely cavernous. Again Pilgrim followed instruction.

He blinked as light blossomed in front of his eyes.

Dacey must have snapped a lucifer with his thumbnail. Above the rumbling, the pattering of dust and small stones, Pilgrim hadn't heard the other tiny sound.

They were in another cave, smaller than the outside one which could be called the 'parent' one. Dacey held a battered storm lantern aloft. It must have been there all the time.

'Better put that cover back,' Dacey said, 'in case folk find their way here.'

'Our horses are way back,' muttered Pilgrim. He hoped the posse — or posses — didn't commandeer them.

Dacey went past him after placing

the glowing lantern on the floor. He manipulated the rock back into place, said, 'Don't worry. It'll shift again. I know the way. But no light will escape outside now. I found this place by accident when I was exploring these hills. Mebbe I was lookin' for secret places.' He gave a little spurt of laughter. 'Injuns love secret places. 'Specially Yaquis. The lantern was here then. It's been here a long time I guess. I had to get oil for it.'

He pointed upwards. 'There are some thick cracks up there like in the other chamber. I was up top when I caught my heel in one of them and wondered if there was anything else. I came round into the main chamber with a light and, probably just by accident, found this secret place. Now look over here, Joe.'

He led the way to a corner of the small cage where there was a hole, a small pile of soil beside it. This was a foreign place in the rock floor with stunted bits of dried colourless vegetation peeping out here and there.

Dacey placed the lantern beside the hole and dug down with his one hand and brought forth soil. Holding it to the light, he let it trickle through his fingers.

It was black, but specks of gold shone through, some of them adhering to Dacey's fingers.

'That's gold, Joe,' the big man said. 'Not fool's gold, real gold. I reckon a bag of the stuff was buried here and the bag leaked a mite, lettin' some of the stuff through to the soil.'

'Yeh, looks that way,' said Pilgrim. 'But where's the bag now?'

Dacey chuckled, not much humour in it. 'Well, I ain't got no bag. Nor no gold. There ain't enough here to put in your eye. It's worth shit. It's gone, the big loot. Mebbe it's been gone a long time. Who can tell? I ain't even got a finder's fee. Anyway, you're the first person I've told about this, let alone shown it to. I even began to think that the Tiller tale, the legend or whatever you'd like to call it, was a barrel of horse-shit, something cooked up by somebody an' passed around as legends are.'

'Yeh, the West's full of 'em,' Pilgrim said. He chuckled, didn't sound too amused. 'Injun ones an' all.'

'This Injun don't believe in legends,' Dacey said. 'Did the gold go in the lake? Or did somebody take it, making fools of everybody who has looked for it since an' even prospected in these hills and found nothing?'

'I guess somebody still figures there are goodies still around here someplace,' Pilgrim said. 'I don't think all that torturin' and killin' was for plumb nothin'.'

'You're durn tootin'. And it all seemed to start when you came to Tiller's Watch an' Bill an' Knocky braced you. But who was behind Bill an' Knocky, tell me that, Joe?'

'You know this territory and its folks better than I do,' said Pilgrim pointedly. 'You tell me.'

'I can't.'

'Is this where you planned to bring me in the first place?'

'No. If that posse, that bunch with that little son-bitch Snuff hadn't been on our heels I'd've taken you someplace else.'

The inevitable question was poised on Pilgrim's lips then; but Dacey went on quickly, his voice lowered, 'There's somebody in the other place.' He blew out the lamp. They both froze. They heard footsteps, voices.

14

The two men in the little cavern couldn't hear any actual words from the front part, only mumbling, scraping, small thuds. But suddenly the thuds became louder, violent even, crashing against the rock walls, resounding in the smaller chamber. There was a pattering of dust falling on the two men who waited in the darkness.

And then, as suddenly as they had started, the greater sounds died. The sounds became sort of furtive.

Dacey went slowly over to the bulwark which separated their small space from the larger one. He was silent for a moment and then he returned to Pilgrim, said, 'I think they've gone.'

Matching his companion's low voice, Pilgrim said, 'Best hang on a bit anyway. We don't want to walk out of that big cave an' into a hail of lead.'

Dacey said, 'I don't think the posse'd start shootin' like that.' Then he added as if as a concession to his companion, 'But, yeh, mebbe that little bastard Snuff might.'

They were silent for a short time and they didn't hear any more sound. Earlier, they hadn't heard horses or men approach. Now they didn't hear them go away. The cave walls were thick, and they were in the inner part after all.

Eventually, still keeping his voice low in case somebody had an ear pressed to a wall, Pilgrim said, 'Y'know, I've got mighty keen hearing an it didn't seem to me there was a whole lot of folk came into that big cave. Maybe even only one — an' a lotta echoes.'

'I dunno. Anyway, I don't expect the whole goddamn bunch would get in there. Two bunches in fact.' Dacey was suddenly away from Pilgrim again, moving to the big boulder. He was quiet for a bit, and then he hissed, 'I can't hear a thing.'

Pilgrim joined him, pressed an ear to the cold rock, said, 'Naw. You're right.'

'Stand back, Joe. I'll shift this.'

Pilgrim got out of his way, heard him pulling, manipulating. But the wall didn't seem to move as it had done on the other side, letting them in. It didn't seem to move at all.

'It's stuck,' hissed Dacey. Pilgrim moved to help him.

'Here,' Dacey said. 'Here!' They used all their strength, straining, panting.

'They've blocked it somehow on the other side,' Dacey said. 'We're stuck.'

Something rumbled. Dust pattered. It was as if they, too, had brought about some change.

But still the rock wouldn't move.

'I guess it'd help if the lamp was lit again,' said Pilgrim caustically.

'Oh, sure. I left it by that hole.' Dacey turned, went off in the darkness. He'd been catlike but suddenly, wasn't catlike any more. He knocked the lamp over and Pilgrim heard the glass break and, though what had happened was certainly not a good thing, couldn't suppress a smile, which Dacey couldn't see of course.

The would-be omnipotent big man was suddenly getting his balls all in a tangle.

He was silent. But the snap of a lucifer had a savage sound about it in the ghostly darkness. The flame blossomed. The lamp was lit, flickered. But there was no draught and the glow blossomed through the shattered glass.

'Thanks be to that,' said Dacey, and there was laughter in his voice now and Pilgrim warmed to him anew.

* * *

'I saw somep'n,' said Snuff, halting, crouching low, pointing.

Beside him Jules said, 'Don't go off half-cocked. I'm warning you. No shooting 'less I say so.' The young deputy had taken on a new authority

141

and he was being backed by his posse-members, a mite more numerous than Snuff's lot, barflies all.

He was being backed also by Snuff's friend and mentor, big Saratoga Jack, who had caught up with the rest of them and was climbing manfully.

Jack said, 'Heed what he says, Snuff, me boy.' And that clinched things it seemed.

'I didn't see anything anyway,' said Jules.

'Me neither,' said Jack.

Nobody else had a comment to make. The men were spread out, striving, panting, their horses way below them.

Many of Snuff's friends were lagging behind, wishing they were back in town with a cold flagon of beer in front of them. In Dacey's Place even, though Dacey wouldn't be there right now. He was up in these hills someplace, they didn't know where.

Snuff's main friend, Jack, was up front with Jules and more of the volunteer law deputies and they were the first to break out in the clearing.

Jules said, 'There's a cave here, I remember that.' He pointed.

* * *

Their faces and eyes gleamed in the lamplight. Dacey was on his knees, Pilgrim squatted beside him. Dacey said, 'This doesn't look the same. It's almost as if something's been pushed in from the other side. I think we were blocked in deliberately anyway. But I don't guess the posse would do that.'

'Snuff might.'

'But there are the others.'

Dacey broke off, began to use his hands, passing small boulders back to Pilgrim who cleared a space, dragging the stuff back. Soon he was able to help. They worked like beavers.

Then they rose to crouching positions, deciding to push.

They pushed.

The flame of the lantern flickered,

went out. 'That's the oil gone I guess,' said Dacey.

'It's goin',' said Pilgrim. But he didn't mean the lamp.

'Watch it,' he shouted and they both staggered backwards in the pitch darkness as the wall almost fell on them.

Dust enveloped them and they coughed, cursed, spat. But they saw a faint light ahead.

They broke out. Dacey almost fell over the stout bough of a tree which had obviously been used as a lever. More rocks were piled out here. 'Somebody tried to tomb us in,' Dacey said. 'Bury us for good.'

They went out through the big cave, the sun, though it was less powerful now, almost blinding them. Blinking, they stopped dead, facing ranks of armed men. Two dirty, dishevelled scarecrows.

'Godalmighty,' said Saratoga Jack. 'What happened to you two?'

'How long have you been here?'

demanded Pilgrim hotly.

'I'll ask the questions,' said Deputy Jules, importantly.

Suddenly he was king of the heap. And, compared to the two bedraggled ex-fugitives, he was downright immaculate.

'We'll go back to town with you boys,' said Dacey. 'And I ain't saying a thing about anything till we get there.'

'I'll go along with that,' said his companion.

'I will say one more thing, though,' said Dacey, and everybody seemed to be looking at him expectantly.

This was no lynch-mob. This was a sizeable bunch of tired, dusty polyglot individuals who had worked off their spleen over a long, rough, *climbing* trail and were too damn weary for an argument.

Dacey said, 'Yeh, I'll tell you one more thing. Pilgrim here didn't kill Tim Creegan, an' I know that for a fact. You can take my word on it.'

Nobody knew his real name. He'd had many names. Then, years ago, somebody dubbed him 'Preach' because of the way he looked. It stuck and he didn't seem to mind it.

He was an old man now. But he still dressed the same as he'd always done, as far as anybody remembered that is — and many of his contemporaries were long gone. And if he'd ever been a kid 'twas said he'd been spawned by a snake colder than any snake could be.

He was six foot two and thin to the point of emaciation but straight as a ramrod. He wore a black coat just a mite too large for him, easier for fast movement, ruffled shirt and black string tie, tight pants and polished high riding boots which came almost to his knees.

He wore only one gun in plain sight, a big modified Remington groomed to his own specification, loose on his thigh in a long holster tied down with a whang-string, a small thong on the hammer too.

The rig wasn't too ornate, just solid, and wickedly workmanlike. It was known by some folks that he carried other weapons, but they were cunningly out of sight and didn't seem to weigh him down none. He still walked like a loping cat, though maybe stiffer than he used to — until he heard a call to action.

He'd had many calls like that through his long and checkered career. It was bruited that he'd killed thirty men; but who was counting?

Just after the arrival in Tombstone of the old killer with the skull-face and expressionless basalt eyes, Sheriff Lou Salliwell of Tiller's Watch turned up there. He was visiting his friend County Sheriff Jack Behan.

The town marshal at this time was Virgil Earp whom Lou had met and liked. Virgil pointed out killer Preach to Lou.

Lou had heard about the man — who

in the southwest hadn't? — but hadn't actually seen him before. He figured that Preach didn't know Lou from Adam.

Tombstone and the silver-mining territory of San Pedro around it which had caused its inception from a sun-baked nothing to an up-and-coming town, was being plagued by claimjumpers, conmen, rustlers and assorted stick-up artistes.

Virgil Earp was waiting for his brothers Wyatt, James and Morgan — and Wyatt's gambler friend John 'Doc' Holliday — to turn up, hoping they would be of some help to him in his law-bringing.

Although he had never met other members of the Earp clan, Lou Salllwell had certainly heard of them — particularly Wyatt who had made a law-rep for himelf as a sort of constable in Dodge City, helped somewhat, it was murmured, by his friend, Doc.

Lou Salliwell thought, with all the Earps, and some of their cohorts, in

Tombstone, there was bound to be more trouble, but he didn't dwell on it: none of his business anyway.

He figured there'd be a lot of politicking going on in Tombstone territory ere long — and he didn't hold with too much of that going hand in hand with law-bringing.

When tall old Preach left Tombstone, Lou followed him at a discreet distance.

Come to think of it, there'd been a recent rumour that Preach had started to have his highly paid professional killing done for him by other folk, only turning up himself for straightforward and often unpaid challenges, jealously living up to his terrible reputation. But there'd been fewer challenges of that kind in recent years.

Preach took a trail that Sheriff Salliwell knew extremely well.

Though it was night Preach didn't veer at all.

Maybe he'd had good directions given to him.

Or maybe he'd been this way years

ago. That was likely.

It was past dawn when he skirted the lake. Lou watched him from a dip of ground just past the hills on the approach to Tiller's Watch, and he saw that the tall upright man on the rawboned brown horse didn't go right into the town, but reined up outside a house on the edge and entered through its front door.

15

Tiller's Watch was under a sort of miasma of anti-climax. On their way after recapturing the two fugitives — if they could still be called that — the tired conglomeration of voluntary roughriders hadn't talked much. Who could call 'em a posse now? Or two posses, to which was added Saratoga Jack, a one-man posse who now said he felt awful, wished he had stayed in bed.

Somebody had said something about seeing somebody up on the bluffs before Pilgrim and Dacey came out of the cave. Nobody from the pursuing bunch had been up there. By that time they were all pretty much together.

And it couldn't have been the fugitives, could it? At that time they would've been in the cave — or would they? But nobody seemed to actually want to start an argument. It was just a sort of whining . . .

Anyway, it was Snuff, in the lead at the time, who'd said he spotted somebody. Nobody else had, or didn't admit that they had. And now, with his friend Jack sort of peeved with him, Snuff was in disfavour with the company, which spread every-which-way when it got to town.

Deputy Jules, Joe Pilgrim and Obe Dacey got together in the law office, but Pilgrim wasn't put back in his cell. It was full dark and the lights were gleaming. Sheriff Salliwell hadn't returned yet.

Although Pilgrim and Dacey couldn't figure how two, maybe three of the posse-members could possibly have tried to entrap them in the inner cave, they hadn't divulged the fact to anybody that they had been incarcerated for a while. They didn't tell Jules about this even in the privacy of the office.

The young man was quite tractable now and he certainly wasn't scared

that these two desperadoes might turn
on him.

He had a question to ask, however,
one that had been eating at him all the
while during the weary ride back from
the hills.

* * *

Lou knew the house, knew the woman
who lived there.

A woman alone whose name was
Greta Boilon.

Lou didn't like to think of Preach
being with her. What was that old,
degenerate killer doing there?

There was a small grove of trees to
the right of the house. Lou made a
detour and approached them from the
side, as far away from the building
as possible, hoping his horse's slowly
moving hoofbeats wouldn't be heard.

He left the horse hidden in the
trees and made another sweep and
walking lightly, carrying his big bulk
well, approached the house from the

back. There was no light on in the kitchen area. He had already ascertained that there was a glow downstairs at the front.

There was no cover now between him and the house except a privy and a small hut which he knew contained odd household tackle. It wasn't the first time he'd been around here.

The woman's husband, Lemuel Boilon, had been the local blacksmith and Lou's good friend. He had been kicked in the head by a crazy horse and his senses had fled from him. His wife, Greta, had nursed him through a sort of early dotage with the help of Lou and others, until he'd died and was laid to rest in a spot on boothill which caught the morning sun, reminding the townsfolk how big genial Lemuel had always sat before his shop in the early mornings when the sun was kind, greeting everybody who passed before he began his day's work.

The couple had had no children and, it seemed, nobody could take

154

Lemuel's place in Greta's eyes. Lou remained Greta's best friend, and later they became discreet lovers. But she would not marry him. And she stayed at the handsome frame house on the edge of town, the home that Lemuel had built for the two of them.

Although Lou knew this back way so well, he had never approached it so silently or secretly before.

It wasn't till he was in the kitchen that he realized he'd been discovered, and by then it was too late.

He began to turn in the blackness as he heard the swishing noise. He must have reached for his gun also in a desperate reflex action. But the blow on his head was like a tree falling upon him, its leaves blanketing, smothering him, bringing a greater darkness, an absolute ending.

The ending did not last and he was acutely aware of that as pain stabbed at his head. Also, he soon realized, he couldn't move, was tied hand and foot. He was gagged too, could only make smothered sounds that made his headache worse.

He still lay on the floor but, rolling painfully, he saw the greyish light of an uncurtained window — curtains undrawn anyway — which lessened the blackness but gave him but little relief.

Smells assailed his nostril, and they were not unpleasant. He realised he was still in the kitchen, lying on the floor. Rush threads tickled his hands as he struggled with his bonds. But the rawhide was tight, cutting into his wrists. He was lying on one of the rush mats in the kitchen. Maybe the one nearest to the sink. He remembered those rush mats well.

He thought he heard voices in one of the other rooms. This place was very strongly built, the walls thick and cool and pretty soundproof.

His mystification grew. And then his rage.

He struggled frenziedly, using all the strength of his big body. But this only made him madder, frustrated, more mystified.

★ ★ ★

Preach said, 'I ought to slit his throat.'

Greta said, You can't. I won't let you. Unless you want to slit mine first.'

'I can't, you know that.' He sat in his shirt-sleeves with his collar open and his string tie loose and dangling. He sat opposite the comely, dark-haired woman at the big dining-table her husband had made. Lemuel had been a pretty fine carpenter as well as the town's best tarrier and blacksmith.

Greta said, 'You can't do anything to him. I warn you, don't try.'

'You'll have to keep him here then. Can you do that?'

'I can try. I don't want him hurt. I don't want either of you hurt.'

'I can look after myself.' He rose. 'I should be back by nightfall.'

'You're — you're not going into town?'

'No, I'm not going into town,' he echoed, flatly. He was tying his tie, putting on his coat, taking his gun gear from the back of a chair.

★ ★ ★

In answer to the question from Jules, Dacey said, 'I know Pilgrim didn't kill Tim Creegan. I know! Maybe Lou Salliwell knows now but, even if he does, he ain't here to tell us, is he?'

The natty young deputy suddenly gave signs of being quicker on the uptake than the others had given him credit for. He said, 'Lou knew you wouldn't let anything happen to Pilgrim, didn't he?'

'Maybe he did,' said Dacey. Pilgrim looked from one to the other of them without speaking.

Jules went on, 'His break-out — ' he jerked a thumb in Pilgrim's direction — 'that was kind of a set-up, wasn't it?'

'Not exactly. I didn't know Saratoga

Jack was gonna act the way he actually did — whoever knows with Jack? I certainly didn't think Jack's sidekick Snuff was gonna go off half-cocked the way he did. That even took Jack by surprise, and he's made up for it since. I didn't know that you were gonna get yourself some target practice in the backyard. That was Linda show-off stupid wasn't it?'

Jules smiled. 'Kinda, I guess.'

'I had to act then,' said Dacey, 'before the whole town went haywire.'

* * *

'You're not going yet,' said Greta firmly, barring his path. 'I want Lou in the bed upstairs so I can tend to him.'

Preach smiled thinly, his dark eyes pitiless. 'I guess he's been up there before, huh?'

'None o' your business. You do as I say. I'll stay here till it's done and you can be on your way.' Greta's voice was suddenly scornful. 'You got your mighty weapons and you've got him as well. He's not gonna bite you. But I don't want him harmed again, y'understand?'

'I hope you know what you're doing. If he yells or gets away . . . '

'He's bound and gagged, isn't he? All you have to do is untie his legs and make him walk. I'll do the rest. I've got a gun as well.'

'I don't believe you'd use it.'

'You can believe what you like. You're wasting time.'

'All right.' He turned and left the room.

Not much later, riding across the open prairie, he had time for reflection. Should he have gone to the other place first, not to Greta's place? Maybe he should have stayed away from Greta this time. But that son-bitch had been on his tail — he'd only spotted the man towards the end of the journey — so maybe he shouldn't have led him to the other place, might've caused complications.

More complications was something he didn't want. If it wasn't for complications he wouldn't be here now.

Was he getting soft in his old age? Should he have handled Greta differently?

He told himself that he was still the same old Preach. He could draw as swiftly as he'd ever done, could shoot as straight, could kill without compunction because that was what he did best. He was prepared to do it again.

But there was a conflict of interest . . .

Greta Boilon found herself in a similar predicament.

Up in her bedroom, as Sheriff Lou Salliwell half-reclined in her bed, she had tended his head. His legs had been left unbound but otherwise he was in the same state as before.

She had told him that she would remove his gag if he promised not to yell. He had shook his head vehemently, his eyes accusing her.

Although she reviled herself in her mind, she was glad that he'd refused her offer. She didn't want to hear his questions, didn't want to give her answers.

She told him to rest, and she went downstairs. He didn't seem too bad, but still she wondered if he needed a doctor. But she knew Doc McTreen, a good friend to both of them, would have questions to ask, wouldn't be still about anything.

Lou had no other woman to look after him, only her. He had been married once, she knew, although she had never seen the girl and he never alluded to her any more. She had left him; there had been no offspring.

There was a knock at the door. She was startled.

Then she remembered: it was Tuesday. Reba Dacey, wife of Obediah, and Debbie Clandell, wife of Jabez, always visited her on a Tuesday and had coffee and a chat. Debbie, in the little gig, always went to Dacey's Place first and collected Reba and brought her out here.

The kitchen door was unlocked. And if Greta didn't answer the knock — there was the second one! — they'd just open the door and walk in, calling out in their warm, cheerful fashion.

She went out to the door.

16

Greta had closed the bedroom window. Even so, Lou wouldn't have been able to make himself heard anyway. He had chewed at his gag but hadn't been able to shift it.

He was somewhat punch-drunk but his brain wasn't addled. He had certainly been in the wars lately though, as the saying was. His wounded shoulder had healed fine but, with him struggling, had begun to ache. That and his head seemed to be vying with each other for consideration and Lou cursed them both from beneath his gag.

But then he began to hear things.

The closed window didn't cut out all sounds, although no noises from the town could be heard on the edge here: Lou had made note of that before. Even when the town was jumping when the cowboys were there at night this spot was a quiet place.

But now he thought he heard the sound of wheels. He strained his ears. These wheels were squeaking, badly needed oiling. But now he could distinguish soft hoofbeats.

And they stopped below, and the squeaking stopped too, and he heard the back door open and female voices.

Suddenly he remembered what day it was. Tuesday. He knew that Greta always had a visit from her two friends Debbie and Reba on a Tuesday. She visited Reba pretty frequently in town and sometimes the two of them went out to the Clandell place and Debbie, though not so often: that was understandable, of course.

Lou's legs were free. He used them as sort of leverage and began to struggle with all his might.

Suddenly he was rolling. Then he was off the edge of the bed. His big body hit the floor, shaking it mightily.

He lay there, his head swimming none too gently. But he managed to have a sardonically humorous thought: he had been in this bed before but this was the first time he'd fallen out.

He heard clattering footsteps on the stairs and strove to rise, didn't make it.

Reba Dacey burst into the room. She'd always been the feistiest of the three ladies. In her fist she had a small nickel-plated derringer. 'Jehosophat,' she said. 'What in tarnation's happening here?'

Greta came through the door behind. The younger lady, Debbie Clandell brought up the rear.

* * *

Small, squint-eyed Snuff was peevish and at a loose end. He had been to see his friend Saratoga Jack who was still resting up. Jack had told him to take his ass outa there an' bury it.

Snuff stood at the bar and looked about him and scowled. He'd already had a few quick drinks and was feeling sorry for himself and fed up right to the back teeth by his fellow townsmen who, to his mind, had let a killer slip through their hands like molasses in the sun. That the killer was back in the jailhouse was no consolation to Snuff right then.

He brightened when five Cross U boys came to the bar. One of them said, 'Sounds like we missed all the fun.'

So somebody had been talking already!

Pity they hadn't come earlier, Snuff thought.

'You shore did, boys,' Snuff said.

The Cross U was a horse ranch and this bunch were cayuse-breakers, wranglers, roughriders. Hard men. Harder than the average cowpuncher even. Men who liked taking chances at work and out of it. Particularly out of it, meeting trouble more than halfway and relishing it.

They were more than willing to listen to Snuff, who had the reputation of a nasty little sidewinder. A friend of notorious Saratoga Jack he was also, and that must mean something.

Jack wasn't around yet but maybe he would be. The boys knocked back their drinks as fast as ever, as was their way. And then Snuff — Jack or no Jack — led them. And they followed him. Not like sheep. More like wolves, noisier than usual, just looking for sheep so they could have a tearing, racing, chasing, happy game.

Jostling each other, pushing each other from side to side like children, they went down the street with Snuff at their head. Oh, they were hard men all right; but young. Snuff was much the eldest and they followed him. They had boozed very quickly, whereas Snuff had had plenty of time. He was much the most vicious.

A few barflies tagged behind. They had taken part in the other march on the jail and nothing had come of it. Maybe now they had another chance. Really they didn't care one way or another, were just going along for the fun of it and maybe a chance to kick a few heads.

The old jailer had been in the saloon, had gone along the backs of town to warn the three men in the jail office. was a surprise to the crowd to see the four men out on the stoop, all with ready guns.

It brought them up short, but so inebriated were they that it caused them some merriment also, and they began to slap each other again in boisterous byplay and stagger in all directions.

Snuff had no use for such jollifications, however. He pointed his finger at Joe Pilgrim and shouted, 'There he is. There's the killer. He's out here free as a bird. Whatdyuh think o' that?'

'You're like a burr in a burro's ass, little man,' Pilgrim said, his voice rising. 'Go back there an' take your drunken friends with you.'

'You heard what the man said,' shouted Deputy Jules. 'Get away from here. The first man who steps on this sidewalk gets peppered, I promise yuh.'

Snuff began to hop up and down like a monkey on a see-saw with a bag of manure on the other end. The biggest young jasper among the horse-breakers began to clap his hands in some sort of rhythm, but getting nearer to the sidewalk all the time in a hoppity sort of way, nearer in fact to Pilgrim.

Then he suddenly gave a wild Injun yell and flung himself at the so-called 'killer'.

Pilgrim wasn't to be caught that easily. He swung his borrowed Colt and its barrel cropped the big young man solidly along the side of the head. He went down like a felled tree, raising the same sort of dust that a tree might, and staying down also.

Obe Dacey had a shotgun. He let off both barrels, the charges screaming over the crowd. And, as the echoes died, Jules yelled, 'Stand still, all o' yuh!'

They stood.

'Raise your hands!'

They raised 'em.

The big feller, who had a head like a boulder, was rising slowly to his feet. His eyes were glazed and he shook his head slowly from side to side.

'I've been slugged,' he said thickly. 'I wanna make a complaint. Where's the sheriff? Where's that damn' sheriff?'

One of his pards gave a howl of laughter. 'I saw the sheriff earlier,' he said. 'Outa town. I saw another gent too, like a skelington — on a big horse. Black. Him not the horse. Looked like a preacherman. Him not the horse. Looked like the sheriff was tailing the tall skelington man in black. He went in the nice frame house on the edge of town. Then the sheriff sort of made a detour and came round back o' the house.'

'How come you saw all that, Clem?' asked another feller owlishly.

'I was tryin' to catch a little wild cayuse weren't I? An' the li'l bastard gave me the slip after all.'

171

'Preach,' said Pilgrim. 'I know him.'

'Sounds like him,' said Dacey. 'And that house is Greta Boilon's place. She's a good friend of Lou's. She's a good friend of my missus too. Hell, it's Tuesday. Reba could be there now. They meet for a chinwag on Tuesdays. An' Debbie Clandell.'

They left Jules and the oldster to hold the jail. The crowd was making back for the saloon, shouting jocular insults backwards and forwards, and exchanging a few with their pards also and various unshaven townies. Even the snappy Snuff had made himself scarce, mightily disgruntled no doubt.

17

They made a gap between them as they approached the back of the house. The Clandell gig was there, the pony cropping grass contentedly, not evincing any interest in the new arrivals. The place was quiet. They came closer together and approached the kitchen window and looked in.

They saw a sight they hadn't expected to see and Dacey hissed, 'Godamighty.'

Debbie and Reba were seated at the kitchen table and facing them with a shotgun was their friend Greta who didn't look at all friendly now.

The men backed off and Pilgrim said softly, 'Go round the front an' knock the door. I'll take it this side. Trust me.'

'All right.' Dacey moved lightly for so big a man.

Pilgrim went back to the window.

He drew his gun. He didn't, of course, hear the knocking on the door but he saw all three women start.

The woman whom Pilgrim didn't know, the one who had been referred to as Greta, half-rose, her head turning.

Pilgrim unlatched the door and moved in. 'Drop that gun, honey,' he said. 'Or I'll have to shoot you.'

'He means it, Greta,' said Reba Dacey.

Wide-eyed with shock, Greta lowered the weapon to the floor. As she rose again Pilgrim saw that her face had been smudged with tears and there was still a suspicious brightness in those wide eyes. What the hell?

'Go and open the door for your husband, Reba,' he said.

'Right, Joe.'

The third, and youngest pretty woman, Debbie Clandell, watched her two friends and didn't say a word.

Pilgrim looked at Debbie and Greta in turn, waiting for one of them to speak. Neither of them did. Both of them looked as if they had awakened from a dream, were not with the real world yet.

Reba returned with Obe who asked, 'What the hell's been happening here?'

Then, strangely, it was Debbie who spoke up, beating her friend Reba to the punch it seemed.

'Sheriff Salliwell is upstairs. He's hurt and he's tied up. Greta wouldn't let us help him.' Her voice was toneless. She sat with her hands demurely in her lap as if on a polite visit. It *had* been a polite visit, a friendly, affectionate one! It had turned into a nightmare.

'Watch 'em, Obe,' said Pilgrim and he found the stairs.

★ ★ ★

Lou Salliwell said he didn't feel so bad, considering.

With Pilgrim he joined the others in the kitchen; and then the revelations poured forth in a halting sometimes uncertain way.

Preach was Greta's brother, real name Ted Crane, once known as Dollar Crane. He hadn't visited his sister often: her husband Lemuel hadn't liked him there. She didn't know what special reason he had had for coming to this territory at this time.

Even Lou Salliwell hadn't known Greta's maiden name. But the name Dollar Crane struck a chord in Pilgrim's mind.

He knew Preach, of course. It might be said that they were in the same kind of business.

Debbie Clandell came out with another revelation, though a small one that she hadn't thought to mention beforehand to either of her friends. Greta, of course, hadn't mentioned her brother's visit. But when Debbie had been coming in with the gig before picking up Reba she had passed the man on the trail, though she hadn't realized he'd been coming from Greta's place.

An imposing-looking oldish but very

176

straight man, who had courteously tipped his hat to her, on the trail that could take him to her place, or to what was left of the tragic Tim Creegan's place, or on further to the horse ranch called the Cross U or way past there to smaller settlements that were dotted around on the wide prairie. One of those. Or on to Tombstone.

But he'd come from there, Sheriff Salliwell explained. He'd tailed Preach from there but hadn't been circumspect or clever enough; and he had a headache to prove it.

Pilgrim had been thinking hard. He said he thought he knew where Preach had been going.

Dollar Crane, yes. The name chimed in with two other names. Names from the past. Jeremiah Tiller, elderly prospector. His young partner, Caleb Tripp. And Tripp's friend, Dollar Crane who might or might not have been responsible for Jeremiah's death. Jeremiah, the 'watching' man who had, indirectly, given the neighbouring town, then unbuilt, unknown, its descriptive name.

A seated skeleton with skull looking out at the placid waters of a lake which had been thought to hold a rich secret in its waters. But probably didn't . . .

Greta Boilon was openly weeping, kept saying brokenly, 'I'm so sorry. *I'm so sorry* . . . '

Obe Dacey would go with Pilgrim.

His wife would go back to town, look after the place, was quite used to doing this while Obe was a-roaming. Pretty young Debbie, sweetly forgiving, said she would stay with Greta.

Pilgrim wasn't sure that Debbie staying was a good idea, though maybe it wouldn't be wise to leave Greta on her own. He hoped nobody else didn't turn up there unexpectedly.

He decided not to say anything about his doubts. He and Obe left, waving Reba on her way in the opposite direction.

★ ★ ★

When Reba got back to the place in Tiller's Watch it was to learn that the Cross U horse-breakers were still there — and it looked as if more trouble could be brewing. But this was not now in the lap of those jovial boys who'd been sampling the culinary delights of the establishment. These, today, in Reba's absence, had been in the hands of her protégé, a young Indian girl called Suley-Ann, who was turning out to be almost as good a cook as the madam was.

Suley-Ann was being complimented by the boys under the watchful eyes of the big barman — his shotgun at his elbow — ready to step in if anybody got a mite too familiar. Nobody did. The boys had had their fun — hell, they hadn't expected to hang anybody anyway; they were sober after their meal, they were replete, they were smoking, they were relaxing like beeves browsing in the twilight after a bellyful of the best cud they could find.

It wasn't twilight yet, though, only

almost — when little squint-eyed Snuff revealed himself to the boys once more, staggering and shouting, as drunk as a turkey that had gobbled a sour-mash pie.

He screamed, 'What is the matter with you yeller-bellied skunks? Ain't any of you got any stomicks at all? You let a killer get away from you an' he's wild an' loose now an' ready to kill again. I tell yuh, all o' yuh, a bunch o' lily-livered sonbitches like yuh just ain't welcome in my town.'

There was more of the same, but Snuff got garbled, inarticulate, out of breath. And the boys, their boisterousness at an end, the little Indian cook retreating behind them, the big barman lifting his shooter. Well, the boys, they were on their feet, advancing in a ragged half-circle. And that was when Snuff's friend, Saratoga Jack, turned up and said, 'Leave this to me, my friends, if you please.'

And the barman shouted, 'Do as he says. Back off now.'

The boys backed off.

''Lo, Jack,' Snuff said owlishly.

'I tol' you an' I tol' you,' Jack said, and he picked Snuff up in his huge arms like a baby.

'Put me down, Jack,' Snuff protested. But Jack just carried him through the batwings.

The horse-ranch boys followed. And the big barman came out from behind his counter and even left his shooter behind.

'Oh, hell, Jack,' said Snuff plaintively. Then Jack dropped him into the horse-trough on the edge of the boardwalk.

Reba Dacey, who'd walked back from the Boilon place, turned up just then, right then in fact, catching some stray water from Snuff's splashing.

'What did you do that for, Jack?' the lady saloon-keeper wanted to know.

'Wa-al, Miz Reba, I guess I just figured he needed a bath.'

18

When Pilgrim and Dacey got in sight of the Clandell place the light was failing. The front of the house looked out towards Tiller's Watch but even in good light, the town or the lake couldn't be seen from here.

There was no sign of movement, no kitchen smoke coming from the chimney. There was a quietness.

Pilgrim said, 'We'll make a detour.'

So they came in on back of the place.

There was no horse in the corral. A quietness out here too.

But this was suddenly despoiled with explosive violence. Bullets zipped over the heads of the two men with a snap of a rifle from the house, mellowed then by the echoes, floating off in a sinister way.

They took cover, Dacey behind a

convenient horse-trough on the edge of the corral, Pilgrim behind a pile of damp hay which didn't smell too pleasantly.

The echoes were gone. There was silence again. Dacey said, 'Whoever that was he was shootin' kind of high. I'm gonna try somep'n.' He raised his voice, yelled, 'Halloah, the house! That you, Jabe? This is Dacey and Pilgrim.'

Nobody appeared. But a voice replied, 'Come ahead, easy.'

'That's Jabe,' said Dacey and he rose, holstered the gun he'd drawn automatically. Pilgrim followed his example.

Their horses were behind them on the back end of the corral. They moved to the pile of hay which Pilgrim was glad to get away from. The two men left them there and walked.

The kitchen door was unlocked. They opened it and went through. Jabez Clandell sat in his wheelchair before the window with a rifle on his lap.

It was pretty dark in the kitchen now but the diffused light from the partially open window Jabez hadn't had to smash panes in order to get his rifle-barrel through — illuminated the man's face. It was drawn and sweat-bedewed.

There was blood on his neck, soaking his collar, his shoulder. No wonder his shooting had been high! He explained, 'I didn't know it was you, light too bad. An' I guess maybe I ain't shooting very straight. They were just warning shots.'

'Let me take a look at that neck,' said Dacey, starting forward. 'Is anybody else here?'

'No. Debbie's gone to Greta Boilon's place. I was expecting her back.'

'She's still at Greta's place. We've seen her. She's all right.'

Dacey said the wound was shallow but bleeding badly. There was a sodden, bloody rag on the floor. 'I was doing the best I could. Then I saw you.' Jabez chuckled bitterly.

Dacey took off his own bandanna. 'Hold that to it. I'll get some water.'

Pilgrim said, 'Tell us about it.'

Jabez seemed to be marshalling his facts together.

Then he started.

The man called Preach had been here to visit Jabez's brother, the ex-Ranger and noted gunfighter known as Trace. Debbie had gone and Jabe had been out on his wheelchair 'just sort of browsing in the late sunshine'. Coming back he'd heard Preach and Trace arguing hotly. He'd come into the kitchen where they were sitting taking coffee and Preach's face had been turned fully towards him.

'I recognized him. I recognized him right away. It was like a revelation. I — I didn't think I ever would. He was the man who was responsible for this.' With his free hand Jabez indicated his ruined legs. 'I didn't see him properly and it was a long time ago an' we're both older now. I didn't think I'd know. But I did. And something clinched it. He knew me. I could see it in his eyes. I'd heard of Preach o' course, but didn't think I'd ever seen him. I didn't know this visitor was Preach until Trace called him by that name. Still, maybe way back he had another name . . . '

'He did. He was called Dollar Crane.'

'I've heard that name too. But I guess that was a long time ago as well. I've been waiting. Like hell! I knew him. *I knew him*, and he knew me too!'

Dacey was ready with his ministrations. And the story went on.

Involuntarily, Jabez had drawn on Preach. But the old killer had been faster and, if Brother Trace hadn't grabbed his arm, would have probably drilled Jabez dead centre. But, as it was, the bullet had only torn a groove in Jabez's neck, bloody and sickening but not lethal.

Preach had taken off. An unexpected thing for that killer to do, Pilgrim had

186

thought. But he didn't say so.

Trace had gone after him. They'd both gone in the opposite direction to the town.

'I'll be all right,' said Jabez. 'Thanks, Obe.'

Pilgrim said, 'So you don't know why Preach came here, Jabe?'

'No. Like I said, I wasn't here when he arrived and, if they were arguin' — and it sounded like that — I don't know what they were arguin' about. Trace didn't tell me anything before he lit out after Preach.'

'Stay here an' keep that rifle ready.' Pilgrim exchanged glances with Dacey. 'We'll be on our way.'

'I guess Debbie will be back soon,' said Dacey.

★ ★ ★

They figured they were on the right trail. The hills were bathed in moonlight. They had both been shot at from these hills before. Both seasoned campaigners,

187

they took no chances now.

They left their horses behind rocks. They used rocks. Separating but keeping within sight of each other, they took devious routes through the foothill, weaving, crouching.

They used their senses, all six of them. They knew they hadn't run into any false trail when the bullets winged at them and the echoes rolled. But then both of them were in cover and slugs whined off the rocks and made other strange sounds and ricocheted.

The shooting stopped as quickly as it had begun and they made their own two ways slowly upwards again. And then somebody was calling and Pilgrim remembered how somebody else had called from these hills — and that had been Knocky Dowson who had since been murdered. That seemed a long time ago, but really it had been no time at all.

This was like tragic history repeating itself, lit by moonlight as if from great lamps on a huge stage. Sibilant noises only, from scraping heels and slithering dust. In these hills Knocky Dowson's partner, Dill Rickles, had been killed by a slithering sidewinder. Pilgrim's thoughts were running away with him. Was it all a long time ago? Hell, no, it wasn't. *And here was now.* Here in the quietness under the moon was danger and death.

Dacey found Trace Clandell lying among a jumble of rocks. Pilgrim caught up, to hear Trace say, 'My ankle's busted. I lost my gun. That old bastard left me.'

He had given himself away, Pilgrim thought. Seemed like he had caught up with the other and they had been together.

'I didn't do any shooting,' Trace said.

Could he be believed?

'Watch him,' said Pilgrim. 'I'll go on.'

★ ★ ★

He reached a clearing. These hills seemed to have various clearings. Pilgrim remembered the one where the cave had been. Where Dill Rickles had died from a rattlesnake bite as the tortured Tim Creegan lay in the cave.

There was no cave here, just a cleared rock and scrub-floored place surrounded by boulders. From one of these hidden places a voice issued, 'Stay right there and drop your gun.'

Pilgrim dropped the gun, held his hands away from his sides, braced himself. So the son-of-a-bitch wanted to talk — he hoped so!

'So you're Pilgrim.'

'You know me?'

'I've seen you. But not in action. You're quite a shooter it seems.'

'I do my best.'

The voice became conversational. 'I didn't kill anybody in this territory you know. That was done by your friend back there, Mr ex-Ranger and paid killer, Trace Clandell.'

'But you were behind him, weren't

you?' said Pilgrim. 'He was your front-man here. And I guess you didn't get any gold anyway, did you, Mr Dollar Crane?'

Preach didn't answer the question. But he came out from behind his rock, tall and black-clad in the moonlight, his skull-face grinning without humour.

'You're an astute *hombre*, aren't you, Pilgrim?'

'Like I said, I do my best. And I tell you somep'n else, Dollar, or Preach, or whatever you like to call yourself.'

'Preach will do.'

'If you ain't got the gold I don't guess you have much to live for, an old coot like you.'

'So you'd like to put me out of my misery?'

'Sure, why not?' I've got him, thought Pilgrim, the arrogant, show-off old bastard — but could I haze him?

'You think you're better than me, huh?' said Preach.

'Oh, hell,' said Pilgrim. 'Quit the play-actin' will yuh? If you aim to blast me, do it an' get it finished with.'

'Bend and pick your gun up slow and easy and put it back in its holster.'

'Yeh, I never did like tricks.' Pilgrim did what was asked of him.

Preach pouched his own weapon.

They stood erect, facing each other. Preach was taller than Pilgrim. An old gunfighting killer, like a soldier, straight as a ramrod. Full of pride.

'Take me,' he said.

The skull face and the dark eye gave nothing away. The moonlight slanted down. Pilgrim could watch the face, the eyes . . .

But not in this case. Preach was a right-handed man: Pilgrim watched the right shoulder.

He saw it drop; and he let his own right shoulder drop, his arm with it, but not all the way. Crooked, the hand closing over the butt of the gun — a borrowed gun but a prime one — and lifting it, and levelling it in one smooth motion, knowing instinctively that he had a slight edge but crouching, half-leaning, but not too much either way.

The hammer, the trigger: the old, familiar movements; and the hot lead speeding on its way. He saw it hit, and Preach was staggering, his own gun booming, the slug plucking Pilgrim's shirt on the left shoulder.

Pilgrim fired again, moving the barrel a little. And Preach was falling, two bullets in his chest, just a few inches between them, driving into the area of the heart. Trying to rise, fingers trying to grasp a fallen gun, not making it, subsiding with a great sigh.

The smoke was quickly dispelled, the smell. The moonlight bathed the scene, not a harsh moon, a prairie and mountain moon.

And Pilgrim looking down at a worthy adversary, but one who had deserved to die.

'So be it, old men,' he said.

19

He took the gunbelt and draped it over his shoulder, after putting the big and borrowed ivory-gripped Colt .45 back in its holster. He took another gun from the back of Preach's belt, a smaller Smith & Wesson like one he'd once toted himself, likewise a double-barrelled derringer from an inside pocket, a sort of improvised sheath inside the dark-grey woollen vest.

He found a jack-knife too, with a sort of spring catch. You didn't take stones from horses' hooves with an implement like that: it was a killing instrument.

He went through Preach's pockets and found a notebook which told him nothing, a stub of lead pencil and an old leather wallet stuffed with enough greenbacks to choke an elephant.

He distributed the whole lot, weapons

and all, around his own person.

Preach had gotten his horse part way up here. Pilgrim found the beast, brought it back, piled the body over the saddle. He wondered how Obe was faring with Trace Clandell.

He got a prime shock when Trace suddenly appeared before him, limping like all hell, but with a gun in his hand. Lopsided, though, on uneven ground, so that his first shot missed its target and hit the corpse of Preach that was draped over the saddle. The body jerked, then stayed firm. And then Pilgrim was in cover of the horse his own gun out, triggering over the beast's neck.

Trace spun around, his gun flying from his hand, sparkling beneath the moon. He sprawled on his side. Gun levelled, Preach's gear still draped over his shoulder, Pilgrim somewhat unsteadily advanced on the man.

Trace didn't move. He had been plugged in the side. His head had hit a rock.

Instinctively, Pilgrim whirled, gun levelled, as rocks pattered. It was Obe Dacey and he was holding his head. A thread of blood, black in the bright moonlight, ran down the side of his face.

He said, 'The bastard foxed me. He hit me on the head with a rock.'

Reaching the standing man and the prone one, he lowered himself slowly towards the latter.

'Keep him alive,' said Pilgrim harshly. 'I want to hear him talk.'

* * *

Jabez Clandell had Debbie with him when the cortège got back to the little spread. Greta Boilon had not returned with her friend, so as yet Pilgrim and Dacey didn't have quite so much explaining to do as they might have expected.

Trace was moaning but, it seemed, not yet fully conscious. Dacey had fixed the wound in the man's shoulder.

Pilgrim, hard as nails now, had a sneaking suspicion that Trace might be playing possum.

Pilgrim could wait.

Trace was carried up to the small bedroom he occupied while staying with Debbie and Jabez. Debbie got to work on the wound where Dacey had left off.

It was as if, for the moment, she and husband were scared to ask questions.

Pilgrim had plenty of questions to ask. Trace wasn't going to die, and he couldn't play sick possum forever.

He wasn't going any place. Not yet.

Pilgrim stayed at the Clandell place, bunking on a couch in the living-room. Before that he reckoned Dacey should return to Tiller's Watch and notify Sheriff Salliwell of what had happened. Then Obe could rejoin his wife, Reba. After all, they did have a thriving business to run.

The place quietened. Maybe Pilgrim dozed. But he certainly didn't sleep.

In the small hours he went upstairs.

Trace Clandell awoke to find Pilgrim sitting at the bedside watching him.

And Trace laughed.

'You know nothing,' he said. 'Preach's dead. He can't tell you anything.'

Pilgrim said, 'He blamed you for everything anyway.'

Trace said, 'Hell, I should've finished you off in the fire at Tim Creegan's place. But I've always been too damn' devious for my own good. I pretended to find you. Way I figured it, you'd be blamed later for that job. And you were, weren't you?'

'It didn't wash, though.' Pilgrim was smiling thinly as if this was a chatty conversation between two friends. There was nobody else in the small room.

Pilgrim went on. 'I stuck. I stuck right from the start. A bad move of yours, hiring those two apes, Dill and Knocky, to warn me off. They thought it was fun. They learned different. You should've tried another way. Preach would've.'

'Preach wasn't here.'

'No, he was too well known, wasn't

198

he? Your brother knew him, for one. Preach hired you to handle things here. But you didn't get the gold, either of you, did you?'

'Hell, maybe there ain't any gold,' Trace snorted. 'It was an interesting go-down anyway.'

'Your last, bucko.'

'You can't prove anything.'

'You took some damnfool chances at that. You killed Knocky Dowson in case his pard, Dill Rickles, had told him too much. An angry sidewinder had already taken care of Dill for you. You were searching Tim Creegan's place when he caught you, and you killed him. But maybe the fire was an accident, somep'n you hadn't planned. You were devious all right, always ridin', searchin', watchin'. You tried to bury Obe an' me in that cave.'

'Creegan knocked the damn' lamp over . . . As for the cave — well, that was a chance too good to miss.'

'You're gonna hang, bucko,' said Pilgrim. They were certainly talking at cross purposes now.

'Horse-shit!' snorted Trace.

The bedroom door opened. Trace's brother, Jabez, was there, in stockinged feet, leaning heavily on the doorjamb.

His face was full of pain. 'Oh, yes,' he said. 'I can move about if I set my mind to it. Slowly, taking it easy. I've been out here some while, listening. I heard everything.'

Trace's hand appeared above the bedclothes and in it was a gun that Pilgrim immediately recognized. His own big Starr pistol, the one Trace had stolen from him as he lay unconscious at the scene of the fire at the Creegan place. He must have kept it in this room since then.

'I'm lightin' outa here,' said Trace. 'And I'm takin' Debbie with me.' He began to ease himself out of bed.

Pilgrim said, 'You'll never make it.'

'Don't try an' stop me. I'll shoot both of you if I have to, you know that.' He struggled to get his pants on. This was something he had had in his mind all along, a desperate killer ready to grab at any eventuality.

He was bandaged. He was awkward. But he managed, got his boots on, held the lethal gun steadily, walked.

'Get out of my way, Jabe.'

'Damn' your worthless hide,' said the disabled brother. But he moved, if awkwardly, and let Trace through the door and on to the landing. Debbie appeared, tousle-haired, sleepily pretty, clad in a long colourful dressing robe that looked like authentic Navajo.

'You're coming with me, honey,' said Trace.

'What's going on?' A trite question — as she stared at her brother-in-law, her husband, their new friend, Joe Pilgrim. So many people in such a small place. So bewildering.

Her brother-in-law, Trace, the man who'd always made such a fuss of her. With a gun pointing at her now.

Like a grim stranger . . .

'Down the stairs, Debbie,' said Trace. 'Move!'

20

They were outside, Pilgrim and Jabez. 'We've got to get after them,' the latter said. 'Help me on this horse. Dammit, I can ride. I can ride.'

The gig, with Trace and Debbie side by side on the narrow seat, was little more than a small dust-cloud now. But the two horses could go faster. And Jabez was in the middle, Pilgrim, after helping him, mounting then his own horse. They rode. They lessened the distance between them and the fugitives, the spinning wheels.

Trace had cleared the place of all the weapons he could find. And he still had Pilgrim's gear which he had taken earlier.

He had missed a rifle that Jabez had had wrapped in a tattered rug in the corner of the kitchen behind the well-cushioned rocking chair in which

Jabe sat sometimes as a change from his wheelchair. He'd said that rocking gave him an illusion of movement in his poor legs. He had no self-pity. And he was striving now.

The rifle was an old Henry, well cared for though, in prime condition. Jabez had it across his saddle.

The speeding gig was becoming clearer to the sight of the two pursuing horsemen. And suddenly Jabez cried, 'She's fighting him. Debbie's fighting him.'

But then the man and the girl were apart on the narrow seat and Pilgrim saw the glint of the gun in the man's fist. God, so they were so much nearer now! And Pilgrim didn't have a weapon. And there was the girl. What would happen to the girl?

She was in deadly peril, but she had guts.

She was struggling with Trace again — and Pilgrim couldn't see the gun any more.

Suddenly, she was out of the gig.

She was sprawling in the dust.

Pilgrim turned his head wildly, yelled, 'I could take him. He's your brother, but I could take him. With the rifle. *I could take him!*'

Like a screaming parrot!

'He's a murderous skunk,' said Jabez. 'And he took Debbie. *Take him!*' He threw the rifle.

Pilgrim caught it, reversed it.

He raised it to his shoulder, cushioned the butt, a solid, satisfying feel to it.

Trace was turning, gun in hand. Was he aiming to shoot back?

Was he aiming to shoot the girl? The vicious bastard!

Pilgrim saw the vicious face. Not too indistinct.

The lifting, levelled gun.

He lowered the rifle a little and squeezed the trigger.

The Henry, well cushioned, bucked satisfyingly against his shoulder. He knew, with a sort of cool exhilaration, that his aim was straight.

It was almost as if in slow motion

that Trace came off the seat of the gig.

He pinwheeled. He hit the dust and jerked and rolled a bit. Then he lay perfectly still. Pilgrim kept the rifle on him, however, riding slowly towards him.

Jabez was in front a mite, but veering off, not in the line of fire, making for Debbie who was rising to her feet, seemed unhurt.

Trace lay curled up, his face away from Pilgrim. Was he playing possum: he seemed to be good at that? There was no sign of a gun.

Keeping the rifle levelled at the still form, Pilgrim climbed down from the saddle.

He skirted the prone form of Trace quite widely. There was no movement.

He had a full view.

It had been a good shot. Plumb in the heart. Trace must have been dead before he even hit the ground, any movement a sort of reflex, a chicken tremor.

Trace stared sideways, uncomprehending.

Pilgrim bent and closed the lids over the unknowing eyes and straightened up.

Jabez had fallen hastily from his saddle rather than climbed down from it. Debbie had been quicker, had run to him. Now they were both down in the dust, hugging each other.

Not far from them, something glinted. Pilgrim recognised the shape of it. His own big Starr pistol which Trace had toted, even might have used, if the old Henry he had overlooked hadn't barked first. A good old long gun, Pilgrim thought. He patted the barrel absently — and I ain't so bad myself, he thought.

He strode to the Starr hand-gun, picked it up, tucked it in his holster. It was good to have the big hogleg back.

Debbie and Jabez were on their feet, still holding on to each other.

Pilgrim said, 'You two get on the gig. I'll bring in the horses. And the body.'

'I can't understand . . . ' Debbie began, tailed off.

'C'mon, sweetheart,' said Jabez. 'We'll do as Joe said.'

Pilgrim helped the girl on to the seat of the gig, then they both gave her husband a lift. Weapons littered the floor. Pilgrim held on to the Starr and the Henry. 'Go ahead,' he said, and Jabez clicked his tongue, jerked the reins.

Pilgrim did what he had to do; then he followed.

21

Later.
Tiller's Watch.

The body from the Clandell place. The body — though not in such good condition — from the hills.

Preach — who had once been known as Dollar Crane.

Trace Clandell, ex-Texas Ranger.

Two killers lying side by side in the undertaking parlour, a sight to see, and the populace standing in line.

The news soon got around of course. There were newspapermen. And a photographer who had been doing some work in the growing town of Tombstone turned up with his contraption that looked like something made by a mad scientist fictioneers were featuring in recent times.

He bribed the undertaker and his young assistant to bring the bodies out on to the boardwalk. He bribed a local carpenter to make frames on struts against which the bodies could be propped and he took shots while a newspaper colleague of his made notes.

The main street of Tiller's Watch began to resemble a travelling circus, complete with a boom-time, vociferous audience.

The photographer desired to take pictures of the notorious gunfighter who had brought the two miscreants down, and the newspapermen wanted to interview same.

At length they found Joe Pilgrim — who had taken no part in the street celebrations — in Dacey's Place. He said if they got too near to him he'd shoot their feet off, and they beat a hasty retreat.

Then Pilgrim disappeared. It was Obediah Dacey's idea. He was doing more business than he'd ever done before, but seemed restless, said Reba and the big barman, with two added helpers, could look after the place.

As for Pilgrim: he was a restless individual anyway and people *en masse* got on his nerves after a while.

Obediah said he had had a brainstorm. Whatever that was!

A few folks who might have been of the same mind as the two friends, the saloonkeeper and the range detective-cum-gunfighter, who avoided noisy sensation-seekers, saw the pair leave town on Dacey's wagon which seemed to have shovels and stuff in the back.

They, the townies, might have wondered whether there had been another of those pernicious rumours about a gold-strike (they never came to anything anyway!), but they didn't follow Dacey and Pilgrim. The pair weren't the kind of people you could follow with impunity, were best left alone to get on with their business, whatever that was.

★ ★ ★

210

The area around what was left of the late Tim Creegan's small spread was quiet and desolate. Joe and Obe hadn't seen anybody. They'd caught sight of the Clandell buildings in the distance but there didn't seem any life there either, so maybe Debbie and Jabe still had their heads down. They had suffered a lot in a short time. But so had other folk in Tiller's Watch territory, the two partners had to reflect — and some of them hadn't lived to tell the tale.

The ruins of the Creegan buildings were like a reflection of a bundle of sober and tragic facts. But, as Obe commented, maybe there was a possibility of a silver lining someplace. More than that: a golden one.

And was this to be the place?

No smoke now. Of course not. Just blackened timbers and ashes. Black dust blowing and drifting in a small wind.

The small corral, without a single occupant, looked pathetic. Nobody had bothered to knock down the fences and cart the timber away. Compared to what had once been the house, the corral was still workmanlike. But who would use it? It didn't look as if anybody had been near the place since the fire.

'Like somep'n in a ghost town,' Obe said.

'I've seen worse,' said Joe. 'Well, if we're gonna do it, let's get at it. And don't forget it's your idea.'

'I won't. But, if we find anything you'll take half, don't forget that.'

'I'll try not to.'

They ground-hitched the horses. They used their hands, clad in work gloves to move charred timbers and stuff that came apart in their paws. They scratched and delved. And they used the shovels.

Obe said, 'Evidently there wasn't a root cellar or anything like that.'

Joe said, 'Yeh, I noticed that.'

He coughed, the dust in his throat. Both men were smudged with dirt; they were dusty, sweaty.

Joe thought, if we find any gold that Tim Creegan hid what would I do with it? Buy a ranch? Hell, his dad, old Marshal Joe had a ranch on the Pecos. Young Joe was part of that any time he wanted to be. But, an inveterate fiddlefoot and an addict of close chances, he enjoyed what he did.

Well, Obe could buy himself another saloon — or him and that delectable lady, Reba, could retire and live a life of luxury. Back East maybe . . .

Nah, they were both Westerners through and through!

Obe had brought a miner's pan along with him, and canteens of water. He was now down on one knee doing some real prospecting. Near as damnit anyway.

He began to cough. Finally, spitting, he got some words out.

'Nothing,' he said. Vehemently repeating that. '*Nothing*.'

Then he started coughing again,

rising staggering, dropping the pan.

Joe moved forward.

Obe waved him back. 'I'll be all right.'

'Let's get out of here then.'

As Joe's words finished, so did Obe's coughing. And he started to laugh.

'Jackass,' said Joe, and he turned and made for the wagon.

Obe wasn't slow, caught him up. They climbed on the seat. Obe still shook with laughter, but it was almost silent now.

'Git up.' Joe jerked the reins.

They rolled.

'Goldseekers,' Joe snorted. 'More like damn' scarecrows.'

'I guess ol' Tim made fools of all of us,' Obe said.

'I guess he did.'

But Joe was remembering how Tim had told him about the jewellery that his aunt had left him. Maybe Tim hadn't been desperately looking for gold after all. But two killers, and other assorted desperadoes, had been doing so. Tim had wanted protection.

Joe thought, did I let him down?

No, Tim had let himself down more like, had been too greedy, vengeful, completely self-centred.

Had he stuck his own neck in a noose after all, in a manner of speaking?

Now you're going all high-falutin' again, bucko, Joe thought.

Obe said, 'Maybe the legend of Tiller's Watch was never a real legend after all.'

Joe said, 'It makes you think, huh?'

If that was a question there was no answer to it.

They rolled along in silence except for the sound of steadily drumming hooves and creaking, hissing wheels.

Tiller's Watch came into view under the sun, folks moving around, horses, wagons. It didn't look like anything resembling a ghost town.

Or even a legendary one . . .

RIDERS OF RIFLE RANGE
Wade Hamilton

Veterinarian Jeff Jones did not like open warfare — but it was there on Scrub Pine grass. When he diagnosed a sick bull on the Endicott ranch as having the contagious blackleg disease, he got involved in the warfare — whether he liked it or not!

BEAR PAW
Nevada Carter

Austin Dailey traded two cows to a pair of Indians for a bay horse, which subsequently disappeared. Tracks led to a secret hideout of fugitive Indians — and cattle thieves. Indians and stockmen co-operated against the rustlers. But it was Pale Woman who acted as interpreter between her people and the rangemen.

THE WEST WITCH
Lance Howard

Detective Quinton Hilcrest journeys west, seeking the Black Hood Bandits' lost fortune. Within hours of arriving in Hags Bend, he is fighting for his life, ensnared with a beautiful outcast the town claims is a witch! Can he save the young woman from the angry mob?

GUNS OF THE PONY EXPRESS
T. M. Dolan

Rich Zennor joined the Pony Express venture at the start, as second-in-command to tough Denning Hartman. But Zennor had the problems of Hartman believing that they had crossed trails in the past, and the fact that he was strongly attached to Hartman's Indian girl, Conchita.

MEDIA, TECHNOLOGY AND EVERYDAY LIFE IN EUROPE

Media, Technology and Everyday Life in Europe

From Information to Communication

Edited by

ROGER SILVERSTONE
London School of Economics and Political Science, UK

ASHGATE

Published by
Ashgate Publishing Limited
Gower House
Croft Road
Aldershot
Hants GU11 3HR
England

Ashgate Publishing Company
Suite 420
101 Cherry Street
Burlington, VT 05401- 4405
USA

Ashgate website: http://www.ashgate.com

British Library Cataloguing in Publication Data
Media, technology and everyday life in Europe : from
    information to communication
    1. Information society - Europe 2. Information technology -
    Social aspects - Europe 3. Digital media - Social aspects -
    Europe
    I. Silverstone, Roger
    303.4'833'094

Library of Congress Cataloging-in-Publication Data
Media, technology and everyday life in Europe : from information to communication /
edited by Roger Silverstone.
        p. cm.
    Includes bibliographical references and index.
    ISBN 0-7546-4360-3
    1. Information society--Europe. 2. Information technology--Social aspects--Europe.
3. Digital media--Social aspects--Europe. I. Silverstone, Roger.

    HN380.Z9I565 2005
    303.48'33--dc22

2004027234

ISBN 0 7546 4360 3

Typeset in Times Roman by N²productions
Printed and bound in Great Britain by MPG Books Ltd, Bodmin, Cornwall.

Contents

List of Tables and Figures

List of Contributors

Anne-Jorunn Berg is Senior Scientist at the Institute of Social Research in Industry (IFIM), SINTEF. Her current research interests cover the exploration of memory-work as method, post-colonial studies, studies of ICTs and everyday life, and new developments in the 'co-construction of gender and technology'. Recent publications include: 'Low-voiced Embarrassment: racialisation, whiteness and memory work', *Kvinneforskning*, nr.2, 2004, 'Challenging Gender Studies – reflections on three 'post-'s', *Kvinneforskning*, nr.1, 2003, and *Naming whiteness – feminist memory-work as method*, SINTEF, Trondheim 2002 (with Kirsten Lauritsen).

Thomas Berker is Research Fellow at the Norwegian University of Science and Technology. He is the author of *Internetnutzung im Alltag. Zur Geschichte, Theorie, Empirie und Kritik der Nutzung eines "jungen" Mediums*, Campus, 2002, a book on the history of the internet in the early 1990s. More recently he has published on the everyday life of transnational knowledge work and domestic energy consumption.

Marc Bogdanowicz is Senior Scientist at the Institute for Prospective Technological Studies (IPTS), one of the seven joint research centres of the European Commission DG JRC. He holds a degree in Education Sciences and Postgraduate diplomas in Organizational Sociology and Group Dynamics Communication. Before joining the IPTS, he was in charge of the Technology Assessment Unit of the Laboratoire d'Etudes des Technologies de l'Information et de la Communication at the State University of Liège (Belgium). For the last two years he has worked on the information society issue in new Member States and Candidate Countries.

Kees Brants is Senior Fellow at the Amsterdam School of Communications Research and Director of the MA programme in European Communication Studies, both at the University of Amsterdam. He also holds a special chair in political communication at the University of Leiden.

Jean-Claude Burgelman is Principal Scientist and Project Manager at the Institute for Prospective Technological Studies (IPTS), one of the seven joint research centres of the European Commission DG JRC. He holds a PhD in Social Sciences and a Master in Science and Technology Dynamics from the Free University of Brussels. He was Professor of Communication Technology Policy at the Free University of Brussels, where he created and directed the SMIT (Studies on Media Information and Telecommunications) research centre. His main research area is the socio-economic impact of IST in Europe. (See http://fiste.jrc.es.)

Bart Cammaerts is a political scientist and media researcher working as Marie Curie Research Fellow at the London School of Economics and Political Science, UK. He holds a PhD in social sciences and his research interests include: information society social discourses, alternative media and the use of the internet in terms of formal and informal political processes. His current and recent writing centres on political jamming, e-democracy, the problematic nature of a transnational public sphere and civil society participation in multi-stakeholder processes.

Dorothée Durieux is Advisor in Organisation and Human Resource Management in the administration of Liège. She was a researcher in the Department of Organisation and Human Resources Management within LENTIC in the Faculty for Economics, Management and Social Science at the University of Liège, Belgium. She worked in the area of organisational and social studies of information and communication technologies and innovation processes, with a focus on the management of ICT innovation, participative design and the social implications of ICT use.

Valerie Frissen is Senior Researcher at TNO, where she is head of the department ICT and Policy. This department investigates the social and economic impact of ICT developments and its implications for policy. She is also Professor in ICT and Social Change at Erasmus University Rotterdam, Faculty of Philosophy.

Myria Georgiou is a Lecturer in International Communications at the University of Leeds. Her research interests are in the areas of transnational communications, diasporic identities and media consumption. Her publications include: (2001) 'Crossing the Boundaries of the Ethnic Home: Media Consumption and Ethnic Identity Construction in the Public Space. The Case of the Cypriot Community Centre in North London', *Gazette*, 63(4); (2002) 'Les Diasporas en Ligne: Une Expérience Concrète de Transnationalisme', *Hommes & Migrations*, Num. 1240, and *Diaspora, Identity and the Media* (forthcoming, Hampton Press).

Maren Hartmann is currently working at the University of Erfurt, Germany. She taught and researched at several UK universities before she moved to the VUB in Belgium for the EMTEL Project. Current research foci include youth and new media, internet cultures and media use in everyday life. She has recently published *Cyberflâneur and the Experience of 'Being Online'* (Reinhard Fischer Verlag, 2004), and is currently co-editing a book on domestication.

Caroline Pauwels is a full Professor at the Free University of Brussels (VUB) and is currently head of the Department of Communication Sciences. She holds a PhD in Social Sciences and lectures on national and European communication policy. Her main area of expertise is in the field of European audiovisual policy making, the entertainment economy and in convergence and concentration issues in the media industries. She is also director of SMIT, a research centre focusing on social, economic, cultural and political aspects of ICTs (http://www.vub.ac.be/SCOM/smit).

François Pichault is full Professor at HEC-Business School, University of Liège and is also currently associate Professor at the ESCP-EAP Business School in Paris. He chairs LENTIC, a research centre located in Liège and focused on the social, economic and organisational aspects of information technologies. His main publications concern organisational change linked to information technologies, for example, 'A Political Model of Change in Network Organizations', *European Journal of Work Organizational Psychology*, 1998, and, more generally, the human aspects of organizational change processes, for example, 'HRM Practices in a Process of Organisational Change: A Contextualist Perspective' (with F. Schoenaers), *Applied Psychology. An International Review*, 2003.

Paschal Preston is Professor in the School of Communications and Director of the Technology, Society and Media (STeM) research centre, a multidisciplinary research centre focused on the changing interfaces between society, technology and mediated communication, based at Dublin City University. He has been engaged in several multi-country projects dealing with production, user and policy aspects of digital media developments over the past five years. He is the author of *Reshaping Communications: Technology, Information and Social Change*, Sage, 2001.

Yves Punie is Research Fellow at the Institute for Prospective Technological Studies (IPTS European Commission DG JRC) in Seville. He holds a PhD in Social Sciences from the Free University of Brussels (VUB). His doctoral thesis was on the use and acceptance of ICTs in everyday life. Before joining IPTS in 2000, he was interim Assistant Professor at the VUB and Senior Researcher at SMIT (Studies on Media, Information and Telecommunications). Punie has worked and published on the social and technological aspects of ambient intelligence in everyday life, on the future of the media and the media industries, on social capital in the knowledge society and on privacy, security and identity in the future information society.

Roger Silverstone is Professor of Media and Communications at the London School of Economics and Political Science. He was the Co-ordinator of EMTEL. His recent publications include *Television and Everyday Life*, Routledge, 1994; *Why Study the Media?*, Sage, 1999; *E-Merging Media: Kommunikation und Medienwirtschaft der Zukunft* (edited, with Axel Zerdick et al.), Springer, 2004. His latest book, *Morality and Media*, Polity Press, will be published in 2006.

Knut H. Sørensen is a Professor in the Department for Interdisciplinary Studies of Culture at the Norwegian University of Science and Technology in Trondheim. He has published widely in the field of technology studies, including *Making Technology our Own: Domesticating Technology in Everyday Life* (edited with Merete Lie), (Oslo: Scandinavian University Press, 1996), *The Spectre of Participation. Technology and Work in a Welfare State* (Oslo: Scandinavian University Press, 1998) and *Shaping Technology, Guiding Policy: Concepts, Spaces and Tools* (edited with Robin Williams), Cheltenham, UK: Edward Elgar, 2002).

Katie Ward is a Research Associate in the School of Health and Related Research (ScHARR) at the University of Sheffield, UK. Before joining ScHARR, she was engaged in research with the EMTEL 2 network, where her main interest focused on the use of media technology in the domestic context. For the past two years her research interests have covered health technologies, gender and identity.

List of Original EMTEL Project Reports

Berker, Thomas (2003) *Boundaries in a space of flows: the case of migrant researchers' use of ICTs*, NTNU, University of Trondheim.

Cammaerts, Bart and Van Audenhove, Leo (2003) *ICT usage among transnational social movements in the networked society*, ASCoR/TNO, University of Amsterdam.

Durieux, Dorothée (2003) *ICT and social inclusion in the everyday life of less abled people*, LENTIC, University of Liège and ASCoR, University of Amsterdam.

Georgiou, Myria (2003) *Mapping diasporic media across the EU; addressing cultural exclusion*, Media@lse, London School of Economics and Political Science.

Hartmann, Maren (2003) *The web generation: the (de)construction of users, morals and consumption*, SMIT-VUB, Free University of Brussels.

Punie, Yves (2003) *A social and technological view of ambient intelligence in everyday life*, IPTS (EC DG JRC), Seville.

Ward, Katie (2003) *An ethnographic study of internet consumption in Ireland: between domesticity and public participation*, COMTEC, Dublin City University.

Preface

The research from which this book emerges was conducted over a three and a half year period, between May 2000 and October 2003, under the auspices of a grant from the EU within its 5th Framework Programme. EMTEL, *the European Media Technology and Everyday Life Network*, was funded under grant HPRN-CT-2000-00063 as a Research Training Network.

EMTEL brought together senior and – because it was a training network – junior researchers in seven laboratories within the EU to investigate what we announced as 'the realities and dynamics of the user friendly information society in Europe'. The research was designed to explore the underbelly of that society, the everyday lives and practices of its members, as citizens and consumers, as they made their way into the supposedly revolutionary new world of technologically driven social, political and economic organisation. The questions that we posed to each other as well as to our respondents, in what for the most part was qualitative research, had been developed over a number of years. EMTEL had had an earlier incarnation, with overlapping, but not identical partners, in the mid-1990s. In the work we did then, something of the present intellectual and methodological agenda was developed, but most of all what emerged was an understanding of each other's perspectives, despite being initially separated by culture and first language. Above all what was developed was a trust in each other as researchers, and even more importantly, as human beings.

EMTEL 2, as we called it, allowed us to bring into the network young, mostly post-doctoral, research fellows who were required under the EU regulations for the programme to work in a country other than their own. This was, for many, a considerable undertaking, one that was added to the already significant challenges of entering a new field and of developing new research projects which they would have responsibility, albeit under supervision, for conducting. It is a pleasure to report that all those who completed their projects in the network have subsequently moved on to academic posts, as researchers or teachers or both, and all are building their careers and writing their publications on the basis of resources which EMTEL encouraged them to develop and within a field which the network itself was significantly involved in developing. So, in many respects, and for the young researchers certainly, this book marks a beginning; one in which the EU in its drafting of the programme and in its fine judgement in including us in it, can well take some pride.

This book, therefore, is the product of the collective work of seventeen European scholars from diverse social science disciplines whose shared agenda over three years of collaborative work it expresses. The field is a relatively new one: the concern with the dynamics of everyday life in the confrontation with new technologies and new media, and the implications of that confrontation for a further understanding of socio-technical change and for its management. Indeed the research was always looking over its shoulder at policy and market makers as they continued, in an otherwise untroubled way, the construction of technologically defined visions of the future. We hope that the contributions to this book, both severally and together, will at worst give pause, and at best encourage a more sensitive and informed understanding of what really does emerge at the interface of the social and the technological in the lives of ordinary people within Europe's polymorphous societies.

We leave the notion of Europe open. The research was conducted before the enlargement of the EU, and refers to the dynamics of information and communication technology use in all of its then member states. But Europe as a possibly problematic socio-political category remains on one side, as does any attempt to provide a formally comparative framework for the study as a whole. Indeed it would be fair to say that this book does not represent in any strict sense a study 'as a whole', since it is precisely the diversity of experience across and within European societies that it is designed to illuminate and explore.

Two people otherwise invisible on these pages are owed a huge acknowledgement. Wainer Lusoli, who by the time these pages are read will be Dr Lusoli, was a key individual during the life of the network in his role as Administrator. He was efficient and cordial and dedicated. These characteristics also describe Anita Howarth who has worked on the editing of the manuscript for the book with great application and patience. EMTEL as a whole is immensely grateful to both. We would also wish to thank Ralf Rahders of the European Commission for his supportive management.

Chapter 10 has previously been published in the journal *Communications and Strategies*, 57 (1), 2005, and appears here with the permission of the publisher.

List of Abbreviations

AmI	Ambient intelligence
EARC	Experience and Application Research Centres
EMTEL	European Media Technology and Everyday Life Network
ESDIS	The Employment and Social Dimensions of the Information Society
ICT	Information and communication technology
ISTAG	Information Society Advisory Group of the EC
IT	Information technology
S&TRM	Science and Technology Road-mapping

Chapter 1

Introduction

Roger Silverstone

> If we accept the argument that developing technological capabilities does involve a complex, endogenous process of change, negotiated and mediated both within organisations and at the level of society at large, it is obvious that policies cannot and should not be limited to addressing the economic integration of technological change, but must include all aspects of its broader social integration. We thus reject the notion of technology as an external variable to which society and individuals, whether at work or in the home, must adapt (*Building the European Information Society for Us All*, Final Policy Report of the High-Level Expert Group, European Commission, 1997).

The work of the *European Media Technology and Everyday Life Network* over the last three years has addressed the *problematique* which the above quotation identifies. What is at stake is the significance of social processes for the nature, direction and speed of technological change, and the significance of the everyday as a context for the acceptance of, or resistance to, new communication and information technologies. Such a perspective has, potentially, radical implications, for it demands a different view of the so-called European Information Society than the one which commonly informs both research and policy in this field at both European and national levels. It is one that is grounded in a requirement to investigate, and in that investigation to privilege, the ways in which the user, the consumer, the citizen, the worker, incorporates or fails to incorporate the new and the technological into the familiar, ordinary and more or less secure routines of his or her life in contemporary European society.[1]

For it seems to us quite clear that it is at this level, the level of social action and experience, where the decisions and risks are taken which enable or disable access to, and participation in, this society. It is here where individual and collective judgements are made which affect the realisation of individual and collective capabilities. And it is also here where the material and symbolic resources are or are not available to engage with what many still believe is the brave new world which digital technologies are capable of creating.

This book is a synthesis. It is also an argument. In its first ambition it summarises a range of empirical and conceptual work which seven young researchers have conducted within a framework of training and support provided by senior researchers in the field at seven different centres in Europe. In its second ambition, it intends to present a case for the importance of the detailed investigation of the everyday for the capacity subsequently both to understand and to direct the complexities of socio-technical change which the latest generation of information and communication technologies are currently creating. In the latter context it will suggest that what takes place in the everyday life of all those within European society is a crucial determinant of what takes place, or will take place, in this context in Europe society as a whole. And it will suggest that all those involved in directing policy, or developing markets in this emerging digital world, will, likewise, need to take what ordinary people are doing in their everyday relationships to communication and information technologies, in cities, suburbs, provincial towns and rural areas, across Europe, entirely into account. This report will be structured in the following way.

The first part will elucidate the significance of everyday life as a frame for approaching the European Information Society and the dynamics of socio-technical innovation which may or may not be producing it. The second section will present the key findings and arguments from the individual research projects. The third and final section will identify issues, consequences and questions.

Everyday Life

It is within the sphere of everyday life that individuals and groups can be agents, able, insofar as their resources and the constraints upon them allow, to create and sustain their own life-worlds, their own cultures and values. It is within the sphere of everyday life that the ordinariness of the world is displayed, where minor and often taken-for-granted activities emerge as significant and defining characteristics. We take everyday life seriously because it is precisely in its distinctiveness and its generality that we can see and understand how meanings that sustain as well as challenge its taken-for-grantedness are generated and communicated. And it is in the conduct of everyday life that we can begin to observe and try to understand the salience of information and technologies in humanity's general project of making sense of the world, both private and public.

Perhaps the most useful way to approach the distinctiveness of the everyday as a frame for understanding the dynamics of the information society will be to indicate what kinds of questions it allows us to ask – questions, perhaps to put it too bluntly, which are asked from below, rather than from the more familiar *de haut en bas*.

What does it mean to be part of the information society? What does it offer, what does it refuse, its citizens? How might participation in its direction and access to its claimed benefits be achieved? What are the constraints on, and what individual or socially provided resources might be needed for, that participation? What new skills or competencies will be needed, what literacies? Will new communication and information technologies improve or undermine the quality of daily life? Can we use these technologies meaningfully to change the relationship between work and leisure, work and play? What scope might there be for the marginalised or the excluded to claim a place in the mainstream, and will the new media reinforce or undermine the existing barriers to membership and citizenship? How far will the primary institutions of modern society, the family, or the community be affected by new technologies; and how far will they be able to mould them to their own cultures? Will the new information and communication technologies increase or reduce anxiety, dependence, and the capacity to manage the ups and downs of life in the twenty-first century?

These are questions – and there are others – which emerge with some clarity once a perspective on the everyday is taken. But to ask these questions from below in turn requires that their answers also must be premised on the requirement to take into account the quality and the character of the everyday.

First of all the answers must understand, as we have already intimated, that it is within everyday life that individuals and groups are agents, active, insofar as resources allow, in their ability to create and sustain their own life-worlds, their own cultures and values. Our answers must take into account everyday life's uncertainties and its contradictions. They must recognise the significance of cultural differences and the inequalities of access to the symbolic and material resources necessary for participation in European society. They must acknowledge that for many Europeans, both in the new and the old Europe, as well as the young and the old, life in the emerging Information Society is hard, and there is scepticism as well as enthusiasm, fear as well as hope, opportunities denied as well as offered, in their engagement with it. Our answers must take into account the specificity of the individual and the local as well as the generality of the national and the global. They must understand, finally, the particularity of information and communication technologies, which are central to the conduct of everyday life, not just as material objects, as technologies, but as objects of desire or dismay, and through whose use individual identities, as well as social networks and communities, are defined and defended.

We therefore presume the importance of information and communication technologies to the conduct of everyday life in contemporary Europe. But we remain sceptical as to their precise significance. Such scepticism leads to, and informs, our particular social scientific approaches to their investigation. We argue, and aim to demonstrate, how an approach grounded in studies of the ordinariness of the everyday, and in the experiences and practices of ordinary people, the included as well as the excluded, will illuminate the otherwise easily ignored realities of the information society.

Illumination, however, is not the only possible consequence of this interrogation. For it is in the investigation of the ordinariness of the everyday that one can also begin to offer a critique of the everyday and, in this context, dissect the limits and misunderstandings embedded in the rhetoric of the information society. Above all, our inquiries aim to challenge the presumptions of rationality and efficiency (operationalised as they so often are in a discourse of consumer need) which impose themselves on the way we are encouraged to think about the relationship between information and communication technologies and social change, and which are grounded, always, in an equally pervasive, but equally ill-founded, assumption that technological change rules. The ordinariness of everyday life is not therefore to be found only in the mundane but also in our not infrequent capacities for transcendence, evidenced in the kinds of creativity that emerge both with, but also against, the grain of technological innovation, and which never fail to surprise innovators and policy makers alike.[2]

This is a challenge which we would regard as important and long overdue. There are four dimensions of this approach which require brief comment: the empirical; the epistemological; the methodological; the political.

The Empirical

The world of everyday life is a specific domain. It is where groups and individuals act together and separately, in harmony and in conflict. It is where decisions are or are not taken: to work or to play; to participate or not to participate; to move or to stay put; to be sociable or to remain solitary; to communicate or not communicate. It is where the structures of the social: institutional power, the presence or absence of material and symbolic resources, are most keenly felt. It is in our everyday lives where we confront the most profound and challenging ambiguities, contradictions and insecurities. The tools we have to help us manage these challenges have become increasingly technologically enhanced. Indeed we have become increasingly dependent, over the last century or so, on a range of technologies, predominantly our information, communication and media technologies, which have come to provide us with a framework for making sense of the world in which we live. And for those of us without those resources, without basic access, but more significantly without the reasons, skills and literacies to take advantage of what that access enables, the consequences are profound. These frameworks, the frameworks for personal security as well as social and cultural participation, the frameworks of meaning and practice which are a precondition for full participation in contemporary society, are potentially and often actually disabled.

Everyday life is an empirical domain in which our relationships to information and communication technologies are worked out and worked on. Both meaningful access to information resources and the equally meaningful capacity to engage in communication are preconditions for its conduct. The ability to make sense of the world, both within and beyond the range of individual experience, has become dependent on the mediations that flow through the various electronic channels – of broadcast radio and television, the internet, the cellular phone – which are ever present in the daily lives of most citizens of European society. Everyday life is lived both in face-to-face and in the often contradictorily technologically mediated spheres, where battles for control – over privacy or surveillance, for example – are central. Much of our everyday life is involved in the management of that interface and, as we have already suggested, in both its transgression and transcendence.

The Epistemological

Framing everyday life as an empirical domain of this kind involves an equally distinctive approach to its investigation. The research reported here for the most part draws on an epistemology which is derived from two substantively converging approaches to an understanding of communication and information technologies. Both media and communication studies and the social studies of science and technology have, over the last decades, developed epistemologies which depend on seeing both media and other technologies as being socially constructed. This process of dematerialization, and the reconfiguring of technologies as symbolic objects and products has directed attention to information and communication technologies as being constituted in and through the everyday practices of both production and consumption. Without underestimating the institutionalised power of such technologies as they are introduced and sustained as significant means of information dissemination and communication, this approach challenges any simple or linear account of technologies as being determined either in their design and development or in their consumption and use. The particular complexity of information and communication technologies, that is their double articulation as both objects of consumption and as media of consumption, and their distinctive status – precisely – as key technologies for the conduct of everyday life, requires a way of seeing and understanding them as subject to the daily exigencies of social and individual action.[3]

One major consequence of such an epistemology is the requirement to acknowledge the open-ended nature of technological innovation, its provisionality, its unintended directions and consequences. Since such innovation is subject to the actions of all those involved, albeit with different power and resources, then it is essential that the trajectory of social change is not just read off from the trajectory of technological change (as if that itself was easily readable). It is equally essential that one accounts for the specificity of these technologies, that they are produced and consumed both as machines and as media, and as such that they are particularly vulnerable to their definition and redefinition through the human capacity to make meaning and order in the world. It is of course equally essential to recognise and understand technology's capacity to mould that world in its own image, or the image at least of those who design, market and regulate it.

Methodology

The methodologies developed and mobilised by researchers within the network, again for the most part, derive from these sets of theoretical assumptions and perceptions, as well as the continuous tensions between them. In practice this means a focus on qualitative approaches to the study of everyday life. If everyday life in the information society is constituted through the actions and meanings that individuals and groups produce in their interaction both with each other and with the technologies that, at least in principle, enable that interaction, then an understanding of that process requires the researcher's focused attention on meaning and significance. While this does not preclude quantitative approaches, it nevertheless privileges those methodologies which seek to get beneath the surface of everyday life and practice, to explore the dynamics, the ambiguities and the contradictions as well as the certainties, of the relationships we create and sustain with our information and communication technologies, both old and new. For without this sensitised investigation of the dynamics of the everyday and of innovation as a contested process of social as well as technological change, we will misread and misunderstand the realities of innovation and the implications of those realities for policy.[4]

Inevitably the kinds of findings produced by close attention to process and meaning are not easily amenable to mechanical generalisation. The case studies that comprise much of the research of the network are designed both to complement, and to be complemented by, quantitative investigation. It is important to point out however that such latter kind of investigation is likewise limited insofar as it does not address the dynamics and complexities of the realities it purports to be describing. It is our contention that methodologies need to be implemented in social research that engage with meaning and agency as constitutive of both technology (as technological practices) and everyday life, and that such methodologies are defensible in their attention to detail, in their capacity to generate theory and in their ability to challenge the taken for granted assumptions, perhaps in policy and technological discourses above all, that the world is as it is, and can be legislated into existence from on high.

Two dimensions of our methodology need further comment. The first is the scepticism built into the approach. The social dynamics of everyday life (society as it is experienced and constructed) get in the way of technological change, just as technological change poses both particular and general challenges for the conduct of everyday life. The mutuality of this disruption, and the uncertainties as well as the strains that it generates for all participants in the process, needs to be inscribed into the way in which research into the information society is conducted.

Likewise the relationship between action and communication in online and offline spheres. It has been a recent commonplace of research into, especially, the character and significance of the internet to presume that it can be investigated on its own terms, without reference to the social context in which access and engagement takes place. Notions of cyberspace signify such otherwise arbitrary attention to life online as if it were understandable *sui generis*. As so much in everyday life, this is not sustainable. Recent research has pointed to the ways in which everyday life online and everyday life offline are mutually constituting. There is a complex social dynamics within and between the 'real world' and its cyber equivalent, which needs to be addressed. Such mutuality, and the need to recognise its significance for an understanding of both life online as well as off it, is a precondition for effective research in this area.

Politics and Policy

The quotation from the High-Level Expert Group on the Information Society which acts as the epigraph to this report begins with a statement about policy, and ends with a statement about epistemology. So far, we have moved in the reverse direction. But the point to be made is the same. Both the politics of, and the policies for, the European Information Society need to recognise what it is that makes the society, in its lived reality; that is, what the information society is, and what it is not. The everyday is the ground upon which both through individual and collective action, and through individual and collective action that in its frequency and generality (as well as its uniqueness and originality) becomes significantly social in its consequences, the much dreamed information society will or will not be built.

Indeed there is a politics as well as a policy discourse to be addressed. In relation to the first, politics, there are recognisable struggles over access to, and increasingly, and properly, participation in the so-called information society. Further, if the information society is coming to be, as many argue and believe, the expression of a new kind of social formation in which access to immediate and accurate information and advanced communications are the *sine qua non*, then the capacity to participate, the struggle to be included, but also the struggle over its control, are becoming, and will remain, a crucial component of European political life, both at union and national levels. And if such politics is to be advanced and those who wish to participate in its advancement, but even more significantly in its direction, are to be heard and given the opportunities that are required, then national and European policies will need to be developed which go beyond the narrow confines of existing information or communication policy (Burgelman and Calabrese, 1999). They will need to treat information and communication as social goods, and ones that can only meaningfully be mobilised in the context of Europe's diversity of cultures and the persistence of inequalities of access to both material and symbolic resources. They will need to address the dynamics of the appropriation and rejection of new information and communication technologies as well as the consistencies of economic and cultural inclusion and exclusion. We will return to these issues in the final section of the report.

Media, Technology and Everyday Life

We have suggested, in a framework paper, that the European Information Society can be seen as under construction (Silverstone, 2001). By this we meant that it was still in formation and that its emergence was neither consistent, nor confidently predictable. We also argued that no established single social theory would be adequate to encompass the full range of its variations and complexities; above all there was no single theory (either that privileging social or privileging technological determinism) which could provide an explanation for the relations between social and technological change that might otherwise seem quite straightforward.

Our research has addressed these relationships from a number of different perspectives. In its original formulation it was framed through two primary concerns. The first was with inclusion and exclusion. Here the concern was with the particular implications of information and communication technologies for enabling participation in European society. It has commonly been presumed that they have that potential, and that access to technologies, networks and services is on its own sufficient to compensate for the otherwise disabling and excluding consequences of social and economic disadvantage. The second focus was on flexibility and the quality of life. Here again the innate characteristics of new information and communication technologies in particular are often seen to be able to provide for new possibilities for choices in the conduct of everyday life, and the presumption is that those choices, freely made and enhanced by such access, will lead, individually and collectively, to a more satisfying and productive existence.

During the course of the research a third, albeit subsidiary, theme emerged which cuts across these first two. It is that of mobility and belonging. Here the issue is the particular role information and communication technologies have in the context of a significantly mobile Europe, one in which mobility is expressed through the migration of groups and populations as well as through the individual's capacity to breach the hitherto clearly bounded dimensions of public and private space.

Inclusion and Exclusion

This theme emerged as a primary focus in three studies, though it should be restated that questions of participation, citizenship, and exclusion are ubiquitous in our research as indeed they should be in all research on the relationship between technological and social change.

We explored this theme through specific projects on work, political activism and the culture of ethnic minorities.[5]

One crucial issue in the debates on the capacity of information and communication technologies to make a difference to the ability to participate in contemporary society centres on questions of skills and training, as well as on issues of access. The project from Liège and Amsterdam focuses on a range of initiatives designed to create facilitating institutional frameworks for involving the less abled and disadvantaged (principally in this study, the unemployed and the physically or mentally impaired) in work that would meaningfully connect those involved to the mainstream of social life. A training programme in IT skills and a call-centre specifically organised around the recruitment of the less abled were examined in order to evaluate their success in becoming conduits for meaningful participation and for personal contribution amongst those recruited to participate as trainees or employees. The study also assessed the implications for such involvement on the quality of the participant's everyday life, and above all the degree of transferability of skills and competences in the use of information and communication technologies into their own private spheres.

Skills in using information and communication technologies were found to be necessary but not sufficient for such participation. Organisations established with specific commitments to enable that participation found themselves, under commercial and other institutional pressures, increasingly unable to provide sustainable training or experience that could be translated into the wider domains of everyday life. Such failures could be differently understood.

First of all, the reasons were found to lie in the absence of links between the organisations concerned and other facilitating environments which would provide continuity and connection for the individuals beyond the specific locations of direct work or training, so that few opportunities were available for trainees to take what they had learned meaningfully into the wider world of work, or develop or apply their newly learned skills in the open job market. Or, in the case of the call centre, the level of training and the pressures of work were such that it became a less than satisfactory experience, sufficiently unrewarding for those involved to feel that their involvement with technology should remain confined to the workplace. Secondly, and to a degree consequently, the reasons were found to lie in the wider culture and character of everyday life, where there was often little reason either to invest or experiment with computers or the internet, given the existing level of participation of these already marginalised individuals in ongoing society. It was at this individual level where choices were made or not made, rationally and reflexively, on the basis of judgements of self-interest, need, competence and confidence, that were central in defining the degree and character of participation that information and communication technologies are seen to be able to provide.

The second study, from Amsterdam, addressed the issue of participation and inclusion in the context of political actors in global civil society. Here the issues and questions were obviously different but there is also some convergence in the issues raised with the previous study.

The focus of the research was on the role and significance of the internet for transnational social movement organisations, in their own project of generating civic engagement and influencing political processes. The research analyses the dynamics, in four such organisations with their headquarters in Europe, of some current attempts to shift the political agenda to what might be called an embryonic global public sphere. It also addresses the capacity of such organisations to provide frameworks and settings for inclusion and participation, both among other subsidiary groups but also among individuals.

Here, too, the findings were premised on a recognition of the ambiguities and the complexities of the relationship between life and activity online and life and action offline. Each of the organisations surveyed, each with its distinct agenda, organisational infrastructure and transnational character, used the internet in different ways and with different consequences for their own organisational capabilities. Their capacity to reach, and communicate with, a wide range of partners and participants around the world was in effect the internet's primary function. It was less useful as a way of genuinely mobilising participation in specific tasks or projects, and at all times what took place online was conditioned and translated by communication and action in the real world. Organisations too have their everyday lives. And in this context the transnational political organisations studied clearly found the internet vital as a decentralising tool for communication and organisation, and perhaps to a lesser degree and more problematically, as a tool to enable the construction of public or semi-public fora for online discussion and debate.

Yet the question arises in such a study as to the effectiveness of such online discourse and organisation when it comes to meaningful political action in both local and national contexts. And here is where the realities of power and agency in the public and private, everyday worlds of individuals and organisations intrude, and significantly determine the effectiveness and transferability of both online discourse and the capacity of transnational organisations to intrude into the public conflicts of offline life-worlds.

The third, London-based, study investigating inclusion and exclusion, engaged with the increasingly significant presence in media, communication and information environments of diasporic minority groups in European society. This research, which involves both a mapping of the current context of minority media production and consumption in the 15 member states, as well as a number of more detailed case studies, effectively focuses on the cultural as a major dimension of exclusion in European society.

A sizeable and rapidly changing proportion of the population of the European Union have their origins in recent migration, creating, albeit unevenly, an increasingly multicultural society which is posing significant opportunities and challenges both for the Union and for its member states. Sources of, and reasons for, migration, vary enormously. Likewise the economic resources commandable by migrants. Their status in what are called their host societies also varies, in part depending on the age of the migration as well as its origins and its dominant ethnicity. The experience of migration is different for men and for women, for the first generation and for the second. It varies too from country to country, depending on national policies both on immigration and integration.

The research sought to establish the significance of minority media in European culture, and to investigate the significance of media cultures for a wider understanding of social inclusion and exclusion. Particularistic media, appearing in print, broadcast and digital forms, are produced locally and globally, yet are for these populations consumed locally. At issue is their role in creating and sustaining networks and communities, and the relationship between those networks and communities and the national majority cultures within which they conduct their everyday lives, the wider European society, and the ethnically distinct global culture in which the minorities become majorities.

The questions raised by this research go to the heart of the European project of inclusion, and suggest a greater importance in public discourses should be given to dimensions of culture and particularly mediated culture in forming policies appropriate to the creation of more inclusive and tolerant societies.

Flexibility and the Quality of Life

We have suggested that European society has become progressively a fluid society (Silverstone, 2001). As a result of greater affluence, technological change, greater opportunities for social and geographical mobility, and the spread of neo-liberal ideologies, a culture has emerged which has increasingly valorised, and for those with the appropriate resources delivered, a world of greater choice and greater opportunities for self-determination. Indeed in contemporary discourses focusing on the quality of life, these are the dimensions – personal freedom, choice, the ability to control one's own private sphere and to manage one's own life course – which prevail.

The issues for us in this changing environment are two-fold. The first concerns the specific role of information and communication technologies in both disabling, and enabling the management of, such a world. The second is the capacity and consequences of individuals to appropriate new technologies and services into their everyday lives.

Three studies directly approach this agenda, and do so from complementary perspectives. The first, based in Dublin, undertakes an examination of the ways in which the internet is being used in a local setting by a predominantly sedentary and well-established community. The second, based in Trondheim, effectively asks the same question of a highly mobile, cosmopolitan population of scientific researchers based, albeit temporarily, in either Norway or Germany. And the third study focuses on what is sometimes called the web-generation, that group in society, between childhood and 'settling down', who have constructed patterns of appropriation and use of ICTs, especially the internet and the mobile phone, as key resources to manage their own fluid, mobile, and flexible lifestyles.

In each case the focus is on consumption, considered as a dynamic process of engagement with the mass-produced products of contemporary global capitalism. From a perspective of everyday life, such processes are seen as creative, insofar as individuals and groups can adapt the affordances of new information and communication technologies to the exigencies of their own lives. Consumption involves active engagement with the intended functionalities of new technologies and services. Consumers engage with the new from a perspective honed by their everyday life experiences with familiar technologies, and from within a framework of their own values and perceived needs.

The study of neighbourhood life and the internet in Ireland focuses on how the domestication of the internet by families and households in a small seaside town in turn reveals how the technology and its possibilities are moulded to fit local and private cultures, while at the same time challenging the existing boundaries between public and private spheres. Here the internet is being significantly privatised. It is being used to provide a private communication space linking families and friends otherwise out of reach. It is being incorporated into family cultures, particularly in those households with children. But it is barely being used as a tool for local civic engagement. So although the internet has the potential to become or significantly facilitate a democratic public sphere, it has so far failed at this local level to operate as a fully inclusive, interactive forum.

What are seen as the second generation of internet users have, in this local context, come to terms with the sweeping information and communication functionalities of the internet in particular, manageable and individual ways. Such domestication indicates, perhaps, a much slower and less determined process of innovation. It also indicates the power of the cultures of everyday life to incorporate the new on different terms, often, than those envisaged by designers and policy makers, while at the same time seeking and mostly succeeding in protecting the established patterns and structures of their private lives from the possible disturbances caused by too rapid or dramatic technological innovation.

The study of the cosmopolitan offers related but differently inflected perspectives on the internet and its significance at the interface between public and private spheres. A population of international researchers was investigated to establish how the networking and communicational potential of the internet was used by such displaced individuals both in their professional and private lives. A number of issues become central: the relationship between the electronic and the face-to-face as modes of communication; the salience of the local as opposed to global cultures; the relationship between home and work; and perhaps most significantly the extent to which the internet can be seen as a resource to enable the mobile to sustain their identities and their security in strange and sometimes temporary spaces.

It becomes quite clear how significant the internet is for the conduct of professional life, in the communication with scientific colleagues and its status as a research tool. It becomes much more problematic in the context of everyday life and the constitution of a personal and private sphere, where the importance of the local and the face-to-face looms large. The research reveals a collective portrait of a group of people at the forefront of the information society and whose own lives express the flexibilities enshrined and often celebrated in the space of flows of the network society, yet who use the internet (but also refuse to use it) in specific ways precisely to compensate for, and manage, the consequences of their displacement.

The internet has become incorporated into the mix of media that enable the sustaining of personal relationships in both local and trans-local spaces. Amongst this group of researchers, information and communication technologies (principally the internet, satellite radio and television, the mobile phone) are treated instrumentally and domesticated into their everyday lives in ways that both enable the management of flexible work and likewise enable the 'policing' of private and personal space when work threatens to extend its otherwise acceptable boundaries. Everyday life becomes a site of struggle, for connection and disconnection, and for the control and management of its space and times. These technologies are, then, both tools and troubles. They are immensely facilitative in many professional and personal settings and activities, but at the same time they become threats. Users will develop responses that extend from a refusal to use them at all under certain circumstances, to strategies of using one to manage the disturbances caused by another.

This theme of the role of information and communication technologies in the management of personal space reappears as a central one in the study, conducted in Brussels, of the so-called web-generation and their use of the internet. This generation is often heralded as being in the forefront of the information revolution, socialised into the technology from an early age and developing lifestyles which both depend on and extend the inherent fluidity and flexibility of everyday life which characterises the postmodern condition. These are, we are led to believe, the vanguard generation.

This research brought a number of key issues to light. The first was the centrality of personal availability for members of this group. The second is these technologies' centrality in the life-project of constructing and managing identity and self-hood. The third was their role in creating a sense of belonging. And the fourth was the much more evolutionary, rather than revolutionary, process underway in the socialisation of the new.

But none of these findings are simple or singular in their significance. The everyday lives of this generation manifest the same kind of contradictions that are present in the lives of their parents, and information and communication technologies have the same ambiguous role in their conduct. For example personal availability was central but still needed to be managed. Face-to-face relationships were still preferred over mediated ones, and provided a base-line morality against which certain kinds of stigma were attached to meetings and friendships online. It also became clear that, in a related way, in the case of the internet but also the mobile phone, that the immediacy and directness which these technologies afforded would be seen as more of a disguise than as a means for openness; they became screens for the self as well as windows on the self. The sense of belonging is extended, though not always unproblematically, through the communicative networks created and sustained through text-messaging and the sending of email as well as through located action in the face-to-face and the neighbourhood. However it was clear that in establishing such a kind of mediated culture, this generation was struggling with the need to create a set of conventions and rules which increasingly came to be seen as having moral status. Their own uses of the technologies, but even more the uses of others, were subject to constant discussion and examination. Here issues of trust, both in interpersonal relationships and in the mediated relationships that might emerge, in e-commerce or other ways, with institutions became increasingly salient.

The seventh study, from IPTS in Seville, consists of an analysis of ambient intelligence, and its social and technological future in everyday life in Europe. Its technological assessment is linked closely with the work of ISTAG (Information Society Advisory Group) of the EC, but it subjects that assessment to a critical review grounded in perspectives adopted by the research in the EMTEL network as a whole and from arguments based in the domestication approach.

Ambient intelligence is the next big thing. It is the object of considerable attention and investment within the 6th Framework programme. The AmI vision is to bring computing into the very fabric of everyday life (both literally and metaphorically); to make it invisible but at the same time to make it responsive to the information and communication needs of individuals in both private and public spaces, but most especially the former. Fabric, environments, even dust particles, will carry sufficient active and reactive intelligence to enhance the quality of everyday life, by making both environment and context infinitely sensitive and responsive. Rather than a route leading to virtual reality, or indeed even to artificial intelligence, ambient intelligence (or ubiquitous computing as it is sometimes called) seeks to extend human reach, in the way that Marshall McLuhan would have understood well when he talked of the capacity of media technologies to extend the human sensorium, into the micro-regions close to home and close to bodies.

Such visions are not, generically, new. Nor are they likely to be fulfilled in every respect. Research in this report reverses our usual epistemology by drawing on existing work both within the EMTEL network and outside it to challenge the presuppositions that inform the technological agenda. Everyday life is not biddable to the desires of technology. The AmI visionaries recognise that the emergence of such supposedly enabling technologies will depend on a sophisticated understanding of the human, but fail, it is argued, to address the human as fully and as frustratingly social as it is and will always be.

The discourses of and from everyday life, consequently, speak to and debate with technology in a number of different ways, posing particular challenges to its otherwise determining claims. In this case they raise questions that are grounded in the nature of family and domestic life (conflictful and political rather than harmonious, and a sphere of housework as well as leisure); in the capacities of technologies to work, to work consistently, to be trusted to work, and to be accepted as workable in environments where they will both challenge as well as enhance individual control; and to provide a manageable balance between rigidity and flexibility in the design and delivery of innovative software and hardware.

This project presents, we believe, a coherent case for bringing the empirical research of the kind that has been undertaken within the EMTEL network into the technological design process itself.

Issues, Consequences and Questions

A number of issues have emerged during the project. They illustrate the complex inter-relationship between information and communication technologies and everyday life. They raise questions both for further research and for the formation of future policy. Above all they reflect the significance of the domain of everyday life as being central for an understanding of the dynamics of technological innovation in this area. These can be identified briefly.

The Nature of Change

Despite the discourses of revolutionary change that have accompanied the emergence of a number of new technologies over the last decades, and the implication of their convergence or over-determination, as constituting a technologically led transformation of the nature and quality of life in modern societies; and despite too the utopian endorsement as well as the dystopian denial of those claims, the actual processes of social engagement with new technologies has proved to be evolutionary rather than revolutionary, contradictory rather than linear. Technologies may change rapidly, societies and cultures change much more slowly. The absence of synchronisation reflects a complexity and indeterminacy in the social, and above all in the practices of everyday life, which too rarely are taken into account in the plotting of future scenarios as well as in the management of the present.

New technologies, services and content are appropriated into ongoing ways of living and being, sometimes easily and without much consequence for the rituals and behaviours of the everyday, sometimes after a struggle and with quite significant changes to the quality of private or public life. Not all their functional properties will be accepted, and many will be transformed in use, as messaging transformed the mobile phone as a communication device. New information and communication technologies take their place alongside the old, which rarely disappear, but whose patterns of use might be transformed by the new. Neither the new nor the old are entirely new nor entirely old. Functionalities evolve and their acceptance is dependent both on the characteristics of everyday social practices where they may be, or may not be, found a place, and on the pre-existing relationships to media which new technologies may offer to deepen or extend, as well as make obsolete.

But everyday life also changes. Both adaptation and resistance to new technologies generate, often, quite profound shifts in the ways in which, both in public and in private, we conduct ourselves and relate to others similarly and differently placed to us. Our capacity to respond creatively, indeed our capacity to respond and engage with technological change at all, will depend on our financial but also on our educational and cultural resources. The first uses of a new technology are not always the last, nor are they likely to be uniformly spread across all sections of the population, or even among those sections of the population most likely to gain from them.

Domestication

We are arguing that technological change is evolutionary because it depends on social action, and on social action that takes place in multiple domains and in uneven and often contradictory ways. The acceptance of new technologies into the sphere of everyday life, both in public and private (of which more soon) can be understood as an active and, in the broadest sense of the term, as a creative one. Individuals, families and groups make choices on the basis of their own perceptions of their needs and values, and on the often unconscious frameworks which guide their actions and interactions.

This process, which has been called *domestication*, has emerged as an important dimension of the information society (Silverstone and Haddon, 1996; Lie and Sorenson,1996). It is clear that in the case of the individual and his or her appropriation of the internet or the mobile phone, the family or household, as well as that of the larger organisations, social processes are underway which transform and make more complex the innate characteristics of these new technologies, and disturb the singularity of their projection in the public discourses of both policy and advertising.

The research has suggested that the concept of domestication needs to be extended and deepened. Firstly in respect of the need to attend to service and content issues. Secondly in respect of the need to recognise the significance of the transformative work of everyday life in public as well as in private spaces. In both these respects, however, the work of appropriation remains significant. The relationship between technological and social change is dialectical, and both technologies and cultures change in the process. At the heart of this relationship is a struggle over control, and over the capacity of individuals in their primary groups (family, community, and possibly neighbourhoods and networks) to create a sustainable moral space for themselves in which judgements of appropriateness and practices of use are legitimated. Information and communication technologies pose substantial challenges and opportunities to the conduct of everyday life, precisely because they affect the core meaning making and communicating components of social life. Managing them and positioning oneself in relation to them and what they offer as resources for communication and as tools for understanding the world, are arguably some of the key socio-cultural challenges of the twenty-first century.

Changing Boundaries

It is a commonplace of much contemporary social theory that everyday life, both in its structuring and in its living, has become liquid. Social life is no longer clearly bounded and such hitherto taken for granted categories of experience, identity and community perhaps above all, neither any longer have any real meaning nor the capacity to provide the kind of securities they once did. This postmodern world, for better and for worse, is a fluid one (Bauman, 2000; Castells, 1996; Urry, 2000).

Technologies, and in particular information and communication technologies have contributed to these ontological shifts, though there are other factors, both economic and political, to be taken into account. Likewise technologies can be seen to be both boundary breaching and breaking as well as the use of – and this is of course the important point – boundary restoring and securing.

We suggest that boundaries are still important in everyday life. There are socially and individually defensible and defended boundaries between the strange and the familiar, between the past, the present and the future, between the individual and the collective. Three boundaries in particular have emerged as particularly salient in the conduct of the research in this programme. The first is that between public and private spheres and spaces. The second is that between the worlds of online and offline social interaction and political action. And the third is the boundary between ourselves and others.

Each, of course, can be seen to be increasingly porous and fragile in an information society, yet each is subject to practical work as individuals and groups in their ongoing relationships to information and communications seek to preserve and protect the private, the face-to-face, and what is seen as their own, within the conduct of their everyday lives. Each is defined, or sought, through a trade-off, for example, between security and surveillance, or between proximity and distance.

It is a truism to report that information and communication technologies are key mechanisms in the erosion of the boundary between public and private spaces. Media bring the public world into the living room. Mobile phones and transistor radios bring private conversations and media consumption into parks and railways carriages. Yet the porosity of this boundary should not be overestimated. The transition of media into private spaces does not go by without significant interruption and transformation, as families and households seek to control what they might see as unwelcome intrusions into their private spaces (just as so-called celebrities seek to control by other means the media's intrusion into their private lives). This is the case in the domestication of the internet; it is the case in the ways in which young adults manage their own mobile culture; it is the case amongst international researchers trying to protect themselves from the creep of work into their leisure time; and it is the case, though differently expressed and valued, in the context of the absence of the transferability of skills in the households of the less abled, where their private culture is unable to sustain what has been learned in public.

The relation, and boundary, between everyday life online and everyday life offline also goes to the heart of what is presumed to be distinctive in the information society. For it is the opening up of new communication and information spaces, and the expectation that users will flock to them with a range of expectations in no way defined by the customs and values forged in the short and long durées of their everyday lives, which has had both methodologically and substantively such a powerful effect on the construction of the idea of cyberspace. Our research suggests that this boundary remains a salient one in the conduct of everyday life, and that increasingly our capacity to construct relationships and meanings in both contexts depends in turn on our capacity both to understand and manage them as perpetually intertwined. Not only are the online and offline sociologically and politically inseparable, but they can only be explained in relation to each other. And when it comes to value, as perhaps surprisingly the study of the web-generation suggests, and perhaps less surprisingly the study of transnational social movements reveals, it is the offline, the face-to-face, which is seen both to be in need of defence, and still the precondition for effective political action.

And finally to the boundary that separates ourselves from others, a boundary that is, or should be, also, a bridge. That boundary is also central to questions of identity and culture in the information society; central too to both perspectives and policies, when it comes to multicultural society. Indeed it is the overlaying of the one on the other in Europe which provides for some of the most profound social and political challenges, ones which our research can hopefully illuminate, but which it will take concerted and informed political action to resolve.

Mobilities

We have suggested that the theme of mobility and belonging has emerged as an increasingly significant one during the course of the research. Perhaps it should not have been as surprising as it turned out to be, for as we have just argued, questions of fluidity and change have long been part of the debate on the character of late modern society. However it would be fair to say that this unexpected finding was not a matter merely of visibility, for we were investigating mobility in direct ways, but a matter of its density, complexity, salience and its implications.

Mobilities are first of all plural. They manifest themselves at many levels. We have observed them, for example, at the level of population movements, that is migrations. We have observed them in terms of the freedom of individual and collective movement between public and private spaces. In both of these cases mobilities, both at the macro and the micro levels, are geographical. We have observed mobilities between roles and identities, and between the spheres of work and leisure. In both of these cases mobilities are social. We have observed mobilities between online and offline communication and interaction, and between personal and social spaces. These mobilities are both technological and cultural. And we have observed mobilities in both individual and collective identities, and in the instabilities of belonging and identification. Here we are confronted by psychology as well as by anthropology.

The so-called information society, at least insofar as it has emerged in EMTEL research, is one in which information and communication technologies can be seen, principally, to be enabling these mobilities, though in ways that are neither uniform, nor uniformly acceptable. Insofar as this is a sustainable observation then, we would argue, we need to attend to a range of consequences, not least among which is the fundamental characterisation of the nature of the social change and the social challenge that these technologies are required to address.

EMTEL research suggests, consequently, that the information society could well be a misnomer, and that what needs, on the contrary, now to be addressed is Europe as a *Communication Society*.

Notes

1 We wrote, in our initial proposal, the following: 'The social acceptance of new information and communication technologies is not just important from the point of view of social policy but it is crucial to the development of a broadly based information economy. Indeed innovation is a social process and not just a technological and an economic one. Technologies do not emerge without active involvement of the consumers and users who have to accept them as relevant and useful in their everyday lives. Technological change is itself mediated. Technologies change in their social acceptance, and societies change as new technologies are accepted. But some technologies are resisted and some groups within society are excluded from participating in the benefits that are expected.'

2 The recent, grand, obvious and familiar examples are those of messaging and file sharing; but the capacity for transcendence is not limited to these market shaping (or undermining) initiatives, as we will show in the account of the research that follows.

3 For a discussion of media technology's double articulation, see Silverstone and Haddon (1996).

4 This approach clearly needs to be differentiated from one that depends in whole or in part on benchmarking as a strategy both for research and implementation, since it eschews the *a priori* and self-consciously reflects on the normative, for example EC COM (2002) 655 Final, *Communication from the Commission to the Council and the European Parliament: eEurope 2005: Benchmarking Indicators*.

5 Full references to each of the projects to be discussed over the next few pages can be found at the beginning of this book.

References

Bauman, Z. (2000) *Liquid modernity*, Cambridge: Polity Press.

Burgelman, J-C. and A. Calabrese, (eds) (1999) *Communication, citizenship and social policy: rethinking the limits of the welfare state*, Lanham, Md.: Rowman and Littlefield.

Castells, M. (1996) *The rise of the network society*, vol. 1 of *The information age: Economy, society and culture*, Oxford: Blackwell.

EC (2002) *Towards a knowledge-based Europe: the European Union and the information society*, Europa.eu.int/information_society/newsroom/documents/catalogue-en.pdf (downloaded 5/08/03).

Lie, M. and K. Sørensén, (eds) (1996) *Making technology our own? Domesticating technology into everyday life*, Oslo: Scandinavian University Press.

Silverstone, R. (2001) *Under construction: new media and information technologies in the societies of Europe*, A Framework Paper for the European Media Technology and Everyday Life Network (EMTEL 2), www.lse.ac.uk/collections/EMTEL.

Silverstone, R. and L. Haddon (1996) 'Design and the domestication of information and communication technologies: technical change and everyday life', in R. Mansell and R. Silverstone (eds) *Communication by design: the politics of information and communication technologies*, Oxford: Oxford University Press.

Urry, J. (2000) *Sociology beyond societies: mobilities for the twenty-first century*, London: Routledge.

Part 1
Inclusion and Exclusion

Chapter 2

Inclusion and Exclusion in the Information Society

Kees Brants and Valerie Frissen

Introduction

Recent policy discourses in Europe strongly emphasise the need to build what is called an 'inclusive information society'. With the current widespread diffusion and use of ICTs in all domains of everyday life, ICTs are increasingly considered a fundamental and necessary resource for every European citizen, the socio-economic effects of which will resonate across the continent. The strategic goal for Europe in 2010 – worded forcefully by the European Council in its Lisbon strategy – is: '... to become the most competitive and dynamic knowledge-based economy in the world, capable of sustainable economic growth with more and better jobs and greater social cohesion' (European Council, 2000). While access to ICTs is considered crucial for participation in and enhancing the qualities of that society, there is, at the same time, an accompanying nervousness that it might sow the seeds for a new exclusion, a digital divide quite distanced from the dream of an all inclusive society.

The policy discourse adequately reflects a wider debate on inclusion and exclusion, which is wavering between a sombre and a shining vision. The pessimists in this debate point to the tendency of ICTs to create a new domain of exclusion, which strengthens the already existing divides and inequalities based on class, gender, ethnicity, etc. The optimists claim that ICTs function as a new means of overcoming traditional forms of exclusion and inequality, and refer to ICTs as *enabling technologies*, leading to greater social justice, equal opportunities and empowerment of citizens. The two positions are not necessarily mutually exclusive and both seem to be inspired by a certain technological determinism, but both are also forceful in their claims.

This introductory chapter addresses both the policy and the academic debate about inclusion/exclusion and the need for conceptual clarity of an otherwise ambiguous dichotomy. At the same time, it aims at debunking some of the underlying rhetorical assumptions while arguing that the concept needs to be approached in a more dynamic way, with a clear sense of its multi-layered nature. In doing so, we hope to set the tone for the following, more empirical chapters on diasporic media across Europe, the use of ICTs in transnational movements and the benefits of ICTs for the less abled.

The European Policy Context[1]

Social issues – such as social inclusion and social cohesion – have been introduced only gradually in the European IST (information, science and technology)-policy agenda. Before 1995, the focus was mainly on technological and economic aspects, more specifically on the de-regulation and liberalisation of the telecommunication market. Social issues were addressed only marginally and usually in quite an optimistic tone of voice. This is, for instance, illustrated in the following quotation taken from the report of the High-Level Group on the Information Society, better known as the 'Bangemann' Report. 'The information society has the potential to improve the quality of life of Europe's citizens, the efficiency of our social and economic organisation and to reinforce cohesion' (High-Level Group on the Information Society, 1994, p.5). Or, the following comment in the 1994 Action Plan about the European information society. 'The information society promises to create new jobs, enhance social solidarity and to promote Europe's linguistic and cultural diversity. However, if not adequately framed, it could create new social and economic discrepancies' (European Commission, 1994, p.13).

After 1995, social issues were addressed with greater emphasis in the European IST-related policy documents and actions. The work of the Forum on the Information Society must be mentioned here. In its first annual report, the Forum stressed the need for a shift from 'technology to people'. Although the authors are conscious of the fact that the potential of ICTs will not become a reality by itself, the report expresses an overtly optimistic view of the information society and on social inclusion. 'If we create life-long learning systems and decide that access to the skills and information that people need will be universal and affordable, then there will be more jobs, more social cohesion and more personal fulfilment' (Forum on the Information Society, 1996, p.6).

Another important report in this phase was *Building the European Information Society for us all*, by yet another High-Level Group of Experts, chaired by Luc Soete. In this report, the issues of inclusion and cohesion were addressed with more emphasis. The expert group states that in order to enable inclusion, technologies must be adapted to human needs. However superfluous this statement may sound, it is not so self-evident if we consider that the EC-policy had been quite technology-driven hitherto. The expert group also states that 'the IS [information society] should not *create* new categories of exclusion; they should be put to use to improve social integration and the quality of life of European citizens' (High-Level Expert Group, 1997, p.59).

These issues were taken up by the EC in its Green Paper *Living and working in the information society – people first* (European Commission, 1996). Here, the issue of inclusion is mostly dealt with in terms of employment and work-related objectives. Cohesion is particularly linked with the potential of ICT to reduce the disadvantages of less favoured and more peripheral regions. There are also concerns about the development of a two-tier society of information 'haves' and 'have-nots' (Ibid., p.23). Lastly, what is interesting is that this document highlights the identity of Europe in relation to information society issues: social issues are considered to be an expression of what is called the 'European model', built both on competition between enterprises and solidarity between citizens and member states. By labeling the social agenda as crucial for European identity, the social has moved from the margins to the core of the European policy discourse, at least for the moment.

We can observe this move in the current policy phase which we may label 'e-Europe and beyond'. In this phase, policy is focused on the objectives that are better known as the Lisbon strategy and its translation in several action plans and programmes. While in the e-Europe 2000 programme, social cohesion and inclusion were still translated in a quite limited way into actions focused on 'e-participation for the disabled', in the e-Europe 2002 action plan, the concept of e-participation was broadened to 'participation for all in the knowledge-based economy'. This action plan also covered the fight against 'info-exclusion'. This is an interesting move, as it broadens the focus from policies aimed at improving access to ICT-*infrastructures* to access to *information structures*. The e-Europe 2005 action plan (with the title, *An information society for all*) particularly aims at translating the increased connectivity in Europe into increased economic productivity and improved quality and accessibility of services, based on a secure broadband infrastructure available to the largest possible number of people. In this plan, the social agenda seems to be less visible again and is predominantly framed in terms of economic goals. Special attention to the e-inclusion theme is assured by the instalment of a task force on the Employment and Social Dimensions of the Information Society (ESDIS), which has produced a special report on this subject. The focus in this report is on physical access to ICTs as well as access to *capacities* via education.

In conclusion, the development of the IST-agenda of the EC shows that access to ICTs is considered one of the key drivers for realising social and economic policy goals. Closing the digital divide is a social objective, as it is assumed to improve the possibilities of European citizens to participate fully and on equal terms in society. It is also an economic objective, as it is assumed to raise the competitiveness and productivity of regions and nations. When we look closer, the social goals are often also phrased in narrow socio-economic terms: there is a tendency to frame the inclusion issue in terms of the classical agenda of the Employment Directorate General, which implies a bias towards citizens' participation in the labour market and on the skills they need to improve their position here.

The Academic Debate on Inclusion/Exclusion: Conceptual and Political Ambiguity

The digital divide may be seen as the ICT translation of a wider debate on *social exclusion* and poverty. Both are problematic in the sense that they seem to suffer from a certain one dimensionality, framed as they are in predominant (socio-)economic terms. Particularly in policy discourses, it is often assumed that social exclusion is a condition experienced by marginalised groups and mainly caused by a lack of *financial resource*. That is, social deprivation leading to poverty, ill health and bad education is merely a consequence of the *economic* circumstances people are in.

In academic literature, other related dimensions of exclusion are pointed to, as well. Some stress the *capabilities* that are needed to fully function in society (cf. Sen, 1992). Others also refer to *cultural qualities*, *mutual acceptance* and *well-being* as factors that correlate with social inclusion and exclusion. Elias (1994) has pointed out that the main deprivation people suffer when in degrading positions of social exclusion is not so much lack of food, money or work, but rather a deprivation of value, meaning and self-respect, which leads to stigmatisation impeding full social acceptance. Postmodernists have moved away from the more structural, objective explanations of exclusion to social meanings attributed to inclusion and exclusion, from categories of class, gender and ethnicity to identities and subjectivities, thus emphasising a theoretical and empirical dichotomy between structure and agency (Wyatt et al, 2000). From these different positions, it becomes clear that the processes and dynamics that may lead to exclusion are often intertwined and strengthen each other. These include: work and income, food and living conditions, health and social security, knowledge and mobility, (communicative) skills, non-discrimination.

From a historical perspective, control over, distribution of and access to past and present technologies has always been exemplified as showing the dissonance between assumed and thwarted emancipation, between expectation and the many realities of inequality and strengthened deprivation. The 'digital divide' – as a specific form of exclusion – is commonly described as the gap between those who have access to computers and the internet and those who have not. This divide is both seen as a *result* of the other forms of social exclusion – those who suffer from a lack of financial resources, skills or capabilities will also have trouble accessing ICTs and handling the information that is accessible through ICTs – and as a *factor that will aggravate* the other dimensions of social exclusion. As ICTs become increasingly important, if only in rhetoric, for citizens to participate in and enjoy the 'blessings' of modern society, those who lag behind in this respect will also become increasingly marginalised in social, economic and political respects. It is therefore not a surprise that the digital divide *problematique* has caused a lot of concern among both academics and policy makers.

The concept of the digital divide is, however, highly problematic for a number of reasons. Firstly, the concept is theoretically vague and is thus confusing in what exactly it tries to describe or explain (see for instance, Cammaerts et al., 2003; Frissen, 2003). It is defined and operationalised in a multiplicity of ways but this is often unsystematic and lacking in clarity. Norris (2001, p.23) speaks of a '*multi-dimensional* phenomenon' and distinguishes between a global divide (the divergence of internet access between industrialised and developing societies); a social divide (the gap between the information rich and poor in each nation); and a democratic divide within the online community (signifying the difference between those who do and those who do not use the 'panoply of digital resources to engage, mobilise and participate in public life'). Cammaerts et al. (2003) have observed that the concept refers not only to the social exclusion mechanisms of individuals, but also to the political exclusion of NGOs and the economic exclusion of small enterprises. Van Dijk (1999) criticises the one-sidedness in limiting the divide to computer access, whereas basic skills, insufficient user-friendliness and unevenly distributed usage opportunities are equally important in understanding the multi-faceted and true nature of existing barriers to access.

In fact, the notion of 'access' itself, which is often taken for granted as being at the heart of the divide, is also rarely well defined. Sometimes it is referred to as 'availability', sometimes as opportunity; often the context of specific use is ignored, whereas physical access does not necessarily imply that people actually feel able to make use of these opportunities. Selwyn (2004, p.348) notes that, instead of speaking of either having or not having access, one should speak of a hierarchy that reflects more complex questions of levels of connectivity in terms of the capability and distribution of the access concerned. He also points to Wilhelm (2000), who distinguishes between various 'shades' of marginality between 'core' access, 'peripheral' access and non-access.

Secondly, the existence of a digital divide is based on the empirically unsound assumption that lack of access to ICTs automatically leads to, or sharpens, other forms of exclusion and thus is a barrier to the opportunities for citizen participation. This assumption leads too easily to policies in which access to ICTs is promoted as the answer to all our troubles. Western governments, along with international institutions and non-governmental organisations, are seeking to increase their profile in this area by declarations to the effect that reducing the digital divide is an absolute priority.

Thirdly, the notion of digital divide is based on empirically unwarranted assumptions about how and why citizens use or do not use ICTs (Cammaerts et al, 2002). It refers in a sense to a static situation, which is in fact sometimes very dynamic and can alter rapidly for specific groups. In this sense, identified gaps are changing all the time, which is highly problematic for policies aimed at targeted social groups (and many policies are designed like that). For example, women and senior citizens are catching up very fast in the area of the internet. Moreover, the enormous success of mobile services among all strata of the population demonstrates that the digital divide discourse is too one-sidedly focused on specific technologies, such as the PC and internet. The explicit connection made between the digital divide and exclusion – *if you are not online, you do not belong* – ignores other reasons given for the non-use of a particular technology. Research has shown that non-users also point to other explanations than the classic 'victim' arguments, such as a lack of skills or financial resources. Negatively perceived functionality, techno-fear and an aversion technology play an equally prominent role (Punie, 2000, p.398), and – from a critical consumer perspective – some of these negative attitudes towards technology are certainly quite warranted.

Fourthly, data on market-penetration, ICT-ownership and subscriptions to the internet are often correlated with socio-demographic characteristics of potential users, such as levels of income, education, skills, etc. These figures can be helpful in determining which groups in society are lagging, but also tend to stigmatise groups that are already marginalised. They do not tell us much about the skills and capacities or other dimensions of the everyday life of the stragglers. Qualitative parameters – what it is that users *do* with ICTs, what functions these ICTs have in their everyday life and what they mean to their users – are rarely investigated. Precisely these factors may shed an interesting and possibly different light on the dynamics of exclusion.

Lastly, a double fallacy of democratic participation appears inherent in the digital divide argument. Emphasising the virtues of a deliberative democracy, made possible and enhanced by the application and use of the internet and inspired by the Enlightenment ideal of rational-critical debate, can very well exclude different groups in society, for example, many women, minorities, the uneducated, etc. (Benhabib, 1996). Moreover, the implicit connection made in the digital divide discourse between ICT use and participation is too simplistic and fails, also, to take into account other forms of participation and other forms of exclusion which may be quite structural. Research shows that citizens' social participation or involvement in, for example, voluntary organisations has been increasing over the last decades without any clear (positive or negative) correlation with the use of ICTs by these citizens (Elchardus, et al. 2000; Frissen, 2003). There is no clear evidence that access to ICT-technology, content and skills will automatically have an effect on other forms of exclusion. Cammaerts et al. (2003, p.304) state that to a large extent social exclusion has a structural character and mere access to ICTs is not able to change this complex situation, caused as it is by a multiplicity of interconnected and mutually reinforcing exclusion mechanisms.

Prerequisites for the Study of Inclusion-Exclusion

The ambiguity in the digital divide concept calls for an approach to inclusion-exclusion that takes into account its multi-dimensionality, the complex relationships between the different dimensions and its variety across different contexts. Furthermore, such an approach should be sensitive to the subjective experiences and processes of meaning construction underlying inclusion/exclusion and to the normative assumptions that are often underlying the inclusion/exclusion discourse. Let us take a closer look at these requirements.

Inclusion/Exclusion is Multi-dimensional

We have argued that, particularly in the policy debate, ICT-related exclusion is often discussed in a rather one-dimensional sense, that is, in relation to participation in economic life. However relevant, exclusion can take place in many other dimensions of everyday life as well: the political, cultural, social as well as the economic. From civic engagement and political rights such as voting, to be elected in a representative function or to demonstrate, cultural citizenship or the right to express and enhance one's own identity, to ordinary processes that take place in everyday life, social welfare and well-being – all are areas and aspects of the everyday where inequality and exclusion can take place. Strategies that focus on ICT should take all these different aspects of exclusion into account, including of course the exclusion that relates to communication, information and signification.

The Relationships Between Different Dimensions of Inclusion/Exclusion are Complex

As Wyatt et al. (2000, p.4) have noted equality is often 'judged by comparing one particular aspect of an individual, such as income, wealth, health, happiness or education with the same aspect of another'. They approvingly quote Sen (1992, p.2), who has concluded that equality in terms of one variable may not necessarily coincide with equality in another. For example, equal opportunities can lead to very unequal incomes, and equal wealth can coexist with unequal happiness. In the same vein, digital 'exclusion' may well coexist with a sense of well-being. Furthermore, those who are marginalised in a socio-economic sense may still be quite well equipped with ICTs. This raises difficult questions, such as: how can one 'weigh' the relative importance of inclusion in, for example, political processes *vis-à-vis* exclusion in wealth? How can it be explained that digital inclusion increases the potential for social networking (social inclusion) while at the same time decreases the inclusion of citizens in political processes? In short, in order to get a clear picture of what we actually refer to when talking about inclusion/exclusion, it is important to investigate how, within specific contexts, the different dimensions of inclusion and exclusion affect each other.

Inclusion/Exclusion is not Static

Over time, the hierarchy of basic needs of goods and services, which differs between people, will change. Not so long ago, ownership of a mobile telephone, a home computer and access to the internet were more desires than needs for self-actualisation. Now, they function more or less as aggregate statistical indicators of inequality between social groups, and all walks of life feel them and 'live' them as basic needs or as life style signs of inclusion, of being part of a social group. Thus, the importance of specific dimensions of exclusion may change over *time*. Moreover, the implications (dimensions) of inclusion/exclusion may vary considerably in different *contexts*.

Inclusion/Exclusion is both Objective and Subjective

Inclusion/exclusion has an objective and a subjective component, a material and a symbolic aspect. The objective aspect is usually based on aggregate, quantitative data, mapping structural factors that impede social inclusion. A conclusion that may be valid here is that the unequal uptake of ICTs seems to coincide with other forms of inequality. Digital exclusion thus seems to manifest itself particularly among those social groups or regions that are already at the short end of the stick (Frissen, 2003, p.18). However, the subjective aspect usually builds on more qualitative and ethnographic data, on the experiences and meanings underlying inclusion/exclusion. Thus, on the basis of certain social or structural criteria or indicators, someone may be considered excluded, but 'feel' quite differently and may even be happy with his lot, seeing that others are worse off. An analysis of access to ICT should thus go beyond the strictly material, and include the experiential – what does it mean to have or not to have access to ICTs? In other words, the analysis of social structures underlying inclusion/exclusion should be complemented with a study of social meanings and the way these are embodied in culture, identity, subjectivity and individual agency (cf. Wyatt et al., 2000, p.7).

Inclusion/Exclusion is a Normative Concept

Lastly, inherent in the inclusion/exclusion dichotomy is that being socially excluded is defined as bad and inclusion the preferred state of being, worth striving for and putting an effort into. Emphasising human agency runs the risk that inclusion will not only be seen as a right, but also as an obligation: empowerment as an *opportunity* to participate is propagated as a *necessity* to be active too. That begs for inbuilt disappointment, when barriers are lowered and access is improved but 'nothing happens'; not everyone is a social or political animal driven by an urge to articulate and to mobilise. Non-participation, inactivity and even exclusion may reflect a voluntary individual choice (cf. Bhalla and Lapeyre, 1997, p.415). Moreover, low-key forms of participation such as 'lurking' in fora or news groups are often considered to be a problem or at best a secondary level of involvement, while they could also be seen as a way of learning and engaging, and a style of non-participatory communication certainly worth studying.

An Alternative Approach

Both the complexity of the inclusion/exclusion concept and the discourses underlying the debate on the digital divide, which are strongly based on empirically unwarranted and highly normative assumptions, point to the need for an alternative approach towards inclusion/exclusion. This approach needs to focus on different dimensions of inclusion/exclusion, and on the way these dimensions relate to and interact with each other in a specific context. It also needs to include a subjective or experiential dimension, as these experiences may give us clues, which in turn uncover sometimes-surprising reasons for exclusion. Studying the role and position of ICTs in this complex situation should also take into account that they can be considered a tool or a strategy to overcome exclusion and to be included, but also a new domain of inequality in itself.

To do justice to the multi-dimensionality of the concept, the studies presented in the next three chapters focus more or less on three different dimensions of inclusion/exclusion: the *socio-economic*, the *political* and the *cultural*. All of them also criticise the assumption that giving access to technology leads automatically to (social) inclusion. The potential of ICTs for participation is recognised, but the use of these technologies is not seen as an absolute condition guaranteeing inclusion.

If we then look more closely at the findings of Myria Georgiou's study on diasporic communities (Chapter 3), we see it underpins the highly ambiguous nature of inclusion/exclusion processes. This study gives an indication of how problematic it is to reach unitary conclusions about the degree of cultural inclusion/exclusion within these communities. She argues that the implications of ICTs in the production of minority media and in the increase of content that interests niche and often-segregated ethnic groups are complex.

On the one hand, the possibilities for production expand as cost decreases and as autonomy and access to ICTs broaden. This becomes directly visible in the increasing numbers of such products and in the growing success of online and transnational satellite television in ethnic/diasporic media. These media projects open up possibilities for alternatives to the mainstream content, including products in minority languages, information regarding migration and integration and links between transnational diasporic communities. In offering information about local, national and transnational events, in allowing people to communicate in their first language and in feeding their everyday repertoires with ethnic cultural products, it can be argued that minority media offer their users *knowledge* and *power to participate* as more equal players in local, national and transnational communities, in ethnic and multiethnic public spheres.

On the other hand, the *voluntary exclusion* or *exclusivity* within the ethnic group may limit and even hinder integration or inclusion of these diasporic communities in the autochthonous community. Furthermore, this study introduces differentiation on yet another contextual level, namely *the local*, *the national* and *the transnational*. On the local level, it makes clear that there are many informal local projects and initiatives taking place, resulting in a highly differentiated new kind of multicultural public space, both in a physical sense (internet cafes, call shops, radio stations, etc) and in a virtual sense (cultural content, websites, etc.). Indeed, this can be understood as inclusion, as media and ICTs offer minorities many possibilities for voicing, representation and identification. On the transnational level, this empowering potential is evident as well; ICTs and media enable these communities to exist and to expand across national boundaries and to create a cultural space of their own, and thus live and enrich their diasporic existence. Particularly on the national level, however, we can also see that, although these minority media offer an alternative to the mainstream, the latter is not really challenged. The exclusion of minorities from the mainstream has not changed at all. In this sense, the use of ICT here seems to stimulate the rise of a separate but not a more inclusive public sphere.

Bart Cammaerts' findings (Chapter 4) show that the use of ICTs by transnational movements has an *empowering* (*inclusive*) and at the same time a *disempowering* (*excluding*) effect in political terms. In most cases studied here, the internet can be seen as an enabler, allowing transnational CSOs (Civil Society Organisations) to organise themselves more (cost-)efficiently, mobilise beyond their constituency, build networks with like-minded organisations, facilitate participation and control their own information flow. The linking of local branches within the transnational network and internal organisation ICT is especially significant. The internet also enables short-term as well as result-oriented and issue-oriented participation through mailing lists, public forums and other interactive tools. However, although this potential of ICT increases the possibilities of these organisations to do what they want to do and to do that well – and thus to be potentially *included* in processes of opinion formation, political pressure, etc. – the political impact seems to be limited. This, after a while, can become a reason for disengagement. Moreover, the organisations described in this study are, to a certain degree, self-excluding. It is quite clear that only a limited number of people actively participate and there is a gender gap too, as most of the participants appear to be male.

A major constraining factor is the unequal distribution of technologies and capabilities, between, and even within, transnational CSOs. Some have considerably more human and financial resources, which allow them to develop more dynamic and interactive services and thus empowers those that are already capable. Yet, another indication for exclusion is that it is questionable, according to the author, whether ICTs actually contribute to the political power of CSO's organisations, and thus whether we can actually speak of political inclusion. This underlines the relative character of inclusion/exclusion and certainly the ambiguous character of the concept.

Finally, from Dorothée Durieux's study (Chapter 5) we may conclude that the inclusive potential of ICTs for the 'less abled' is clearly there. ICT is experienced as an opportunity to be active, to (temporally) structure one's life, and to create new social relationships. More specifically, it allows the unemployed to get in touch with the reality of working life and to see employment as more accessible. On the other hand, this study clearly shows that the *subjective* experiences related to ICT use are quite different in different contexts. The elderly, the unemployed and the less abled vary substantially in their perception of ICTs. The unemployed see ICT as an enabling technology, which is functional in their search for a job. The less-abled attribute more varied meanings to ICT: in their everyday life it is seen both as a tool for practising their job and as an instrument for communicating with others. They seem to be less 'utopian' regarding the potential of ICT as a means to become more included. For the third group, the elderly, the attitude towards and perceptions of ICT are more critical: they seem to be wavering between conflicting meanings such as 'not to be a slave of technology' and 'not to be outdated' at the same time.

It is not self-evident what these ambiguous experiences actually tell us conclusively about being included or excluded. However, the findings of this case study show the relevance of an approach which points to both the *contextual* and the *experiential* as important elements in understanding processes of inclusion and exclusion. This may lead to the conclusion that it is not enough to focus on mere access to ICT or on the improvement of ICT skills in order to enhance (socio-economic) inclusion. We have to know how ICTs are experienced in the contexts of people's everyday life in order to define adequate policy strategies.

Note

1 For this section we are indebted to Dr Jo Pierson (TNO and SMIT/Free University of Brussels), who has analysed the social agenda within the European IST-policy for SOCQUIT, a project on ICTs, social capital and quality of life, commissioned by the EC (http://www.eurescom.de/socquit/).

References

Benhabib, S. (1996) 'Toward a deliberative model of democratic legitimacy', in S. Benhabib (ed.), *Democracy and difference: contesting the boundaries of the political*, Princeton: Princeton University Press.

Bhalla, A. and F. Lapeyre (1997) 'Social exclusion: towards an analytical and operational framework', *Development and Change*, 28 (3) pp 413–433.

Cammaerts, B. (2002) *Social policy and the information society: an assessment of the changing role of the state, social exclusions and the divide between words and deeds* (in Dutch), Doctoral thesis, Vrije Universiteit Brussel, Brussels.

Cammaerts, B., L. van Audenhove, G. Nulens and C. Pauwels (eds) (2003) *Beyond the digital divide*, Brussels: VUB Brussels University Press.

Cammaerts, B., M. Georgiou and D. Durieux (2002) *Exclusion and ICT: beyond binary assumptions, beyond technological determinisms?* Paper for EMTEL meeting in Seville, 2002.

Elchardus, M., L. Huyse and E. van Dael (2000) *Het maatschappelijk middenveld in Vlaanderen: een onderzoek naar de sociale constructie van democratisch burgerschap*, Brussels: VUB Brussels University Press.

Elias, N. (1994) *The established and the outsiders. A sociological enquiry into a community problem*. London: Sage.

European Commission (1993) *Growth, competitiveness, and employment: the challenges and ways forward into the 21st century*, White Paper, Vol. COM(93) 700 final, Brussels.

European Commission (1994) *Europe's way to the information society: an action plan*, Communication from the Commission to the Council, the European Parliament and to the Economic and Social Committee and the Committee of Regions, Vol. COM(94) 347 final, Brussels.

European Commission (1996) *Living and working in the information society – people first*, Green Paper, Vol. COM(96) 389 final, Brussels.

European Commission (1997) *Cohesion and the information society*, Communication from the Commission to the European Parliament, the Council, the Committee of Regions and to the Economic and Social Committee, Vol. COM(97) 7/3, Brussels.

European Commission (2000) *e-Europe – an information society for all*, Communication on a Commission initiative for the special European Council of Lisbon, 23 and 24 March 2000, Brussels: Commission of the European Communities.

European Commission (2001a) *e-Europe 2002 – impact and priorities*, Communication from the Commission to the Council and the European Parliament, Brussels: Commission of the European Communities.

European Commission (2001b) *e-Inclusion – the information society's potential for social inclusion in Europe*, Brussels: Commission of the European Communities.

European Commission (2002) *e-Europe 2005 – an information society for all*, An action plan to be presented in view of the Seville European Council, 21–22 June 2002, Brussels: Commission of the European Communities.

European Council (2000) *Presidency conclusions*, Lisbon European Council 23 and 24 March 2000, Lisbon: EU.

European Council (2001) '"e-Inclusion": exploiting the opportunities of the information society for social inclusion', Council Resolution of 8 October 2001, in *Official Journal of the European Communities*, No. 2001/C 292/02.

European Council & European Commission (2000) *e-Europa 2002 – an information society for all*, Action plan prepared by the Council and the European Commission for the Feira European Council, 19–20 June 2000, Brussels: Commission of the European Communities.

Forum on the Information Society (1996). *Networks for people and their communities: making the most of the information society in the European Union*, First annual report to the European Commission from the Information Society Forum, Brussels: European Commission.

Frissen, V. (2003) 'The myth of the digital divide', in B. Cammaerts, L. van Audenhove, G. Nulens and C. Pauwels (eds) *Beyond the digital divide*, Brussels: VUB Brussels University Press.

High-Level Expert Group. (1997) *Final policy report – Building the European Information Society for us all*, Brussels: European Commission.

High-Level Group on the Information Society (1994) *Europe and the global information society*, Brussels: European Council.

Norris, P. (2001) *Digital divide. Civic engagement, information poverty and the internet worldwide*, Cambridge: Cambridge University Press.

Punie, Y. (2000) *Domesticatie van ICT. Adoptie, gebruik en betekenis van media in het dagelijkse leven: Continue beperking of discontinue bevrijding?* Doctoral thesis, Brussels: VUB.

Selwyn, N. (2004) 'Reconsidering political and popular understandings of the digital divide', *New Media & Society*, 6 (3) pp 341–362.

Sen, A. (1992) *Inequality re-examined*, Oxford: Oxford University Press.

Van Dijk, J. (1999) *The network society: social aspects of new media*, London: Sage.

Wilhelm, A. (2000) *Democracy in the digital age*, London: Routledge.

Wyatt, S., F. Henwood, N. Miller and P. Senker (eds) (2000), *Technology and in/equality. Questioning the information society*, London: Routledge.

Chapter 3

Mapping Diasporic Media Cultures: A Transnational Cultural Approach to Exclusion

Myria Georgiou

Introduction

Cultural diversity, perceived in some quarters as a threat to harmony across Europe, has recently come under attack while at the same time ideologies of assimilation and forced integration have been making a significant comeback. At a time when such discourses assume an interconnection between difference and segregation and between diversity and inter-ethnic conflict, the vast majority of minority populations experience a very different reality. On one hand, minorities face old and new forms of exclusion and, on the other hand, they become active participants in the production of cultural repertoires of identity, community and belonging[1] that only marginally relate to segregation and inter-ethnic conflict and mostly reflect the struggles for self-representation and participation in broader societies and distinct communities.

The growth in European diversity raises a number of key questions that challenge arguments about cultural clashes and which invite us to think about the social, cultural and communicative elements of participation and inclusion in Europe. The issues emerging in the study of exclusion/inclusion cut across two axes with theoretical and methodological implications. First, there is a sociological question about Europe. Is Europe reflexive and inclusive of cultural diversity or does cultural difference become a point of more or less intense conflict and exclusion? In addition, there is a communication-related question. How is the growing cultural diversity across Europe expressed/communicated and with what consequences?

This chapter focuses on a study of the inter-relation of the two axes – the sociological and the communicative. Mediated communication – increasingly central for the shape of contemporary cultures – brings the issues of representation, exclusion and inclusion closer together. The two axes meet when investigating questions about the role of media and communication technologies in projects that involve the political and cultural representation of minorities. The area of communication, as part of the cultural sphere, becomes the main terrain where the symbolic representations of a society are produced and consumed. In mediated culture, perceptions and actions around inclusion and exclusion are produced and communicated. The question then becomes who is a member of the society and who has the right to belong, to be included and to be represented. The important role of the cultural sphere in general and of communication in particular in advancing or restricting inclusion and participation have rarely been addressed in academic and policy debates.

The research discussed here investigated the links between exclusion and the cultural sphere as they emerged in mediated communication and in the context of everyday life. Diasporic and migrant minorities experience economic deprivation, and research shows that they are among the groups facing high levels of exclusion.[2] While relevant data suggests that minorities are extensively excluded from economic progress, little has been said about how everyday cultural experience and communication shape and is being shaped by marginalisation, exclusion and participation. If the debates around social exclusion and the possibilities for participation are to be meaningful, there is an urgent need for developing a discourse that considers informal and communication practices that take place in everyday life as much as formal and institutional processes – for example, employment, education.

The tense relationship between the sociological and the technological, as illustrated in diasporic communication practices, underlies the theoretical and empirical elements of this research. Diasporic media cultures develop as mediation becomes increasingly central to social and cultural life. Everyday culture has become media culture (Silverstone, 1994; Alasuutari, 1999). Representations, communication and information are increasingly mediated by television, radio and the internet. Media cultures develop and diversify as technological developments expand the potential for media production, for access and control of personal and communal communication flows and for trans-spatial connections. Such developments do not take place just because technology is available or for the sake of technological progress. The social appropriations of communication technologies give meaning and social significance to technological progress. For example the engagement of different groups with ICTs and the media – as producers, receivers, as neither or both – has multiple implications for the possibilities for participation in media cultures and, inevitably, in European societies. This will be explored in more detail later in this chapter. Furthermore, as mediated communication crosses boundaries and communication technologies are appropriated in transnational spaces and by spreading communities, cultural life becomes less defined and bounded within singular nation-states and more complexly shaped in the interweaving of different political, social and cultural spaces (Harvey, 1989; Urry, 2000). This research focuses on just such developments, that is, the communicative and the social are at its core, rather than the informational and the technological.

The research this chapter draws from is a unique attempt to map diasporic media cultures across the EU. Theoretically and empirically, such an attempt becomes a demanding challenge. Such an undertaking cannot be an objective, quantified and complete map of mediation and diversity; it can only be a cultural, suggestive and interpretative grasp of European diversity and mediation as these relate to diasporic minorities and their experience of exclusion and participation. Diasporic media maps are constantly changing and they are extremely diverse in terms of production and consumption, especially when they are studied across states and groups. This mapping addresses some common issues around inclusion and participation that surpass the particular[3] and which relate to mediation. In doing so, it draws from 13 national reports[4] and from a series of case studies, either produced for this research or drawn on as secondary sources. The research primarily focuses on diasporic media production because it:

(i)   Reflects a cultural presence of different communities within broader local, national and transnational media cultures.
(ii) Partly reflects the cultural identity of diasporic groups (for example, in terms of mono-lingual or multi-lingual media; local and/or global media).
(iii) Allows us to investigate how media production interweaves with media consumption in complex communicational relations that cannot be grasped in linear analyses of the 'sender-receiver' relationship or in techno-centric approaches.

Diasporic Media Cultures in the European Context

The population of peoples who at some stage in their history migrated from an original *homeland* and settled in European Union (EU) countries is estimated to be as high as 8 per cent of the population of the EU. In addition, millions of members of older diasporas – Jewish, Roma, Armenians – have become integral players in Europe's past and present, even if their experience of Europe has sometimes been of pain and persecution. More recently, hundreds of thousands of refugees have been settling in the EU and though their numbers are minimal compared to the world refugee population (for example, only 3 per cent of world refugees reach the UK), refugee mobility is central in debates on the future of Europe. Given that only 3 per cent of the world's refugees reach the UK and that in most EU countries migrant populations do not exceed 2 per cent of the population (Council of Europe, 1993), the interest in migrant and diasporic populations is not merely a reflection of a numerical phenomenon.

The cultural richness of Europe has long been part of public debate. The ethnic differences between communities in the EU have been presented as a positive indicator of the pluralism of the continent (Gatling, 1989). Yet, a discourse that celebrates diversity has not always been significantly and meaningfully inclusive. As Gatling argues (1989), in the EU there is a discussion on diversity within unity, but such unity often has racist overtones. The idea of Europeanism and the celebration of the European Judeo-Christian values and the Greco-Roman political heritage are together supposed to focus on the characteristics that are shared across the continent, but they actually reflect specific elements of mainstream and dominant cultures. In the dominant ideologies of Europe and European diversity, the heterogeneity of diverse and multicultural societies is seen as a threat, while heterogeneity has often been pathologised. Hobsbawm and Ranger argue that this tension is partly created in the invention of tradition as an integral task in the nation-state's reproduction of its continuity: 'There is then an inherent tension between the invented "heritage" which roots national identity in history, and the change and heterogeneity that characterises the contemporary western Europe nation-state' (quoted in Husband, 1994, pp.6–7).

Why Diaspora?

This project focuses on diasporic communities because they often face high levels of exclusion, but also because diasporic particularity reveals some of the spatial and cultural complexity of inclusion and participation in highly mediated societies. In Gillespie's words, 'a diasporic perspective acknowledges the ways in which identities have been and continue to be transformed through relocation, cross-cultural exchange and interaction. The globalisation of cultures is deeply implicated in this process' (1995, p.7).

A defining characteristic of diaspora is a strong and continuing sense of sharing collective identities among dispersed populations (Cohen, 1997), but also the sense of a *changing same* (Gilroy, 1995). That is, collective identity does not imply similarity but instead recognises heterogeneity and diversity (Hall, 1990). Media and ICTs become particularly relevant to diasporic transnationalism. Diasporic populations are increasingly dependent on and benefit from communication and transportation technologies for sustaining connections across the many countries where they are settled. Diasporic mediated transnationalism is a case of particular interest for the present discussion. On one hand, there are strong indications of continuing diasporic participation in distinct communities (as they develop across local, national and transnational spaces) and, on the other hand, there are many restrictions in the participation of such populations in European societies. The empirical findings discussed here will show that these two contradictory elements of diasporic life are closely interlinked, especially as media production and mediated everyday life challenge the closure of both the mainstream and of diasporic communities and advance various forms of self-generated participation and inclusion.

Here, the concept of *diasporic* is preferred to *diaspora* for two reasons. Diaspora implies a long experience of settlement in a host country, a feature that does not characterise many of the populations who have migrated in recent times. Yet, the key characteristics of diasporic condition – that is, transnationality, a sense of ethnic commonality, myth and memory of a common original *homeland* – are present and significant for the populations who have migrated to the EU and who experience exclusion because of ethnicity. Furthermore, the concept of diasporic rather than diaspora challenges any attempt for closure that would assume that the populations in question are by definition and forever attached to a *homeland* and to certain identity. The diasporic condition is contextual (Dayan, 1998) and the possibility of change and challenge to diasporic identification is always present.

The Politics of Exclusion and Why Everyday Life Matters

The now popular concept of social exclusion was initially introduced within a discourse of static and singular definitions of poverty. As a concept, social exclusion reflects a shift in both academic thinking and policy making from a focus on 'being' poor to recognition of the complex processes that lie behind 'becoming poor'. Social exclusion has unfolded a broader agenda that highlights the different mechanisms of inequality and links poverty to social divisions such as gender, ethnicity, age, etc. (Anthias, 2001). Diasporic and migrant minorities experience economic deprivation and are considered to be among the groups facing high levels of social exclusion (Social Exclusion Unit, 2000). Thinking through the concept of social exclusion is the first step in understanding how inequality and discrimination are complex conditions and not singularly defined sets of economic relations. Even though the concept and the studies of exclusion highlight complexity, the cultural, communicational and the everyday remain at the periphery of the dominant debates.

Media and communication technologies become involved in processes of participation and inclusion in formal, informal, symbolic and practical ways. John Urry (2002) argues that participation expands as the media broaden imagined and virtual co-presence with the increase of links, interaction and exchange of information and images across space. Physical co-presence emerges as people come together to consume the media, that is, 'a socially inclusive society would elaborate and extend the possibilities of co-presence to all members' (Urry, 2002, p.270). The development and sustaining of social capital and social relations is extensively dependent on connections – or restricted connections – to populations with a cultural commonality living within proximate localities, across the national and across global spaces. According to Urry's analysis, seeking co-presence through imaginative and physical travel is growing among diasporic populations, while restrictions on physical and mediated initiatives for expanding co-presence can increase and intensify a sense of exclusion and marginalisation. This sense – and experience – of exclusion is growing as other social groups enjoy extensive mobility and growing possibilities for co-presence with other members of their social groups.

Co-presence, physical, virtual and symbolic, informs the sense of belonging (to societies and to distinct transnational communities). In everyday life, exclusion is challenged as new networks emerge. These are networks of social support and information exchange – about social and political developments in the host society and the broader diaspora. However, they also include cultural projects of self-representation that challenge exclusion from the mainstream media and appropriate communication technologies in impoverished migrant neighbourhoods. The examples of such diasporic practices discussed here challenge the conceptual and policy limitations of exclusion and invite us to think of exclusion, media and ICTs:

(i)   Beyond a strictly functional perspective of access to technology (for example, for developing skills for employment).
(ii) In relation to group, community and identity dynamics and differences that shape differentiated interests, agendas and ways of getting involved in the use of ICT and the media.[5]
(iii) Through a multi-level analysis that aims at developing communicational strategies that take cultural exclusion – the elements of exclusion that relate to communication, representation, identity and community – into consideration as much as socio-economic exclusion.
(iv) In multiple spaces and beyond the singularity of the nation-state as a context for exclusion/inclusion.

As will be shown in the next section, a multi-spatial approach is key for this re-conceptualisation of exclusion.

A Spatial Approach: Mapping Cultural Exclusion/Inclusion and Diasporic Media Cultures

Diasporic minorities live within specific locales – urban places especially – and in national and transnational spaces. The social interaction and communication within the diasporic communities, among dispersed populations and with others take place in and across spaces. Some of those spaces (also defined as ethnoscapes and mediascapes by Appadurai, 1990) are grounded in very specific places – such as the neighbourhood – while others exist virtually and in non-places (Urry, 2000). Social interaction and relations are no longer dependent on simultaneous physical co-presence. There are also relations developing with the 'absent other' through new communications. When this happens experience of time and space becomes distantiated (Giddens, 1990) and diasporic communities can break off the specificities of space and extend their communication potential. In this context, there are fewer possibilities for a neat equation between culture, community and geography (Gillespie, 1995) and more space for 'imaginative geography and history' (Said, 1985). The connections and relations of 'absence' between places are greatly strengthened by ICTs, which have augmented a sense of diasporic awareness. Diasporic communities sustain and partly depend for their communal shared sense of identity on transnational communication. But the national and local context where diasporic populations live are equally important for the development of links, for sustaining community and identity, as well as for the experience of participation and exclusion from the formal and informal social life. Furthermore, the national and the local still have distinct characteristics (for example, physical co-existence, national laws, local social demographics), even when they are shaped in dialogue with the global (Morley and Robins, 1995). For this reason, the local, the national and the transnational are studied in their co-existence, but also in their autonomy.

European diasporic media are numerous, extremely diverse and include national newspapers, local pirate radio stations, transnational satellite television and fast-growing websites of semi-professional character. Our mapping included diversity in terms of cultural, political and linguistic appropriations of media and communication technologies, as well as diversity in terms of viability, success and level of

Table 3.1   Examining Exclusion from a Cultural Perspective

The Local	The National	The Transnational
The (Re-)construction of Urban Space	The National and the Policy Context: Enabling or Restricting Minority Voices	The Satellite Television Map: The Transnational as the Alternative
The Multicultural and Mediated Local – Multicultural Media Projects	Minority Media as a Challenge to the Mainstream National Media	The Internet: Active Participation in a Community

professionalism. The focus on the relation between media and diasporic exclusion/ inclusion in local, national and transnational spaces meant that many of the particularities of diasporic media projects surpassed our objectives. The mapping focuses on six themes that emerged as the most significant in the analysis of the national reports and the case studies.

The Local

Everyday life is primarily experienced in locales; media are integrated in everyday life and technologies are appropriated to meet interests, needs and cultural, political and social goals. Experiences of mediation in local spaces recorded in our research reveal some of the most interesting – yet unexpected – elements of participation and the dialectics of inclusion/exclusion.

The (re-)construction of urban space One of the most significant forms of participation and connection within media cultures is that which is relatively invisible to the mainstream, but visible in multicultural neighbourhoods. Internet cafés and communication centres[6] mushroom in multicultural neighbourhoods; internet access points are also very popular with migrants and members of diasporic groups. According to Cammaerts (2001), 18 per cent of the users of the internet in Belgian public libraries are members of such groups; in multicultural big cities – such as Antwerp – the percentage reaches 50 per cent. Other ethnographic data from Greece (Georgiou, 2002b) indicates how communication technologies – including telephony – mediate processes of construction of local social and communicational spaces in multicultural urban space. They also function as bridges to the country of origin and diasporic communities around the world. Telephone and internet centres and diasporic video clubs have grown rapidly in multi-ethnic neighbourhoods. These communication centres both reproduce and sustain mediated minority co-presence, as well as direct and face-to-face communication. The visitors of such public spaces not only use the communication technologies offered; the centres also become social spaces for local interaction, with people just using them as meeting places. That is, their visits become more than functional. This example indicates how online communication is experienced and involves offline forms of socialisation. It also shows how media converge in their use and how symbolic value is shaped in the everyday mediation experience. The character of some of these internet cafés and communication centres in multi-ethnic neighbourhoods reflects new dimensions of (inter-)ethnic public space and of ethnic identity performance in public. An internet café in New Cross (South London) is at the same time an Afro-Caribbean hair salon. Another one in Seven Sisters (North London) is a supermarket selling *ethnic* food for its primarily North African clientele.

Yet, the diversity and revival[7] of such neighbourhoods – where communication centres thrive – reflect only one side of the experience in the urban space. Another side is that of degraded inner city ghetto-isation and a very different experience of the subversive appropriation of communication technologies. The entry and settlement of migrants in the city reflects their economic position and the level of social and cultural integration. Not all migrant experience is the same. For example, Nigerians – who form one of the very few black groups in Greece – are highly marginalised and usually live in poor quality inner-city accommodation. This community depends extensively on the informal economy and on pirate CD/DVD/video tapes traded in street commerce. Interestingly, for the much-marginalised Nigerian community, ICTs are central as everyday reference.[8] A large number of Nigerians become ICT-literate as such literacy is a necessary tool in the reproduction and commerce of pirate audio-visual products. The boundaries between the professional and the personal use of ICTs are constantly blurred. ICTs are used for their own personal communication and information needs – especially email and surfing on (Nigerian) websites – but also for sustaining a very particular, ethnic and informal economy, that is, producing pirate CDs, DVDs and video tapes. It is interesting to observe how ICTs economically sustain the majority of this community – most of its members are excluded from the mainstream economy, as they are illegal immigrants. ICTs use has led to the emergence of a very particular form of economy that, though informal and illegal, has become an integrated part of the urban everyday culture.

The multicultural and mediated local – multicultural media projects   In the local – especially in the urban context – diasporic cultures and public performance become visible and often develop around specific diasporic media and communication practices. Furthermore, the local is where inter-ethnic co-existence takes places and where collaborative media projects develop. As well as the media produced and consumed by specific groups, a growing number of new generation multicultural programmes has emerged. These programmes address at the same time people of different cultural backgrounds, both minorities and majorities (for example, *Couleur Locale*; Belgium; *Radio Multikulti*, Berlin, Germany; *Radio OneWorld*, Ireland; *Colorful Radio*, The Netherlands; *Sesam*, Sweden). Most of these multicultural projects are radio stations/programmes, although there are some examples of multicultural television across Europe, like in Aarhus, Denmark. Common to these projects is the sharing of a particular frequency or channel by different groups – diasporic minorities, but also non-ethnic minorities (for example, women, youth groups). These mediated spaces reflect and represent multi-ethnic spaces across Europe in ways that most national media fail to do. Different languages, different kinds of music, different religions and minority political and social groups find a space of representation.

Such multicultural broadcasting is gaining popularity *vis-à-vis* the separate/separatist diasporic media and – though it does not form a harmonious space and there are, for example, tensions around frequencies and time-slots, inner ethnic oppositions – it does form a significant element of contemporary European mediascapes. The increasing number of such programmes reflects:

(i)   A temporal change, as new generations take over.
(ii) A political project of integration and the development of a multicultural public sphere.
(iii) A top-down approach to multiculturalism, which promotes media integration (for example, public service).
(iv) A political top-down attempt to cover the lack of autonomous minority media, especially in countries where migration is a new phenomenon (for example, in Spain).

The National

The national context: enabling or restricting minority voices A cross-national comparison of diasporic media production across six EU countries shows that many of these media are produced locally and some are outcomes of inter-ethnic co-operation – the most characteristic being community media projects (especially relevant in the case of Sweden and Germany). The reason for focusing on these countries is that they offer some of the most accurate relevant data. This small-scale comparison is informative and indicative of the interrelations between:

(i) The length of groups' experience in the diaspora and the extent of their media production.
(ii) The length of their experience in the diaspora and the spatial positioning of their media.
(iii) The extent of the experience of exclusion and the extent of media production (for example, does limited access to media production relate to extensive exclusion? Does political exclusion lead to more extensive media production?).

Table 3.2 A Cross-National Comparison of Diasporic Media[9]

Group	Belgium	Greece	Germany	Spain	Sweden	UK	Total
Arabic	3	4	5		17	11	40
Indian					5	58	63
Pakistani					2	6	8
Chinese	1		3			3	7
Black African	6				24	11	41
Caribbean						14	14
North African	4			1			5
Spanish	4						4
Italian	19		1				20
Greek	5		3		4	5	17
Turkish	6	11	22		12	3	54
Kurdish	2		4		38		44
Jewish			2		1	6	9
Iranian			2		57		59
Polish	4	1	8		6		19
Serbo-Croat	1		5		13		19
Other E. European		11	19		22		52
Latin American	3			1	36		40
Other Group		4	6	1	22	3	36
Multicultural	28	2		18	7	1	56
Total	86	33	80	21	266	121	607

Table 3.2 reveals some of the elements of diasporic media diversity across Europe. The first and most significant conclusion that can be drawn is that the countries with the most developed multicultural policy framework and which are the most supportive of minority media projects (that is, The Netherlands and Sweden) are the two countries with the richest and most diverse minority media availability. The UK – a country that advocates the multicultural model and which hosts an immensely diverse population – has a surprisingly small number of minority media. This is primarily an outcome of a restrictive and highly controlled broadcasting system and the lack of support (for example, in the form of subsidies) for community and minority media projects. The limitations of the nationally framed media are challenged by transnational media production – especially satellite television – and internet production and use (which is impossible to quantify, but which is evidently of growing significance) across Europe.

The visible inequalities between different groups relate to numerical unevenness (for example, the largest groups have the highest production), but also to the complexity of diasporic experience (for example, cultural traditions, politics within the group, as well as to the level of literacy and economic affluence of the group). The direct link between cultural and social exclusion – for example, employment, education – becomes visible in this numerical presentation. In many ways, economic deprivation restrains cultural production of certain groups or leads to the concentration of such production (and power) in the hands of the few privileged members of diasporic groups.

Minority media output as a challenge to the mainstream national media   Data from the UK (Dodd quoted in Georgiou, 2002a), Denmark (Hussein, 2002) and Ireland (Ugba, 2002) shows that for the vast majority of the non-minority populations, familiarity with minority cultures is mediated. In Denmark, 80 per cent of Danes have no interpersonal relationships with migrants, while in the UK two-thirds of those asked said that they get their information about Muslims from the media. Though this data indicates the increased role of mediation for inter-cultural dialogue and understanding, it also reveals a grim picture about the representation of multicultural society in mainstream media. The Runnymede Trust report on multicultural Britain (2000) found that at senior decision-making level in the BBC, Channel 4 and ITV there were even fewer Black and Asians in 2000 than there had been in 1990.

In discussions on minority representation in the media, two dimensions or questions require special attention. Firstly, what kinds of representations, if any, are available to all members of the public about minorities (Malonga, 2002)? Secondly, what kinds of representations are available to the minorities about themselves? Both areas are linked to questions of inclusion. On one hand, fair and visible representation of minorities in the mainstream is a reminder of the multicultural character of European societies and can lead to further understanding and acceptance of diversity. On the other hand, fair and visible representation of minorities for the minorities can become an everyday reminder of their active participation in the societies where they live and enhance communication and participation within the particular diasporic communities. Much has been said elsewhere on the significance of fair representation of minorities for majorities (for example, ter Wal, 2002; Malonga, 2002), but very little has been said about the role of minority representations for minorities in processes of their inclusion. The focus of our project was on self-representation and on the alternative and the subaltern production. What our data indicates is that different alternative minority media projects can challenge exclusion and they can engage in projects of minority participation in multi-ethnic societies. One of the themes analysed in the report is briefly discussed here in relation to a specific case study.[10]

Visibility   Cultural inclusion implies visibility, that is, the ability of the members of the society to see their ethnicity, identity, cultural and political activities reflected in social representations. The case of the *Perşembe* press supplement in Germany is one of the few and significant examples where minorities make a visible presence among – and as part of – the mainstream national media and remind both the majorities and the minorities of the existence of alternative cultural identities, agendas and interests in national societies. This weekly supplement was established in September 2000 and was sold every Thursday with the German daily *Die Tageszeitung* (Rigoni, 2002). The initiative only lasted for a year, but its existence is of great importance. Written in German and Turkish, *Perşembe* was the only supplement attached to a mainstream newspaper addressing Turkish audiences. Furthermore, it was not attached to the media industry in Turkey and so qualifies as a national minority media project. Integration and inclusion – the major minority concerns in Germany – were central to the paper's agenda, though it also covered a diverse repertoire of the everyday life and politics of the Turkish minority. With its agenda, *Perşembe* became a constant reminder that Germany is a country of immigration and that the young people of migrant origin have the right to economic, political and cultural inclusion (Rigoni, 2002). The inability of *Perşembe* to remain part of the mainstream and compete with the media industry indicates the inequalities and the exclusions that minorities face in the struggles for participation in the competitive and financially demanding European mediascapes. For such small or autonomous initiatives, the competition comes from both the German mainstream and the Turkish mainstream (media produced by the major conglomerates based in Turkey). The difficulty projects like *Perşembe* have competing raises concerns about the exclusions emerging in the established power relations in diasporic and European mediascapes.

The Transnational

As diasporic production on the web is growing, as email turns into one of the few uncontrolled, decentralised and participatory means for diasporic communication[11] and as satellite television emerges as a challenging counter-point to mainstream broadcasting, the transnational diasporic mediascapes are becoming increasingly involved in interaction and in the production of information and knowledge. Increased, decentralised and participatory communication can have implications for the ways diasporic populations construct their identities and communities as informed citizens, participating members and knowledgeable discussants. The potential development of transnational spheres challenging national boundaries and the hierarchies of the nation-state are issues that relate to media production and appropriation of technologies across geographical borders. The attempt to undertake systematic mapping of transnational media had to contend with the restrictions inherent in diverse, fast-changing and fast-growing global communication. These challenges become even more acute given the vast, uncontrolled and popular online diasporic products and make online production and communication almost impossible to record. Satellite television allows a much more systematic approach than online production. Though the two media are rather different, in the context of this research their study had a common aim: to understand how transnational production and appropriation of communication technologies in diverse and interconnected spaces becomes involved in processes of (selective and uneven) inclusion and participation.

Satellite television map: the transnational as an alternative to the mainstream One of the key communication technologies to be homologous to transnationalism is satellite technology. Our comprehensive and comparative mapping of satellite production has illustrated a radical change in transnational communication achieved with satellite television. With satellite technology, television produced in the *homeland* has become a media product available across the globe. Additional satellite channels have emerged in transnational spaces aiming to attract particular transnational diasporic audiences, which come from more than one country (for example, Al Jazeera and MedTV). The connectedness, simultaneousness and sharing of common images and narratives between the country of origin and the different positions of diasporic groups reinforces and reminds these dispersed populations of the existence of a transnational community which is – potentially – inclusive of all those groups around the globe. The consequences of satellite television originating in the *homeland* for community and identity are discussed elsewhere in further detail (Ogan, 2001; Georgiou, 2001; Aksoy and Robins, 2000; Madianou, *in press*). This mapping emphasises the significance of satellite television as this relates to questions of inclusion/exclusion. It investigates how the availability of diasporic satellite television challenges the mainstream and commercial television (and its exclusionary approaches to minorities and minority cultures) and how diasporic satellite television is characterised by diversity and unevenness, which creates inequalities in the development of cultural products and projects of inclusion across different minorities.

In many European countries, diasporic communities have introduced and/or increased the popularity of satellite television. The density of satellite dishes and cable television subscription is higher in migrant households compared to Austrian households (note Böse, Haberfellner and Koldas, 2002). Similar findings appear in countries with large migrant communities (for example, Germany and Greece), while access to diasporic satellite television is becoming an area of political decisions with unpredictable consequences. Local authorities in a growing number of EU countries (for example, Austria, Denmark and The Netherlands) have introduced restrictions in the installation of satellite dishes that allow the reception of diasporic channels. Such restrictions can increase the sense of exclusion within minorities (who are on the receiving side of such policies) and reinforce a sense of 'otherness' among them. At the same time, the growing popularity of diasporic satellite television shows that the nation-state can only partly control communication maps.

The quantity and quality of satellite television varies extensively. The common element is the fast-growing number of such channels which either broadcast from the original *homeland* or various places across the world. These channels might be public, state-run and state-controlled or commercial initiatives. Our systematic mapping showed that there are immense inequalities in the satellite mediascapes. Turkish satellite production is the largest production originating in only one country with more than 35 channels. There are more than 30 Arabic channels, while the Russian and other East European channels reach similar numbers. A couple of dozen channels address Eastern Asian audiences and comparable numbers of South American channels aim at reaching Spanish-speaking and Portuguese-speaking global audiences. The apparent inequality in satellite television production becomes even more important when the above numbers are compared with the channels broadcasting from African countries. In this case, the numbers drop radically and if Northern African channels are excluded, the African transnational broadcasts become almost non-existent. Such inequalities are reminders of the reproduction of social inequalities in mediascapes. Limited production and access to media production can jeopardise the participation of smaller and poorer diasporic groups in transnational public spheres, as well as the functioning of global public spheres themselves. It can also undermine minorities' sense of visibility and increase their subordinate position in the increasingly mediated European cultures.

The internet: active participation in a community?   If we accept that the internet is a social space (Poster, 1997), then it becomes particularly relevant to question the nature of diasporic inclusion. The internet – as an environment for transnational as well as localised communication, for public and private connections, for the exchange of information, entertainment and for interpersonal attachment – has often been discussed as a space for transnational, interactive and decentralised communication among dispersed populations. A series of themes emerged from our research. They highlight significant and distinct characteristics of the diasporic internet and explain why and how online diasporic communication relates to inclusion in transnational communities and multi-ethnic societies. These themes become apparent in the public uses of the internet and of course, other issues emerge when it comes to interpersonal and private communication.

Though most members of diasporic populations, like any others, use the internet primarily as a tool for email communication (Castells, 2001), there are certain distinct characteristics of diasporic online communication. Diasporas, as transnational communities, have always depended on mediation and networking for sustaining relations and communication across distance. Until recently, the telephone and snail-mail served this role and now email has become a powerful competitor of the telephone and post. With online communication, the exchange of everyday, banal news has increased. Many people say that they regularly share their daily news with relatives and friends living in other positions within the diaspora, while among the most commonly exchanged attachments are intimate products, such as family photos. Sharing the banality, the routines and the common activities of everyday life (De Certeau, 1984) increases the sense of belonging to a community and furthers the limits of the imagination of sharing (Georgiou, 2001). In addition to the personal and ordinary, which forms a major area for diasporic everyday communication and for reconfirmation of belonging, the internet has also taken further the possibilities for developing long-lasting diasporic cultural projects. Initiatives for sustaining languages and dialects of diasporic minorities in transnational web projects, cultural initiatives for exchanging music across the diaspora and cultural knowledge databases have brought closer together spread expertise on formal and informal diasporic cultures (which are usually excluded from the cultural history in the countries of settlement). Such examples include the European Sephardic Institute (www.sefarad.org), the Latino cultural portal http://www.mundolatino.org/cultura, based in Spain, and the Kurdish encyclopaedia, which calls for contributions on Kurdish culture, language and dialects (http://www.kurdistanica.com). In both the cases of the personal and the communal, the image and sound of commonality become virtually confirmed. For communities such as the diasporic, which are characterised by disparity and diversity, the construction of shared imagination largely takes place through the mediated images and sounds of their commonality (Anderson, 1983).

The third area that destabilises the condition of exclusion of diasporic populations is that of political action and representation. The diasporic internet challenges in multiple ways the limitations in expression and political participation set by the nation-state – both of the host country and the country of origin. For example, The Muslim News (http://www.muslimnews.co.uk), which is based in the UK, claims a role as an independent news provider; a news provider that is ultimately diasporic and transnational as it attaches itself to no particular Muslim country or government. Then there are a few other active and popular sites, directly challenging state control and dependence. The Arabic internet Media Network (http://www.amin.org) defines itself as an 'uncensored' bilingual (Arabic and English) professional journalism' site, while the Arab Press Freedom Watch (http://www.apfwatch.org/en) benefits from its transnational diasporic position to struggle for press freedom in Arab countries.

The internet not only creates competitive spaces for communication beyond state control, but it also challenges concentration of power and control in singular points within the global. There are numerous examples illustrating this virtual shift from concentrated power to more decentralised spaces of dialogue. For instance, there is the case of the PALESTA network (Palestinian Scientists and Technologists Abroad – website www.palesta.gov.ps). PALESTA, in its short life, turned from a network, fully controlled by the centre – the Palestinian territories – to a diasporic multi-positioned network with multiple flows of communication among its dispersed participants. Through tensions and long debates about the role of a diasporic network like PALESTA, eventually the centre lost its original, fundamental and unchallenged role as the heart of a global community (Hanafi, 2001). The network members demanded and succeeded in communicating from within different positions in the diaspora, without this communication being controlled and co-ordinated by the centre/*homeland*.

The internet is a space of contestation and struggles of power of the offline world reflected online. Additionally, other new struggles emerge around the control of technology and of mediated communication flows. While expression in online spaces cannot be celebrated as *de facto* democratic and participatory, the growing visibility and activity of diverse groups on the internet certainly destabilises the concentration of representation within diasporic groups and within European societies.

Conclusions

This brief review of the key findings of a cross-European research seeks to illustrate the various ways in which media cultures challenge homogenising and exclusionary discourses in local, national and transnational spaces. The themes discussed highlight two main points in relation to media and communication technologies. Firstly, minority media cultures do not usually emerge around a singular medium or technology – rather they are shaped in the combined, multiple and complex engagement of people with the media and in the convergence of the media. Different media and technologies – including the very *new*, like the internet and satellite but also the radio, local (analogue) television and ethnic press – shape diasporic media cultures. Media cultures are diverse, but media also converge and co-exist. This leads me to the second important point. Media and technologies have their specificities, but their significance lies not so much with the technologies as with the range of practices that cross a range of media, and as such produce a kind of common denominator within the processes of communication and mediation. Such an approach is less technology-driven and more concerned with the implications of diasporic media for culture and everyday life. It also argues for the role of media cultures in the wider social experience of inclusion and participation. In this context, three key arguments are made.

Participating in the Local, the National and the Transnational

Diasporic space is a multi-positioned space and includes three interweaving – and competing – elements: the local, the national and the transnational. Media are increasingly taking the role of the mediator of the triangular spatial context of diasporic belonging: in the locality, in the host country, in connection between the country of origin and the global diasporic community. Radio, television, the internet – but often no less the press – are becoming mediators of the triangular spatial context of diasporic belonging. The interplay among these three spaces and the mobility of people across them – either in real or virtual terms, cultural and psychological – sustains communities and alternative publics. Diasporic media can help the development of *imagined presences* (Urry, 2000), of '[non-national] communities of sentiment and interpretation' (Gilroy, 1995, p.17); they shape scenarios of identity and diasporic consciousness (Iordanova, 2001). Needless to say, the media themselves do not always promote fair representations, nor do they necessarily promote democratic engagement. As they destabilise the mainstream mediascapes and their exclusionary (for minorities) hierarchies and representations, they allow more space for tense and intense dialogue across and within European cultural spaces.

Representation and Self-representation

In diasporic media, representations which are alternative to the mainstream can become dominant, as diasporic media are more inclusive of (some) marginalised expressions of identity and as they promote positive representations of otherwise invisible and stereotyped cultural behaviours. Online diasporic communication defies – or at least challenges – boundaries set as identifiers and social margins around communities. Exclusion, marginalisation and racism have always created and depended upon the ascription of single-dimensional identities and upon the drawing of clear-cut boundaries that divide groups between *us* and *others*. In the rich and diverse diasporic online presence, singular identifications and stereotyping of minorities are directly and actively challenged. The construction of self-representations of diasporic groups and subgroups challenges the exclusionary discourses of the mainstream (in communities and societies) creating a setting for increased participation through difference.

Some examples from diasporic communication presented here have highlighted the growing challenges to homogeneity and stereotyping of groups from the mainstream and from the dominant powers within diasporic groups. Mainstream and dominant diasporic projects of homogenising and of (self-)stereotyping of diasporic groups (for example, the national satellite television from the country of origin) are constantly challenged by alternative voices within the group (for example, Al Jazeera, PALESTA). In these cases, even if the battle is unequal, bottom-up, decentralised and marginal agendas and cultural repertoires can destabilise the set hierarchies reproduced by the nation-states (of the host country and of the country of origin).

Finding a Voice

The struggle around the occupation, ownership and control of mediated space is an element that should inform the debates on mediation, exclusion and inclusion. Diasporic media, in their interactivity, transnationality and diversity, may allow the development of more open, and less controlled by singular centres, communication (and cultural) spaces. In diasporic mediated spaces, there is a possibility for the emergence of a *global commons* (Silverstone, 2002) – a space which is of course contested – but which allows those marginalised from the mainstream groups to find a voice: to talk and to perform on media and around the media.

Minorities within minorities – women, sexual minorities, subgroups that distantiate themselves from the *homeland* – are neither voiceless nor invisible anymore; community hierarchical relations of marginalisation are now directly challenged. As Franklin writes about the Pacific female diasporic online communication:

> ... the internet/www allows them [women] an oral space, through access to online forums. They press on and loosen gendered conventions and hierarchies of the right to speak by making use of the more permissive features of online debate; (quasi)anonymity, informal syntax and the immediacy – and safety – of posting a message for instance (Franklin, 2001, p.400).

As it becomes apparent, a discussion on diasporic media and inclusion cannot be a discussion on media *for all* and *by all*; this is not only utopian, but it also reproduces exclusion in thinking of minorities as homogenous. Not all representations in diasporic media projects reflect and express everybody's agenda and identity within particular groups; not everybody is included and is equally represented. Some of these projects promote exclusion and discrimination. Diasporic media cultures are spaces of mediation and like any other such space, they are not harmonious. Otherness within diasporic groups exists as much as it exists in the relations between these groups and the mainstream. In emphasising difference and even more in thinking of difference as threatening and exclusive, otherness becomes a point of conflict and a point where boundaries are raised. The project of inclusion is a constant struggle for understanding and tolerance. Inclusion is a project for lateral recognition and participation; it is a project of differentiated communication (Kymlicka, 1995).

Notes

1 Saying that, community and identity are neither stable nor harmonious; struggles of power take place around them. Such tensions, however, have more to do with minorities' internal politics and the politics of difference and less with the disintegration of the European societies.

2 See for example Anthias, 2001 and Social Exclusion Unit, 2000.

3 The particular and the specific, usually studied through in-depth qualitative research, are very important. The present choice to focus on the cross-European is strategic and it relates to the main research questions. This research, in its breadth, is still informed by case studies and qualitatively collected material.

4 The thirteen reports cover an equal number of EU member states: Austria, Belgium, Denmark, Finland, Greece, Germany, Italy, Ireland, The Netherlands, Portugal, Spain, Sweden and the UK. This research was conducted before the recent European enlargement. The national reports, as well as a number of case studies, were produced by a network of researchers across Europe and myself. I am indebted to all contributors for their participation (all the reports produced for this research are available online: http://www.lse.ac.uk/collections/EMTEL/Minorities/minorities.html).

5 See also Cammaerts (Chapter 4) and Durieux (Chapter 5) in this volume.

6 These are small shops that offer internet access and cheap international calls/fax service. Their character varies. They might offer just these communication services or they might also sell all kinds of different merchandise (for example, groceries or gifts).

7 Examples from countries of the periphery (for example, Greece, Spain) show that migrant communities have brought more life to degraded neighbourhoods.

8 This is described by an informant, who spends most of his working time among migrant communities.

9 This mapping does not include transnational media (unless their output is integrated in local/national media) and internet use and production. These will be discussed in the following section.

10 A number of themes are discussed in the project report but due to limited space, only one appears here.

11 Needless to say, only for those who have access and are computer literate.

References

Aksoy, A. and K. Robins (2000) 'Thinking across spaces: transnational television from Turkey', *European Journal of Cultural Studies*, 3 (3) pp.343–65.

Alasuutari, P. (1999) 'Introduction: three phases of reception studies', in P. Alasuutari (ed.) *Rethinking the media audience*, London: Sage.

Anderson, B. (1983(1991)) *Imagined communities: reflections on the origins and spread of nationalism*, London: Verso.

Anthias, F. (2001) 'The concept of "social division" and theorising social stratification: looking at ethnicity and class', *Sociology*, 35 (4) pp.835–54.

Appadurai, A. (1990) 'Disjuncture and difference in the global cultural economy', in M. Featherstone (ed.) *Global Culture: Nationalism, Globalization and Modernity*, London: Sage.

Böse, M., R. Haberfellner and A. Koldas (2002) 'Mapping minorities and their media: the national context: Austria', http://www.lse.ac.uk/collections/EMTEL/Minorities/reports.html.

Camauer, L. (2002) 'Mapping minorities and their media: the national context: Sweden', http://www.lse.ac.uk/collections/EMTEL/Minorities/reports.html.

Cammaerts, B. (2001*) Een kwantitatieve analyse van de internet-gebruikers en het internet-gebruik in de Vlaamse Openbare Bibliotheken,* Unpublished thesis, SMIT-VUB, Brussels.

Castells, M. (2001) *The internet galaxy: reflections on the internet, business and society*, Oxford and New York: Oxford University Press.

Cohen, R. (1997) *Global diasporas: an introduction*, London: UCL Press.

COSPE (2002) 'Mapping minorities and their media: the national context: Italy', http://www.lse.ac.uk/collections/EMTEL/Minorities/reports.html.

Council of Europe (1993) *Political and demographic aspects of migration flows to Europe*, Strasbourg: Council of Europe.

da Cunha, M.A. (2002) 'Media and Portuguese in France', http://www.lse.ac.uk/collections/EMTEL/Minorities/case_studies.html.

Darieva, T. (2002) 'A map of Russian media in Europe', http://www.lse.ac.uk/collections/EMTEL/Minorities/case_studies.html.

Dayan, D. (1998) 'Particularistic media and diasporic communications', in T. Liebes and J. Curran (eds.) *Media, ritual and identity*, New York: Routledge.

De Certeau, M. (1984) *The practice of everyday life*, Berkeley, LA and London: University of California Press.

Featherstone, M. (ed.) *Global culture: nationalism, globalization and modernity*, London: Sage.

Figueiredo, A. (2002) 'Mapping minorities and their media: the national context: Portugal', http://www.lse.ac.uk/collections/EMTEL/Minorities/reports.html.

Franklin, M.I. (2001) 'Postcolonial subjectivities and everyday life online', *International Feminist Journal of Politics*, 3 (3) pp.387–422.

Gatling, J. (1989) *Europe in the making*, London: Crane Russak.

Gaya, B. (2002) 'Mapping minorities and their media: the national context: Spain', http://www.lse.ac.uk/collections/EMTEL/Minorities/reports.html.

Georgiou, M. (2001) *Negotiated uses, contested meanings, changing identities: Greek Cypriot media consumption and ethnic identity formations in North London*, Unpublished thesis, University of London.

Georgiou, M. (2002a) 'Mapping minorities and their media: the national context: the UK', http://www.lse.ac.uk/collections/EMTEL/Minorities/reports.html.

Georgiou, M. (2002b) 'Mapping minorities and their media: the national context: Greece', http://www.lse.ac.uk/collections/EMTEL/Minorities/reports.html.

Giddens, A. (1990) *The consequences of modernity*, Cambridge: Polity.

Gillespie, M. (1995) *Television, ethnicity and cultural change*, London: Routledge.

Gilroy, P. (1995) 'Roots and routes: black identity as an outernational project', in H.W. Harris et al. (eds) *Racial and ethnic identity: psychological development and creative expression*, London and New York: Routledge.

Hall, S. (1990) 'Cultural identity and diaspora', in J. Rutherford (ed.) *Identity: community, culture, difference*, London: Lawrence and Wishart.

Hanafi, S. (2001) 'Palestinian community networks in Europe and new media', http://www.lse.ac.uk/collections/EMTEL/Minorities/case_studies.html.

Harvey, D. (1989) *The condition of postmodernity: an enquiry into the origins of cultural change*, Oxford: Basil Blackwell.

Hobsbawm, E. and T.O. Ranger (1992) *The invention of tradition*, Cambridge: Cambridge University Press.

Husband, C. (1994) *A richer vision: the development of ethnic minority media in western democracies*, Paris: UNESCO.

Hussein, M. (2002) 'Mapping minorities and their media: the national context: Denmark', http://www.lse.ac.uk/collections/EMTEL/Minorities/reports.html.

Iordanova, D. (2001) *Cinema of flames: Balkan film, culture and the media*, London: BFI.

Kauranen, R. and S. Tuori (2002) 'Mapping minorities and their media: the national context: Finland', http://www.lse.ac.uk/collections/EMTEL/Minorities/reports.html.

Kymlicka, W. (1995) *The rights of minority cultures*, Oxford: Oxford University Press.

Madianou, M. (in press) 'Contested communicative spaces: rethinking identities, boundaries and the role of the media among Turkish speakers in Greece'. To be published in the *Journal of Ethnic and Migration Studies*.

Malonga, M-F. (2002) 'Ethnic minorities: which place and which image in French television', http://www.lse.ac.uk/collections/EMTEL/Minorities/case_studies.html.

Minority Rights Group (ed.) (1997) *World directory of minorities*, London: Minority Rights Group International.

Morley, D. and K. Robins (1995) *Spaces of identity. Global media, electronic landscapes and cultural boundaries*, London: Routledge.

Ogan, C. (2001) *Communication and identity in the diaspora: Turkish migrants in Amsterdam and their use of media*, Lanham: Lexington.

Ormond, M. (2002) 'Mapping minorities and their media: the national context: Belgium', http://www.lse.ac.uk/collections/EMTEL/Minorities/reports.html.

Poster, M. (1997) 'Cyberdemocracy: the internet and the public sphere', in D. Holmes (ed.) *Virtual politics: identity and community in cyberspace*, London: Sage.

Raiser, U. (2002a) 'Mapping minorities and their media: the national context: Germany', http://www.lse.ac.uk/collections/EMTEL/Minorities/reports.html.

Raiser, U. (2002b) 'Selection of minority web sites in Germany', http://www.lse.ac.uk/collections/EMTEL/Minorities/case_studies.html.

Rigoni, I. (2002) 'Turkish and Kurdish media production in Europe: an overview', http://www.lse.ac.uk/collections/EMTEL/Minorities/case_studies.html.

Runnymede Trust, The (2000) *The future of multi-ethnic Britain: the Parekh Report*, London: Profile Books.

Said, E. (1985) *Orientalism*, Harmondsworth: Penguin.

Silverstone, R. (1994) *Television and everyday life*, London: Routledge.

Silverstone, R. (2002) 'Finding a voice: minorities, media and the global commons', in G. Stald and T. Tufte (eds) *Global encounters: media and cultural transformation*, Luton: University of Luton Press.

Social Exclusion Unit (2000) *Minority ethnic issues in social exclusion and neighbourhood renewal*, London: Cabinet Office.

ter Wal, J. (2002) (ed.) *Racism and cultural diversity in the mass media*, Vienna: European Monitoring Centre on Racism and Xenophobia (EUMC).

Ugba, A. (2002) 'Mapping minorities and their media: the national context: Ireland', http://www.lse.ac.uk/collections/EMTEL/Minorities/reports.html.

Urry, J. (2000) *Sociology beyond societies: mobilities for the twenty-first century*, London and New York: Routledge.

Urry, J. (2002) 'Mobility and proximity', *Sociology*, 36 (2) pp.255–74.

Chapter 4

ICT-Usage Among Transnational Social Movements in the Networked Society: To Organise, to Mobilise and to Debate

Bart Cammaerts[1]

Context

In recent years, the literature on the many usages of information and communication technologies (ICTs)[2] in everyday contexts has increased exponentially. The different perspectives in studies on ICT-use seem to suggest that this communicative technology permeates every aspect of everyday life. If this were the case, then it would be logical to suggest that – in addition to the socio-economic sphere – the cultural and the inter-personal, the political and the democratic systems are also being affected. There are of course many ways of looking at the usage of ICTs in political terms. An important distinction that emerges here is between the use of ICTs in more formal political processes and their use in more informal political processes. This case study looks at ICT-usage from the latter perspective and more specifically posed questions as to how (transnational) social movements appropriate and use these technologies for different purposes. It is, however, necessary to stress beforehand that although the use of ICTs was the starting-point of this case study, a technology-centred approach was rejected. It is too easy to herald the new potentials of the internet in democratic terms as revolutionary – able to change politics and the nature of political participation. We need to remain critical of unsubstantiated claims and assumptions that ICTs would (or have already) change(d) our lives in a radical way – economically, socially, culturally and politically.

In many ways things have changed, of course, and ICTs enable or facilitate certain (political) processes, but these processes are very much embedded in an historical context, which is always a story of combined patterns of continuity and discontinuity. That is why this case study on ICT-usage by transnational social movements also needs to be linked to the existentialist crisis that faces (formal) representative democracy as well as to changing meanings of citizenship and to changes in participation.

Debates on the crisis of representative democracy usually refer to low voter turnout at elections, declining membership of political parties and old social movements, as well as an increasing number of protest voters. The crisis of representative democracy can also be explained against the backdrop of the partial withdrawal of the welfare state in many countries and long-term processes of globalisation and regionalisation, which have undermined the sovereignty and power of the nation states (Rosenau, 1990; Hirst and Thomson, 1995; Held et al., 1999; Axtmann, 2001). It is possible to argue that this power-shift from the nation-states towards regional/global political or economic institutions and the lack of or weak democratic control over these 'higher' levels of governance, has prompted civil society organisations – and more specifically social movement organisations – to organise themselves beyond the nation-states in order to critically question the legitimacy and policies of international economic and political actors (Anheier et al., 2001; Florini, 2000; Guidry et al., 2000). Transnational civil organisations allow citizens to link up with a community of interest and action beyond their own nation-state. As such, transnational civil society could be perceived as resulting from 'globalisation from below', an attempt to counter-balance the globalising economic, political and cultural spheres that increasingly escape the sovereignty of the nation-states.

The citizenship notion has, of course, also evolved considerably since the Greek city-states or the formation and consolidation of the Westphalian nation-states. Although citizenship is theoretically, but also empirically, still very much linked to and conceptualised within the 'boundaries' of the modernist nation-state, the increased globalisation of the world economy, revolutionary innovations in communication, transport and mobility, ecological and demographic pressures, as well as ethnic and nationalistic forces have considerably undermined the sovereignty and legitimacy of that nation-state, the core of the bounded notions of citizenship (Harvey, 1989; Lash and Urry, 1994; Held et al., 1999). These social, economic and political transformations would suggest it is fair to conceive of citizenship as more complex and diverse then a classic understanding linked to rights and nationality. In political theory, this is exemplified by the emergence of several concepts of citizenship that could be called unbounded and go beyond the nation-state (van Steenbergen, 1994; Bauböck, 1994; Hauben, 1995; Linklater, 1999; Sassen, 2002). Examples of these are: ecological citizenship, net.citizenship, transnational citizenship, cosmopolitan citizenship or denationalised citizenship. Without going into the conceptual differences between these alternative notions of citizenship, they do have a commonality in that they point to the distinctiveness, but also – possibly conflictual – co-existence of, or even tensions between, on the one hand, the citizen as a legal subject, linked to welfare state rights, and on the other hand, the citizen as a normative subject, linked to social, sexual or cultural identities and action. Citizenship thus becomes, to use the words of political theorist Chantal Mouffe (1992, p.231), a 'form of identification, a type of political identity; something to be constructed, not empirically given'.

This approach suggests that the primacy of a liberal representative democracy that reduces political participation to voting in a political elite once every few years is no longer tenable. We need to develop new ways to enrich our democracy and complement representativeness with more participatory 'models of democracy', to use the title of David Held's famous book (1987). Civil society – local as well as transnational – can play an important role in this process of increasing participation by acting as an interlocutor or mediator between citizens and state. When this is applied to the global or international level, it becomes necessary to acknowledge that civil society actors – as well as business actors for that matter – have manifested themselves increasingly as legitimate actors in processes of global governance.

However, this does not mean that the voice of civil society is being listened to (Cammaerts and Carpentier, 2005). At the same time, the number of issues requiring global solutions has also increased and became more prominent on the political agendas of citizens, civil society organisations and (some) governments. Examples of such issues are: child labour, ecology, security, mobility, migration and human rights.

It is within this complex political context that the use of ICTs by transnational social movements should be situated. Studies of the different usages of interactive communication technologies by social movements have identified three main categories of use. Firstly, social movements use ICTs to organise themselves and to interact with their members, sympathisers and core staff. Secondly, use relates to mobilisation when ICTs are used to lobby within formal politics or to foster social change through online as well as *offline* direct actions. Thirdly, there is the potential of strengthening the public sphere through the mediation of political debate. Here the internet is considered by many scholars as a potential means to extend the working of transnational social movements geographically, to organise internationally, to build global or regional coalitions with like-minded organisations, to mobilise beyond their own constituencies, to spread information on a global scale independently and thereby support the development of global or transnational public spheres (Scott and Street, 2001; Dahlberg, 2001; Norris, 2002; Bennett, 2003; Kahn and Kellner, 2004).

Selection of Cases and Methodology

The selection of transnational social movement organisations for a more in-depth analysis of these different usages was based on a typology that distinguished between umbrella organisations, platform organisations, portal organisations and web organisations.[3] This typology provides a useful tool for the selection of a diversity of cases that embody the multitude of issues raised by transnational civil society organisations, the variety of organisational structures and the different levels of governance they address (Dahlgren, 2000). It should, however, be noted that – like every typology – this typology is an ideal type. In reality, the different cases often perform different functions at the same time, such as platform, portal and web organisation. The problematic nature of typologies – as a construct – and the selection of only one case per type make it difficult to formulate generalisations about differentiated types of virtual organisations. Furthermore, the selection of the specific cases, although guided by the typology and with an eye on diversity and the transnational character of the organisation, is necessarily subjective. Despite these problems, four cases were selected.

WWW.APC.ORG (Umbrella)

The Association for Progressive Communications (APC) functions as a network of networks and has been active since 1990. It can be regarded as a transnational non-profit umbrella organisation linking 24 national or regional computer networks and serving the needs of the social change sector. It was established to facilitate co-operation, information-sharing, and technical inter-operability among its members. APC not only promotes the development of non-commercial online spaces for and by

Table 4.1   Typology and Features of Selected Cases

Type	Characteristics	Selected Case	URL
Umbrella Organisation	Advocacy, representative, promoting use of ICTs, pooling expertise and resources.	APC	http://www.apc.org
Portal Organisation	Intermediary, sometimes with editors, mostly issue-oriented, directs towards others sites and organisations.	LabourStart	http:// www.labourstart.org
Platform Organisation	Platform for interaction, organisation and communication, interactive development of counter-discourses.	ATTAC	http://www.attac.org
Web Organisation	Forums, mailing-lists, networking, mobilisation, virtual communities, alternative source of information.	Indymedia	http:// www.indymedia.org

NGOs, but also lobbies for the inclusion of the information and communication needs of civil society in telecommunication, donor and investment policy.

WWW.ATTAC.ORG (Platform)

At first ATTAC – *Action pour une taxe Tobin d'aide aux citoyens* – pleaded for the introduction of a Tobin-tax to counter financial speculation and re-regulate the markets. But ATTAC also pursues the much broader goal of altering the dominant global neo-liberal economic framework. ATTAC could be described as a transnational coalition of local entities acting in accordance with a common agenda and developing alternative discourses. It has branches in 48 countries and has a web-presence in 33 countries. However, major differences exist between local branches, with regard to resources, volunteers and popular support. The transnational level serves more as a common frame of reference and less as an organisational structure.

WWW.LABOURSTART.ORG (Portal)

The LabourStart page can be considered a very dynamic portal site dedicated to labour-related news and the international labour movement. It was originally developed by Eric Lee and is supported by Labour and Society International, an independent organisation that aims: 'to link the trade union movement with other parts of civil society and to help unions to develop a wider agenda'. The case of LabourStart indicates that the internet allows for widespread transnational activity with little or no resources. LabourStart, although based in London, is also transnationally organised. LabourStart exists in nine languages and is supplied with material by almost 150 correspondents located in some 30 countries. Correspondents also communicate with each other through email and a mailing list. Overall, LabourStart can be considered to have a very strong transnational basis, given its presence on all continents and, even more importantly, given the fact that it provides content in different languages.

WWW.INDYMEDIA.ORG (Web)

Indymedia is a worldwide network of independent media organisations through which several hundred dedicated journalists and activists cover grassroots activities and actions, thereby explicitly distancing themselves from corporate interests. Although supported by organisations in civil society, Indymedia is largely a virtual platform bringing together both individuals (activists) and organisations. It uses new technologies to provide an alternative and organic public space that also functions as a space for steering and promoting civic action. Indymedia is active in over 40 countries and combines a global view with news on local action. Indymedia can be characterised as a transnational coalition of independent local initiatives with a common aim – to provide alternative news and support direct actions. The emphasis, however, is placed on the local organisation and on the reporting on local struggles, embedded in and/or linked to similar struggles at an international or regional level. As such, the geographical spread of Indymedia is rather strong, with a presence on all continents. The cultural spread, on the other hand, is moderate given that Indymedia is to some extent dominated by the Anglo-Saxon culture.

A diversity of methodologies was used to assess ICT-usage on the part of these transnational social movement organisations for organisation, mobilisation and debate. Table 4.2 provides an overview of the different methodologies.

This study examined organisational usage in terms of the degree and nature of transnationalisation within each organisation and the degree of online and *offline* interaction or virtualisation within each organisation. The respective websites were analysed and a number of secondary sources relating to the different organisations

Table 4.2   Overview of Methodologies

Methodologies	
1. Organisation Degree of transnationalisation Degree of *online* and/or *offline* presence	Analysis of web presence In-depth interviews Documentary desk-study
2. Mobilisation Policy-influence vs political influence Online and *offline* mobilisation	Analysis of web presence In-depth interviews Documentary desk-study
3. Debate Web-Forums of LabourStart/Indymedia and a mailing list of ATTAC	Content analysis of web forums and discussion mailing list

was studied. This was complemented by in-depth interviews with key persons from each organisation. Mobilisation was explored firstly in terms of the political strategy of each organisation and then in terms of specific instances of online and *offline* mobilisations with the aim of assessing the precise role of ICTs in mobilisation. The same methodologies as those used to analyse organisational usage were applied. Lastly, the usage of the internet to foster debate was examined through an analysis of the web forums of LabourStart and Indymedia as well as a mailing list of ATTAC.[4] Content analysis was used to get an idea of the variety of participants, the degree and nature of interactivity and the diversity of debated issues.

For a more in-depth overview of the research please consult the respective research-reports on which this chapter is based (Van Audenhove et al., 2002; Cammaerts and Van Audenhove, 2003).

ICTs and Organisational Usage

The study posed two basic questions within the context of the organisational use of the internet by the different organisations selected. On the one hand, it was necessary to determine the nature and degree of transnationalisation of the different cases and to establish whether certain patterns emerge. On the other hand, there was the question as to whether this could be linked in some way to the degree and nature of interaction online versus *offline* of the different organisations.

Degree and Nature of Transnationalism

All the organisations can, of course, be defined as transnationally organised as they were selected on this basis. The results of the analyses, however, show that a distinction can be made between APC or LabourStart and ATTAC or Indymedia. APC and LabourStart, unlike ATTAC and Indymedia, do not have locally based relatively autonomous branches. Transnationalisation is, therefore, much more integrated in the case of APC and LabourStart. ATTAC and Indymedia are more embedded in a local or national context and see the transnational as linking up different local initiatives into a common frame of meaning, reference and, at times, action. The degree of transnationalisation in the cases of ATTAC and Indymedia should therefore be qualified as rather moderate, while it is much stronger and more unbounded in the cases of APC and LabourStart. In addition to the differences that occur on the organisational level, the unbounded-ness of transnational organisations also has to be graded in terms of geographical spread and cultural ties.

As Figure 4.1 illustrates, although all organisations have a considerable international presence, developing countries are often under-represented. Indymedia, for example, is active in most Western countries, but is only present in three English-speaking African countries (Cameroon, South Africa and Nigeria), two Middle-Eastern (Israel and Palestine) and two South Asian (India and Indonesia). ATTAC has an important presence in Europe, covers five African countries and six Latin American countries, but is noticeably absent in Asia and the Middle East.

In addition to the geographical disparities, there are also cultural divides that determine the nature of transnationalisation. Although all organisations make efforts

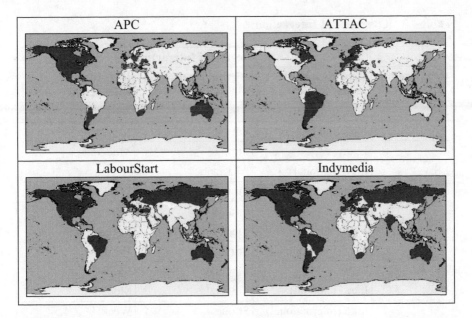

Figure 4.1   Geographical Spread of Organisations

to provide information in multiple languages and often have a considerable number of volunteer translators at their disposal, language barriers, nevertheless, remain an important problem. The dominant language is often English or – in the case of ATTAC – French. The absence of an independent media centre in French Africa is revealing about the influence of language on transnationalisation, although other factors may also play a role in this. The same applies to ATTAC, which is present in four African countries, but all are French-speaking. Its presence in English-speaking countries, on the other hand, is rather weak. Here, it is also telling that all four organisations were founded in Western Europe.

All this raises questions about the nature of the transnational civil society. Aside from the geographical and cultural divisions observed and the still dominant position of the West, it is possible to argue that organisations like ATTAC and Indymedia start from the local 'bounded' context and link local issues to global or transnational causes and solutions. APC also comprises local independent organisations – its members – but it is clearly organised in a transnational decentralised manner, going beyond the national 'bounded' context. Whereas, an organisation like LabourStart starts at a transnational level and brings in the local, bottom-up perspective through its dispersed correspondents, thereby bypassing the national 'bounded' context (cf. labour news from China or Iran).

Table 4.3   Overview of Interaction

		Degree of Interaction	
Organisation	**Organisational Level**	**Virtual Interaction**	**Real-life Interaction**
APC:	Intra (national)	Absent	Absent
	Intra (international)	Strong	Moderate
	Extra	Strong	Moderate
LS:	Intra (national)	Absent	Absent
	Intra (international)	Strong	Weak
	Extra	Exclusively	Absent
ATTAC:	Intra (national)	Moderate	Strong
	Intra (international)	Strong	Weak
	Extra	Moderate	Strong
IMC:	Intra (national)	Moderate	Moderate
	Intra (international)	Strong	Weak
	Extra	Strong	Moderate

* *Gradation: Absent, Weak, Moderate, Strong, Exclusive*

Degree of Interaction

Table 4.3 provides an overview of the degree of virtual and real-life interaction per organisation, analysed at the organisational, national and international levels, both internally and externally.

This assessment, based on web analysis and in-depth interviews, gives rise to a number of common themes that elucidate the degree of virtuality in the different cases and the importance of real-life interaction between activists and within these organisations.

Firstly, differences were observed within those organisations that have local branches. For example, while internal virtual interaction in Indymedia Germany is quite strong, real-time interaction is quite weak. In contrast, Indymedia Belgium still holds weekly editorial real-life meetings because they are a much smaller organisation. Similarly, ATTAC in France is quite a big organisation with over 30,000 members, while in Belgium it is a rather small-scale organisation where face-to-face interaction is much more important.

Secondly, the *offline* remains very important or even crucial. APC, for example, is highly virtualised internally, using closed newsgroups to conduct regular online meetings, but will nevertheless have at least one real-life meeting a year. This points to the importance of face-to-face interaction, social ties and the building of trust amongst activists. The real-life representation of the APC staff within political

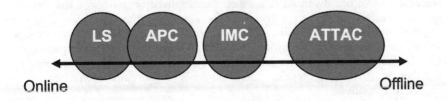

Figure 4.2   Relative Importance of *Offline* and Online

structures at the international level is high as well (cf. World Summit on the Information Society). ATTAC is an organisation that has many *offline* events for its members, sympathisers as well as core-activists. It thus seems that social movement organisations, although using ICTs extensively, are seldom totally virtual. Even an organisation such as LabourStart, which organises itself almost exclusively online, did have a (social) get-together event for their correspondents in London (in 2002). These findings confirm other research suggesting that the most successful virtual communities are those that not only interact virtually, but also in real life (Diani, 2001, p.121). Nevertheless, as Figure 4.2 indicates, a distinction can be made between the different cases as to the importance of the online versus the offline

Lastly, it is of course useful to look at what makes ICTs and the internet in particular so attractive for social movement organisations. Where do these interactive technologies make a real difference? Here, it has to be noted that many of the usages by organisations for internal or external interaction relate to what social movements have always done, only more efficiently, quicker, cheaper, etc. The provision of information, transnational networking, mobilisation, or advocacy are not new to social movements, but the internet makes it easier to inform independently, to enlarge their scope and constituency, to link up with other organisations in strategic or short-term networks and last but not least to bridge time and space. This last feature is probably one of the most revolutionary potentials of the internet. It allows organisations to decentralise work and to rely on the voluntary work of dispersed sympathisers and activists. In the case of ATTAC, Indymedia and LabourStart this means that people from different countries, with different backgrounds, can contribute to what could be called a virtual and transnational public sphere, disseminating alternative information, developing alternative discourses and/or engaging in common strategies of action. In the case of APC, the internet allows this organisation to be run from different locations worldwide and nevertheless be efficient and very active at the transnational or global level of governance. As such, the internet sometimes provides relatively small organisations with new means of cheap, highly flexible and instantaneous communication, making organisational decentralisation and at the same time co-operation and integration possible.

The findings in this study show that those organisations that are typically seen as examples of the virtualisation of civil society only have virtual social relations in specific circumstances. Organisations such as ATTAC and Indymedia – even when using the internet extensively – have local branches where members participate and socialise in real life. Even APC, a much decentralised organisation, has meetings and real-life activities. Very often individuals active at the transnational level in organisations such as Indymedia, ATTAC, LabourStart and APC are actively engaged in local branches of the organisation or in other civil society or political organisations. Last but not least, the need to meet face-to-face in order to build confidence and togetherness is always present in a social movement organisation even when they are organised virtually.

ICTs and Mobilisation

Another popular assumption that is often made is that the internet plays an increasingly important role in mobilising civil society and citizens. Before addressing the role of ICTs in the mobilisation for online and/or *offline* direct action, it is necessary to address and identify the different political strategies adopted in the selected cases.

Political strategies

It does not come as a surprise that transnational social movements pursue diverse strategies. However, these strategies aimed at formal politics and/or in terms of being politically involved become even more complex if we take into account the distinction between online and offline, as can be observed in Table 4.4.

Three basic strategies were identified: firstly, engaging with formal political actors; secondly, disengaging and pursuing their aims through direct action, public opinion formation and/or changing lifestyles; and thirdly, a double strategy combining lobbying with direct action and opinion formation.

Table 4.4   Political Strategies

Organisation	Strategy	Political Strategies	
		Virtual	**Real-life**
APC	Lobby	Strong	Strong
	Direct Action	Absent	Weak
LS	Lobby	Weak	Moderate
	Direct Action	Moderate	Absent
ATTAC	Lobby	Weak	Strong
	Direct Action	Moderate	Strong
IMC	Lobby	Absent	Absent
	Direct Action	Strong	Strong

* *Gradation: Absent, Weak, Moderate, Strong*

APC and ATTAC lobby extensively. APC, as an advocacy organisation, is especially strong in this regard, both in the real world and in the virtual. It can thus be characterised in terms of a strong involvement and commitment towards civil society participation in processes of global governance (APC & CRIS, 2003). ATTAC prefers the real world when it comes to lobbying, which it does mainly by networking with other organisations in a platform. For example, on how to get some form of Tobin-tax implemented through national parliaments. As a portal-organisation LabourStart is not very active politically, but it does point to the (local and international) lobby-structures of the labour movement in the real world and the networks they have. In contrast, Indymedia disengages itself explicitly from formal politics, as it does not believe that a 'dialogue' is possible.

When it comes to direct action, ATTAC follows a double strategy, being strong in lobbying, but also in terms of direct action, foremost *offline*. Indymedia can also be considered strong in direct action and *online*, but also by being present and visual at demonstrations and actions. Direct action is, of course, one of its hallmarks. LabourStart does not engage in direct action in the real world, but does have action alerts through the internet. APC is not that involved in direct action.

In other words, for those organisations that do engage with formal politics and policies, the online does not seem a very efficient realm to lobby. Here, the real world and face-to-face contacts are preferred. Furthermore, it seems to be easier for organisations with a local base, such as ATTAC, to be involved in *offline* direct action, than it is for dispersed organisations. It is, however, possible to develop alternatives through online direct actions, such as LabourStart does. Lastly, another strategy, pursued by Indymedia, consists of disengaging from formal politics and lobby-networks and aiming to change public opinion and lifestyles through direct actions, be it online or *offline*.

The next section will develop two cases further in order to identify more precisely the enabling and constraining factors of ICT-use in mobilisation. The first relates to the online action alerts as developed by LabourStart and the second relates to ICT-use in terms of *offline* direct action. A specific direct action will be analysed, namely the occupation of a forest in Bruges (Belgium) in which both Indymedia and ATTAC were involved.

Online Actions: LabourStart's 'ActNow!'

A section called 'ActNow!' can be found on the LabourStart site.[5] This provides action alerts in connection with the jailing of labour activists or the boycotting of businesses that exploit their employees. Users and sympathisers are asked, through the site and through email, to act or respond. Email is a very efficient means of reaching large numbers of people rapidly, crossing borders and at a relatively low cost. The viral characteristics of email, forwards and mailing lists also make it relatively easy to set up a campaign that has the potential to make citizens aware of certain injustices or events and, through online action, put those governments and/or companies under pressure.

Examples of successful actions include the coercion of the Sydney Hilton in Australia in 2002 to make concessions to employees fired because of renovation works to the hotel. The receiving of more then 3000 emails from all over the world protesting against their practices played an important role in this decision and helped to make the international management team aware of what was initially a local labour conflict. Mark Boyd, a representative of the local union declared afterwards: 'The union understands that the hotel is so aware of the effect of the email campaign that they plan to write to all 3000 people, individually, to tell them they have made peace with the union and their workforce' (quoted in LHMU, 2002).

Also in 2002, the suitcase manufacturer Samsonite was targeted by a worldwide email campaign protesting at the illegal firing of employees in Thailand and demanding the right of employees to be members of a labour union (ICFTU, 2002). Jaturong Sornroong, a local labour activist, stated: 'It is clear that without the solidarity action launched by Campaign for Labour Rights, Solidarity Center, AFL-CIO, ICFTU, Clean Clothes Campaign and LabourStart, based on the information provided by the workers through TLC and CLIST, it would not have been possible for the case to be settled with this positive result' (quoted in Cleanclothes, 2002).

Other examples highlight pressure on the state, for instance, the stopping of the stoning of the Nigerian woman Amina Amal (Amnesty International Campaign) and the reluctance of the US to execute Mumia Abu Jamal, a Black Panther activist on death row.

Despite successes like these, it is clear that the efficiency of email campaigns is dwindling fast. Firstly, the dramatic rise in so-called spam mails[6] and the inflation of such e-actions, make citizens less responsive to e-mobilisations. Secondly, those usually targeted by such actions – companies or governments – have also developed counter-strategies. They are much less impressed by the huge numbers of mails and are using filter- or anti-virus software to block the protest mails. Eric Lee (2003) from LabourStart recognises this: 'For more than a decade now, trade unions and others have used email as a powerful tool for *online* campaigning. Despite some notable successes, it is now becoming clearer by the day that this tool is becoming less and less effective.'

To conclude, online action and mobilisation does play a role in making citizens aware of certain issues, events and actions and can have some success, but the increase in spam and the increased number of e-mobilisations are counter-productive for this form of direct action.

Offline Direct Action: The Occupation of the Lapperfort Forest

Activists also intensively use email, mailing lists and the worldwide web to organise and mobilise for *offline* protests and direct action. The success of a direct action is dependent on a variety of interacting factors, of which a media strategy plays an important role, but should also not be exaggerated. This study examined the case of the occupation of a forest by a number of young environmentalists near Bruges (Belgium) to show this complex interplay. In August 2001, activists occupied the forest, which was due to be cut down to make way for roads and an industrial park. The activists stayed there for more then a year after which the owner took them to court and the mayor decided to evict them forcefully from the forest. In the meantime, a coalition of 76 civil society organisations, political parties, unions, ecological movements and other organisations such as ATTAC, had been set up to support the activists. The activists were evicted, but the Green minister of the environment started negotiations with the owner of the forest to buy and thus subsequently save the forest.

The main question posed in this chapter is what precise roles the internet played within this direct action. Firstly, the activists had set up their own site.[7] This allowed them to communicate independently with their sympathisers and the 'outside' world. Secondly, the activists of the Lappers' Front also communicated regularly through the site of Indymedia-Belgium, which is – like many IMCs – geared towards being an interface for direct action. Indymedia itself also reported extensively on the occupation, the court decision, the eviction and the protests that followed.[8] Thirdly, the internet also played an important role in mobilising a wider population at short notice and in the preparation of the actions that followed the eviction from the forest.

> The Lappersfront launches a call to all sympathisers: To those who can make themselves available when the police clears the forest, we ask to leave an email-address or a telephone-number to Pat; CALL or EMAIL: mA.f@pandora.be, 0497/XX-XX-XX. You will not have to be in the forest yourself, but you can help by forming a buffer (Indymedia, 2002a: *translation by the author*)

Another message on the Indymedia site illustrates how quickly a mobilisation can be organised. Only an hour after actual eviction started, calls were made for a demonstration later in the afternoon: 'URGENT MOBILISATION: 16h00 Town Hall Brugge – Emergency protest meeting for the saving of the Lappersfort forest (…) Please forward this message to as many people and post it on as many lists and websites' (Indymedia, 2002b: *translation by the author*).

Also, ATTAC-Flanders mobilised for a protest at the headquarters of the owner of the forest (cf. the energy company Tractebel) in Brussels. In total, both alert-protests attracted some 250 people, but in the evening, another demonstration was organised in Bruges, which attracted 500 people and the weekend after between 4,000 and 5,000 turned out, depending on the source. Citizens demonstrated in the streets of Bruges to express their sympathy for the occupiers (Indymedia, 2002c and d). It thus became apparent that the activists and their objectives could count on a considerable degree of support from the local population and that it was not the internet *per se* that played an important role in terms of mobilisation and the success of the action. The (positive) attention in the mainstream media, cultural events during the summer that drew many local people and the personal involvement of the Green party – that is, formal politics – played a much bigger role.

The Lappersfort case shows how a group of young activists, all-in-all rather marginal and radical, can nevertheless be very present in the public sphere and influence the political agenda by tapping into transnational strategies and struggles, in this case forest preservation, while at the same time ensuring that they have a local base and support for their direct action. It also shows that the passive involvement by citizens, local as well as from other places in Belgium, can be transformed into active engagement by protesting against the eviction, thereby showing that public support for the preservation of the forest was strong. However, apart from its potential to inform the outside world independently and as an instant alert-medium to mobilise through Indymedia, email and mailing lists, the internet was not crucial for this action to be successful.

ICTs and the Public Sphere

Another claim often made is that the internet – in particular online discussions and more recently blogs – enriches the public sphere. An inter-related claim suggests that public forums and discussion mailing lists allow for a transnational public sphere to thrive and global citizens to emerge. However, the evidence from the three cases[9] of interactive spaces analysed here suggests otherwise. Before returning to this, the different cases will be introduced through a short assessment of the variety of participants, the transnational character of the issues discussed and the degree and nature of debate or interaction between participants.

LabourStart Web Forum 'Terror and the War on Terror'

The LabourStart web forum had at the time of analysis some 1,400 registered users. Out of a total of 35 forums, only nine had more than 50 postings and 15 more than 20 postings. It is fair to say that most forums were not used at all. There were, however, a few exceptions. The forum 'Terror and the War on Terror' is an example of such a 'popular' forum created by LabourStart itself. This LabourStart forum was analysed during a period of three months.[10] Of the 454 postings made by some 40 participants, 212 were actual contributions, the other 242 postings were reactions to these contributions. Contributions originated from six countries, the US, the UK, the Netherlands, Canada, Australia and finally India. The number of participants from those countries differs but it is fair to say that the majority of participants come from the UK and the US. Some participants from other countries have, however, been very active in posting contributions. In so far that it was possible to determine, almost all participants in the forum appeared to be male. The language used was English. The transnational character of issues could be described as rather moderate as the content of the online forum focused both on issues linked to a local/national context, such as the American and British stance and war efforts, and more transnational issues such as the socio-economic and geo-political reasons that make terrorist activity flourish or international law and rights. In terms of debate, only a small group of participants really engage in discussions with each other – about 30 per cent of messages were real debate and exchange of arguments between participants. Also, 70 per cent of the posted contributions (reactions not counted) came from five very active members of the forum. Overall, the discussions could however be qualified as being of a high level. Confrontations and arguments were sometimes heated, but never became seriously enflamed. This latter observation may be due to a common ideological framework from which most participants developed their opinions. It was also apparent that most participants were also politically active in the 'real' world.

ATTAC.be Mailing List

ATTAC uses mailing lists a lot for internal organisation and as a discussion platform. Several local branches have discussion mailing lists where members and non-members can discuss current issues. In order to subscribe to one of these ATTAC lists the user has to register with an email address. Some mailing lists ask users to present themselves, others are more open. The discussion mailing list of ATTAC-Belgium was analysed during a period of three months.[11] During that period, some 40 active members posted 410 messages. About the same number of subscribers (46) were 'passive'. The participants were mostly sympathisers of (French-speaking) ATTAC-Belgium and thus embedded in a local context. Most active participants were male and the dominant language was French, but there were also messages in Dutch posted. Who the passive subscribers – or so-called lurkers – of this discussion mailing list are and what they do with the messages they receive is in a sense a black box, requiring additional research. Some might trash them or read selectively, others might forward some messages to their own networks or even to other mailing lists. The issues raised by the members of the mailing list were very diverse and mostly related to transnational issues. They were heavily influenced by what happens in 'the world', although very little was said about Africa and Asia. The favourite topic during the period of analysis was definitely the conflict between Palestine and Israel, which led to heated debates and outspoken opinions. Of the more than 400 messages, only a third could be attributed to real discussion and debate among the members of the list. Discussion between participants on the mailing list only occurred on a limited number of issues; the conflict between Israel and Palestine, globalisation, the repression of demonstrations by police forces and privacy. Debate itself was, however, rather sterile, as it often only took place between a limited number of very active members of the list and – as was the case with the LabourStart forum – it was also located within an ideologically homogeneous framework of reference. Nevertheless, points of view, especially on the Middle East conflict, were sometimes opposed, but flaming did not occur.

Indymedia Spontaneous Forum on the Murder of Pim Fortuyn

Lastly, one might say that almost every article published by Indymedia could potentially develop into a forum, as it is possible to react to the posting, as well as to reactions of others. This way of integrating interactivity within an alternative news site has a relatively low threshold to participate in discussions and can be considered as stimulating debate and participatory communication. Some posted articles stimulate much reaction and develop into a fierce debate among the 'readers', turning into 'participants'. A short article on the Dutch site of Indymedia about the murder of the Dutch right-wing populist leader Pim Fortuyn provoked some 270 messages in one week, posted by about 110 participants.[12] As most postings used a pseudonym and were therefore anonymous, it was in theory difficult to determine where the participants came from. Content analysis revealed however that there were two main categories of participants, Dutch people, of different opinions, and Dutch-speaking Belgians, eager to make the comparison with the North Belgian fascist party Vlaams Blok. There were also a few comments from Spain and UK, but this did not prompt the 'Dutch-speakers' to switch into another language and engage with the 'foreign' comments! Although difficult to prove empirically, the fluid character of the Indymedia format also seemed to attract more participants who were not politically active in the 'real' world. In addition to the discussion between Dutch participants and Belgian participants – which referred mainly to local contexts – the debate expanded into, perhaps more interesting, discussion on the defence of democracy against anti-democratic forces and more specifically whether it is justified to use violence in the fight against fascism and other extreme right-wing movements in society. Populism and the rise of fascism are phenomena present in many European countries. Within this context, the transnational character of the issues addressed could be described as moderate, relating to a local context but also going beyond. About two-thirds of the participants posted only one message in reaction to the article or to a posting by someone else; 25 participants posted between two and five messages, while only nine out of 110 participants posted more than five messages. One participant posted 25 messages. The way this spontaneous forum unfolded shows the fluid character of ICT-mediated participation. During the one-week timeframe of the analysis, new participants kept coming in, most only posting one message, but some staying on and throwing themselves into the ongoing discussion. The debate between the participants could be characterised as hefty and at times very argumentative. Most comments condemned the murder, many referred to the personality of Fortuyn and the ideology he personified, but some participants to the spontaneous forum went so far as to justify the murder by stating, 'a good fascist is a dead fascist' or 'who's next?'. Such strong views were however countered by other participants. The result were some severe insults – 'you are a shortsighted ASSHOLE' or 'Be careful, doomsday will come!!! All left-wing activists must fear for their life'.[13] This kind of flaming of course had its effect on the ongoing debate and made some participants quit the forum.

Assessment

It has to be noted that the use of the internet for interactive debate and the construction of a transnational public sphere is burdened with many constraints.

The degree of interactivity or real debate is often rather weak. The forums and mailing lists are also used to inform or to mobilise. Furthermore, often only a limited number of (male) participants really discuss issues with each other. The analysis of the ATTAC mailing list as well as the LS forum confirms other studies that found online engagement in forums is cyclical, tends to be dominated by those already politically active in the *offline* world and functions within a homogeneous ideological framework (see Hill and Hughes 1998; Wilhelm, 2000). The spontaneous Indymedia forum differs from the two other examples in many ways. It shows that one sensitising issue can attract a diversity of participants and opinions in a short period. It can also be assumed that most of the Indymedia forum participants are not politically

Table 4.5   Constraints on the Construction of a Public Sphere

	Number of Participants	Variety of Participants	Transnationality of Issues	Degree of Debate
LabourStart	Low	Moderate	Moderate	Moderate
1480ATTAC	Low	Low	High	Moderate
Indymedia	High	Low	Moderate	High

active *offline*. However, this also led to insulting postings and rows within the spontaneously emerged forum. Here, it is necessary to bear in mind that passions, conflict and opposed ideological views – certainly towards anti-democratic forces and essentialist discourses – relate more to political debate in the 'real' world than discussions between like-minded participants reasoning within a more or less common ideological framework (Mouffe, 2002).

However, it is fair to state that (politically active) citizens engaging in a forum or discussion list do contribute to ongoing debates within the public sphere on local, but also on a whole range of transnational or unbounded issues. Here the internet does facilitate short-term, as well as longer-term interactive civic engagement, which can be rather passive (receiving mails from a mailing list) or more active (posting messages, discussing). The internet as a medium is also well adapted to accommodate the present fluid nature of political engagement. As such, interactive forums and mailing lists potentially contribute to an emerging transnational public sphere and the development of ideas of unbounded citizenship. But, it has to be noted that in online debate linguistic and cultural boundaries play an important role. English was dominant in the case of the LabourStart forum, French in the case of the ATTAC mailing list and Dutch in the case of the Indymedia-forum. It is also crucial to mention global, regional and national digital divides, as constraints on increased engagement and participation in (transnational) debates. This is certainly relevant in view of the overstated claims about the development of a transnational public sphere. There is also a much more dynamic relationship between the local and the transnational. While participants may be active within a local context, the issues they discuss and relate to can be qualified as transnational, as was the case with the ATTAC mailing list. While the list and its participants were clearly embedded in the local and even regional context of French-speaking Belgium, the issues being discussed and debated were not.

Conclusions

This chapter discussed three main categories of use – to organise, to mobilise and to debate. Each type of specific ICT-use revealed that the often optimistic assumptions and claims, but also the very pessimistic ones, regarding the internet, participation, social movements and democracy need to be shaded and put into an historical, political and inherently social perspective. On the one hand, the potential is there, borne out by indications that (transnational) civil society is becoming ever more adept at using the internet to organise themselves internationally, to network and mobilise at that level and to provide spaces for interactive debate. On the other hand, there is also clear evidence that most of these movements are still rather Western-dominated and also that local cultures or language often still play a major role. In many other ways throughout the analysis a similar double image appears. Although the internet is essential for some of these transnational organisations, the *offline* remains a very important factor, even if they are transnational and dispersed. Social factors, such as trust and the importance of face-to-face contact in a social setting, cannot be ignored, although size of the country and of the organisation does influence the degree of virtuality. Many social movements also use the internet to do what they have always done but by other means. At the same time, the internet is an interactive real-time communication tool that does allow for decentralisation and co-ordination. The internet, as well as transnational strategies, are also being used for organising local struggles and informing about them, but the Lappersfort case showed that for a direct action and/or a mobilisation to be truly successful, the mainstream media, local constituencies and an active civil society mediating between activists and formal politics are also crucial.

The same shaded perspective emerges with use of ICTs for debate. The empirical analysis of the interactive spaces for online debate shows that the notion of an emerging transnational public sphere is highly problematic. While the issues addressed might be transnational, participants are often located in the Western hemisphere, discussion often happens between like-minded activists and the importance of language, local cultures as well as the potential for flaming, conflicts with the conceptualisation of a unified – Habermassian – transnational public sphere. Another observation is that the dynamics between the national or local and the transnational are much more complex then often presented. Both 'identities' are present within all of us. They co-exist, compete and sometimes even conflict with each other. The internet does, however, allow us to reach out, to go beyond our local-national bounded setting, without however completely detaching ourselves from that local context.

Each time we find a pattern that points to conflicting findings. Discontinuity and agency in some practices, and at the same time (structural) continuities in others. In order to fully get to grips with the nature of ICT-use and the roles that ICTs play within transnationalised civil society organisations we need to combine patterns of discontinuity – such as the increased and more decentralised network capabilities for social movements, alert-mobilisation, facilitation of interactive debate or even the open source software movement, with patterns of continuity – such as user practices, the importance of face-to-face contact, but also the unequal distribution of access and capabilities, the commodification of information, conflicts of interest at a local, national as well as global level and thus structural power relations within society. In this regard, we also need to start asking the non-media centred question: does it make a difference?

Notes

1 The author would like to thank Leo Van Audenhove, Kees Brants and Valerie Frissen for their valuable contributions to the research-project and the report.
2 Although the term ICTs implies more than the *internet* (cf. mobile technologies, etc), this case study will focus foremost on the *internet* and its uses as an interactive information and communication medium.
3 This was loosely based on a typology developed by Bekkers (2000) to frame the notion of virtual organisations.
4 APC only uses interactive tools for internal online meetings, to which we did not get access for analysis.
5 See: http://www.labourstart.org/actnow.shtml.
6 Unsolicited mail.

7 http://www.lappersfront.tk (not online anymore because of too many hits), http://
   www.geocities.com/lappersfort/ (mirror-site).
8 For an overview (in Dutch) go to URL: http://www.indymedia.be/ and type 'Lappersfort'
   in the search-engine.
9 APC has no forums or discussion mailing lists that are public; they do use these for internal
   organisation purposes.
10 Analysis from 11/11/2001 till 19/02/2002.
11 Analysis from 3/03/2002 till 6/06/2002.
12 Analysis from 6/05/2002 – the day of the murder – till 15/05/2002.
13 Translations by the author.

References

Anheier, H., M. Glasius and M. Kaldor (eds) (2001) *Global civil society*, Oxford: Oxford
   University Press.
APC & CRIS (2003) *Involving Civil Society in ICT-policy: the World Summit on the
   Information Society*, Johannesburg: APC.
Axtmann, R. (2001) 'Between polycentricity and globalisation: democratic governance in
   Europe', in R. Axtmann (ed.) *Balancing Democracy*, London: Continuum.
Bauböck, B. (1994) *Transnational citizenship*, Aldershot: Edward Elgar.
Bekkers, V. (2000) *Voorbij de virtueleorganisatie? over de bestuurskundige betekenis van
   virtuele variëteit, contingentie en parallel organiseren*, Oratie, Rotterdam: Erasmus
   Universiteit (Beyond the virtual organisation).
Bennett, L. (2003) 'New media politics', in N. Couldry and J. Curran (eds) *Contesting media
   power*, Boulder: Rowman & Littlefield.
Cammaerts, B. and N. Carpentier (2005) 'The unbearable lightness of full participation in a
   global context: WSIS and civil society participation', Media@LSE Working paper,
   forthcoming.
Cammaerts, B. and L. Van Audenhove (2003) 'ICT-usage among transnational social
   movements in the networked society: to organise, to mediate and to influence', EMTEL Key
   Deliverable – unpublished report, Amsterdam-Delft: UvA-TNO.
Cleanclothes (2002), 'Thanks from Light House workers union and supporters', 25/09, URL:
   http://www.cleanclothes.org/urgent/02-09-26.htm.
Dahlberg, L. (2001) 'The *internet* and democratic discourse: exploring the prospects of online
   deliberative forums extending the public sphere', *Information, Communication & Society*,
   4 (4), pp.613–33.
Dahlgren, P. (2000) 'The *internet* and the democratization of civic culture', *Political
   Communication*, 17 (4), pp.335–40.
Diani, M. (2001) 'Social movement networks: virtual and real', in F. Webster (ed.) *Culture and
   politics in the information age, a new politics?*, London: Routledge.
Florini, A.M. (ed.) (2000) *The third force: the rise of transnational civil society*, Washington:
   Carnegie Endowment for International Peace.
Gitlin, T. (1998) 'Public sphere or public sphericules?' in T. Liebes and J. Curran (eds) *Media,
   ritual and identity*, London: Routledge.
Guidry, J.A, M.D. Kennedy and M.N. Zald (2000) *Globalizations and social movements:
   culture, power, and the transnational public sphere*, Ann Arbor (Mich.): University of
   Michigan Press.
Harvey, D. (1989) *The condition of postmodernity: an enquiry into the origins of cultural
   change*, Oxford: Blackwell.

Hauben, M.F. (1995) 'The netizens and community networks', URL: http://www.columbia. edu/~hauben/text/bbc95soch.text.

Held, D. (1987) *Models of democracy*, Cambridge: Polity Press.

Held, D., A. McGrew, D. Goldblatt and J. Perraton (1999) *Global transformations*, Cambridge: Polity Press.

Hill, K.A. and J.E. Hughes (1998) *Cyberpolitics: citizen activism in the age of the internet*, Lanham: Rowman and Littlefield.

Hirst, P. and G. Thomson (1995) 'Globalisation and the future of the nation state', in *Economy and Society* 24 (3), pp.408–42.

ICFTU, (2002), 'A victory for trade union solidarity in Thailand', 16/9, URL: http:// www.icftu.org/displaydocument.asp?Index=991216489&Language=EN.

Indymedia (2002a) 'Alternatief ontruimingsplan: gefaseerde en vrijwillige opkuis lappersfort', 13/09, URL: http://www.indymedia.be/news/2002/09/31187.php.

Indymedia (2002b) 'Lappersfort: dringende mobilisatie', 18/09, URL: http://www.indymedia. be/news/2002/09/31568.php.

Indymedia (2002c) 'Lappersfort: honderden betogers in en om Brugge', 16/10, URL: http:// www.indymedia.be/news/2002/10/34152.php.

Indymedia (2002d) 'Betoging behoud Brugs Lappersfortbos', 20/10, URL: http://www. indymedia.be/news/2002/10/35188.php.

Kahn, R. and D. Kellner (2004) 'Internet activism and oppositional politics: a critical/ reconstructive approach', paper presented at ICA-conference, 28-31/May, New Orleans.

Lash, S. and J. Urry (1994) *Economies of signs and space*, London: Sage.

Lee, E. (2003) 'What to do when email campaigns no longer work', 03/11, URL: http:// www.ericlee.me.uk/archive/000061.html.

LHMU, (2002) http://www.lhmu.org.au/lhmu/news/761.html.

Linklater, A. (1999) 'Cosmopolitan citizenship', in K. Hutchings and R. Dannreuther (eds) *Cosmopolitan citizenship*, London: Macmillan Press.

Mouffe, C. (1992) 'Democratic citizenship and the political community', in C. Mouffe (ed.) *Dimensions of radical democracy: pluralism, citizenship, community*, London: Verso.

Mouffe, C. (2002) 'For an agonistic public sphere', in O. Enwezor et al., *Democracy Unrealized*, Documenta11_Platform1, Kassel: Hatje Cantz.

Norris, P.: (2002) *Democratic phoenix: political activism worldwide*, Cambridge: Cambridge University Press, URL: http://www.pippanorris.com/.

Rosenau, J. (1990) *Turbulance in world politics, a theory of change and continuity*, Princeton: Princeton University Press.

Sassen, S. (2002) 'The repositioning of citizenship: emergent subjects and spaces for politics', Keynote at conference, *Race and ethnicity in a global context*, 7 March, Berkeley Journal of Sociology, Berkeley: University of California.

Scott, A. and J. Street (2001) 'From media politics to e-protest? The use of popular culture and new media in parties and social movements', in F. Webster (ed.) *Culture and politics in the information age, a new politics?*, London: Routledge.

Van Audenhove, L., B. Cammaerts, V. Frissen, L. Engels and A. Ponsioen (2002) *Transnational civil society in the networked society: a study on the relation between ICTs and the rise of a transnational civil society*, study in the framework of TERRA 2000, EU Project under IST 2000 for Institute of Infonomics.

van Steenbergen, B. (1994) 'Towards a global ecological citizen', in B. van Steenbergen (ed.) *The condition of citizenship*, London: Sage.

Wilhelm, A. (2000) *Democracy in the digital age: challenges to political life in cyberspace*, London: Routledge.

Chapter 5

ICT and the Everyday Experiences of Less-abled People

Dorothée Durieux[1]

Introduction

This chapter is based on research that raises questions about the potential social impacts of ICT on inclusion processes and citizens' participation in the new economy and society. Discourses on the information society afford ICTs contradictory positions that range from utopian to the dystopian. On the one hand, ICT use is considered a prerequisite for participation in the information society; on the other hand, it is seen as creating new forms of exclusion from different social processes. An extension of the first position is evident in various action programmes at European and national levels that view ICTs as inclusion 'tools', capable of integrating people whose involvement in education and labour markets is made difficult by lack of physical abilities, lack of skills and qualifications, lack of incomes, ageing, etc. The research outlined in this chapter questions the capacity of ICT-based programmes within two privileged fields of everyday life – the training and the working spheres – to ease integration of the less abled.

This chapter analyses two case studies as part of an exploration of the potential in ICTs for meaningful participation in the information society: firstly, an ICT training programme offered by a non-profit organization for unemployed people with very low qualifications and, secondly, a call-centre employing physically disabled people. The findings reveal limited inclusive capabilities within the two programmes and suggest these constraints come from the absence of links between different organisations that would create a wider 'facilitating' environment. But they also emerge out of the culture and character of the everyday life of individuals at the level where choices are made or not made. The everyday life of less abled people reflects a complex reality where ICT use or non-use takes place in contexts other than the working and training spheres and are incorporated in a more or less extended range of activities through different kinds of attitudes. Individual stories raise the multi-dimensional reality of less abled people who participate in ICT experiences, and these in turn suggest various implications for the quality of life and for the various efforts to transfer skills and competences from the specific work settings to the private sphere. This chapter presents the main findings of this research project as it relates to the inclusion and exclusion experiences of the less abled in everyday life and to the specific role of ICTs in those experiences.

Research Context

There is growing concern among academics and politicians about the increasing presence of information and communication technologies in different spheres of everyday life. Concerns range from social impacts, the digital divide between 'information-rich' and 'information-poor' as well as the participation of citizens in the new economy and society. These concerns highlight two specific limitations in current political and even academic discourses. The first relates to the utopian belief that ICT use has essentially positive implications and affects diffusion actions in a range of areas; the second relates to the definition of social inclusion or exclusion. This is often based on the 'hetero-designation' of specific categories of people targeted in inclusion programmes.

This chapter addresses a hypothetical distance between, on the one hand, political objectives formulated in European and national programmes about the necessity to give all categories of citizens equal opportunities to access ICTs, to the use of ICTs as a prerequisite for digital and social inclusion; and on the other hand, individual and social representations about technology, the need to develop *e*-skills and to participate in socio-economic processes. In other words, it questions the belief in the potential of ICTs for social inclusion.

The Social Role of ICTs in the Political Agenda

This concern about a potential divergence between political aims and everyday life or contextual realities has emerged from different observations of European and national political discourses as presented in such documents as the eEurope Action Plans of 2000 and 2002: *Strategies for jobs in the information society* (European Commission, 2000b), *eEurope 2002: An information society for all* (Council of the EU, Commission of the European Communities, 2000), *eEurope 2005: An information society for all* (Council of the EU, Commission of the European Communities, 2002). With *e-Inclusion. Le potentiel de la société de l'information au service de l'insertion sociale en Europe* (Commission des Communautés Européennes, 2001), policy makers also target the 'information-poor' in society and lay out proposals to provide equal opportunities for people to participate in society and to acquire skills needed in a knowledge-based economy.

Other documents – such as *Building an inclusive Europe* (European Commission, 2000a) and *Strategies for jobs in the information society* (European Commission, 2000b) – recognize the importance of tackling structural barriers to social inclusion and propose to strengthen job creation in the information society through 'further articulation between employment, economic reform and social cohesion' (European Commission, 2000a). Nevertheless, the focus of these initiatives remains 'the potential new forms of social exclusion, which may emerge with the move towards the knowledge-economy and society' (European Commission, 2000b). Although such discourses also reflect concerns about other aspects of social inclusion besides employment or level of income – such as social rights, health, education – the main emphasis is on ensuring access to technology and promoting participation in the information age.

In order to reach a better understanding of how a specific awareness of ICT and social exclusion entered the European agenda, it is useful to consider some observations made in research for the European Commission (European Commission, 1997, pp.40–45). The *Social exclusion* report suggests that initially European policy sought to fight long-term unemployment through the creation of the European Social Fund (ESF) in 1957. Until 1974, European programmes primarily focused on economic aspects of exclusion or poverty. But later policies attached greater importance to social aspects of employment and the European labour market, through co-ordination and exchange of experiences between member states. Then in the 1990s, social cohesion was officially included in political plans and priorities were formulated in terms of housing, health, ageing, etc. However, key actions were still focused on integration into the labour market and on improving the working conditions of different categories of population. Action Programmes like *Integra* or *Horizon* – the basis of the second case study referred to in this chapter – were launched during this period. The priority attached to economic aspects of inclusion may be perceived as reductive in terms of the development of social inclusion in the everyday life of discriminated groups. A more comprehensive perspective on social exclusion will be presented in the following sections. Central themes explored include the potential divergence between political discourses as well as their translation into European and national action programmes and everyday life experiences.

Translation into Action

Member states, when dealing with European strategies and political aims for the development of the information society and increasing social inclusion, also translate European objectives into their own political agendas. So for instance, the ESF favours local initiatives within the framework of European-funded national programmes. Different action programmes – such as *Objective 3*, *Horizon* or *Equal* – have been launched in Belgium, a country where the national context is fairly representative of ICT penetration rates in the EU and of various social exclusion indicators. Indeed, Belgian figures of ICT penetration into households and among citizens are close to the European averages. A survey in 1998 showed home PC penetration rates in Belgium to be about 33 per cent, while the European mean is 30.8 per cent for PC use at home and 40.5 per cent for workplace use (Eurobaromètre 50.1, 1999). Internet penetration rate among Belgian citizens was about the same as the EU average of 8 per cent in 1998 (Eurobaromètre 50.1, 1999). In 2002, 41 per cent of Belgian households had access to the internet at home compared to 40 per cent of European households (Flash Eurobarometer 125, 2002).

However, if the Belgian context as a whole is representative of the European average, the same cannot be said of Walloonia – the main French-speaking region of Belgium – in terms of social, economic or technological indicators. Indicators for the Walloon region diverge from those for Belgium as a whole both in terms of ICT penetration rates and in terms of wider social and economic factors. A survey in 2000, by the Walloon Agency for Telecommunications (*Agence Wallonne des Télécommunications*, 2001) showed favourable penetration rates of home PCs –

44 per cent of Walloon citizens compared to 44.3 per cent of European people in 2001 – but a lower penetration of the internet – 23 per cent of Walloon citizens were internet users in 2000, compared to a European average of 34.3 per cent in 2001. Furthermore, the Walloon labour market suffers from a higher unemployment rate than the European market. In 1998, 13.5 per cent of the Walloon population was unemployed, compared to a European average of 10.1 per cent and 9.2 per cent in Belgium as a whole (*DOCUP Objective 3 Wallonie-Bruxelles*, 2000). Moreover, Belgian experts highlight regional divergences and an widening gap between Walloonia and Brussels, on one side and Walloonia and Flanders on the other side (*DOCUP Objective 3 Wallonie-Bruxelles*, 2000). The same study found that the long-term unemployed represent a higher proportion of unemployed people in Walloonia (70 per cent) than in the EU (48.6 per cent) and in Belgium (58.5 per cent). There are also differences between Flanders and Walloonia in terms of the presence of multinational corporations, the development of small enterprises, the level of income, etc.

This particular social and economic context may explain why various local initiatives have focused on employment, education and vocational training and specific attention has been given to the development of technological use and skills to improve participation in the new economy (*DOCUP Objective 3 Wallonie-Bruxelles*, 2000). That is also the reason why EU-funded action programmes in the Walloon region have tended to give a higher priority to ICT-based proposals that focus on work and education. The aim is to improve social inclusion of less favoured groups such as the disabled, the unemployed, ethnic minorities, etc. Although many ICT-based action plans aimed at discriminated groups have been launched at the local level, there is only a limited understanding of the relationship between socio-political objectives and perspectives on inclusion processes, on the one hand, and their everyday life experiences, on the other hand. Little attention has been paid to the specific context within which these groups find themselves, their real technological or social needs and the structural causes of their social exclusion. There is also only a limited understanding of the durability of the positive impacts of such initiatives on the everyday lives of the targeted people or of their inclusion or exclusion trajectories in relation to ICT use.

Fieldwork

This research took as its starting point political discourses and assumptions, then used these to explore the relationship between ICT use and inclusion or exclusion experiences in the everyday life of 'the so-called discriminated' groups. It sought to counter utopian and deterministic perspectives by considering 'human agency' (Loader, 1998) and the social construction of technology (Bijker and Law, 1992). This meant investigating inclusion experiences through the analysis of individual stories and collective experiences in the context of European-funded initiatives. The suggested approach tends to reflect interactions between social, local and individual constructions of the potential of ICT in inclusion experiences.

The Less Abled

The research focused on groups which are 'designated' as excluded or are said to be at risk of social exclusion. These groups are often targeted in specific initiatives launched under the framework of European policy but translated into national programmes. Here, the notion of 'less ability' refers to political discourses about exclusion, which tend to designate vulnerable groups as excluded or at risk of exclusion because of such factors as lack of skills, lack of income, age, gender, disability, etc. This conception of exclusion reflects many diverging groups and experiences but does not consider individual or social definitions.

The study therefore sought to identify specific groups that are often targeted and 'hetero-designated' in social inclusion policy or ICT action programmes at European and national levels, in order to investigate if they were 'self-designated' as included or excluded in their everyday context, irrespective of their everyday use of ICTs. This approach meant 'less-abled' people may still belong to various categories, such as elderly people, unemployed people, disabled people or ethnic minorities, and a selection had to be made.

Selection of Case Studies

The starting point was data from the ESF, whose mission is to develop human resources and to improve work and education systems in each country of the EU. The ESF funds national programmes, particularly social inclusion-related ones. In Belgium, such actions are more specifically launched in Walloonia because of the social, economic and technological context outlined earlier in this chapter. The other main region of Belgium, Flanders, was not targeted in the research for linguistic, methodological and contextual reasons.

Two specific cases in the training and the working sphere were chosen from among existing ESF programmes in order to reach the less abled who are targeted by such actions. One of these programmes, namely *Objective 3*, focuses on the adaptation and modernisation of education, training and employment systems. It includes prior actions for improving socio-professional insertion and social inclusion, notably through ICT-based training programmes for unemployed people. Thus, the first selected case was an action funded under *Objective 3* and was an ICT 'pre-qualifying' training programme provided by a non-profit organization for unemployed people with very low qualifications. The project aims to enable inactive people to reintegrate into a training trajectory through the development of ICT skills and other basic skills, like a basic knowledge of the economy, labour market and social rights. In the long run, the organisation intends to provide them with sufficient skills and knowledge for re-integrating a working life. Other programmes, such as *Adapt* and *Employment*, which operated between 1995 and 1999, also developed specific actions for improving social inclusion among various groups such as women, young people without qualifications, disabled people and people excluded from work. Some interesting projects funded under the heading of 'Employment', have become permanent and are still operating. This is the case of a social enterprise that employs disabled workers within a call-centre. The project was launched under *Horizon*, part of the 'Employment' programme funded until 1999. The call-centre was developed as a social enterprise in collaboration with a telecommunications company because this was seen as a way to integrate disabled people in a 'normal' working life.

Both cases were used to reach two specific groups of less-abled people affected by such ICT-based initiatives, namely unemployed people with very low skills and disabled people. A third group was also chosen in line with raising concerns about ICT use among older people, especially older workers or retired people. This group is increasingly targeted in *e*-strategies at European and national levels and is also 'designated' as a group at risk of exclusion from the information society. It comprises people aged over 50 and mostly retired, who do not fall within any specific initiative but are the focus of political concerns and are of interest because of the way they may appropriate the social potential of ICTs in their everyday life.

Understanding the Social Potential of Diffusion Actions

The first criticism of utopian arguments on ICTs centres on the absence of investigations into the process of translating political aims into specific and contextual actions and their transfer to everyday experiences through appropriation processes. In other words, the analysis starts from a 'diffusion-based' position that defends ICT social impacts on social inclusion and tends to highlight constructivist processes that incorporate ICT use into inclusion or exclusion trajectories. The research on which this chapter is based is more in line with recent studies that highlight the necessity to go beyond one-dimensional perspectives on social exclusion (Anthias, 2001; Bhalla and Lapeyre, 1997; Chapman et al., 1998; Commins, 1993) and to question the prevalence of the economic sphere over other dimensions of everyday life (Goodwin and Spittle, 2002). In it, the researchers have highlighted the multi-dimensionality, dynamics and the contingence of inclusion processes. Lastly, this perspective was integrated into a constructivist approach of ICT use and innovation processes with the purpose of analysing the social construction of ICT in everyday experiences.

Translation and Appropriation Processes

The researcher, through the analysis of 'diffusion-based' initiatives, has attempted to highlight how organisational factors and project management might influence the translation of political aims in a specific context of use and how various interests – political, local, organisational, and individual – were translated over time, to facilitate inclusion or exclusion of less-abled people. This translation perspective does not present innovation as a linear process of propagation (Rogers, 1995) but rather as an operation that creates interest among actors and whose success is strongly related to the specific context where managers of an innovation have translated their project at different levels, according to technical, social, economic and organisational factors (Akrich, Callon and Latour, 1988). This perspective was used to better understand the key factors in the success or failure in the management of ICT-based initiatives over time and their convergence or divergence *vis-à-vis* initial aims. The ability to construct appropriate networks of innovators; to 'choose the right stakeholders' (Akrich, Callon and Latour, 1991); to translate a project into different levels of action and to redefine alliances during the process are crucial for the success of an innovation process. Furthermore, the actions of stakeholders may influence innovation projects in the achievement of their original 'political' goals – in the cases studied here, it was social inclusion through ICT diffusion in the socio-economic fields. This translation perspective may be understood as an 'improvisational model' that recognises that technological change 'is typically an ongoing process made up of opportunities and challenges that are not necessarily predictable at the start' (Orlikowski and Hofman, 1997, p.20).

Secondly, the analysis of 'subjective' factors related to such initiatives may highlight the reflexive role of ICT users. The potential of ICT may also be constructed through mental and symbolic representations of participants and appropriated through inclusion experiences. This approach seeks to understand how values incorporated into ICT use through appropriation by the less abled may contribute to the construction of an inclusion trajectory. In the study detailed here I am questioning the way ICT use experiences may create inclusion or not depending on individuals' appropriation in specific contexts of use and on the potential transfer of experience between various spheres of everyday life – for instance, from their training experience to leisure activities. The studies investigated this human potential to appropriate ICT through various forms of being and acting with ICT. They extended Bakardjieva's continuum from consumers to communitarian usages for the internet to also apply to wider ICT use. Indeed, rational values inherent in the attitudes of consumers – such as efficiency or usefulness – may either be incorporated into internet use through infosumers' behaviours (Bakardjieva, 2003, p.7), or into computer use through 'jobs-oriented' or 'skills development' attitudes. In parallel, if the internet is a privileged space to develop new kinds of sociability or community, mediation or social values may also be incorporated into the domestic use of a PC, especially through inter-generational, professional or friendly relationships.

This conceptualisation meant both cases were analysed from two starting points. First, was the everyday life of the less abled where ICT use took place at a certain moment in time. From this experience of ICT use, some individuals appropriated ICT in other spheres of their everyday life or in their own domestic space. (Domestic here refers to different potential activities that are interrelated in everyday life – leisure, family, training, political participation, etc). Second, was the social impacts of ICT in terms of inclusion or exclusion within the specific contexts of training and working, but also in other aspects of less-abled everyday life since 'technologies potentially affect all spheres of life such as work, home, and leisure' (Lie and Sørensen, 1996, pp.13–14). But what is social exclusion?

From Social Exclusion to 'Self-designated' Inclusion

Social exclusion is a relatively new concept and few definitions reflect the complexity of the phenomenon. Previously, one of the main problems was the one-dimensionality of the concept, which tended to limit it to participation in economic life. Now, current academic discourses mostly agree on its multi-dimensional characteristics.[2] Exclusion is conceptualised through different social dimensions: political, cultural, social or economic. More and more authors (Anthias, 2001; Bhalla and Lapeyre,

1997; Chapman et al., 1998 and Commins, 1993, in Phipps, 2000) highlight the multi-dimensional sources of social exclusion and call for an integrated approach.

However, the concept, even from a multi-dimensional perspective, still contains persistent problems (Anthias, 2001, pp.838–9). Firstly, there are concerns about different levels of inclusion or exclusion and the possibility of experiencing both at the same time in one or several dimensions. Like other related concepts, exclusion may be viewed as relative. For instance, Sen points out that equality in terms of one variable may coincide with inequality in terms of another variable – for example, income, health, education, etc. (Sen, 1992, in Wyatt et al., 2000, p.4). Secondly, there are problems with the assumption of a binary division between those who are included and those who are not. Here, exclusion may include relative as well as 'dynamic and contextual' (Anthias, 2001, p.839). This suggests a more qualified view on inclusion or exclusion processes, with potential for 'in-between' cases or differential processes. Thirdly, the literature tends to distinguish between active and passive members of society, as if being included or participating would necessarily mean active. Phipps, writing from within this perspective, conceives of social inclusion as 'bringing in' disadvantaged individuals, groups and communities, and involving them in decision-making, enabling and empowering them to develop and fulfil their potential in the full range of their social, community and work activities' (Phipps, 2000, p.54).

Thus, many arguments about exclusion processes remain 'systemic', as if exclusion from each of the different dimensions depends only on 'system failures' (Phipps, 2000, p.43). Such arguments lead to perspectives based on the 'hetero-designation' of certain groups or individuals, who are defined as 'the excluded'. Few authors consider the human potential to construct 'inclusion' within one or various everyday spheres, what could be called 'self-designation' processes. Therefore, the everyday life perspective was used in our study to understand inclusion processes as a multi-dimensional experience. Everyday life is usually defined as a set of routine activities of human existence. 'Routines, rituals, traditions, myths, these are the stuff of social order and everyday life' (Silverstone, 1994, p.18). Moreover, everyday life may be viewed 'as something that is related not to a specific sphere of life, but rather to critical assessments of functions or activities making connections between them in an individual's life' or 'a social space, which the individual citizen is able to oversee and manage' (Lie and Sørensen, 1996, p.15).

Therefore, the everyday life of the less abled was explored as a multi-dimensional reality, which embeds various activities from routine to non-routine activities, from public to private activities, and which combines 'systemic' processes of inclusion or exclusion, as well as self-designation processes. Indeed, if ICTs may be the source of social and economic developments, there is a real danger in viewing them as the means of increasing social inclusion, whereas the exclusion problem is much more complex than just 'giving access' even to an adequate technology. A disadvantage is relative and varies according to historical, social and cultural contexts (Wyatt et al., 2000, pp.5–6). Drawing on theorisation put forward by Giddens (1984), Wyatt et al. (2000) also consider that social structures and material aspects constitute conditions for experiencing dis/advantage and that there is no strict dichotomy between social structures and social meanings in the analysis of inequality or exclusion. Drawing on Loader (1998), the research on which this chapter is based tends to combine both perspectives in an analysis of inclusion or equality within the information society:

> whilst the negative implications of exclusion are examined in a range of contexts, the overall argument [...] is that 'inclusion' must be a process which is the result of the 'human agency' of the many diverse individuals and cultural or national groups who should help shape and determine, and not merely 'access', technological outcomes (Loader in Wyatt et al., 2000, p.15).

The study investigated how 'human agency' may influence inclusion processes and the social construction of technology. Both were explored within a wider framework of structural factors and social contexts and within which human potential is able to play a role. Here, structures are understood as 'specific formal and informal, explicit and implicit "rules of play", which establish distinctive resource distributions, capacities, and incapacities and define constraints and opportunities for actors depending on their structural location' (Kleinman, 1998 in Klein and Kleinman, 2002). However, this research pretends neither to understand all structural aspects of social inclusion processes in relation to ICT, nor to give individual reflexivity all potentialities; but rather to understand the dialectical relationship between 'agency' and structure as a space where ICT use may be constructed and negotiated towards social inclusion.

The everyday perspective tends to combine reflexive and contextual aspects of ICT use where ICT is conceptualised as only one element of the everyday life of the less abled. That means that ICT use is investigated from a user's perspective, on the one hand, and in a contextual way, on the other hand. Thus, ICT use is not isolated in a 'virtual' sphere that would be independent from the other everyday fields. ICT use is an experience, which may exist in different spheres of everyday life, may inter-relate them and may be appropriated in various ways depending on social or structural constraints and on human strategies. This perspective of ICT use in everyday life follows such authors as Wellman and Haythornthwaite (2002) who insist on the evolution of internet research towards the investigation of internet use – in our research, of ICT use – as an embedded part of users' everyday life. In combining this conceptual framework of a critical approach to the social potential of ICTs, I analysed how specific social networks manage innovation processes over time through the translation of various interests and how appropriation strategies of users or non-users participating in such networks may influence the construction of ICT use in everyday experiences of inclusion or exclusion. This perspective suggests ICT use may converge with individual interests in some fields of everyday life rather than others, depending on the way that the network has been constructed and the process managed. Therefore, our analytical perspective tends to highlight how ICT-based initiatives are translated in one specific field of everyday life, as a starting point, and in other spheres of everyday life through users' appropriation – or non-appropriation. It also seeks to understand interactions between translation processes and appropriation strategies. The main empirical findings from both case studies and the three sets of interviews are presented in the rest of this chapter.

From Diffusion to Inclusion: Successes and Failures

The analysis of both cases – the training programme and the call-centre – highlights that translation processes operating over time may influence the relative success or failure of diffusion projects. They partly succeeded in giving less abled people a first opportunity to participate in socio-economic processes. But they partly failed in the achievement of their original goals in terms of inclusion. Comparative results point out the many obstacles in translating political aims into everyday inclusion experiences.

In the two fields, the management team initially developed a project to answer European political aims. The training programme – or TeC project – tended to address this through the insertion of unemployed people into ICT-related careers; the social enterprise was created to favour the introduction of disabled people in 'traditional' jobs. In both cases, those initial intentions have been translated into actions according to the interests of local stakeholders. The training programme was conceived around ICT-oriented courses in response to the technological interests of the trainers and in order to maintain their position within the organisation by attracting trainees. Therefore, the project answered personal and organisational interests. The social enterprise and the call-centre were developed to answer management interests in developing new kinds of activities, mainly commercial. And the call-centre became rapidly the most significant department, so that its profit and productivity became crucial for the survival of the social enterprise. Those internal and organisational aims became more important than inclusion objectives. Consequently, both cases increasingly diverged from the European political aims in response to internal needs.

However, the two cases may be distinguished in terms of how they have been translated and the social consequences of those translation processes. Indeed, the training programme was further translated according to the needs of the less abled and the educational team reviewed the programme in order to help unskilled people re-integrate into a training trajectory. Therefore, each programme has been assessed according to trainees' comments and needs. Thus, if the programme diverged from European initial objectives, this evolution not only served personal or organisational interests but also the interests and needs of trainees to be coached, to be better informed about ICT-related jobs and training, to be educated about different aspects of the labour market, etc. The team also translated European criteria for the development of social inclusion when they thought that they were not adapted to specific needs and contexts of less abled people and that other actions were needed in order to have a real impact on socio-professional insertion or inclusion. For example, the selection of a less 'computer-oriented' and 'computer-literate' public seemed more appropriate for the construction of a more 'realistic' professional project that would help them find a new position within society, even though such an orientation strayed from the initial project definition aimed at the reinsertion of job seekers into careers related to ICTs.

Thus, the case illustrates how a translation process may create interest among actors (Akrich, Callon and Latour, 1988) and produce convergence between various interests, notably those of the trainers, European and national authorities and the less abled in the construction of inclusion. But it also highlights how this success is strongly related to the specific context within which managers have translated their project, an organisational context where profit is not necessary and a training sector where such a structure may work.

Hence, the real consequences of the project in terms of everyday and multi-dimensional experiences are not so clear and optimistic. Firstly, one may observe a 'correlation' between the level of skills of some trainees and their inclusion trajectories in the training or working spheres. Indeed, the analysis shows that the 'least' abled tend to remain excluded, in the structural or political sense of exclusion. Interviews with members of the educational team also raised other issues related to the heterogeneity of the groups of participants in terms of level of skills, but also of cultures and personal stories. The absence of follow-up after the training also contributed to the failure of the trainees to achieve insertion aims. According to the educational team, some of the participants were not capable of using their time effectively and were unable to find an activity – whether another training or job – that enabled them to develop their own trajectory or to use the skills that they developed during the training. They had a tendency to sell themselves short and forget all the work accomplished. According to trainees' discourses, their main frustration was probably because they realised they still lacked technical skills. Four or six months after the training, some trainees paid a visit to the trainers who observed that they were still a bit lost, did not know if they had to accept a job to earn a living or continue their education to evolve, without any guarantee of a successful outcome. These frustrations were sometimes aggravated by the fact that they had no real professional life project. Here, individuals' appropriation of the training or ICT use into their everyday experiences was crucial for their further inclusion process.

At another level, the divergence of interests within the training sector itself constituted another important obstacle. Specialised training programmes – which usually follow 'pre-qualifying' ones in training policies – are often provided by large organisations where there are many applicants and the selection process is very strict. This gap between 'pre-qualifying' and specialised programmes reflects diverging interests among key-actors and weak ties between various organisations of the training network, which seem to be targeting different categories of unemployed people and not necessarily the 'less abled' as they are designated in inclusion policies.

At odds with this attempt to improve inclusion of unskilled people, the call-centre management did not develop new kinds of actions in accordance with inclusion objectives. Commercial objectives and organisational performance were more significant in the everyday life of the structure. Even if managers of the call-centre were more tolerant than other employers would be, the 'inclusion' project in itself does not exist anymore and the current enterprise works as a traditional commercial structure following economic interests.

A general profile of the workers highlights the diversity of their educational background, personal stories and experience of disability. Individual interviews revealed that for many of the disabled employees this had been their first employment experience since their illness, accident or other 'medical' story. However, the social impacts of their experience in the call-centre were mitigated and strongly related to the working conditions. The social enterprise operates with a schedule that is set and flexible at the same time; it is regular, organised in shifts from 6am to 8pm depending on the workload. Individual interviews with disabled workers and observations highlight that work conditions are very stressful in the call-centre.

The client company, Telecom, determined working time and the procedures to be respected, realised the control of everyday production statistics and productivity reports for the social enterprise managers. Break times were also pre-determined and scheduled based on a common planning with the client's call-centres, without any adaptation to the potential physical problems of disabled operators. Similarly, some of the workers felt management gave no special consideration to their physical problems and thought that they were considered as 'normal' workers despite having been hired because they are disabled. On the one hand, they were said to work in a structure adapted for them, had been given the opportunity to work again and to be treated with care. On the other hand, the wages were very low, work was subject to high standards of productivity and the technical infrastructure was not adapted to physical impairments. Calls from clients were often difficult to manage for them and some operators suffered from depression.

In this context, being 'innovator' or 'early adopter' (Rogers, 1995) did not help much in appropriating ICT in the construction of an inclusion experience. The only scope for them to express their identity and individual interests or projects was either to develop deviant uses or to construct another trajectory out of this enterprise. Individual interviews with several operators revealed how some had left the call-centre to work elsewhere and how others had stopped working there for medical reasons.

In this case, the translation process was conducted through the interests of a few stakeholders, namely the co-ordinator and representative of the community and managers of the call-centre. It did not generate interest among disabled workers because they were not considered 'actors' in the project. Indeed, 'actors', as defined in translation theory, should be implied through enrolment and mobilisation in the innovation process (Amblard et al., 1996). As a result, most of the disabled workers remained excluded from 'traditional' jobs and even from satisfying work conditions. Also, the commercial structure and the work conditions imposed constraints on the achievement of workers' needs and interests as well as on their reflexive potential. Working conditions did not necessarily give any opportunity to develop individual strategies, especially for people who had experienced more or less long periods of loneliness and unemployment. As with the first case study, one may wonder if this kind of initiative has real implications for inclusion in the long run. Disabled people may be more vulnerable in the labour market than other categories of unemployed or unskilled people. And this case highlights how ICT potential for inclusion depends on different translation processes operated through interactions between individuals, contexts and the actions of various stakeholders.

Successes and failures, as observed in both case studies, highlight that translation processes conducted over time may produce inclusion, as well as exclusion. But in the specific contexts of both initiatives, individual processes also play a crucial role for the construction of inclusion experiences in other everyday dimensions. Some findings about individual constructions are developed in the next section of this chapter.

The Appropriation and Inclusion Experiences of the Less Abled

A comparison of individual appropriation processes across the three sets of inter-views suggests common processes probably related to the characteristics of being less abled as outlined at the beginning of this chapter. Appropriating ICTs from specific experiences to other contexts of everyday life was not only related to the translation process of both projects in terms of socio-professional practices. The incorporation of ICT use into domestic space also reflected reflexive processes of incorporating value into ICT use. And those values would be seen to influence the way that the less abled appropriated ICT-based initiatives and transferred this specific experience into their everyday experience. Interviews with the elderly underscored that they also intervene in common processes of appropriating ICT in everyday life contexts.

The comparison of various individual interviews raises the question of the incorporation of specific values through the appropriation of ICT use. Those values were used to distinguish three transversal categories representing three specific appropriation modes or ways of acting in relation to ICT (Bakardjieva, 2003) that were observed among the three groups and among people having various socio-demographic profiles. Appropriation modes also reflected different constructions of inclusion trajectories through contrasted temporalities in the development of ICT use. So, those 'self-designated' trajectories could be seen to diverge from usual 'hetero-designation' processes implying a higher potential for appropriation among more favoured categories of people.

The 'Utopian' Attitude

The first category considers 'utopian' people who develop various ICT usages (from computer use to information or communication tools) and incorporate a wide range of values in ICT (from rational values of usefulness to social or communitarian meanings). Their discourse provides a positive appreciation of ICT in their everyday life and highlights an individual and social identity strongly related to technological use, notably through the construction of ICT-related professional projects or ICT-based activities related to a professional experience or a technical 'feeling'. Here, three unemployed trainees wished to find a job in the ICT sector after the TeC programme; one disabled worker (Christian) left the call-centre to construct a new career as a webmaster in a town administration; one retired interviewee was still developing software, while two others spent most of their time using a computer for managing their holidays and accounting or communicating with children.

Their appropriation in various spheres and the relationships created between contrasted activities of their everyday life also tends to support the construction of a multi-dimensional inclusion process. For instance, Christian was able to construct a new inclusion trajectory through the creation of a negotiated space between rational and social values incorporated in ICT. Rational values were evident in his appropriation of ICT as an insertion tool and social values in his appropriation of ICT as a relational and communication tool.

However, such utopian attitudes may also create new forms of exclusion when the beliefs of the less abled in the potential of ICT diverge from social constraints. Then, it may create a limited space for human agency and produce perverse consequences in terms of exclusion. This was the case of one of our retired interviewees for whom ICTs became a main activity and a source of isolation from social and relational activities. Unemployed people who wished to be active in the ICT sector failed to achieve their professional projects, notably as a result of a lack of social support.

The 'Rational' Attitude

The second category comprises 'rational' individuals who appropriate ICT for specific purposes and in relation to specific values. They incorporate an activity-based usefulness in usages that are not necessarily related to any professional or personal project – for instance, it may be job research, home banking, or surfing on the internet. Their social usages reflect indirect mediation processes – social networks around them influence their motivation to communicate – or more active use aiming at supporting existing social networks or participating in collective debates via ICT.

Their appreciation of ICTs centres on specific usages and they expressed some reluctance *vis-à-vis* 'useless' aspects of technology (for instance, chat-rooms or games). Their usage reflected the construction of an inclusion experience in relation to specific dimensions of their everyday life rather than others, notably social relationships, leisure activities or job research activities. Their appropriation and human agency was limited to specific spaces of their everyday life where ICT is appropriated, while their self-designated inclusion trajectories are constructed in divergence from utopian beliefs in the overall social potential of ICT as an enabling technology. Here, self-designated trajectories are partly constructed in relation to ICT use and partly in relation to other dimensions and experiences of their everyday life.

The 'Dystopian' Attitude

The last category represents the most 'dystopian' attitude *vis-à-vis* ICT. Here, less abled people were developing very limited use of ICTs. The unemployed and disabled in this category did not appropriate ICT outside the specific training and working initiatives or developed a very low level of use. The three groups incorporated very few rational or social values in using ICT and they usually preferred other everyday and social activities that were not technologically mediated – for instance, social face-to-face communications, leisure activities and visiting the family.

Their view of technology was quite negative and they were reluctant to make the most of some usages, namely chatting, sending emails, realising transactions, searching for information. In their case, ICTs reflected a very low inclusion potential and their own representations of ICTs strongly diverged from utopian beliefs. Their 'negative' values may be related to structural or socio-demographic constraints since those interviewees had no extended social networks, no friends to communicate with via the internet, no family or friends using ICT, and sometimes no economic resources to access technology.

But what was more significant was the absence of any interest on their part in using technology, and the non-incorporation of values in using ICTs for constructing their inclusion trajectory. Their 'self-designated' trajectory was constructed without any reference to ICT. Their inclusion trajectory was not constructed through the appropriation of ICT and those less abled defined themselves through categories and relevant dimensions of social inclusion familiar in hetero-designation. They did not attribute social or inclusion values to ICT and constructed their own trajectories outside such a perspective, in relation to other experiences such as family, leisure, home, etc.

Conclusions

The attempt in this EMTEL study to go beyond, utopian beliefs in ICTs, highlighted how diffusion programmes in the working and training fields may be translated over time and may result in failures in terms of socio-professional or 'hetero-designated' inclusion. But the findings also underline how the individual experiences of the less abled incorporate interests and values in ICT use and everyday life experiences. They showed how ICTs might be appropriated in the construction of social networks, as well as in the construction of new socio-professional projects. ICTs are used in many ways to express human agency in everyday processes and particularly to construct communication processes through or around technology.

This constructivist approach of collective and individual experiences through the comparison of two specific cases and three different groups highlights multiple constraints and opportunities – that is, the conditions where the less abled may or may not construct a 'self-designated' inclusion trajectory. Experiences such as the realisation of professional projects, the communitarian use of ICT or the non-use of ICT suggest many ways to construct ICT potential for inclusion. Social factors and norms define social inclusion as a 'hetero-designation' process, yet contextual and organisational conditions may be translated in ways that make possible spaces for 'human agency' and 'self-designation' processes; they may also constitute constraints where little space is given for innovation and reflexivity. This constructivist approach to inclusion and exclusion within the information society may be used to raise key questions about the development of European eInclusion strategies and make innovative suggestions as how to better address everyday experiences in the specific contexts of the less abled. Namely, the need to question the realism of ICT-based projects for an inclusion policy in the everyday life of the less abled.

Indeed, the non-appropriation of ICTs, in these cases, highlights the difficulty of diffusing ICTs among the less abled, but also the irrelevance of diffusion actions *vis-à-vis* some individual experiences where structural sources of exclusion are not solved and where individual support is needed. Given some of the inclusion failures of the diffusion-based initiatives and the various appropriation processes observed among the less abled, one suggestion would be to go beyond ICT use as a tool for accessing the working and training spheres and instead to favour ICT use as a 'support' tool for personal projects and evolution in different spheres of everyday life (professional, educational, cultural, etc.). Maybe such projects would gain by expanding diffusion actions to other kinds of personal trajectories and inclusion processes? Similarly, reinforcing ties within local networks may be a way to develop political strategies based on communication processes and social relationships that may support everyday experiences of inclusion.

Notes

1　This research project was conducted in ASCoR (Amsterdam School of Communications Research) at the University of Amsterdam and LENTIC (Laboratoire d'Etudes sur les Nouvelles Technologies de l'Information et de la Communication, l'Innovation et le Changement) at the University of Liège.
2　The conception of exclusion developed in this section is inspired from a reflection conducted by three EMTEL research fellows during the process of their research.

References

Agence Wallonne des Télécommunications (2001) *Enquête sur les usages TIC des citoyens et des PME en Wallonie*.

Akrich, M., M. Callon and B. Latour (1988) 'A quoi tient le succès des innovations? 1. L'art de l'intéressement', *Gérer et comprendre*, 11, pp.4–17.

Akrich, M., M. Callon and B. Latour (1991) 'A quoi tient le succès des innovations? 2. L'art de choisir les bons porte-parole', *Gérer et comprendre*, 12, pp.14–29.

Amblard, H., P. Bernoux, G. Herreros and Y-F. Livian (1996) *Les nouvelles approches sociologiques des organisations*, Paris: Seuil.

Anthias, F. (2001) 'The concept of "Social Division" and theorising social stratification: looking at ethnicity and class', *Sociology*, 35 (4), pp.835–54.

Bakardjieva, M. (2003) 'Virtual togetherness: an everyday life perspective', *Media, Culture & Society*, 25 (3), pp.291–313.

Bhalla, A. and F. Lapeyre (1997) 'Social exclusion: towards an analytical and operational framework', *Development and Change*, 28 (3), pp.413–33.

Bijker, W. E. and J. Law (eds) (1992) *Shaping technology/building society. Studies in sociotechnical change*, Cambridge: MIT Press.

Chapman, P., E. Phimister, M. Shucksmith, R. Upward and E. Vera-Toscano (1998) *Poverty and exclusion in rural Britain: the dynamics of low income and employment*, York: Joseph Rowntree Foundation/Arkleton Centre for Rural Development Research.

Commins, P. (1993) *Combating exclusion in Ireland 1990–1994: a midway report*, Brussels: European Commission.

Commission des Communautés Européennes (2001) *e-Inclusion. Le potentiel de la société de l'information au service de l'insertion sociale en Europe'*, avec le soutien du groupe de haut niveau 'Emploi et dimension sociale de la société de l'information' (ESDIS), Bruxelles, Document de travail des services de la Commission.

Commission Européenne, DG Emploi et Affaires sociales (2000) *DOCUP Objectif 3 Wallonie-Bruxelles*, en partenariat avec le Gouvernement wallon, le Gouvernement de la communauté française, le Collège de la commission communautaire française de Bruxelles-Capitale, 26 juillet 2000.

Commission of the European Communities (2002) *eEurope 2005: An information society for all*, An action plan to be presented in view of the Sevilla European Council, 21/22 June 2002, Communication from the Commission to the Council, the European Parliament, the Economic and Social Committee and the Committee of the Regions.

Council of the EU and Commission of the European Communities (2000) *eEurope 2002 An information society for all*, Action Plan prepared by the Council and the European Commission for the Feira European Council, 19–20 June 2000.

Eurobaromètre 50.1 (1999) *Les Européens et la Société de l'Information*, Rapport rédigé par INRA (Europe), European Coordination Office s.a., pour La Direction Générale XIII 'Télécommunications, Marché de l'Information et Valorisation de la Recherche, géré et organisé par la DGX 'Information, Communication, Culture, Audiovisuel' (Unité "Analyse de l'opinion publique).

European Commission (1997) *Social exclusion in European neighbourhoods – processes, experiences and responses*, Final report, Targeted Economic and Social Research (TSER), AREA III: Research into social exclusion and social integration in Europe.

European Commission (2000a) *Building an inclusive Europe*, Communication from the Commission, Brussels.

European Commission (2000b) *Strategies for jobs in the information society*, Employment and Social Affairs DG, Brussels.

Flash Eurobarometer 125 (2002) *Internet and the public at large*, Realised by EOS Gallup Europe upon request of the European Commission (Directorate General 'Information Society'), Survey organised and managed by Directorate General 'Press and Communication' (Opinion Polls, Press Reviews, Europe Direct).

Giddens, A. (1984) *The constitution of society: outline of a theory of structuration*, Cambridge: Polity.

Goodwin, I. and B. Spittle (2002) 'The EU and the information society. Discourse, power and policy', *New media and society*, 4 (2), pp.225–49.

Klein, H.K and D.L. Kleinman (2002) 'The social construction of technology: structural considerations', *Science, Technology and Human Values*, 27 (1), pp.28–52.

Kleinman, D.L. (1998) 'Untangling context: understanding a university laboratory in the commercial world', *Science, Technology, and Human Values*, 23, pp.285–314.

Lie, M. and K.H. Sørensen (eds) (1996) *Making technology our own? Domesticating technology into everyday life*, Oslo: Scandinavian University Press.

Loader, B.D. (ed.) (1998) *Cyberspace divide. Equality, agency and policy in the information society*, London: Routledge.

Orlikowski, W.J. and J.D. Hofman (1997) 'An improvisational model for change management: The case of Groupware Technologies', *Sloan Management Review*, Winter 1997, pp.11–21.

Phipps, L. (2000) 'New communications technologies. A conduit for social inclusion', *Information, Communication and Society*, 3 (1), pp.39–68.

Rogers, E. (1995) *Diffusion of innovations*, Fourth edition, New York: The Free Press.

Sen, A. (1992) *Inequality re-examined*, Oxford: Oxford University Press.

Silverstone, R. (1994) *Television and everyday life*, London: Routledge.

Wellman, B and M. Gulia (1999) 'Net-surfers don't ride alone: virtual communities as communities', in B. Wellman (ed.), *Networks in the global village: life in contemporary communities*, Boulder, Oxford: Westview Press.

Wellman, B. and C. Haythornthwaite (eds) (2002) *The internet in everyday life*, Oxford: Blackwell.

Wyatt, S., F. Henwood, N. Miller and P. Senker (eds) (2000) *Technology and in/equality. Questioning the information society*, London: Routledge.

Part 2
Consumption
and the Quality of Life

Chapter 6

Consumption and Quality of Life in a Digital World

Yves Punie, Marc Bogdanowicz, Anne-Jorunn Berg, Caroline Pauwels and Jean-Claude Burgelman[1]

Introduction

A popular discourse on technological change claims that the relationship between (new) technologies and quality of life is a straightforward one as new technologies lead to a better quality of life. Technologies are invented to improve efficiency and the overall standard of living as well as to make our lives easier, better and more enjoyable. Consumption in general and the consumption of technologies in particular are seen as an integral part of this increased quality of life. Such a familiar utopian and optimistic view of technology has its dystopian mirror image where technologies are seen as a threat to the quality of life, human values, freedom and even earthly survival. According to this view, the consumption of technologies causes stress, enhances inequality and only serves hyper-capitalism and alienation. In between these extreme positive and negative dimensions of the information society is a myriad of positions, debates and oppositions being negotiated within academic and policy circles (Burgelman, 2000a).

This article contributes to the current academic and policy debate on ICTs, consumption and Quality of Life (QoL). It argues that the relationship between these three notions is complicated, dynamic, ambivalent and far from straightforward. For such an understanding, there is a need to go beyond purely economic conceptions of well-being and QoL and to take into account social dimensions, subjective criteria and human agency. There is also a need to go beyond traditional quantitative studies to understand recent trends in ICT consumption and use. Similar criteria of subjectivity and human agency are seen as important qualitative indicators for ICT-related consumer sovereignty, in contrast with the passive and manipulated television audiences of the 1980s and 1990s. Recent views, however, suggest that an active user is not necessarily to be equated with an empowered user. In this article, alternative views on both QoL and ICT user studies are presented. We also suggest a number of empirical tensions that need to be considered when discussing the ICT potential for QoL.

In doing so, this chapter introduces the section in this volume on consumption of ICT and quality of life. The chapters from Ward (Chapter 7), Berker (Chapter 8), Hartmann (Chapter 9) and Punie (Chapter 10) indeed provide useful insights, based on qualitative empirical research, on how ICT consumption and quality of life are experienced in a world that is increasingly mediated through ICTs. They provide empirical accounts of how ICTs are – or can be – experienced by users and non-users in their everyday life context. Thomas Berker investigates the way in which highly-skilled migrant researchers appropriate and use ICTs to manage the challenges of living and working in a foreign country. These challenges deal with both spatial and temporal flexibility. Maren Hartmann questions the assumption that young people are typical 'early adopters'. Her article suggests that the relationship between young people and ICTs is much more ambivalent than many accounts of the web-generation and similar concepts seem to suggest. Katie Ward looks at the use of the internet in a coastal town in Ireland. She witnesses the rise of a 'second generation' of internet use that adapts the internet to fit local, private and family needs rather than the internet being a distinct virtual world. Yves Punie takes a more prospective view when analysing ambient intelligence (AmI) in terms of visions, technologies, applications and social challenges. He argues that there is a need for a more substantial everyday-life perspective that confronts users in their everyday lives with future visions and technologies. He also gives an indication of how knowledge from an ethnographic 'domestication' perspective could widen and deepen the vision of AmI in everyday life.

These chapters offer relevant case studies on the use and to a lesser extent non-use of ICTs by different user groups in different settings in Europe, such as migrant highly-skilled researchers in Norway and Germany (Berker), the so-called 'web-generation' in Belgium (Hartmann) and internet use in a local Irish coastal town (Ward). A future vision that promises to embrace a human- and user-oriented approach to new technologies is also discussed (Punie). These case studies purposefully cover a wide range of topics, user groups and geographical locations in order to explore the ever-evolving and, in some ways, contradictory relations people develop in everyday life with the technologies they are confronted with. It is the objective in these studies to explore and advance thinking based on particular and small samples rather than present a representative view of users in Europe. Therefore, their concrete findings cannot be generalised but they do offer strong indications that there is a need for new ways of looking at ICTs, and accordingly also a need for more detailed and systematic research along these lines.

To address and contextualise these case studies, we first highlight the shift of views on quality of life and consumption. Secondly, a short overview is given of what user-centred research is about. We pay particular attention to the concept of 'domestication', a notion much discussed and used in this book. It provides an historical context for the approaches developed in the case studies. Thirdly, we outline some issues related to consumption and quality of life, based on the empirical studies of Berker, Hartmann, Ward and Punie on ICT usage and non-usage. Tensions and ambiguities within and across the case studies are highlighted with a view to interpreting them in the more global context of ICT potential for improving quality of life. Lastly, we briefly discuss some implications of an everyday life approach for understanding the relationship between ICTs, consumption and quality of life.

Quality of Life and Consumption

Quality of Life: Beyond an Economic Agenda and Beyond Access to ICTs

Welfare economics argues that economic growth leads to increasing opportunities for consumption and hence increasing welfare. It is assumed that market mechanisms allocate resources efficiently, thus indirectly producing well-being with maximum effectiveness. Economic theories also indicate that technological change – ICTs in this case – is an essential source of welfare growth as it positively impacts on productivity and indirectly on employment. Usually, aggregated numbers of GDP per capita serve as a proxy for well-being in a country or a region, whatever the additional measurement and comparison issues this may raise from a methodological point of view (Tuomi, 2004).

European information society initiatives have been largely inspired by such views. Technological change is seen as having a huge potential for wealth creation because of the strong impact ICTs are expected to have on productivity growth and by extension on the standards of living. So, since the Bangemann Report in 1994 – considered the 'founding' document of European information society policies – the accompanying technological changes have been expected to generate welfare through productivity gains in the economic domain and their resulting beneficial effects throughout society (Pauwels and Burgelman, 2003).

The economic and productivity-related approach has, in the meantime, been complemented by other approaches. Since 1990 for instance, the United Nations' Human Development reports have offered an alternative paradigm for assessing development and, ultimately, quality of life. A coherent intellectual framework for this has been given by the work of the 1998 Economic Nobel Prize Winner Amartya Sen on capabilities. He suggests that the purpose of development is to improve human life by extending the range of things a person can be and do. This is clearly different from extending the range of things a person can possess (as seen in the welfare economics and basic needs approach, which is also understood as Erich Fromm's maxim, 'to have is to be'). Sen argues that policy, rather than on the distribution of income or resources, should enrich people's abilities – what one can do or be in life – and their opportunities (the alternatives for doing something one way or another) in each given context. This approach contrasts explicitly with the economic one, which defines well-being as utility maximisation and neglects – from Sen's point of view – rights, freedoms and human agency (Tuomi, 2004; Fukuda-Parr, 2003).[2]

In addition, at the European level, quality of life as a concept and as a policy target has evolved to encompass both economic and social concerns. The EU's 'Lisbon objectives' for instance aim explicitly at building a competitive, socially cohesive and sustainable European society through – among other means – more and better technologies. The IST program within the sixth EU RTD Framework Programme has similar social and economic concerns and the e-Europe 2005 Action Plan states that the information society has potential to improve the quality of life, to open up social opportunities and to provide more convenient access to information and communication tools. The main focus on access to infrastructures in the first e-Europe plan was the result of Europe lagging behind other countries. The updated e-Europe plans, however, also encompass other issues such as education – beyond the mere penetration rates of PCs in schools – and topics such as e-Health, e-Government and security.[3]

There have been many different attempts to develop indicators for measuring quality of life, such as the one developed by the United Nations Development Programme (UNDP). Recent research (for example, Ling et al., 2004) suggests, however, that a comprehensive view on quality of life should not only take into account objective criteria (for example, material well-being) but also subjective (psychological well-being) ones. Ling et al. also suggest that ICTs do influence quality of life. The empirical accounts that are presented in the remainder of this chapter will make this clear.

Active Consumption, Individual Freedom and Consumer Sovereignty

ICT-related consumption, like all consumption, is often presented as an expression of consumer sovereignty characterised by notions of interactivity and user freedom. However, digital technologies can specifically give users more control over when and what to use. The so-called PVR or digital personal video recorder is a recent example. It allows, among others, TV viewers to record TV programmes but also to pause and fast-forward live TV programmes. Moreover, ICTs enable people not only to receive and consume but also to create and produce digital formats, hence notions like Alvin Tofflers' the 'prosumer'. ICTs do support and stimulate interactivity and user activity, but the idea of consumer sovereignty pre-dates the current widespread diffusion of digital technologies (for example, internet and mobile). It emerged mainly as a reaction against the fairly paternalistic and passive views of media audiences that were developed during the 1980s. Critical theoretical schools such as the Frankfurt School but also positivistic empirical traditions such as the traditional media effects research tend to conceive of the audience as passive and to portray receivers (especially television viewers) as easily manipulated victims (Garnham, 2000).

Several schools of thinking stimulated the idea that the era of consumer sovereignty was about to come. According to Slater (1997), it is strongly linked to the ideals of modernity and neo-liberalism characterised by, amongst others, rational organisation, scientific know-how and individual people acting in a free market. In its more recent version, consumer sovereignty is also supported by postmodernist movements and thinkers for whom paternalism definitely is old-fashioned and idealistic.

Moreover, a tradition of qualitative rather than quantitative audience research dismissed the pessimistic elitist idea of a public made up of passive viewers or consumers who are totally unresisting in their subjugation to television, the ruling classes, ICTs etc. On the contrary, media research and cultural studies proved that the public actively makes its own sense and meaning of media messages, symbols and artefacts (for an overview see Schrøder et al., 2003). Here too, we are close to the idea of the consumer who, if not sovereign, is at least independent or forceful (Pauwels, 1999). Recent studies, however, suggest that an active user is not necessarily to be equated with a sovereign and/or empowered user, thereby arguing for a more realistic assessment in between the extremes of active versus passive audiences or users.

People need both material resources (for example, economic) as well as immaterial ones (for example, social, cultural and symbolic) to be able to accept and use ICTs.

Moreover, consumers sometimes constrain themselves when it comes to the use of ICTs. Recent data (for example, Hargittai, 2004) show possible saturation points in the acceptance of new technologies both at quantitative (for example hours of use) and qualitative levels (for example, pervasiveness of ICTs in all activities).[4] In that respect a possible 'innovation fatigue' could emerge: people become tired of constant and rapid technological innovation (Future Reflections, 2002).

Most chapters in this section address this duality in the use of ICT between the desire for freedom, sovereignty, autonomy on the one hand and (self-)control or being controlled on the other. Moreover, evidence is given that ICTs enable freedom but also generate new struggles of control.

Research on Users and Uses of Technologies

From Diffusionism to the Social Construction of Technology

Many different, isolated and sometimes contradictory approaches to the study of use and acceptance of ICTs have been developed over the last few decades. Until the mid-1980s, diffusionism was the main perspective in innovation research that focused almost exclusively on the receivers/adopters' point of view. The most prominent representative of this perspective is E.M. Rogers with his seminal book *The Diffusion of Innovations*, first published in 1962 and now in its fourth revised edition (Rogers, 1995). Diffusionism focuses on the possible adoption of (technological) innovations by individuals or other decision-making units (micro-level) and on the spread of innovations in a social system (macro-level). Adoption is conceived as a rational 'innovation-decision process' in several successive stages. An individual passes from: (i.) first knowledge of an innovation (ii.) to forming an attitude to the innovations (iii.) to a decision to adopt or reject (iv.) to implementation of the new idea (v.) to the confirmation of this decision.

Identifying stages in the innovation-decision process makes it possible to describe differences among users in the take-up of innovations. This has resulted in Rogers' famous distinction between innovators, early adopters, early majority, late majority and laggards, all showing different degrees of innovativeness in a particular period of time. This temporal characterisation of the diffusion process is also visualised by the well-known S-curve for diffusion.

Various constructivist approaches to the study of ICT criticised this understanding for, among other things, its linear and overtly rationalistic conception of the process of innovation (for example, Punie, 2004; Berg, 1997; Flichy, 1995; Akrich, 1990). Constructivist approaches have rejected the narrow technological determinism that lies at the heart of such theories, where technology is perceived as developing independently of society, having a subsequent determining impact on societal change. Technologies are seen as social constructions whereby 'seamless webs' of social, economic and political actors and factors shape the development of technologies. Social constructivist (for example, Pinch and Bijker, 1987) and social shaping approaches (for example, MacKenzie and Wajcman, 1985) focused primarily on the development and design of sciences in the early 1970s and later, in the 1990s, on the development and design of technologies.

The 'domestication approach' which followed was inspired not only by constructivist approaches to the studies of science and technology, but also by user/ audience research in media studies and by the sociology and anthropology of everyday life. Domestication focuses on the processes of cultural integration of ICTs into everyday life – initially mainly into the household – and emphasises the need for qualitative and subjective approaches to the study of these processes. It gives the user within a specific social context (for example, the household) an active role in the shaping of ICT innovation (for example, Silverstone and Haddon, 1996; Lie and Sørensen, 1994).

Domestication: an Ethnographic Insight into Technology and Everyday Life

The concept of domestication refers to the capacity of individuals, families, households and other institutions to bring new technologies and services into their culture, to make them their own. This approach conceives acceptance and use as contextual phenomena, which should be studied within the context of everyday life, particularly the micro-social context of the household or similar structures. In this approach, the users take part in the process of shaping ICTs through making meaning about/with them, and integrating them into their everyday lives, their social networks, their ideas about themselves, and their value-systems.

Domestication is not necessarily harmonious, linear or complete. Rather, it is perceived as a process borne of, and producing, conflict where the outcomes are heterogeneous and sometimes irresolvable. It is also noted that needs and changes in the household, through ageing, break-up or children leaving the home have implications for the domestication process. Domestication is presented as a struggle between the user and technology, where the user aims to tame, gain control, shape or ascribe meaning to the artefact. As Lie and Sørensen (1994, p.4) argue, there is no technology without action; the premise being that users' actions matter, that when users act they allow a degree of 'interpretative flexibility' when attempting to integrate a new technology into the domestic routine. Artefacts then are ascribed with meaning and functionality, which are bound to the reproduction and/or transformation of relationships.

An ICT innovation is thus not only materially produced but also loaded with symbolic meaning by producers, designers and marketers. Users interact with these meanings when they consider buying a new appliance or when they put it to (non-) use in their everyday lives. Domestication emphasises these meanings as they are constructed by users and non-users in specific contexts.

Key Tensions around ICTs, Consumption and Quality of Life

As argued in the introduction to this chapter, the dominant discourse surrounding technological change claims a relatively straightforward relationship between new technologies and quality of life. Qualitative user research however suggests that this is not the case. The chapters by Berker, Hartmann, Ward and Punie show that people, in their daily routines and practices actively engage with the technologies. Moreover, this engagement is a complicated, changing and often contradictory process. In order to enrich and deepen the debate on consumption and quality of life in the information society, three aspects – or rather 'tensions' – of this complex process will be discussed here. These all deal with the less straightforward aspects of the encounters between ICTs and everyday life.

Early Adopters, Radical Innovations and Everyday Life Normalities

There is a difference between discourses about radical, innovative uses (and early adopters) of ICTs and the ways users (and non-users) think and behave in their everyday life. The discrepancies between ideas about how people ought (and are thought) to behave with ICTs in the information society and the ways interviewees perceive or interpret both their own behaviour and those of other people are striking.

The study by Hartmann on the 'web-generation' provides many empirical examples of this difference. The web-generation discourse assumes that young people today use ICTs extensively, innovatively and without problems. It also assumes that this will have long-term and mostly positive consequences for society overall. Youngsters are meant to push technological and socio-cultural boundaries, rather than accepting limitations. ICTs are (supposed to be) used 'everywhere' and 'anytime'. A general notion of connectivity underlies this image. The web-generation's relationship with ICTs is presented as not only problem-free and smooth, but also confident and playful. Boundaries between work and play are thought to be disappearing for them. In short, the web-generation discourse as analysed by Hartmann is based on the idea of a generational culture that defines itself via ICTs in a fairly conscious and immersive way.

The youngsters themselves do not align themselves fully with this rhetoric. Generally speaking, their attitudes towards ICTs are positive and many of them use ICTs intensively. However, they also experience pressure from ICT discourses and from their peers (friends and also parents) to accept and use ICTs. They sometimes have the feeling that they have little or no choice other than to embrace ICTs. This pressure encourages general ICT take-up by youngsters, but it does not necessarily lead them to explore the full potential (or capabilities) of the new media. (A similar observation of 'ideological pressure' to participate in society via ownership and use of ICTs is made in the study by Ward in which she interviews adult internet users.)

Moreover, the youngsters do not see themselves as pushing boundaries – a perception at odds with web-generation discourse – though this may be related to their specific age group. Hartmann argues that younger teenagers (that is, under 18 years old) might well be more playful and experimental with ICTs than the young adolescents interviewed in her study. This may explain why radical innovations like SMS, peer-to-peer computing and weblogs do take place: they were all 'invented' by teenagers. It could also be that the users themselves do not perceive these uses as innovative, even though they have taken established practices and industries by surprise (for example, SMS, P2P and newsblogs all came as a surprise to the telecom, music and media industry).

Another facet of the tension between discourse and reality is raised in the study on highly-skilled transnational researchers and their use of ICTs. Berker notes that this specific user group can be seen as early adopters, as they are heavy users of ICTs and are highly mobile. At the same time however, he observes a specific form of resistance to ICTs, both in relation to the mobile phone (and to computers at home, as will be shown later). Most of the interviewees have mobile phones but use them only under certain circumstances and in certain places. They always talk about the mobile phone in terms of a justification of their decision not to use it, or only to use it in particular ways. They do not always want to be available. They make excuses and feel it necessary to explain this in detail. When doing so, they actively engage with the dominant discourse of permanent availability and relate their individual choices and behaviour to this. In contrast with the discourse, being available is seen as problematic.

In the Dublin case study, another idealised type of ICT usage is challenged, that is, 'localised' public participation via the internet. The domestic internet users in the study indicate that they rarely look at local web-based content as they prefer traditional modes of communication for participation in local public life. Information is disseminated via the print media and public meetings operate at a face-to-face level. Admittedly, some local organisations and campaigns have developed websites, but these are largely used for advertising purposes rather than as forums for interaction. Thus, according to Ward, it seems that local websites are used to supplement existing and traditional methods of communication rather than to facilitate new forms of connectivity at a local level. In the cases where participants do use the internet for communication about public issues, they tend to go beyond the immediate locale (national or global).

Last but not least, in an analysis of ambient intelligence as a new and future vision of the information society, Punie highlights that even in the vision-building process of new technologies contrasts emerge between idealised types of potential applications and everyday life normalities. It is claimed that the vision of AmI is driven by humanistic concerns, not technologically determined ones, and that the emphasis is on user-friendliness, user empowerment, and support for the informal and unstructured activities typical of much of our everyday lives. A particularly important type of everyday activity in the home, housework, is scarcely – or never – considered in these claims. Initially housework was largely absent in visions and projects about the future of 'everyday computing' while in reality it is still one of the most repetitive and time-consuming tasks carried out in the home. It may not be the most innovative function for AmI but it would probably be a highly valued one, in terms of quality of life. The most recent reports on AmI do indeed emphasise the need for connecting much stronger the technological vision with societal and everyday realities.

Redefining the Boundaries between Work and Home

ICTs are involved in the process of blurring boundaries between what used to be regarded as distinct spheres of life, for instance, public and private; work and home; local and global. They also enable us to bridge some of the limitations of time and space. For instance, increasing flexibility between work and home (for example, telework), is often regarded as contributing positively to changing the way people live and work.

The blurring of boundaries between work and home, enabled by ICTs, is not perceived to be positive all the time however. Berker points out, for instance, that communication media such as mobile phones and internet-connected computers can facilitate private communications but at the same time increase the feeling of availability for work. This makes it hard to resist working from home outside office hours, especially when workloads are heavy. The migrant researchers were clearly looking for a work-free zone in everyday life. Even these highly skilled front-runners of the information society saw the permanent availability of technologies as contributing to stress rather than to relaxation.

ICTs are thus perceived to be rather ambiguous. The extended flexibility enabled by ICTs has – maybe surprisingly – created the need for places, such as the home, where people can switch-off both literally and symbolically (Burgelman, 2000b). The migrant researchers (Berker) are exposed to increasing spatial and temporal flexibility, not only in terms of being knowledge-workers but also because they work in a foreign country. The interviewees emphasise that it is in everyday life – the unspectacular domain of repetition and routine away from-the-work-place – where people look for freedom and control. The intensification of availability that ICTs facilitate raises the question of non-use rather than use. The ambiguous nature of ICTs implies, for the capabilities approach, that ICTs may not only remove obstacles to quality of life, but also may create new ones.

In their everyday lives, people are already developing strategies to deal with these tensions. For example, teleworkers interviewed in the Dublin study, while making special arrangements to accommodate the potential of ICTs, are carefully negotiating spatial and temporal boundaries in order to segregate work from home.

Privacy may become one of the new struggles, as is discussed in the Sevilla study on Ambient Intelligence. The home is usually portrayed as the place where people can live their private lives, the place where they can rest, relax and escape from the pressures of work and public life. The idea that home could become the place where one says no to an over-intrusive AmI environment is worth further exploration. But this notion of home as a sanctuary should not hide the tensions, struggles and inequalities that occur in the lives of most families. To be more precise: certain aspects of private life might be shielded from AmI, while other domains such as AmI for health might not (for example, Cabrera and Rodríguez, 2004), hence current notions of a scalable AmI.

Intrusiveness and the Struggle for Control

The ability of technologies to demand attention just by being there creates disturbances – for example, when they invade social settings, or anticipate action by making you pick up the phone, or 'ping' noisily when a new email arrives. Increasingly policy tries to regulate these problems, for instance, by banning mobile phones from restaurants, introducing silent compartments on trains, and banning mini cameras (on phones) from swimming pools, etc.

In the study of migrant knowledge-workers, the intrusive character of ICTs is much discussed. Ownership of ICTs enabling constant availability should not mean, according to the interviewees, that they are automatically used that way. Users perceive being constantly available as irritating. People make all kinds of rules about when and in what social settings a mobile phone can be used or not. They are clearly trying to create social spaces where being unavailable is valued. The ubiquitous character of ICTs challenges some of the basic notions of having control over one's personal life. The downside of being connected consists of a feeling of being intruded on and thus creates tensions. Users in the case studies sometimes struggle with the management of both connectivity and intrusiveness.

The Brussels study on the web-generation showed a clear tendency towards regarding the mobile telephone as both an interruption in social relations and a facilitator of them. Many of the young people did not feel comfortable with the use of the mobile 'everywhere' and 'anytime', but at the same time, they saw the ubiquitous potential of ICTs as positive, providing they made the right choices (for example, knowing the appropriate times/moments to call someone). There was a general awareness of availability as being problematic, and therefore, it was consciously dealt with, not as a problem but as a choice to be made.

Struggling for control is thus related to issues of how to communicate best with others via ICTs. But it is also related to controlling the technologies as such. The Sevilla study shows that the idea that computing becomes 'invisible' as it is embedded in the environment and in everyday objects, lies at the core of ambient intelligence. This is firstly a physical issue, but it could also become a social practice, that is, a seamless part of normal life.

At first sight, there is a striking parallel with the domestication approach. Ultimately, ICTs are domesticated when they are 'taken for granted', when they are no longer perceived as technologies, as machines, but almost as a natural extension of the self. By claiming to move technologies to the background and people to the foreground, AmI promises the disappearance of the technical artefact and its underlying technologies. As a result, it can be seen as the ultimate stage of domestication. However, domestication also highlights that the process of acceptance and use of ICTs is not necessarily harmonious, linear or complete. Rather it is presented as a struggle between the user and technology, where the user tries to tame, gain control, shape or ascribes meaning to the technological artefact. This is not resistance to a specific technology but rather an active acceptance process.

The material invisibility of technological artefacts –through miniaturisation and/or embedding – may well harm rather than facilitate their acceptance, precisely because they are invisible, and thus uncontrollable. Making technologies disappear, instead of reducing tension, could, on the contrary, make it insoluble. Far from achieving the goals expected, a technological environment perceived as less controllable could generate stress and inefficiency.

ICT and Quality of Life in a Digital World

Domestication approaches rely conceptually on the significance of the everyday and methodologically on qualitative observations of users and non-users of ICTs. They offer insights into how ICTs are experienced by people in their everyday lives. The studies presented here develop a deeper understanding of the evolving and, in some ways, contradictory relations people develop with ICTs. The empirical results confirm that the relationship between ICTs, consumption and quality of life (QoL) is far from straightforward. Rather it can be portrayed as complicated, dynamic, ambivalent and changing. To understand this it is important to take into account that views on both quality of life and ICT acceptance and usage have changed. Views have evolved from linear, mechanic, economic and quantitative understandings of QoL and ICT consumption to embrace more subjectivity, human agency, social dimensions and qualitative approaches. It is not the case that an economic GDP-type approach to QoL has become superfluous. Material resources such as income for instance do still influence QoL but are not limitless, nor do they relate to each other proportionally. Some people in Western societies will, for instance, choose more free time, flexibility or self-realisation over career and money. In fact, recent research suggests that this option may explain the deficit in productivity Europe shows *vis-à-vis* the US (Blanchard, 2004).

Diffusion approaches to the study of innovations that consider the point of view of adopters/users are criticised theoretically by interpretative and subjective approaches, and methodologically by ethnographic and qualitative studies. An important insight from this critique is the message that audiences cannot be seen only as passive victims of powerful media messages but rather as active consumers/users who construct their own meanings and opinions. Yet, this activity is not to be equated with sovereignty and/or empowerment. Users or consumers are constrained by available resources and by different socio-economic positions in society. There is evidence that ICTs are becoming increasingly widespread in society, meaning more diversity in user populations but we can also find examples of ICTs reinforcing social inequality. Interactivity is not without limits. On many occasions, people may just prefer to be passive.

In the case studies presented three tensions emerged. The first tension is the contrast between dominant information society discourses and the effective use and non-use of ICTs. As was observed in other technological areas and with technologies of the past, there is a gap between the core elements of the discourse ('early adopter' or idealised type users: the web-generation, the sovereign consumer, the enhanced home) and the domesticated practice of the relevant user group. The options for the way users can behave are eroded, however, by the normative strength of the discourses. They do influence behaviour but unexpected behaviours develop and grow as well. This interplay provides evidence of the interrelation between agency and structure.

A second tension relates to the ambivalent role ICTs take in the redefinition of basic boundaries such as those of home and work. The extended flexibility of work, and more generally of space enabled by ICTs is evident. However, it seems that a switch-off button is an unavoidable necessity, or at least a 'fading option', both literally and symbolically. The intensification or 'ubiquitisation' of personal availability paradoxically raises the question of a right to non-use, or at least of temporary non-connectivity. Here again, the unexpectedly slow development of distance work might well demonstrate how far ICTs question traditional work relations and organisational models. On the other hand, the unexpected fast diffusion of mobile phones or SMS underlines again the ambivalence in play.

The third tension relates to aspects of control. Contemporary technological trends imply that computing will become invisible as it is embedded in the environment and in everyday objects, hence notions of 'the disappearing computer'. Technologies may thus be taken for granted and become a natural part of everyday life. However, domestication also highlights the fact that the process of acceptance and use of ICTs is not necessarily harmonious, linear or complete. Rather it is presented as a struggle between the user and technology, where the user tries, among others, to gain control over the technological artefact. In the case of ICTs, on the basis of the domestication approach, a fundamental confusion is identified between the physical (and passive) invisibility of embedded technologies, and the mental invisibility that may result from a long and necessary domestication process.

Today's major challenge for information society policies, which were initially aimed mainly at productivity gains (claiming their beneficial effects on the quality of life), is to take on board some of the shifts in the views on quality of life and ICT consumption. The approaches developed by Amartya Sen and Nicholas Garnham invite tomorrow's European information society policy to become much more 'holistic' than it is at the moment, and at the same time much more differentiated if it is to cope with the reality of an enlarged Europe. Information society policies should actively support the development of alternative capabilities, of optional behaviours – and of the freedoms that accompany them. It means also that IS policies go beyond providing access.

Qualitative research can give some answers here as it provides testimonies of people who make use (or not) of ICTs within the regularities and irregularities of their everyday lives. It provides deep insights into what constitutes people's ability to use new ICT, what creative or non-creative use they make of it, and, in general, what the meaning of ICT for the user (and non-user) is. Studies such as the ones reviewed here – although not representative for the populations of Europe – offer strong indications that new ways of looking at ICTs and QoL are needed. Also more and systematic research along these lines would be beneficial.

Notes

1 The views expressed in this chapter are the authors' and do not necessarily reflect those of the European Commission.
2 For an interesting and challenging attempt to introduce Sen into communication research see N. Garnham (1999; 2000).
3 See http://europa.eu.int/information_society/eeurope/2005/index_en.htm.
4 For European data, see for instance the EU initiative on Measuring the information society: http://europa.eu.int/information_society/activities/statistics/index_en.htm.

References

Akrich, M. (1990) 'De la sociologie des techniques à une sociologie des usages. L'impossible intégration du magnétoscope dans les réseaux câblés de première génération', *Techniques et culture*, 16, pp.83–110.
Berg, A-J. (1997) 'Karoline and the cyborgs. The naturalisation of a technical object', in V. Frissen (ed.) *Gender, ICTs and everyday life. Mutual shaping processes*, Proceedings from COST A4 – Granite Workshop, Amsterdam, 8-11 February 1996, Brussels: European Commission (Cost A4).
Blanchard, O. (2004) *The economic future of Europe*, NBER Working Paper No. 10310.

Burgelman, J.-C. (1997) 'Issues and assumptions in communications policy and research in Western Europe: a critical analysis', in P. Schlesinger, R. Silverstone and J. Corner (eds) *International media research. A critical survey*, London & New York: Routledge.

Burgelman, J.-C. (2000a) 'Innovation of communication technologies: some general lessons for the future from the past', in B. Cammaerts and J.C. Burgelman (eds) *Beyond competition: broadening the scope of telecommunication policy*, Brussels: VUB Press.

Burgelman, J.-C. (2000b) 'Travelling with communication technologies in space, time, and everyday life: an exploration of their impact', *First Monday*, 5 (3).

Burgelman, J-C. and M. Bogdanowicz (2003) 'Information society strategies for the candidate countries: lessons from the EU-15', IPTS Report, Special issue, 77 (3) pp.6–13.

Cabrera, M. and C. Rodríguez (*2004, in press*), 'Sociability versus individualism in the ageing society: the role of AmI in the social integration of the elderly', in G. Riva and M. Alcanitz (eds) *Ambient intelligence*, Amsterdam: IOS Press Emerging Communication Series.

De la Porte, C. (2000) 'The novelty of the place of social protection in the European agenda through "soft law"', *Observatoire Social Européen*, Brussels. (www.ose.be).

European Commission (2002a) *eEurope 2005: An information society for all*, An Action Plan to be presented in view of the Sevilla European Council, 21-2 June 2002, Brussels, COM (2002) 263 final.

European Commission (2002b) *Information society technologies. A thematic priority for research and development under the specific programme*, 'Integrating and strengthening the European research area' in the Community Sixth Framework Programme, IST Priority, WP 2003–2004, EC: Luxembourg. http://www.cordis.lu/ist.

Flichy, P. (1995) *L'innovation technique. Récents développements en sciences sociales. Vers une nouvelle théorie de l'innovation*, Paris: Editions La Découverte.

Fukuda-Parr, S. (2003) 'The human development paradigm: operationalising Sen's ideas on capabilities', *Feminist Economics*, 9 (2–3), pp 301–317.

Future Reflections (2002), *Synopsis of interviews and the 7th December 2001 Workshop*, Bournemouth University with the Independent Television Commission, UK, February 2002. http://www.media.bournemouth.ac.uk/documents/frdecsy.pdf.

Garnham, N. (1999) 'Amartya Sen's "Capabilities" approach', in A. Calabrese and J-C. Burgelman (eds) *Communication, citizenship and social policy*, Lanham/Boulder/New York/Oxford: Rowman and Littlefield.

Garnham, N. (2000) *Emancipation, the media and modernity: arguments about the media and social theory*, Oxford: Oxford University Press.

Hargittai, E. (2004) 'Internet access and use in context', *New Media and Society*, 6 (1), pp 137–143

Lie, M. and K. Sørensen (1994) (eds) *Making technology our own. Domesticating technology into everyday life*, Oslo/Stockholm/Copenhagen/Oxford/Boston: Scandinavian University Press.

Ling, R., B. Anderson, F. Thomas, V. Frissen, J. Pierson and J. Heres (2004) *Quality of life, social capital and information society technologies*, Deliverable 6, SOCQUIT Project, EU-FP6, TNO, Delft.

Lisbon European Council *Presidency conclusions*, Press Release: Lisbon (24/3/2000) (100/1/00). www.europa.eu.int.

MacKenzie, D. and J. Wajcman (1985) (eds) *The social shaping of technology. How the refrigerator got its hum*, Milton Keynes/Philadelphia: Open University Press.

Pauwels, C. (1999) 'From citizenship to consumer sovereignty: the paradigm shift in European audiovisual policy', in A. Calabrese and J-C. Burgelman (eds) *Communication, citizenship and social policy*, Lanham/Boulder/New York/Oxford: Rowman and Littlefield.

Pauwels, C. and J-C. Burgelman (2003) 'Policy challenges to the creation of a European Info Society', in J. Servaes (ed.) *The European information society: a reality check*, Bristol: Intellect.

Pinch, T. and W. Bijker (1987) 'The social construction of facts and artefacts. Or how the sociology of science and the sociology of technology might benefit each other', in E. Bijker, T. Hughes and T. Pinch (eds) *The social construction of technological systems. New directions in the sociology and history of technology*, Cambridge/Massachusetts/London: MIT Press.

Punie, Y. (2004) 'Een theoretische en empirische benadering van adoptie, gebruik en betekenis van Informatie-en Communicatietechnologie in het dagelijkse leven', in N. Carpentier, C. Pauwels and O. Van Oost (eds) *Het on(be)grijpbare publiek: Een communicatiewetenschappelijke exploratie van publieksonderzoek*, Brussel: VUB Press.

Rogers, E.M. (1995) *The diffusion of innovations*, New York: The Free Press (Fourth Edition).

Schrøder, K., K. Drotner, S. Kline, and C Murray (2003) *Researching audiences*, London: Arnold.

Silverstone, R. and L. Haddon (1996) 'Design and domestication of information and communication technologies: technical change and everyday life', in R. Mansell and R. Silverstone (eds) *Communication by design. The politics of information and communication technologies*, Oxford: Oxford University Press.

Slater, D. (1997) *Consumer culture and modernity*, Cambridge: Polity Press.

Tuomi, I. (2004) *Knowledge society and the new productivity paradigm: a critical review of productivity theory and the impacts of ICT*, IPTS WORKING PAPER Expert group on socio-economic aspects of the information society, February 2004. http://www.cordis.lu/ist/about/socio-eco.htm.

Chapter 7

Internet Consumption in Ireland – Towards a 'Connected' Domestic Life

Katie Ward

Introduction: Towards Second-generation Internet Use

The household[1] has emerged as a fruitful area of study, in relation to the position of media technology in this environment (Silverstone, 1994, 1999). This type of 'localised' study has developed from perspectives which emphasise the 'social shaping of technology', where the user is perceived to take a dominant role in defining the nature, scope and functions of the technology. This approach aims to question discourses surrounding technological determinism, where technology is perceived to develop independently of society, having a significant impact on societal change.

This chapter is about users and the way in which they shape their internet media to have meaning in their home, family and everyday life. It examines the way in which meaning surrounding internet use is constructed within the household environment and how it is manipulated to complement existing patterns of behaviour, domestic routine and family communication. Using data collected from an ethnographic study carried out in a coastal town in Ireland, referred to as 'Loughrock',[2] I suggest that the participants engage in, what I refer to as, 'second-generation internet use'.

In building a model of second-generation internet use, I suggest that the introduction of new media forms such as the internet – rather then emerging and functioning in isolation – are constructed within an existing media and domestic context (Winston, 1998; Hakken, 1999; Marvin, 1999; Lievrouw and Livingstone, 2002). I define second-generation internet use as having the following characteristics:

(i)   Structured and targeted – participants avoid surfing.
(ii) Embedded within offline communication patterns, routines and needs.
(iii) Integrated into existing consumption habits and practices surrounding 'older' media.

Second-generation Internet Use

Second-generation internet use is personalised and supplements the enactment of existing habits and routines. Such internet consumption involves using the internet in a specific and structured way. The majority of the participants stated that they did not 'surf' the internet. Using a search engine was perceived as too time consuming and many of the websites retrieved were considered irrelevant and unreliable. The time consuming nature of surfing was also considered problematic as the activity engaged the phone line for long periods of time and this was perceived as expensive and inconvenient. Thus, participants tended to use sites they had an address for such as the BBC or the Irish Times. Such 'familiar' websites were seen as supplementary, allowing a different kind of assimilation of information:

> Chris: I'd still buy a newspaper, I wouldn't just go to the Irish Times website. I go especially if I'm away. I look at stuff when I'm away … I look at certain magazines [online] – men's health, GQ. I'd buy them as well though. No matter what, it's the same with newspapers, I generally just read the Irish Times. It is nice to scan the whole page. It's just the way you assimilate the information – you have to have more of a purpose to want to read something online.

The majority of participants were concerned to engage with content that had a personal relevance. For example, participants stated that they used the internet for making travel arrangements and researching their holiday destinations, reading newspapers and checking the weather forecast. Many participants were keen to use the internet as a means to research health issues. They researched their own conditions and those of family members. This involved the consumption of non-interactive material, such as that found in medical journals, or involvement in interactive sites relating to a condition. Overall, participants were less enthusiastic about online shopping and were reluctant to buy online using their credit cards. However, it is interesting to note that the majority of participants would buy from websites they perceived as 'genuine' and 'trustworthy'. Participants considered the Amazon site 'safe', and many people purchased books for themselves and as presents for others using this system.

What is the 'First-generation Internet'?

The first-generation internet has been conceptualised in previous literature by writers who have addressed the nature of the 'reality' emerging online (Baym, 1998; McRae, 1996; Watson, 1997; Jones, 1995, 1997) and much of this literature has been optimistic or utopian in its interpretation (for example, Plant, 1995, 1997). The internet has been presented as an environment embodying democratising and liberating characteristics; contributing to, and perpetuating, a notion that the 'virtual' and 'physical' occupy opposite positions in a dichotomous relationship. Over the last decade debates surrounding the impact of internet media as facilitating a virtual environment have exploded (Featherstone and Burrows, 1995; Shields, 1996; Rushkoff, 1994, 1997; Porter, 1997; Heim, 1998) and the discussion over 'virtuality' and the internet has been fuelled by many enthusiastic proponents of cyber-culture, who have suggested that virtuality has begun to supersede physicality.

Furthermore, as Seidler writes, 'computers can help us imagine different forms of communication'. He regards the net as a 'space of freedom and autonomy where people can … choose the identities they want to live from moment to moment' (1998, p.20). For some scholars then, the internet represents an environment of possibility, where it is argued that the lack of visual and audible cues has the potential to facilitate a post-gender/age/disability/ethnic environment. This view is supported by Plant, who writes:

> The Net has been taken to epitomise the shape of this new distributed nonlinear world. With no limit to the number of names that can be used, one individual can become a population explosion on the Net: many sexes, many species. Back on paper, there is no limit to the games that can be played in cyberspace (1997, p.46).

Internet forums such as bulletin board systems (BBS), emailing lists and Multi User Domains (MUDs) are spaces that consist entirely of text and many have formulated optimistic views about the transformational force of such environments. For example, Young (1994) and Bechar-Israeli (1995) have examined MUDs and suggested that they 'offer new and highly compelling language experiences' (Young, 1994, p.1). In describing the virtual text world, Young takes a 'utopian' view in the sense that he regards the users as having complete control over the presentation of self. He suggests that the user can exercise 'performative language' control, which gives him/her detachment from the environment and the opportunity to create a new self within the virtual environment (also see Danet, 1998).

Approaching the 'Second Generation'

Other work surrounding the internet moves away from an analysis of activity in the 'virtual realm' and suggests that the internet facilitates radical transformations in the way that everyday life is perceived, performed and lived (Dodge and Kitchin, 2001; Castells, 2001). That is, transcending boundaries of the national and international; the local and global; time and space; and the online and offline, or the real and virtual realms. Slevin (2000) adopts what I term a 'second-generation' approach to the internet and he sees it as consumed and produced within localised online and offline contexts. He suggests that in approaching an understanding of the internet and its place in relation to or impact on society, it is sagacious to examine the relationship between 'online mediated experiences' and 'the practical contexts of our day to day lives', allowing an emerging understanding of the mutuality of the relationship between online and offline behaviour, interaction and discourse.

Similarly, other scholars have researched the relationship between the online and offline spheres and new and old media through examining the construction of meaning at local levels and within specific contexts. For example, the role of the internet has been explored in relation to democracy, public life and participation (Tsagarousianou et al., 1998; Schmidtke, 1998; Francissen and Brants, 1998; Dahlberg, 1998, 2001; O'Donnell, 2001); patterns of social inclusion and exclusion (Loader, 1998); the provision of health-based material, goods and services (Meijer, 1998); e-business and globalisation (Castells, 2001; Slevin, 2000); other mass media (Berdayes and Berdayes, 1998; Rausmussen, 1999; Roscoe, 1999; Seiter, 1999) and in the domestic environment (Silverstone et al., 1992; Silverstone, 1994, 1999; Bakardjieva, 2001; Smith and Bakardjieva, 2001).

Merging Online and Offline

Others, in moving towards a conceptualisation of the second-generation internet, have suggested that the shaping of the internet and its consequences for societal organisation are complex. It is perceived to change understandings of mass communication and the boundaries of the 'real' and 'virtual', where the environments overlap in complex and manifold ways (Castells, 1996, 1997).

Hine (2000) avoids the 'mythologising' of virtual culture and perceives the internet as closely tied to 'personal and collective lives'. Miller and Slater (2000) also provide an example of second-generation work and demonstrate the difficulties in distinguishing the online and offline realms. Miller and Slater, in their study of Trinidad, espouse a 'comparative ethnographic approach' towards examining the way in which the Trinidadian people have moulded the internet to make it meaningful in their environment. The authors challenge much 'first generation' literature and suggest that the internet does not exist as a placeless 'cyberspace'. It is argued that the internet, rather than emerging as a 'virtual' phenomenon, is embedded within specific social spaces such as the family, business and religion. For 'Trini' people, the internet is used for practical projects and is seen as supplementing existing forums and this process can be observed in relation to the family. Here it is argued that because of the diaspora, people use the internet to re-construct family living. The internet becomes embedded within family life that is renewed by email and e-greetings. It is argued, then, that the internet allows Trini people to realise their families in an ideal form.

Methods

Since the purpose of this research is to ask what domestic internet users 'do' with their internet media and how they construct it as meaningful in the existing network of everyday life, a qualitative approach has been adopted that prioritises the perception of the user. Similar approaches have been used by Smith and Bakardjieva (2001), where research concerning internet consumption and the domestic environment sought to explore 'behaviour genres' that were established in relation to internet media and their meaning within the domestic context.

Research Location

The research is based on ethnographic data and interviews with 23 domestic internet users,[3] where participants were asked: why they decided to acquire an internet-enabled computer; where the computer was located in the house and why; about their use patterns; who used it and what for; and tensions, conflicts and resolutions surrounding the technology. The research was carried out between January 2001 and January 2002 in Loughrock – a small coastal town in North County Dublin. Loughrock was originally a fishing village, but has recently grown and has a mixed population of older families and commuters; Loughrock has a population of 11,000. Recently, there has been a vast increase in building and construction work, creating new estates and apartments for commuters, while also enabling some of the existing Loughrock population to buy a second house for letting. Loughrock also has a social housing scheme,[4] indicating the mix in social class that currently populates the town. Despite the mixed population, the majority of families in the town consist of a married couple and three children, where the male works full time and the female works part time (Census data, 1998).

Why Appropriate the Internet?

The remainder of the chapter will outline second-generation internet use, beginning with an exploration of reasons why participants appropriated the internet. When asked about why they had chosen to invest in an internet-enabled computer participants most frequently indicated the following reasons:

(i)   It was considered necessary for education.
(ii) Participants felt pressurised to be 'internet literate'.

Educational Benefit

Many participants with children perceived the internet as having educational benefits. The technology is inscribed with meaning and is associated with 'life chances' and quality of life. For example, David had appropriated technology with a specific educational aim in mind:

> The children were getting to an age where they needed a basic understanding of computer skills. I'm involved in education and it was becoming more obvious that kids have keyboard and computer skills at a younger and younger age and it's becoming increasingly typical in schools and education generally.

David was concerned about the education of his children and felt that an internet connection would be beneficial in keeping up-to-date with developments in schools. There is a close relationship between ideology and education and this was recognised by some of the participants. Indeed, in the above example, David presents the following as the reason for appropriating a computer and modem: 'The children were getting to an age where they needed a basic understanding of computer skills.' Thus, in expressing the desire to participate in new educational methods, the household is also making a public statement about its values and priorities.

Many participants cited ideological or educational reasons for investing in an internet-enabled computer. Education was frequently discussed in terms of the infiltration of computer skills into schools. Furthermore, participants were eager to state that they had invested in the computer for educational purposes:

> David: We felt that we had to upgrade because they're using them in school so much now ... well, it's all the thing, isn't it?
> Brian: We got it for the children. Teaching through games. Skills they're learning now will be built upon and develop as communication technology develops ... .
> Katherine: ... Even the youngest is learning how to use a mouse!
> Brian: They use it a lot for their homework ... if they have a project.
> Joe: They use software at school ... 'Webmonkey', I got this laptop and they use it.

Most participants with children were keen to stress that they were aware of the emphasis in schools on computer skills. They indicated that the purchase of the computer had been to enhance their children's education and this was often expressed in terms of providing extra resource materials. Thus, like David, participants were keen to present themselves as having appropriated the technology for a substantial 'educational' reason.

Ideological Pressure

Most participants cited a specific reason for appropriating the internet and this was often driven by a need to engage with societal and technological developments and ideology surrounding the 'information society'. For example, Marie appropriated internet media with an awareness of social change. Her husband, Patrick, and all the five children were computer and internet literate:

> Patrick: In the house, we have three computers, S has one upstairs – he spends a lot of time on the internet. We have the family one and Marie bought this one for herself because the one in the other room was being used a lot … there was always someone on it.

In this situation, the 'family' computer was located in the dining room and perceived as a valuable research tool. It was used by the children of school age (11–17) for homework and projects. The computer located upstairs was appropriated by the oldest son (21). He felt it necessary to have access to his own computer as he had an IT-related job. The third computer was purchased by Marie after completing a computing course at Loughrock community centre. She decided to attend a course as she felt inadequate in comparison with the rest of the family. Furthermore, it was becoming increasingly apparent that she was unable to participate in certain aspects of the 'information society'. She felt a pressure to conform, to learn the language and culture of the internet to continue performing as a competent citizen:

> I bought that for myself [points to computer on a desk], I saved up … I did a course in the community centre and I did this last summer [beginners' course in computing at Loughrock community centre]. We touched on everything and got very good notes … Everyone in this house … here was the mother – the only one … I didn't even know how to switch the computer on, so I said 'I'm going to have to do something about this.' I was beginning to hear web addresses and email on radio, I knew nothing only words, so I said, 'I'm going to try and see if I like it and if I do well and good and practise at home and then do an intermediate course.' That is how I felt, that everyone was computer literate, I felt that I didn't want to lose out. I was missing out.

The extracts from Patrick and Marie illustrate the close relationship between ideology, education and appropriation. Marie describes how she had no experience of using the computer or internet and was beginning to feel 'left behind'. She wished to be as knowledgeable and articulate as the rest of the family. In this instance, Marie was keen to learn a new language and culture that would provide the means to engage with dominant discourse. She implies that her lack of knowledge was hindering her from participating in certain aspects of public culture. Indeed, she states, 'I was beginning to hear web addresses and email on radio, I knew nothing only words.'

Her perceived lack of knowledge prompted her to 'practise at home and then do an intermediate course'. Marie's desire to engage with the information society led her to consume both courses and hardware, which allows her further participation in public culture.

Maintaining Family Contact

'I think the internet has re-introduced our family,' was the confident statement of James when asked whether he used the internet to maintain family contact. James's statement is interesting as not only is it indicative of the type of use that was popular among participants, but also the ways in which internet use can provoke changes in the way in which family membership is perceived and performed. Many participants viewed the internet as a resource to maintain contact with family abroad in places such as Australia, South Africa, United States, Canada and Britain. Some of the participants also produced websites as a means to share family photographs and news.

When families were dispersed, with some members living abroad, two situations emerged. Firstly, contact with dispersed family members was maintained via long distance phone calls and the internet. Typically, when the internet was introduced more frequent contact with the family was maintained via email and the use of website material. Rachel, for example, created 'family websites' as a way to communicate family news, developments and share photographs. For sisters Emer and Rebecca, email exchanges with their cousin in America became integral to their relationship, indicating that a 'virtual' component in the maintenance of family ties had become a 'normalised' and expected part of family life.

Secondly, for some dispersed families the introduction of the internet allowed a 'reunion'. For participants such as James and Patrick, after having no or little relationship with family members living abroad, the internet and email had facilitated contact with dispersed family and a 'new' relationship was formulated. Patrick felt that email had allowed a reunion and was beginning to use the email creatively to send photographs, creating a 'virtual tour' of the house.

Using some of the data relating to family-based internet use, I discuss the ways in which some people had begun to change their patterns of family communication. I felt that the use of email and the participants' vehemence towards the medium's possibilities were intriguing and indicated the emergence of a new dimension to family life. I suggest that while the data does not indicate a radical transformation in family life, internet media has started to allow changes in the ways families think and feel about communication and interaction. More specifically, new outlets for communication and the very process of enacting communication patterns can begin to change what it means to be part of a family, with relationships and communication conducted on a different level.

Changing Communication Patterns

Emer and Rebecca were students and living at home with their parents. They explained that most of their internet use centred on research work for their courses, but they also used email to stay in touch with relatives both in Ireland and abroad. They became enthusiastic when discussing their relationship with their cousin in

America. It transpired that they enacted family relations using both the phone and email and they stressed that, although email had not surpassed telephone use for communication with this cousin, the two communication means were used to facilitate different types of communication. Emer stated that the phone was used every two weeks, for 'quick conversations', whereas email was perceived as a medium for 'catching up' or longer conversations:

> I have a cousin in America and it's (email) so much handier than writing letters … We phone every couple of weeks, but email is better for catching up. I don't think we would phone any more often, if we didn't have the internet; it has not taken over the phone use. We have more contact.

It was fascinating to learn that the two sisters used different forms of communication for the distinct conversation types, but it was also interesting to discover that the internet had not radically changed the existing patterns of communication. In this instance, the internet opened up new communication possibilities. It supplemented other behaviour patterns, mainly phone use and it is clear that the sisters used the internet as part of a network of communication. This addition is perceived to enhance existing communication patterns and this is indicated where Emer states that phone use would not increase if the internet was unavailable. Indeed: 'I don't think we would phone any more, if we didn't have the internet; it has not taken over the phone use.' Furthermore, the short sentence 'We have more contact' reinforces the idea that email, rather than surpassing phone use, has added a new communicative outlet for the performance of family relations.

For Emer and Rebecca, the internet has not radically transformed their behaviour patterns, but it has added a new dimension to family communication. The internet symbolises a gradual change in the way in which family members communicate with each other. In Emer and Rebecca's scenario, where the structure and composition of the family was not radically altered, it is clear that internet use had changed ways of thinking about the family. Meanings associated with family membership had shifted further towards incorporating an electronic, remote element, which can engender specific patterns of communication.

This situation also emerged in conversation with Karen who told me that she and her family shifted between different communication modes, suggesting that while the internet had been introduced as a means to further facilitate family relations, it had failed to radically transform existing behaviour patterns: 'I phone my relatives, I prefer that. We go through phases, we go through about three weeks of emailing and then back to phoning.'

Karen's statement seems to suggest that the maintenance of contact with the dispersed family is highly valued. Her switching between the communicative outlets seems to suggest that she has the option of different types of communication patterns and readily moves between the phone and email. Although Karen indicated that she preferred to phone her relatives, she also stated that she goes 'through phases' of using email and I felt that her enactment of family relations, although largely carried out over the phone, did suggest email provided the possibility for a change in communication pattern and ways of thinking about family relations. Again, as with Emer and Rebecca, the change is not radical and it suggests that the internet is not wholly transforming behaviour, merely supplementing existing behaviour patterns and values, which reinforces the notion that the internet symbolises the beginnings of changing attitudes towards the way in which family life and relations are performed.

For both Emer and Rebecca, and Karen, there was little evidence to suggest that behaviour had wholly changed, but it seemed that the use of email to maintain contact with dispersed family represented a change in communicative pattern. In other words, this virtual element of family life had become normalised, suggesting that the influence and use of the internet within the home had began to incite a gradual change in the way that family relations are thought about and experienced.

In addition to the use of email to maintain contact with dispersed family members, other participants such as Rachel had created 'family magazine'-type websites. Rachel explained that her partner's relatives lived in Australia and that she and her partner had created a website as a means to introduce Loughrock and display recent photographs. Other participants also engaged in similar activities. James explained that his relatives in Australia had established a website for the purposes of maintaining family ties. James's case was interesting as the website functioned to maintain contact between family members and reunite those who had lost touch. Indeed, James explained that their 'family magazine' type website had encouraged the formation of a connected global family: 'There is part of the family in Australia who have a website. They put photos up. We keep up with family all around the world, which is rather nice. We didn't keep up by phone, we lost contact, so this has brought everybody back in line.'

The stories of Rachel and James were thought provoking, as on the one hand they indicated that the meaning of family membership had started to change. Viewing of photographs and news on a website was perceived as 'keeping up with family all around the world' and suggests that this 'virtualisation' of family ties was considered an accepted part of family life. On the other hand, the change in patterns of communication and thinking about family ties was guided by an older set of principles and behaviour genres – for instance, the exchange of photographs; news; and excitement about new houses suggested that while changes in behaviour can be recognised, the shift is not radical: it does not represent a fundamental break from older habits.

New Relationships

For participants such as Emer and Rebecca, the internet had a small impact on the performance of family relations and the meaning of family life. For them, it has allowed a new outlet for communication and started to change the way they think about talking to their relations in America; the implication being that the internet not only allows new outlets for communication, but that the very process of enacting new communication patterns changes what it means to be part of a family.

However, for others, such as James, the use of the internet has had enormous impact on the performance of family relations, in the sense that email has facilitated a 'reunion' with a family member living abroad. It is at this juncture that a significant transformation in terms of what it means to be part of a family can be detected. Similarly, Patrick began communicating with his niece, who lived in Canada, via email, allowing the emergence and perpetuation of a new and/or different family form, where certain family relationships are not performed within the immediate locale or via the telephone. Instead, they are both created and maintained through remote electronic, web-based communication. In this instance, it could be argued that participants are placing trust in the internet as an abstract system and this 'leap of faith' enables a new form, or faction, of the family to emerge.

By way of contrast to those participants, such as Emer, who used the telephone and email to maintain long distance family ties, where the internet was perceived as a supplement to existing behaviour patterns, Patrick and James used the internet to facilitate new relationships that were based solely around email. Email was key in allowing them to formulate new types of family contact and such participants experienced a change in what it meant to be part of a family, not only changing their own perceptions, but playing a role in changing the meaning and symbolic reality of the family. For example, James began discussing his network of family communication and, although he had many relatives both in Ireland and abroad, he also noted that he had used email to regain contact with other family members. Although James had at one time maintained contact with certain relations, he had lost contact and subsequently used the internet both to reconstruct and maintain the family. After discussing all his mundane use of the internet, James stated in a brightened tone that he had been successful in maintaining contact with some aunts and cousins that he had previously lost contact with:

> I think the internet has re-introduced our family. I have one uncle and two aunts and various cousins and I lost touch with my cousin … she came back for a visit and she got in touch with us by email. We began to exchange photographs. Another uncle has joined the circle.

James's 'reunion' typifies the type of scenario that leads to a re-building of a family; allowing family ties to be reconstructed in a new form. Other participants, such as Patrick, in similar situations made contact through email alone. Invariably, they indicated that the internet had allowed the fostering of long-distance family connections, suggesting that while the internet was used to regain contact with family members, its use also produced a set of unintended consequences relating to the meaning and performance of family life. Patrick and his wife, Marie, explained how Patrick had cousins in Canada, with whom they had lost touch, but subsequently recreated contact using the internet. Patrick and Marie both became animated when telling the story of the reunion. Patrick said, 'I've re-established contact with my cousin!'. While Marie added, 'Patrick's niece sent an attachment on her email of photos of the inside of her new house. We're getting to know them and we get to see inside their house!'

Conversation with Patrick and Marie revealed that before using the internet to make contact with the relations in Canada, there had been no previous contact and communication between the relatives. In this instance, the internet had facilitated the formation of a new relationship that was constituted virtually, indicating that this new way of creating family ties was considered a valid and reliable means to conduct familial relationships. This added virtual component had been normalised, indicating that Patrick and Marie had incorporated some new ways of thinking about family ties into their mind-frames:

KW: Did you have contact before the internet?
Patrick: No we didn't actually, we didn't have much. She got a computer and then we started. It does increase your contact with people who before it were too expensive or too inconvenient to get in touch.

Although, the desire to regain contact with a 'lost' family member is not a new phenomena and the story from Patrick and Marie does not suggest a radical transformation in the structure of family life, it does indicate that the couple had adopted a new approach to the performance of some family relationships. This new way of thinking about family relationships was reinforced by the creative approach Patrick and Marie adopted when attempting to make contact with the relation in Canada. Indeed, when asked about the frequency of contact and the type of communication they engaged with, it transpired that Patrick and Marie had used internet media and related equipment in a thoughtful way, using chat-rooms as a means of real-time communication:

KW: Do you stay in regular contact with the family abroad?
Patrick: We were able to make contact with relations in Canada, but the quality of the signal is very bad on the microphone and you have to say 'over', two people can't talk together … that's annoying, so we use real-time chat. It's so cheap compared to the phone. We're thinking of getting a camera as well.

Not only did Patrick note the way in which the internet allowed them to make contact with a distant family member, but it also transpired that other distinct patterns and habits of communication had emerged. For example, Marie stated that Patrick preferred to use email as a means to communicate as he found the medium less pressurised than the phone and more conducive to the type of conversation he wished to foster:

Marie: It's a great way to communicate … very relaxed, if it was the phone. Say we had no computer Patrick wouldn't keep ringing her up. I'd say that goes for a lot of people … it does re-establish family relations.
Patrick: It's very often, you can sit down here and it's nice and quiet. I'll send them something and you can type out a few words and then you send it. Making a phone call, you're thinking, what will I say next, whereas you just send a few lines. So there's not that pressure of being on the phone, there's no long silences.

The above extract is interesting as it indicates the perceived advantages of email-based communication. Patrick notes that he finds the medium more relaxing and less pressurised than the phone. It was felt that the phone demanded a steady flow of conversation, which was sometimes difficult with distant relatives, whereas email masked the tension and created a more comfortable environment for re-constructing the family. Furthermore, this preference for email also reinforces the notion that Patrick had adopted a new way of thinking about family communication. All his previous family communication had taken place at a face to face level, and in this instance his desire to use email suggests that the 'virtualisation' of certain family relationships was rapidly becoming an accepted and integral part of family life.

Conclusion: Contributing Towards a 'Communication Society'

Internet use, which moves between the offline and online realms, allows the beginnings of a re-conceptualisation of society's institutions and other social phenomena, such as democracy, citizenship, the construction of everyday life and the family. The focus of this chapter has been on domestic internet consumption and has explored the way in which the internet has been integrated into the household. The purpose has been to conceptualise second-generation internet use and examine its relationship with family life.

Second-generation Internet Use and Domesticity

The second-generation user focuses on appropriating the internet for specific aspects of daily life and shows a desire to use the internet in a structured and targeted way. Second-generation internet use is flexible, incorporating a set of manifold dynamics that both enable and are re-constructed by user interaction in the domestic environment. This user-driven vision allows the internet to be depicted as embedded into the discourse of everyday life and integrated by the users into their existing social practices and communicative patterns. These characteristics of the second-generation internet can be seen in the ways participants use the internet in the domestic sphere. For example, in maintaining and creating family connections and using the internet for educational purposes, the participants move between the on- and offline realms, using the internet to make connections and changes to the processes of everyday domestic life. These connections and changes remain embedded within established routines, rituals, behaviour and values, but they also contribute to changes within the processes of communication and interaction at the level of domesticity and family life.

Furthermore, not only is second-generation internet use bound closely with the mundane routine of everyday life, it is depicted as crossing boundaries; spanning new and old media and offline and online, or the 'real' and 'virtual', realms. The types of second-generation use that have been highlighted in the paper provide support for the literature, which conceptualises the internet as embedded into the discourses of everyday life. Indeed, there are many points of similarity between the findings reported in this study and those who avoid presenting the internet as a 'cyberspace', or 'matrix' (Hine, 2000; Miller and Slater, 2000; Slater 2002; Slevin, 2000; Wellmann and Haythornwaite, 2003).

Building a Communication Society

Through their adoption and integration of the internet into the household, the participants are becoming 'second-generation' users. Rather than moving into a 'cyberspace', which is disengaged from everyday domestic life, users are shaping the internet in a way that facilitates meaningful connections with existing routines and rituals that define domesticity. The participants' structured and targeted use facilitates connectedness on a domestic level, which contributes to processes of meaningful communication and engagement, rather than consumption of information that has little relevance to the playing out of everyday life and domestic routine.

The apparent desire to use the internet as a means to connect with wider systems such as education and to maintain contacts on a familial level suggests a move towards meaningful communication and engagement that has relevance within existing systems of meaning and routine. This type of second-generation internet use could contribute to a debate surrounding the conceptualisation of the 'European communication society', which would involve examining the ways in which domestic users can both contribute to and benefit from a 'communication society'. This approach allows users to take an active role in the shaping of a 'communication society', which shifts away from the 'top down' emphasis of the 'information society', where policy at national and European level indicates the way in which the user *should* be engaging with internet technologies (see Irish Information Society Commission – http://www.isc.ie), rather than allowing the users to define their own parameters of meaningful, structured and communicative use.

The family: Continuity and Transformation

This chapter has asked questions about the family's use of the internet. Interesting results about the levels, degrees and processes of change have emerged from asking what is the relationship between the internet and family life? How have the family appropriated the internet? And how has the internet changed family relations? The research has suggested that the internet has both facilitated and provoked change in the performance of family life and the organisation of the household, while also indicating that families have maintained a sense of stability via the maintenance of their values systems. This indicates that despite the appropriation and intrusion of the internet, a concerted effort has been made to maintain a continued coherence. Evidence of both transformation and continuity can be recognised on different levels, opening the discussion of the internet and family life to manifold complexities and nuances. The processes of change and continuity can be recognised at a level of spatial and temporal organisation and the use of internet media to perform family relations. The material presented relating to family life and the maintenance of contact with family members reiterates the idea that second-generation internet use is closely bound with the existing patterns of communication that define everyday life and is deeply embedded in the 'familiar' as opposed to creating a new set of dynamics and behaviour patterns.

Notes

1 For a comprehensive exploration of these terms, see Silverstone (1994). In explicating the notion of 'home', Silverstone provides an understanding at a symbolic level: 'Home is a construct. It is a place not a space. It is the object of more or less intense emotion. It is where we belong ... Home can be anything from a nation to a tent or a neighbourhood. Home, substantial or insubstantial, fixed or shifting, singular or plural, is what we can make of it' (1994, p.26).

2 All names have been changed to protect the identity of the participants.

3 All the participants interviewed had access to the internet in their main 'family' home and accessed the internet through a PC.

4 This is a scheme run by the council, where houses are part owned by the council and the buyer, making the housing more affordable. The new estates that have emerged in Loughrock within the last five years, such as 'Loughrock Heights' and 'Kelly's Bay', are a combination of privately owned houses and part ownership.

References

Bakardjieva, M. (2001) 'Becoming a domestic internet user', paper presented at *E-Usages Conference*, Paris.

Baym, N.K. (1995) 'The emergence of community in computer mediated communication', in S. Jones (ed.) *Cybersociety: Computer mediated communication and community*, Thousand Oaks: Sage.

Baym, N.K. (1998) 'The emergence of online community', in S. Jones (ed.) *Cybersociety 2.0, Revisiting computer mediated communication and community*, Thousand Oaks: Sage.

Becher-Israeli, H. (1995) 'From <Bonehead>TO<cLoNehEAd>: nicknames, play and identity on internet relay chat', in *Journal of Computer Mediated Communication*, 1 (2) available: http://www.ascusc.org/jcmc/vol1/issue2/becher.

Berdayes, L. and V. Berdayes (1998) 'The information society in contemporary magazine narrative', in *Journal of Communication*, Spring 1998, 48 (2) pp.109–23.

Castells, M. (1996) *Network society*, Oxford: Blackwell.

Castells, M. (1997) *The power of identity*, London: Blackwell.

Castells, M. (2001) *The internet galaxy*, Oxford: Oxford University Press.

Dahlberg, L. (1998) 'Cyberspace and the public sphere: exploring the democratic potential of the net', in *Convergence*, 4 (1), pp.70–81.

Dahlberg, L. (2001) 'The Habermasian public sphere encounters cyber-reality', in *Javnost: The Public*, 8 (3), pp 83–96.

Danet, B. (1998) 'Text as mask: gender, play and performance on the internet', in S. Jones (ed.) *Cybersociety 2.0, Revisiting computer mediated communication and community*, Thousand Oaks: Sage.

Dodge, M. and R. Kitchin (2001) *Mapping cyberspace*, London: Routledge.

Featherstone, M. and R. Burrows (1995) *Cyberspace/Cyberbodies/Cyberpunk*, London: Sage.

Francissen, L. and K. Brants (1998) 'Virtually going places: square hopping in Amsterdam's digital city', in R. Tsagarousianou, D. Tambini, and C. Bryan (eds) *Cyberdemocracy: technology, cities and civic networks*, London: Routledge.

Hakken, D (1999) *Cyborgs@Cyberspace: An ethnographer looks to the future*, New York: Routledge.

Heim, M. (1998) *Virtual realism*, New York: Oxford University Press.

Hine, C. (2000) *Virtual ethnography*, London: Sage.

Jones, S. (1995, 1998) *Cybersociety: computer mediated communication and community*, Thousand Oaks: Sage.

Jones, S. (1997) *Virtual culture: identity and communication in cyberspace*, Thousand Oaks: Sage.

Lie, M. and K. Sorensen (1996) 'Making technology our own? Domesticating technology into everyday life', in M. Lie and K. Sorensen (eds) *Making technology our own? Domesticating technology into everyday life*, Oslo: Scandinavian University Press.

Lievrouw, L.A. and S. Livingstone (eds) (2002) 'The social shaping and consequences of ICTs', in L. Lievrouw and S. Livingstone *The handbook of new media*, London: Sage.

Loader, B.D. (ed.) (1998) *Cyberspace divide*, London: Routledge.

McRae, S. (1996) 'Coming apart at the scenes: sex, text and virtual body', in L. Cerney and E.B. Weise (eds) *Wired women*, Washington: Seal.

Marvin, C. (1999) 'When old technologies were new: implementing the future', in H. Mackay and T. O'Sullivan (eds) *The media reader: continuity and transformation*, London: Sage.

Meijer, I.C. (1998) 'Advertising citizenship: an essay on the performative power of consumer culture', in *Media, Culture And Society* 20 (2) pp 235–251, London: Sage.

Miller, D. and D. Slater (2000) *The internet: an ethnographic approach*, Oxford: Berg.

O'Donnell, S. (2001) 'Analysing the internet and the public sphere: the case of womenslink', in *Javnost: The Public*, 8 (1), pp.39–58.

Plant, S (1995) 'The future looms: weaving women and cybernetics', in M. Featherstone and R. Burrows (eds) *Cyberspace/Cyberbodies/Cyberpunk*, London: Sage.

Plant, S. (1997) *Zeros and ones: digital women and the new techno-culture*, London: Fourth Estate.

Porter, D. (1997) *Internet culture*, New York: Routledge.

Rausmussen, T (1999) 'New media change: sociological approaches to the study of new media', in J. Jensen and C. Toscan (eds) *Interactive television: TV of the future or the future of TV*, Denmark: Aolborg University Press.

Roscoe, T (1999) 'The construction of the world wide web audience', in *Media, Culture and Society*, 21 (5) pp.637–84, London: Sage.

Rushkoff, D. (1994) *Cyberia: life in the trenches of cyberspace*, London: Flamingo.

Rushkoff, D. (1997) *Children of chaos [Surviving the end of the world as we know it]*, London: Flamingo.

Schmidtke, O (1998) 'Berlin in the net: prospects for cyber-democracy from above and below', in R. Tsagarousianou, D. Tambini and C. Bryan (1998) (eds) *Cyberdemocracy: technology, cities and civic networks*, London: Routledge.

Seidler, V. J. (1998) 'Gender, nature and history', in J. Wood, *The virtual embodied*, London: Routledge.

Seiter, E. (1999) *Television and new media audiences*, Oxford: Oxford University Press.

Shields, R. (1996) *Cultures of internet*, London: Sage.

Silverstone, R. (1994) *Television and everyday life*, London: Routledge.

Silverstone, R. (1999) *Why study the media*, London, Sage.

Silverstone, R. and E. Hirsch (eds) (1992) *Consuming technologies: media and information in domestic spaces,* London: Routledge.

Silverstone, R., E. Hirsch and D. Morley (1992) 'Information and communication technologies and the moral economy of the household', in R. Silverstone and E. Hirsch (eds) *Consuming technologies: media and information in domestic spaces*, London: Routledge.

Slater, D. (2002) 'Social Relationships and Identity Online and Offline', in Lievrouw and S. Livingstone (eds) *The Handbook of New Media*, London: Sage.

Slevin, J. (2000) *The internet and society*, Cambridge: Polity.

Smith, R. and M. Bakardjieva (2001) 'The internet in everyday life: computer networking from the standpoint of the domestic user', in *New Media and Society*, 3 (1), pp.67–83, London: Sage.

Tsagarousianou, R., D. Tambini and C. Bryan (1998) [eds] *Cyberdemoncracy: technology, cities and civic networks*, London: Routledge.

Watson, N. (1997) 'Why we argue about virtual community', in S. Jones (ed.) *Virtual culture: identity and communication in cyberspace*, Thousand Oaks: Sage.

Wellman, B. and C. Haythornwaite (2002) *The Internet in Everyday Life*, MA: Blackwell.

Winston, B. (1998) *Media, technology and society: a history from the telegraph to the internet*, London: Routledge.

Wood, J. (1998) *The virtual embodied*, London: Routledge.

Young, J.R. (1994) 'Textuality in cyberspace: MUDS and written experience', available: http://eserver.org/cyber/young2.txt.

Appendix 1: Tables

Table 7.1 Participating Households

Interview No. and pseudonym	Number in household	Occupation	Ethnic group
1. Katherine and Brian	2 adults; 2 children (under 5)	Accountant; housewife and mature student	White – Irish
2. Peter, Margaret and Robert	3 adults (2 parents and 1 university student)	Housewife; management in ICT sector	White – Irish
3. Mandy, Simon, Jessica and Daniel	2 adults; 2 children (9 and 7)	Clerical worker; taxi driver	White – Irish
4. Janet and Gary	2 adults – children away at university	University lecturer; airport worker and part-time writer	White – Scottish
5. Jenny and Richard	2 adults; 3 children (4–11)	Both running own separate businesses	White – English
6. Sam and Joan	2 adults	Retired	White – Irish/English
7. Lucy and Alex	2 adults; 1 baby	Postgraduate students	White – Irish/ Romanian
8. James and Ellen	2 adults	Journalist; housewife	White – Irish
9. Joe, Mary and Sarah	2 adults; 2 children (4 and baby)	Own business (local shop); wife	White – Irish
10. Tim, Maggie, Emer and Rebecca	2 adults; 2 students (16 and 19)	Teacher; county council – admin	White – Irish
11. Rachel and Oliver	2 adults	Both employed in ICT sector	White – Irish
12. Stephen and Joanne	2 adults; 3 children (under 5)	Artist (own local gallery); housewife	White – Irish
13. Paul and Karen	2 adults; 2 children (8 and 3)	Manager; bank cashier	White – Irish
14. Terry and Liz	2 adults, 2 children (11 and 13 + friends of thirteen yr. old boy	Teacher; citizen advisor	White – Irish
15. Sam, Helen and Chris	2 adults; 1 'grown-up child' (stayed frequently at home, but lived in shared flat in Dublin)	Retired parents; graduate trainee manager – marketing	White – Irish

Interview No. and pseudonym	Number in household	Occupation	Ethnic group
16. Michael and Charlotte	2 adults; 4 children (under 5)	Own business; housewife	White – Irish/English
17. Marie and Patrick	2 adults; 5 children (11–21)	Housewife; manual worker	White – Irish
18. David	2 adults; 2 children (13 and 11)	Teacher; housewife	White – Irish
19. Vicky and Nick	2 adults; 1 child (baby)	Clerical worker; management	White – Irish
20. Jack and Ruth	2 adults; (grown 'child')	Teacher; nurse; (artist)	White – Irish

Chapter 8

The Everyday of Extreme Flexibility – The Case of Migrant Researchers' Use of New Information and Communication Technologies

Thomas Berker

Introduction

A recent European policy document, the *Council Decision on Guidelines for the Employment Policies of the Member States* (2003), promotes flexibility in order to 'facilitate the adaptation of workers and firms to economic change', but it also recognizes the need to aim at 'the right balance between flexibility and security'. There is obviously something attractive and at the same time dangerous about 'flexibility' – not only for European policy makers. In this chapter, I present an empirical study of individuals who live an everyday life of extreme flexibility – that is, migrant researchers. Their ultra-flexible floating-and-switching between places and times is accompanied by the heavy use of all kinds of technology, particularly transportation and ICTs.

The ability of ICTs to facilitate flexible working has been frequently claimed but seldom proved. The relationship between the potential of ICTs, their *uses* and the *consequences* of these uses, is by no means a trivial one and to assume a straight-forward realization of the potentials of the use of any technology is naïve at best. Therefore, this chapter is as much about flexibility as it is about the conditions of technology use in everyday life. Exploring the everyday life of individuals who are heavy users of ICTs and who are living and working in extraordinarily flexible ways yields insights into both phenomena. But it is necessary to first clarify what is meant by the potential within ICTs to increase flexibility in everyday life.

The Meaning of Flexibility

> A kitten is so flexible that she is almost double; the hind parts are equivalent to another kitten with which the forepart plays. She does not discover that her tail belongs to her until you tread on it (Henry David Thoreau).

The policy document referenced above makes a connection between adaptability and flexibility while suggesting that unbalanced flexibility is not desirable. This is in line with dictionary definitions of flexibility, which often stress the ability to bend without breaking and suggest the absence of coherent principles (see the *Oxford Dictionary*'s entry for flexibility). Both meanings refer to adaptation. In the first instance, it is adaptation that keeps the flexible entity intact ('not breaking'); in the second instance, doubt is raised about its integrity (loss of coherence). Thoreau's observation of the kitten's flexibility contains some amazement about her ability to bend, but he also notes that this comes at the price of her becoming fragmented into two parts – until you tread on her tail. In addition to notions of fragmentation and incoherence, there is another problem inherent in flexibility when it is defined as the ability to bend. It is difficult to ascertain the actual degree of flexibility, how far one can bend until one really breaks. Formal definitions of flexibility – for instance, as summarized by Koste et al. (2004) – introduce a quite specific point here. They suggest the need to measure the stress induced by assuming different 'range-heterogeneous' (that is, flexible) states. In other words, not only does flexibility exist until something breaks, but there also needs to be consideration of flexibility in the earlier stages, that is, when bending may be prone to produce negative consequences for the flexible entity, for instance, backache for the kitten when she bends too far.

Returning to flexibility in a work context, we can now ask who or what is bent without breaking, and who or what is in danger of becoming fragmented and penalized. But the relevant research literature frequently, rather than include a proper definition of flexibility, lists different ways to organize work temporally, spatially, and/or functionally – such as part-time, fixed-term and seasonal work, telework and flexi-time agreements, to mention only a few. The single common element in these alternative work arrangements is that they depart from 'normal' work organization in terms of space and time – the normal case being working at one work place provided by the employer, from 'nine to five' and from Monday to Friday.

Hall and Richter (1988) suggest a more precise and concise definition of flexible work. They distinguish between 'boundary flexibility' – the extent to which time and location markers between domains of everyday life are moveable – and 'boundary permeability' – the ease with which the concerns of one domain enter another one. Routines in everyday life are always already ordered in a spatial and temporal sense (Schütz and Luckmann, 1974). In the daily routines of most people, work is a distinct domain defined spatially and temporally. There are considerable efforts to establish and maintain these boundaries (Hardill et al., 1996; Nippert-Eng, 1996; Mirchandani, 1998; Yttri, 1999). Furthermore, there also seems to be considerable dangers of bending them and making them more porous. Martens et al. (1999) found that flexible work is clearly related to health hazards and there are accounts that warn about overworked workers (Schor, 1993; Bratberg et al., 1999) who neglect their homes and children when work takes over their entire everyday life (Hochschild, 1997). These diagnoses assume that there have to be spaces and times that are protected from work. Flexibility is seen as levelling out differences between work and non-work. In terms of the Hall and Richter definition (1988), the boundary between work and non-work is bent until it breaks. The resulting configurations generally seem to be characterized by a loss of coherence and increased fragmentation, but also by new hybrids where work and non-work may emerge as a kind of unity (Tietze and Musson, 2002).

Most studies on failing boundaries acknowledge that the modern separation of work and non-work is neither natural nor pre-given, but subject to 'boundary work' and individual variation. These practices regarding the order of time and space in everyday life are deeply intertwined with the use of all kinds of techniques and technologies, above all with modern means of transportation, information and communication. That there is, for instance, a connection between new ICTs and flexible work arrangements has been claimed since the 1970s (for an early example see Nilles et al., 1976). However, we know little about the actual role of technologies such as ICTs in these processes – beyond the familiar observation that they have an undeniable *potential* to change the spatial and temporal order of everyday life, bending boundaries and/or making them more porous. In this chapter, I present the results of a study of a group of heavy users of new ICTs who work under extremely flexible conditions both in a temporal and spatial sense. The aim is to shed light on the complex relation between space, time and technology in everyday life.

The Space of Technologies

In the Descartian and Kantian tradition, space is seen as a formal container, existing as co-ordinates and measurable distances in Euclidean space. Here, human experience is seen as always and already situated in absolute space. Henri Lefebvre (1991) advocated a different view. He questions the notion of absolute space and prefers instead the notion of a specific form of capitalist production of space that colonizes the space produced in everyday life-worlds. This denaturalization of absolute space is at the heart of every account of *social spaces*, that is, relative spaces created by social interaction and communication. It is no coincidence that the idea of relative spaces should emerge in the twentieth century. From the beginning of this century, mighty machines of transportation and communication have eroded the apparent solidity of absolute space. The development since has been uni-directional and is moving towards substantial increases in scope, affordability and the velocity of these machines. Anthony Giddens (1984) calls this time-space distantiation: the detachment of social interaction from corporeal co-presence and stresses the paramount importance of these processes for modernity.

Although time-space distantiation is inconceivable without technology, when we explore the use of ICTs and their role in ongoing time-space distantiation, we cannot take for granted that they – despite their undisputed potential – really are used in ways which alter social space towards the proposed detachment of social interaction and physical co-presence. Too often, the existence of a technology, and the potential access to it, is confused with its use. We know, for instance, that access to computer networks does not necessarily lead to use (Abels et al., 1996), and this suggests that there are always other variables involved which mediate access and use. Those factors have been explored in in-depth analyses of computer supported collaborative work (CSCW), for example in the comparison of a local and a transnational academic online-network conducted by Koku et al. (2001). They observed that those who work more closely with each other make more use of email. Since email provides access, but not necessarily a reason to communicate, peripheral nodes of the network do not experience a higher degree of inclusion. The study shows not only that frequent email communication is accompanied by frequent face-to-face encounters, but also that email use correlates positively with other ways of communicating. Thus, users maintain social relations choosing a broad range of means of communication including face-to-face encounters.

Matzat (2001), in a study of the use of mailing lists and newsgroups, concludes that the success or failure of electronic communication networks is highly dependent on their adaptation to broader social networks existing outside the electronic networks. The conclusion we can draw from these results is that ties entertained outside the electronic encounters are indispensable for the success of computer-mediated communication. Thus, for ICTs to play a role within time-space distantiation at all, they will have to be embedded in other social encounters, which are also happening under the conditions of time-space distantiation.

Things get even more complicated when we acknowledge that use can change the very technology that is used. Empirical research inspired by studies on 'domestication' (Silverstone and Hirsch, 1992; Lie and Sørensen, 1996) show that the creative appropriation of technology through its users involves a broad variety of actions, which enable it to be fitted into the everyday life of the user. The topic of this chapter – ICTs – which is, in any event, a heterogeneous construct, becomes even less certain, when we include these user activities within the scope of our study. We cannot assume that we know exactly what kind of technology we are studying, and even the most basic assumption – that they play a role within time-space distantiation – is problematic. After all, ICTs can also be used to avoid communication, for instance, through the application of filtering devices. We may also find that, in line with Koku et al.'s (2001) observations, ICTs are often and perhaps preferably used to initiate and organize corporeal co-presence (for example, writing an email to the colleague next door to invite him to lunch). All this is subject to empirical exploration.

Migrant Researchers' Use of ICTs

Despite this complexity and uncertainty, we are still interested in the role of ICTs in time-space distantiation both in terms of what ICTs are and what they do. There is an undisputed technical potential for a reorganization of social spaces, the bending of boundaries, de-territorialization and re-territorialization, which I will explore here. When seeking to approach these processes empirically, it is necessary first to make sure that there *is* use at all, preferably heavy use. Drawing on what was said about the embedding of use in other social networks, the researcher would expect, and wish to study, groups which include heavy users, that is those who are, perhaps most typically, working in professions which involve intensive use of ICTs. Secondly, and again informed by deliberations from the previous section of this chapter, it is necessary to ensure that those individuals included in the study used electronic networks as part of a wider social network, one which covers distances large enough to expect that mediated communication is likely to happen. The decision in this study, therefore, was to focus on migrant knowledge workers, a group which fulfils both requirements particularly well.

The sociology of science acknowledged very early on the crucial role of international and transnational networks in the academic production of knowledge.

These analyses of, for instance, co-authorship in scholarly journals or 'citation networks' show how 'invisible colleges' (Price and de Solla, 1963; Crane, 1972) cross national boundaries, boundaries of institutions and sometimes even disciplines. Given the transnational orientation of modern science, it is not surprising that in the early 1970s scholars were the first users of the internet and its predecessors. When it finally attracted the attention of a broader public, from 1993 onwards, users with high levels of formal education were significantly over-represented among the user population (see the archive of the GVU-Survey, www.gvu.org). The main services provided by the internet were developed as tools for scholars to use remote computing facilities (Telnet); a little later these were also used to co-ordinate these dispersed experiments or just to stay in touch (email, chat); and finally in the late 1980s there emerged the software and the protocols to link and access heterogeneous resources (the web). Universities and research institutions provided their members with email addresses and access to the web very early on. Therefore, this group is the one with the highest proportion of 'internet veterans' in its ranks.

The obvious link between scholarly activities in international and transnational networks and ICTs has been explored since the early 1990s. Similar results have been affirmed in repeated studies. Firstly, communication rather than information has the most far-reaching consequences within academia. Roberta Lamb and Elizabeth Davidson (2002), for instance, describe that the use of the web by oceanographers only marginally, and in rather restricted areas, affects the ways of presenting oneself in the academic community or to a broader public. Furthermore, they maintain that publishing is still a paper affair, largely due to strong institutional pressures. This is in line with Rob Kling and Geoffrey McKim's (1999) insight that the publication of a document not only affords global accessibility, but also the achievement of publicity and trustworthiness. Among the services provided by electronic networks, it is not computer conferencing, mobile communication devices, databases or the web which provide the glue for 'the virtual college'. As every researcher knows from his/her own experience, email is reported to be the most important addition to the broad range of communication channels existing in the academic context. In a quantitative user survey John Walsh and his colleagues (Walsh, 1998; Walsh et al., 1999) observed clear impacts of email use on academic work, in increasing scientific contact, in providing better access to information, and in generating positive impacts on scientific collaboration and productivity (measured in the number of publications, however).

Method

Compared with their stationary colleagues, migrant researchers have additional reasons to use ICTs. Their migration is not forced and they usually have the resources at their disposal to maintain regular and intense contact with their home country, through frequent travel and the heavy use of ICTs (Smith and Guarnizo, 1998; Portes et al., 1999; Vertovec, 2002). The findings presented here, in this chapter, are based on 20 in-depth interviews with such transnational migrants. The interviews were carried out in Trondheim, Norway (twelve interviews) and Darmstadt, Germany (eight interviews) between October 2001 and January 2002. The longest one (Bart) took approximately 130 minutes, the shortest (Leo) 75 minutes. Participants in Trondheim were recruited in three ways:

(i)   An email was sent to all participants of the language summer school 2001 (resulting in six interviews).
(ii)   The personnel department of a large Norwegian research institution forwarded a request to every non-Norwegian employee (four interviews).
(iii) Snowballing resulted in two more interviews.

In Germany snowballing (three cases), personal contact[1] (three cases) and an email to an email list to which 'Erasmus students' subscribed (two cases) were used to recruit participants. All interviews but one were conducted in English. Although the command of English was generally quite good in this group, there were considerable differences, mostly related to age and professional experience. Mistakes were not corrected in the transcriptions.

The interviewees were selected according to the following criteria: they should have worked in research or studied abroad for not less than three months at the time of the interview, and have planned a stay of not less than one year altogether. Despite these 'soft' criteria, the resulting group of participants was relatively homogeneous, at least in some respects. Even though there are 13 nationalities present, most of them were European (Eastern Europe: seven cases; Western Europe: six cases). The youngest participants (24 and older) were students in their final years (four interviews). The largest group consisted of PhD students (eight interviews). The rest was working as a professor (one case), as a post-doctoral researcher (one case) or as so-called senior researchers mostly in permanent positions (six cases). The latter group contained also the oldest participants (of which the oldest was 42 years old). As for the research disciplines the participants were working in, there was a moderate bias towards geology (five cases). Absent from the selection were participants from the humanities and social sciences. This was for one major reason: the two field sites, Trondheim and Darmstadt, are technological hubs in their respective countries with a large technical university in each and several important research institutions. Thus, both cities reveal aspects of what Manuel Castells, exploring the 'New Industrial Space', calls 'milieus of innovation' (1996, pp.386–93). They attract researchers from all over the world and constitute nodes that are rooted in their specific locality within global flows of individuals, goods and information.

The main instrument used to structure the interviews was a thematic interview guide. It consisted of two overarching sections. One was designed to establish a detailed inventory of daily activities in relation to media usage. The second specifically explored knowledge creation and transfer. The interviews, where possible, were conducted in the office of the respondent; this provided additional observational data recorded right after the interview.

Bending and Permeating Boundaries

The interviewees' social networks are, in Manuel Castells' words, 'projected throughout the world'. This has two elements. Firstly, there is generally little contact with locals. Even, in some cases, after many years in the guest country, the informants found it difficult to connect to them. Secondly, significant others and colleagues were often living in other countries, most often the country of origin. Joan, an American geologist living in Trondheim, explained that this degree of separation is not (or not only) because of cultural differences:

> ... a lot of my socializing occurs with people from work. And a lot of them are foreigners and a number of them are like me, single with no children. And so sometimes it is simpler as a group to socialize in the evenings just as a natural process as a lot of folks with small kids can't always come out and so forth.

Joan's partner was living in France. Thus, she was a member of one of the eight dispersed households that were encountered in this study. A closer look at this group of long-distance relationships reveals considerable heterogeneity. There were as many instances where the migrant researcher had left his/her partner behind in the country of origin, as there were cases of the partner living in a third country. Some had met first in this third country, some in the home country, some in the host country. There was even a case where the partners had met in a fourth country, when both had been on holiday.

The existence of dispersed households questions the assumption of a natural siting of households. The physical boundaries around the household are usually imagined as being one with boundaries around the physical home. Within this perspective, being a member of a household that is dispersed represents a case of bending these boundaries, or at least a case of stretching them, to use another metaphor.

In the case of the migrant researchers interviewed here, similar observations were made in the professional sphere. A reoccurring motivation for migration was work-related. The use, maintenance and establishment of international linkages between individuals and institutions were considered as crucial moments within professional activities. Marc, a geologist from Luxemburg, who at the time of the interview had been staying in Norway for a little more than three years, explained this motivation most poignantly:

> You need connections, you must go to meetings, you must maintain connections. It is extremely important to have a network, extremely important. That is the only way you get a job, basically, unless you are extremely good. You get post docs, no problem, you get research, I've had that for ten years. Until I came here it was always two years, three years, one-year contracts, five years was the last one. So that is very easy, but to get a permanent job, where you can develop your research on your own and a research group, is much more tricky and there you need a network.

These considerations about professional careers emerged more strongly in interviews with researchers from Eastern Europe. They were often left little choice but to migrate. Another special trait of migrants from Eastern Europe is that their social networks are even more spatially spread than those of other migrants. Most of their former colleagues and fellow students had migrated as well, and were living all over the globe. Though this was most evident among migrants from Eastern Europe, it also applied to the rest of the sample. Migratory movement *per se* was by no means the only activity of migrating researchers, which involves the crossing of national boundaries. Frequent travel to conferences, workshops and other professional gatherings were commonly accepted as an integral part of the job. Thus, the social space of work reached out far beyond the office, and collaborations with researchers working in faraway places are common. Again, boundaries are being bent and stretched.

Another activity, which involves the routine crossing of boundaries or even continents, is based on the use of a broad range of communication and information devices. Here, the flexibility of usage attracted particular attention. The interviewees, asked to describe which media they are using, when and to achieve what, could go on for hours specifying the broad variety of tools they had used or were using routinely. Maria, a geologist from Italy living in Trondheim, for instance, said that she usually typed her letters to her parents on the PC, printed the letters out, and sent them via fax, because the fax was the machine whose complexity could be mastered by her parents. Other interviewees mentioned the use of intermediaries, such as a brother or sister who delivered emails to offline relatives. The interviewees were usually continuously online at least during the work hours. They were equipped with broadband online access. Those working in Norway, especially, praised the technical equipment provided in the work place.

Email, out of a wide variety of ICTs, was clearly the preferred means of both professional and private communication. Usage was often quite varied and took different shapes, for instance the exchange of long letters, draft papers and articles, but also short messages, which were described by Bart, a Dutch geologist working in Norway: 'Sometimes an email is more convenient; you can just key in one sentence and that's it and then send it. You can do this even when you haven't spoken to a person for a long time.' When Lea, a Lithuanian chemist living in Trondheim, compared email with the telephone, she mentioned another advantage of email: 'I don't use telephone, because I think email is the best for me. When – you know – who will read it when he has time and he will answer me, because you are not sure when you phone, what the person is doing. I don't like this.'

Email is asynchronous communication and considered to be less intrusive. Joan discussed two more advantages of email, which related to the specific situation of migrant researchers:

> … since I'm in this country and sometimes it's people in the United States and I need to contact colleagues, it's not the time difference, 'Are they awake? No. Ok, wait until 7pm.' and so forth. … And also in the Norwegian context – as you will probably know – in the early stages it was such a nightmare talking on the phone. O my god! It was just terrific, because you understand three words out of the 25.

Later in this chapter, I will highlight the concern not to be too intrusive, a courtesy that was also appreciated in return. For now, it is possible to say that email was considered to be the most versatile means of communication; valued for being asynchronous but allowing short response-times, and being text-based but informal.

The research also gave rise to similar patterns of behaviour in relation to information searches as for communication. Again, a broad range of sources was used, including offline sources. Sabine, an Austrian graduate student in geophysics, who lived in Trondheim, summarized a common position, when she said:

... and then we are discussing things and then maybe someone read an article and said: 'Hey Sabine take a look at that thing and it's quite interesting maybe for you as well!' and that makes things easier than to keep the paper. And sometimes you find more stuff if you go to this link by yourself ... and it's quite ok. It makes things much easier and you can get a much more wide-eyed view of things. You are not stuck to one opinion, so if you want you can get more opinions on that.

This particular mix of offline and online sources was very common. In this quotation, Sabine also alluded to accessing scientific literature through the WWW, which was mentioned in every interview. This access was often provided through gateways provided by libraries, but also through the respective professional associations. But in addition, some interviewees routinely used the 'open' areas of the web even though this was generally not considered to be very effective. Ares, an Iranian engineer working in Trondheim put his reservations like this:

... you can easily sit there and just get through it without accomplishing something in just six hours. Just go in <snaps his fingers> an eye blink. I think, that it also could happen that you don't really get [what you were looking for], or that you cannot really educate yourself. You are only wasting your time, so you should be careful.

Almost every respondent listed a broad range of areas where the WWW was used as a research tool. Manuel, a Bulgarian computer engineer working in Darmstadt, probably represented the clearest example of this when he said that he was using it to get 'any information in my private life <laughs>'. He reported that even when he looked for the address of a friend, he just searched his or her name on the Net. Yet, this was only possible because within his circle of friends and acquaintances it was common to publish such information on the web. However, within the group interviewed here, only a minority provided information through the web. Much more common was the use of the web to search for travel-related information, like airfares, connections or regional information about the place to be visited. Interviewees also searched for information about the prices of consumer goods but when it came to buying, with the exception of books, more often traditional ways were preferred.

To sum up, in this section I have sketched the image of migrant individuals who are significantly dispersed throughout the world. They barely socialize with locals and are much more at home in international networks, both in their professional and private life. Their everyday life is characterized by frequent travel and use of a broad variety of technical means of communication and information. In these contexts, they switch between technical and non-technical communication partners and between all kinds of information sources. All kinds of boundaries seem to be seriously weakened.

Problematic Flexibility

But the observations presented in the previous section only tell one of three sides of the story; the other two will be told here. The first of these is based on a series of observations, which in return relate to situations in which flexibility becomes problematic. The episodes and statements cited above suggest far-reaching flexibility – that much is true – but they also highlight factors that pose clear restrictions on these processes.

Not being able to be co-present with a partner and/or a family was a major source of discontent with their current lives. 'Some day', they say, they will move into the country where their partner or family lives. This was commonly expressed by those who lived in dispersed households. At the time of the interview, the desire to be together with partners and family was clearly a factor, which explained the fundamental state of transience in which those interviewees found themselves, even after years of stay in the host country. Borjas' statement that '[i]mmigration is a family affair' (1990, p.177) also applies to this special group. Depending on the situation in which the migrant found him or herself, the location of partners and family could become the main reason for migration. For instance, Tamara and Irina, two of the Russian interviewees, who had applied for jobs in Germany and Norway respectively, had done so to be with their partner.

Even though the wish to reunite households and families encouraged migration and undermined settling in, it also marked a limit to flexibility. The majority of interviewees said that 'at least some day in the future' they *wanted* to end the state of dispersion. This is why they kept open the option to move to their loved ones or facilitate the movement of their loved ones to them. Particularly when it came to a comparison of technically mediated and non-mediated contact with partner and family, the migrants living in dispersed households explicitly stressed the absolute indispensability of physical contact. This, for instance in Joan's case, appeared as a concern for her aging mother, who may have needed the assistance of her daughter in the near future. Marc and Maria, a couple of geologists from Luxembourg/Italy living in Trondheim, stressed that they wanted their children to grow up with their otherwise remote grandparents.

The other side of this story was complaints about too frequent travel. Age seemed to be an issue here: the older the interviewees were, the more likely they were to report having tried to reduce travelling to a necessary minimum. However, this could still mean a considerable degree of mobility, induced by both personal and professional needs.

Another group of observations about the limits of flexibility concern the professional sphere. The interviewees had a significant amount of control over where and when they did their work. This involved a considerable degree of spatial and temporal flexibility, which was, however, in every case restricted by external factors. To be dependent on special apparatuses and equipment meant not only a spatial but also a temporal restriction, because of the need to co-ordinate machine times or to observe ongoing experiments. Jozef – who was working with the most expensive piece of equipment of all, a particle accelerator in Germany – reported that the rhythm of the experiments, which took place only several times a year, fundamentally influenced his work rhythm. Other occasions of similarly restrictive nature reported in the interviews included conferences, deadlines for papers of all sorts, meetings and presentations. Another spatial restriction within the work context – and mentioned in every interview – stemmed from the dependence in scientific collaboration on at least occasional physical co-presence. This meant travel and the need for schedules to be synchronized.

Accounts about the limits of media use were most often about problems of concentration. Email, because of its crucial role, was mentioned most often here. Joan, for instance, had disabled the acoustic signal that would inform her about incoming email, but she still noticed the 'grunting noise' that the hard-drive made when new mail arrived and was interrupted by it. Complaints about not being able to finish job related tasks, which required undisturbed concentration, such as writing papers, were evident in almost every interview, and led to many different strategies and efforts to structure places and times.

These strategies are the third side of the story, which will be discussed in the next section. For now, though, the interviews contain accounts of situations where spatial and temporal flexibility – in terms of personal and professional relationships, work hours and spaces as well as accessibility through all kinds of media – turn against the flexible individual. Then, flexibility – otherwise crucial in the management of everyday life – causes stress and suffering, and is considered, consequently, to be a problem.

Deliberations and Negotiations

Thus far, attention has been paid mainly to dispersed households. Two of the interviewees, Marc and Maria, however, represented the 'minimal dispersion' case. Marc, when he applied for work in Trondheim, had made it part of the deal that his wife would get work at the same institution. Moreover, there was a kindergarten very close to their work place where both children (two and four years old) spent the day. The whole family was united under one roof almost around the clock. As a nuclear family they lived, thus, maybe in an even less dispersed way than the majority of non-migrating families. However, this situation had been actively created in negotiations with the employer. Marc was apparently in sufficiently strong a position to make non-dispersion possible. This, and the nearby kindergarten, explicitly played a role in their decision to move to Norway. However, as was mentioned earlier, Marc and Maria were considering a move back to 'Central Europe', to be closer to the rest of the family.

So, there is constant negotiation and deliberation going on, weighing the advantages and disadvantages of working and living in a particular place. Deliberations about where and how to live, which question even the most basic conditions of everyday life, were present in many of the interviews. Such deliberations focus on the relationship between work and non-work and also on the question of what a home might be. These active orderings and questioning of the spaces and times of everyday routine were closely related to deliberations about where and when to use certain media. The most basic practice observed was the plain refusal to use certain media. Many interviewees refused to use mobile phones altogether, trying to avoid being accessible through this additional channel. Manuel elaborated on the reasons for this:

Maybe I will get one [a mobile phone] later. It's good, sometimes on the weekend when you are out somewhere, reachable. On the other hand, it's an extra source of additional tasks or work, because the more ways you can be reached, the more ways you can get some extra work.

Manuel expected the boundary between work and non-work to be affected by having a mobile phone. In this quote, he discusses the pros and cons. He clearly had thought about it before, but careful deliberation had led to a refusal. Apart from such a plain refusal, other more complex patterns of the deliberate management of media access were more common, for instance, in relation to the answering of email or whether to have internet access at home. These negotiations and deliberations are not without friction and tend to be in constant flux. And, with the next project, with new colleagues and new tasks, with a new ICT (like the mobile phone, for instance), a new challenge may await the interviewees. Experience and age seems to make no difference, since both some of the youngest and the oldest interviewees reported the same problems.

Still, there were some constant factors. The majority of interviewees defended the boundaries between work and non-work and between home and work. Grete, a Danish geologist working in Trondheim, expressed this explicitly: 'I think I have always kept work at work and spare time at home. I find it a bit complicated to start work at home, so you never relax, your brain is never off and I like being off when I get home.'

The likelihood of the separation of work and non-work coinciding with the boundaries of the home was closely related to the absence of internet access at home. Mia put it like this: 'It is kind of made this way [that there is no internet access at home]. My boyfriend, he is also, he does a lot of programming as well. Then we don't want to come home and sit in front of the screen again, that's terrible.' Here, the domestic sphere was deliberately constructed as a place without internet access. In conversation with Joan she noted, with some surprise, that in terms of media there was no way into her home, no telephone, no internet, no TV and not even a radio. In these cases, the traditional boundary between the private and the public sphere was reinforced and made even more impermeable than ever.

In this section, deliberations and negotiations have been explored as the third side of the story about extreme flexibility. The situations in which the interviewees experience flexibility as problematic, such as those presented in the previous section, are the motivation to establish new boundaries and are used as argument and reason in deliberations, arguments and reasons which concern the fundamental structures of everyday life, like where, when and with whom to communicate, to work or to relax.

Cyborgs, Victims and Problem Solvers

The three-sided story told here has a number of implications for time-space distantiation and the role of ICTs.

Firstly, there is the focus on creative aspects of extreme flexibility. The transnational individuals, a hybrid of culture and nationality, that have been described here are switching cunningly between places and times. Where others take a bus to work, they take the plane to meet colleagues from all over the world. Hyper-mobility in work and dispersed households, as well as all kinds of ICTs, are routine elements of their everyday life. An exclusive concentration on their accounts where they talk about their flexible life justifies the conclusion that they represent a group living the everyday life of extreme time-space distantiation.

How these individuals relate to the technologies of information, communication and transport, is best described by Donna Haraway's cyborg metaphor (1991). An everyday life of extreme time-space distantiation does not exist without the significant interference of a broad set of technologies. This indispensability of technology is captured with the cyborg metaphor. If one were to take away the technology, the cyborg would cease to exist; similarly, the hyper-flexible everyday life would turn into something else without technology. This perspective would suggest that the accounts of problematic flexibility as presented here in the second side of the story could be about failing hybridization. Joan, for instance, was completely dependent on email in her everyday life, but she was also distracted by the hard-drive's 'grunting noise'. The 'grunting hard-drive' enabled her to manage time-space distantiation, but it also caused distractions, which obstructed the ability to concentrate on her work.

Deliberations and negotiations – the third side of the story – are, within the cyborg metaphor, a kind of cyborgish self-repair. Joan had deliberately switched off the 'ping', which notified her of an incoming email and she continued to experiment to make all the pieces work smoothly together.

In terms of the second side of the story, the interviewees appeared as victims of time-space distantiation: of mobility and technology. Their suffering and dysfunctionalities were at the centre of attention here. Forced into lives which they often could not handle, they sought refuge with their loved ones and at home. According to this perspective, all deliberations and negotiations are actually about protection and liberation. Indeed, it can also be said that Joan was protecting herself from intrusions forced upon her, when she switched off the email 'ping'. Technology is ambivalent from this point of view, to say the least. It is a necessary evil, which has to be kept at bay at all times. The consequential normative idea of a 'good' life is therefore based on 'real', that is, corporeal, social relations, and not virtual ones.

Lastly, the third side of the story assesses both extreme time-space distantiation including the heavy use of transportation and communication technology, as well as the limiting factors or problems that need to be solved. Here, the kind of everyday life explored in this chapter is characterized mainly by its high degree of reflexivity, one that is always questioning daily routines and never accepting the present. Everyday life can be described as a circle starting with conscious decisions, which then sink into the doxic realm of the unconsciousness of routine, until they re-emerge to be adapted to new circumstances, and so on (Wilk, 1999). The focus on the deliberations and negotiations of everyday life in turn involves a stress on the ability to cope reflexively with routines. Technology, in this version of the story, is mainly seen in its tool-like quality and any limiting dysfuntionalities are interpreted as the result of wrong use or faulty technology.

Tietze and Musson (2002), in their study of professionals working at home, come to a similar conclusion. They too describe individuals with a large degree of reflexivity with respect to the relationship between home and work. According to them, problems resulting from fragmentation of time and unification of space (home and work) are solved by applying self-reflexive coping strategies.

Instances of problematic flexibility appear from the cyborg perspective as failing hybridization, which have to be 'repaired'. From the perspective of the victim metaphor, flexibility appears as threat, and deliberate actions are then seen as defensive and – if successful – liberating. The perspective of pragmatic problem solving, finally, assesses flexibility as a problem and recommends negotiations and deliberations in order to come to the best possible solution.

All three interpretations are based on a particular set of values and fundamental appraisals of technologies, which are widespread not only in technology studies, but also in society. Therefore, it is not surprising that they can be found in the interviews as well. And they all have their respective blind spots: they are all 'wrong' in a certain way. The cyborg metaphor does not account for situations when the interviewees clearly draw a line between themselves and the technologies they use, for instance, when they refuse to let PCs enter the domestic sphere. Exclusively describing the interviewees as victims of time-space distantiation forced upon them does not cover those activities which embrace technologies and put them to instrumental use. Describing migrant researchers, lastly, as self-reflexive problem solvers misses both the cyborg-like incorporation of technologies into everyday life and the episodes where technologies are experienced as irresistible yet adversarial intruders.

Thus, I insist on not reducing the story to one of its sides. These migrant researchers, who live under the condition of extreme time-space distantiation, are cyborgs, victims and problem solvers at the same time. Technologies are an embodied part of their everyday life: they are intrusive forces as well as mere tools.

The same applies to the question of extreme flexibility. Thoreau's flexible kitten becomes aware that her hind part and forepart belong together, when someone treads on her. Similarly, the individuals studied here become aware of limits in their ability to bend when they begin to suffer under dispersion, fragmentation and incoherence. The kitten does not reason and shortly after the unpleasant experience of being kicked, she hunts her hind parts again. The interviewees are more reasonable and try to find ways which allow them to achieve as much flexibility as possible, while admitting as much rigidity as necessary. This work with time, space and technology constitutes the everyday of extreme flexibility.

Note

1 Due to privacy laws it is actually impossible to get lists where foreigners are distinguished from non-foreign employees. So, I walked around at the University of Darmstadt for a while and asked those people I ran into for foreign colleagues.

References

Abels, E.G., P. Liebscher and D.W. Denman (1996) *Factors that influence the use of electronic networks by Science and Engineering Faculty at Small Institutions*, Part I. Queries. *Journal of the American Society for Information Science*, 47 (2), pp.146–58.

Borjas, G.J. (1990) 'The ties that bind: the immigrant family', in G.J. Borjas, *Friends or strangers: the impact of immigrants on the U.S.*, New York: Basic Books.

Bratberg, E., S.Å. Dahl and A.E. Risa (1999) *'The double burden'. Are modern females overworked by career and family?* Bergen: HEB, Program for helseøkonomi i Bergen.

Castells, M. (1996) *The rise of the network society: the information age: economy, society, and culture*, Massachusetts: Blackwell Publishers.

Council of the European Union (2003) Council Decision on 22 July 2003, *Guidelines for the employment policies of the member states* (2003/578/EC) www.europa.eu.int/eur-lex/pri/en/oj/dat/2003/l_197/l_19720030805en00130021.pdf.

Crane, D. (1972) *Invisible colleges. Diffusion of knowledge in scientific communities*, Chicago: University of Chicago Press.

Giddens, A. (1984) *The constitution of society*, Cambridge: Polity Press.

Hall, D.T. and J. Richter (1988) 'Balancing work life and home life: what can organizations do to help?', *Academy of Management Executive*, 2 (3), pp.213–23.

Haraway, D. (1991) 'A cyborg manifesto: science, technology, and socialist-feminism in the late twentieth century', in D. Haraway, *Simians, cyborgs and women. The reinvention of nature*, London: Free Association Books.

Hardill, I., A.E. Green and A.C. Dudleston (1996) 'The "blurring of boundaries" between "work" and "home": perspectives from case studies in the East Midlands', *Area*, 29 (3), pp.335–43.

Hochschild, A.R. (1997) *The time bind: when work becomes home and home becomes work*, New York: Metropolitan Books.

Kling, R. and G. McKim (1999) 'Scholarly communication and the continuum of electronic publishing', *Journal of the American Society for Information Science*, 50 (10), pp.890–906.

Koku, E., N. Nazer, and B. Wellman (2001) 'Netting scholars: online and offline', *American Behavioural Scientist*, 44 (10), pp.1752–74.

Koste, L., K.M. Malhotra and S. Sharma (2004) 'Measuring dimensions of manufacturing flexibility', *Journal of Operations Management*, 22, pp.171–96.

Lamb, R. and E. Davidson (2002) *Social scientists: managing identity in socio-technical networks*, Big Island, Hawaii: IEEE.

Lefebvre, H. (1991) *The production of space*, Oxford: Blackwell.

Lie, M and K.H. Sørensen (1996) *Making technology our own? Domesticating technology into everyday life*, Oslo: Scandinavian University Press.

Martens, M., F.J.N. Nijhuis, M.P.J. Van Boxtel and J.A. Knottnerus, (1999) 'Flexible work schedules and mental and physical health. A study of a working population with non-traditional working hours', *Journal of Organizational Behaviour*, 20, pp.35–46.

Matzat, U. (2001) *Social networks and cooperation in electronic communities: a theoretical-empirical analysis of academic communication and internet discussion groups*, Groningen: University Library Groningen.

Mirchandani, K. (1998) 'Protecting the boundary. Teleworkers insights on the expansive concept of "work"', *Gender and Society*, 12 (2), pp.168–87.

Nilles, J.M., P. Gray, F.R. Carlson Jr and J Gerhard (1976) *The telecommunications-transportation trade-off: options for tomorrow*, New York: Wiley & Sons.

Nippert-Eng, C.E. (1996) *Home and work: negotiating boundaries through everyday life*, Chicago: University of Chicago Press.

Portes, A., L.E. Guarnizo and P. Landolt (1999) 'The study of transnationalism: pitfalls and promise of an emergent research field', *Ethnic and Racial Studies*, 22 (2), pp.217–37.

Price, D. and J. de Solla. (1963) *Little science, big science*, New York: Columbia University Press.

Schor, J.B. (1993) *The overworked American: the unexpected decline of leisure*, New York: Basic Books.

Schütz, A. and T. Luckmann (1974) *The structures of the life-world*, London: Heinemann.

Silverstone, R. and E. Hirsch (1992) *Consuming technologies: media and information in domestic spaces*, London: Routledge.

Smith, M.P. and L.E. Guarnizo (1998) 'The locations of transnationalism', in M.P. Smith and L.E. Guarnizo, *Transnationalism from below*, New Brunswick, N.J.: Transaction Publishers.

Tietze, S. and G. Musson (2002) 'When "work" meets "home". Temporal flexibility as lived experience', *Time & Society*, 11 (2/3), pp.315–34.

Vertovec, S. (2002) 'Transnational networks and skilled labour migration', *Transnational Communities Seminar*: Oxford University.

Walsh, J.P. (1998) 'Scientific communication and scientific work: a survey of four disciplines', *Internet Research*, 8 (4), pp.363–66.

Walsh, J.P., S. Kucker, N. Maloney and S.M. Gabbay (1999) 'Connecting minds: CMC and scientific work', *Journal of the American Society for Information Science*, 51 (14), pp.1295–305.

Wilk, R. (1999) *Towards a useful theory of consumption*, European Council for an Energy Efficient Economy, Paris: ADEME.

Yttri, B. (1999) 'Homework and boundary work', *Telektronikk*, 95 (4), pp.39–47.

Chapter 9

The Discourse of the Perfect Future – Young People and New Technologies

Maren Hartmann

Some stories which researchers analyse are both new and at the same time familiar. The story that is to be told here is the story of young people and new media. The more familiar part of this story is the dominant discourse of the web-generation. In this discourse, young people are described as extensive users of new technologies and as people whose future world will be a radically new one. The discourse, however, provides little actual evidence of these changes. The less familiar part of the story about young people and new media is that told by young people themselves. This side of the story does contain evidence of changes, albeit without the extreme claims of the web-generation discourse.[1] The young people's stories qualify and differentiate the web-generation discourse. For example, their stories clearly show that the young people in question ultimately do not embrace new media on all levels. Indeed, their perceptions often contradicted the expectations that have been raised. Instead, the adoption of new media appeared to be in part frightening and problematic, partly because of the pressure to conform to high expectations. This pressure found an outlet in a clear condemnation of new media use by other people.

New media technologies will, very likely, change our societies in radical ways; therefore, it is important to understand current adoption procedures. Young people's use of new media in general tells us something about these current and future uses, about the specific problems and possibilities that arise from these new media. The young adults were chosen because they have thus far been under-represented in research. In addition, this age group has only partly grown up with new media and therefore occupies a particular position in the adoption process. The research project reported here wanted to engage with the *actual* rather than the *imaginary* web-generation. Tying together a discourse analysis with interviews provided the necessary methodology.

The argument runs as follows. Firstly, what the material shows is that the use of new media by young adults tends to be slightly contradictory – there is a clear embrace on the one hand and a rather problematic relationship on the other hand. Far-reaching adoption into everyday life co-exists with a widespread condemnation of certain kinds of use. This condemnation is usually expressed in a third-person narrative. This seemingly contradictory assessment will be explored below. Secondly, the argument runs contrary to the current notion of a near-ideological divide between the use of information, education and entertainment, while at the same time arguing for a re-introduction of these aspects in different ways, especially in the policy and education sectors.[2] The re-introduction of the latter acknowledges that these different kinds of technologies, applications and uses can indeed serve very different functions and that therefore *all* of them are necessary. Without a playful approach to the new technologies, for example, a lack of confidence and subsequently a lack of use can ensue.[3] A much weaker division between information, education and entertainment seems appropriate and the different value-judgements attached to each kind of use should be (re-)considered. Thirdly, a plea will be made for continued detailed research on young people and new media. The research outcomes presented here, as will be shown, underline once again that media research based on statistics and similar quantitative assessments only tell one part of the story. The production of research that portrays the complexity of attitudes and behaviour requires different research methods and a good deal of time and effort (and potentially a team of researchers). The argument is therefore also one about research politics.

Discourses of Youth

Youth has generally been defined as 'the period of transition from childhood to adulthood' (Eurostat, 1997, p.3).[4] It is a life-phase, but also a social category and – more recently – a lifestyle. As part of the process of becoming an independent and responsible social actor, youth has for a long time been understood as the 'in-between' phase, in which certain types of 'playing around' are still allowed. But changes in the move into adulthood have made clear-cut definitions of youth more difficult in the sense that young people 'build adult destinations which are less definite than they used to be in the past' (IARD, 2001, p.36).

Discourses on youth generally characterise them through engagements with the extremes. Many popular portrayals and academic approaches thus portray youth as a potential *threat* to society, an unruly connection of the uncontrollable.[5] Pedagogic approaches often stress the *potential* that youth embodies. That is, they imply that if youth is taught in an appropriate manner then any future society can be an improvement of the current one. Youth and media research has often repeated these assessments, particularly the negative point of view. The same applies to the web-generation discourse, but it has chosen to take a positive viewpoint, stressing the potential. This positive outlook can serve to orient, to give a framework against which to analyse actual current uses and perceptions, but 'any serious empirical research on this issue … will reveal that this story is not adequate to the complexity of the things going on between young people and networked computing' (Bingham et al., 1999, p.24). Its orientation nonetheless is useful, especially – as will be shown in the end – as a guideline for youth and media policies. A summary of the main points of the web-generation discourse will provide the overall framework.

The Web-generation

The net or web-generation discourse inscribes expectations onto the young and lays the burden of the future on their shoulders. These discourses are familiar to most of us. They are popular discourses that take place somewhere between academia and a mediated popular discourse. Prominent in the mid- to late-1990s, they described a new generation of media users: the young whiz kids, the pre-teenage cyber-experts, as well as the early twenties multi-media multi-millionaires. The web-generation idea expresses both an understanding that these behaviours and attitudes are actually taking place, but also a normative expectation that they *should* take place.

The idea of the web-generation is exemplified through terms such as 'net generation' (for example, Hebecker, 2001; Tapscott, 1998), 'generation@' (for example, Opaschowski, 1999) and 'cyber-generation' (for example, Kellner, 1997).[6] This generation is meant to be connected to the world, adopting new technologies early and using ICTs easily, everywhere and anytime. The web-generation creates its own culture or lifestyle through, and with the help of, ICTs (Opaschowski, 1999, p.18; Kellner, 1997). Young people are seen as leading the way – early adopters of new technologies who show the rest what the future will eventually look like (for example, Montgomery, 2001, p.637). New forms of use and new forms of content are meant to surface, to lead to a new relationship to the world, to knowledge and even to oneself. Many of the authors promoting the web-generation concept assume that this will fundamentally change society (people will communicate differently with each other; they will live in a global world full of possibilities; young people will be creative; etc.).[7] Overall, this generation – which is not clearly defined by age margins – is meant to push boundaries (both technological and social-cultural) rather than accept limitations. Work and play are supposedly not clearly differentiated anymore. Overall, in the web-generation discourse new technologies have been adopted in a far-reaching way with far-reaching consequences for everyday life.

Method

The study detailed in this chapter employed a combination of two methods. On the one hand, a discourse analysis of the web-generation discourse was carried out and, on the other hand, a large range of qualitative interviews with Belgian (mostly Flemish) young adults, aged 18 to 25, was conducted. The interviews took place between December 2001 and February 2002. They were carried out in different locations (most often the interviewees' home) without other people directly present. Most interviews took between 45 minutes and an hour. The main instrument used to structure the interviews was a thematic interview guide.[8]

Altogether, the research resulted in nearly 550 interviews. For limitation purposes, a selection approach was chosen that combined randomness and conscious choice of specific sub-groups of interviewees. The two largest identifiable groups of interviewees (non-students on the one hand and a specific cohort of students on the other hand) were chosen for further analysis.[9] Data analysis was carried out by the researcher and consisted of a qualitative content analysis.[10] The interview analysis presented here has been framed through a number of binary positions because these show the possible range of behaviours and attitudes. Overall, the material provided both width and depth. As a first introduction to the youth and new media topic, an overview of general trends will be provided.

General Overview

Quantitative research shows us that new media use has become commonplace among most European youngsters, including the younger ones. The mobile phone, the computer and the internet are all media that these young people have partly grown up with and use either daily (the mobile phone) or at least once a month (the internet) (ARD-Forschungsdienst, 2003). Belgium more or less represents the median on general internet access and mobile phone ownership within Europe (Eurobarometer, 2001; OECD, 2002; ITU, 2003).

The interview material suggests that the young adults in question let the new media widely influence their everyday life routines. Both temporally and spatially the new technologies are allowed to 'intrude', to be present a lot of the time and to take up permanent (but not necessarily fixed) space in their lives. The mobile phone can be said to take such a role across the board – that is among different social groups, different occupational patterns, etc. There are variations, but they are based primarily on individual experiences rather than on general social dynamics. This is different when we look at computer – as well as internet – use. Nonetheless, even here, at least imaginary domestication, that is, the knowledge about these media and some kind of experience of them, was rather widespread.

More generally, the research material allows some broader observations. Firstly, new media are commonplace in these young adults' lives. Secondly, new media influence their everyday lives, sometimes extensively. Thirdly, new media play an important role in the management of the identities of young adults, but often in unexpected ways. They constantly check and compare their own to other people's uses. Third-person effects are an accepted phenomenon in user research, but the rigidity displayed here is interpreted as particular to both the challenges of the new media and the particularity of the age group (see Hartmann, 2004). Their extreme reactions to new media reveal underlying anxieties and problems in new media adoption. Reasons can be found in the normative discourses that surround new media uses, especially of young adults. These discourses, together with educational institutions, play a major role in the current shape of use and perception. This role needs to be reconsidered if future uses and perceptions of new media should become more accurate (particularly in terms of content-uses). As can be seen below, hesitation about ICTs exits on several levels.

Young Adults: ICT Uses and Attitudes

Hesitate or Embrace?

Overall, one can detect more hesitation about embracing new technologies than an immediate embrace would suggest. This was not an active resistance or Luddism, but a careful 'wait and see', 'not these applications', 'no interest' kind of approach.

> [Referring to online banking transactions] I don't really trust this yet, I'd rather do it myself. Then I'd rather go to a bank and do it there. … It doesn't strike me as really secure yet. …

The risk is simply too great? Yes. Yes, it's still in its infancy, isn't it? (WP3, male, 23, worker – shelf stocking.)[11]

My mother wanted most of all that we could reach her if we were going to be home late or if we had a break-down with the car … It is thus foremost functionalistic, it was not meant to be used for calling extensively and I did not phone much at all in the beginning. (D1, male, 21, student.)

… I can wait until the price falls, that I do. I am not a freak in that respect. I would really like to have them, but I suppress my desire for new ICTs and wait until I can justify buying them. (WO1, male, 22, accountant.)

This 'wait and see' approach was partly a financial matter, but in most cases it was also a lack of interest and a perception of too high a risk. Rich Ling makes a similar point when he affirms, in his own research on mobile phone use amongst adolescent girls and young adult men, that the social context of adoption of new technologies is also shaped by the ideological argumentation of *non-adoption*. Ling mentions, for example, the mobile phone *holdouts*, that is, those who clearly assert non-ownership with different reasons from health to costs and social standing issues (Ling, 2001, pp.8–9). In my interviews, explicit non-use in the absolute sense was rare, even as a discourse. Where it appeared, it was applied primarily to other people's use and here primarily to the (even) younger generation. Children were not meant to own mobile phones too early: 'There is a lot of exaggeration, like in case of small children who run around with a mobile phone. That's usually a toy, but not because they really need it' (WD9, female, 24, personnel administrator in plastic production company).

This chapter will revisit the clear-cut opinions about what is right and what is wrong in new media use as well as the differentiation between play and need (the same differentiation as the information/entertainment/education divide suggests). Important to note is that these young people are not necessarily early adopters of new media. Instead, in my research they presented rather thoughtful and careful accounts of why one should or should not acquire and engage with specific media. They did feel under pressure to conform, to be a part of the supposed network society, of technologically mediated social worlds. This clearly points to ICT use. However, the pressure itself did not make them embrace the overall concept of ICT use very easily. Similarly, their understanding of what should be used showed a range of considerations. Clearly, here too, general expectations, and not just one's own desires and choices, played a role. Many of these expectations had been internalised.

Work or Fun?

'Obviously the computer doesn't stand here only for work, I am also, well I shouldn't say a passionate player but I do once in a while like to play a computer game' (W1, male, 24, student). 'I look at several sites everyday. News as well as sports and relaxation-sites. A site with games, for relaxation' (G1, male, 20, student).

Boundaries between work and fun were beginning to disappear for some. The technologies offered diverse sets of applications and content, especially the computer. It combined different possibilities for work and play within the remit of one technology. In the case of students in particular, the computer was used for university work, but also to look for information that could be both work and pleasure; it was used to communicate with the university, but also with friends; it was used to download information, but also music; and it was used to play games. These things were often intermingled and/or even running in parallel. Thus, the boundaries based on different times and spaces for work and fun (and thus also to some extent for private and public uses) were becoming increasingly porous. Young adults – and here especially those in full-time employment – developed mechanisms to resist this trend:

> Q.: ... is there a reason for that [for not having a computer at home]?
> A.: I see enough of computers at work! I could never really rely on myself to operate the thing correctly if I didn't have a PC support desk ... I'm sure I could work it out but I don't have the interest and I don't have the need because I have a computer at work. (WP1, female, 24, trainee solicitor.)

The mechanisms for resisting the intrusion of the technologies into their everyday lives included certain ways of physically removing them or of switching them off or of controlling who has access to one's contact details – or simply not having the technologies, as Ling has shown. More often, 'resisting the intrusion' included limitations in terms of time or in terms of content or form (SMS instead of phoning; certain websites only; etc.). Thus while everyday life is full of ICTs, they were indeed not used randomly and everywhere, anytime.

> Q.: For what purposes do you use the internet then?
> A.: Pure amusement. Sometimes it is for photography. Usually ... to search for 'rockrally's' [a form of music competition], music. (WR1, female, 21, works in a photography shop.)

> Q.: The internet offers you many advantages, few disadvantages and you use it regularly?
> A.: Daily and not only for my studies, but also a lot for fun.
> Q.: How do you mean?
> A.: I surf sport-sites, I download music, and chat with friends via my webcam. (H2, male, 25, student.)

This went hand in hand with a general perception among some of these young adults that taking care of existing social contacts and of work-related matters was generally permissible, but other content-uses had to be justified. The mixture of work and fun, while practised by some (and encouraged by the technological possibilities), was often described as not 'adult' enough. This shift in behaviour and attitudes was also supported by quantitative studies. It has been documented that, for example, playing games decreases drastically from the late teens to the early twenties (Deutsche Shell, 2000; InSites, 2000).[12] The same applies to the use of MUDs and other chat-/VR-programmes.[13] This underlines the specificity of the young adult age group as an 'in-between':

> Q.: But chatboxes in themselves, no interest in that?
> A.: No, not really. To be honest, I don't have time ... I mean, when I was in university – sure,
> ... I'd use them. Normally about 2 a.m. when I was drunk... and there's the ability to just go

on and talk complete crap to strangers and … But … nah, I mean … on a general level I don't have time and if I did have time I probably wouldn't anyway. (WP4, male, 25, software engineer.)

A.: In the past we sometimes played games on TV, Nintendo or so, but not anymore.
Q.: And why not anymore?
A.: No time. (WD2, female, 23, personnel assistant in the local community.)

The shift was less absolute and subtler than some of the above quotes suggest. There was clearly a tendency that underlined the shift between childhood behaviour (that is, fun) and adult behaviour (that is, work). But there was also a shift in the perception of what is permissible, what 'one should do'. However, this did not always go together with what was actually done.

… And then I waste a lot of time with games – time that I actually need for other, much more important things, and therefore I told myself 'no more games'. (D1, male, 21, student.)

Well, actually I am a bit too old for games, but I think I am now playing more games than I used to do. (D8, female, 20, student.)

The interviews suggest that playfulness becomes increasingly less acceptable. This was translated into actual behaviour – and it came into play in the moral condemnation of other (young) people's ICT uses (see 'Morality or acceptance?' below). Before exploring these moral objections, I want to consider the idea of playing. My impression is that there is a need for a more open-minded approach to new media; we need to take a second look at the education/entertainment distinction. There was a hint already in the quotes above, but there is slightly more to it.

Playing or Learning?

There was actually an underlying suggestion in the interviews that those young adults, who had had a chance to play around with computers in their earlier years (or at least to use them at an age when little serious engagement would be expected), were much more inclined to simply adopt them – partly playfully – into their later lives without much trouble. One of the only MUD-users and computer-self-repair persons in the interviews, for example, had owned and used a computer since he was eight years old (P1, male, 23, student). The same applied to many who were now making a living from new technologies (ranging from Telecom-company staff to the proprietors of internet companies). In general, users who mentioned early ICT- (and here particularly computer) use tended to try out different applications and seemed generally more open towards the idea that new forms of communication and information access are possible with ICTs. Sonia Livingstone asks whether we should not 'learn from how children have fun with ICT in order to understand how they might also learn from it' (2002, p.229). I want to extend that question to young adults. Livingstone's (2002) focus is on computer games and she encourages us to take a closer look at children's engagement with these specific technologies and applications.[14] Others have also called for research on computer games (for example,

Buckingham, 2002) and asked for changes in our understanding of literacy (for example, Kellner, 2002). Aufenanger argues that 'in principle, media literacy should also include aspects of media ethics, for example, questions relating to content evaluation, as well as cover the social consequences of the use of new media, aesthetic design and the experiential dimension of media' (2003).[15]

It is important to stress that playful aspects do not necessarily mean games, nor does every kind of playfulness necessarily suggest creativity.[16] Playfulness is used here in the sense of an experiential dimension, of curiosity-led encounters, of trying out the unknown, of risking being lost or encountering something radically new. Few young adults suggested this as a general approach or even a desired one. Overall, the use of creativity (to create one's own media), of playfulness (to 'play' with the possibilities of the medium) and even of games was limited.

Morality or Acceptance?

A major issue in many interviews was the moral condemnation of other people's new media uses. These other people were not friends or families or other directly known people, but mostly an abstract third person. They did not always differ much from well-known caricatures in popular discourses:

> Now for other people's use. You obviously get these internet-addicts. People who sit in front of their computer the whole day and don't do anything else but internet and looking for things. Those I do find a bit wacky. According to me, they don't really have a social life anymore. (F2, male, 21, student.)

> ... obviously there are a few people who use the internet wrongly. But that happens with all new things that you introduce. There will be a group of people who take it the wrong way, who totally mess up their social life, because they sit the whole time and use chat programmes and I personally think that chatting is actually not a good way to communicate. (WP2, female, 25, works in a socio-cultural organisation in the education section.)

Overall, the judgements tended to be rather harsh and far-fetched. The overall impression of other people's uses appeared to be that they usually took place in the extreme. '[Referring to people's internet use] I think that some, well, pfff, I shouldn't say easy, but ... they use it exactly as if their life depended on it, while others don't use it at all and there is not much middle-ground' (WD10, female, 21, hairdresser). The middle ground was not recognised, although few of the interviewees could count as being among any of the extremes. Furthermore, social life was seen as most worthy of defence – and of condemnation. More extreme was the – well-meant – assumption that certain uses were not good for people with a lower educational status.

> [Asked about the possibility of ordering coffee on the way to a cafe via the mobile (the coffee then awaiting one, paid for from one's phone credit)]
> I think it is actually a good idea – as long as you have a strong personality. People ... who do not think about it – I'm thinking here of people with little schooling – they maybe have no resistance to this, seeing that they can easily buy something and do not have to pay, but then they still get the bill at the end of the month. (WD7, female, 20, stewardess.)

But it was not as if judgements were only applied to others (although primarily so). The young adults also judged their own behaviour via references to others:

> Well, a computer, that was always my opinion, that is for clever people, I think. At home, no one really has much understanding of it, only my father. I know a little bit, but I think you have to be clever for this. To get to grips with this, I find that difficult. (WD4, male, 20, works in supermarket.)

> [Referring to use of new technologies] I think that other people use them much more professionally than me. (WD7, female, 20, stewardess.)

The last quote shows the final step in the line of judging people's behaviours, because here the interviewee's own behaviour is judged according to what she assumes other people do, although she displayed a clear knowledge and use of the technologies in the rest of the interview. The curiosity and even success of the individual interviewee seemed less important than social condemnation. The same could be seen when it came to playing games. Here, too, clear ideas about right and wrong prevailed. This was despite the fact that many interviewees experienced games as a very useful social experience.[17] The social aspects of these games applied more to the male youngsters. The gender difference was most pronounced here – an especially important aspect, if the suggestion of the importance of playing around for learning is true.

Male or Female?

Playing games was still primarily perceived as a 'boys' thing'. The particular behaviour that male friends or family members displayed when engaging with or discussing games or technologies was portrayed by a female respondent as follows:

> I mean, I've seen male friends of mine having incredibly in-depth conversations, sort of really excited conversations about inanimate objects that sit under their TV. It does mystify me a bit. [...] [Referring to the ownership of a Playstation] No ... no ... I wouldn't say that I'd never buy one but it's quite low on my list of priorities. In the various student houses that I lived in, we always had a Playstation ... in 5 out of 6 cases it was always the property of a male rather than a female. But I don't personally have one, no. (WP1, female, 24, trainee solicitor.)

Even the games were referred to as 'male'. '[Referring to a specific game] That is really purely male. I mean that there is nothing female in this game and also when you see this on TV, well, that is definitely aimed at men.' (WV2, female, 21, works as bank teller.)

While the gender differences were most pronounced in relation to games, other technologies were also seen to be used differently by men and women. Often, these differences had to be explicitly asked for in the interviews – they were not stated as a characteristic of the interviewee's own behaviour or of new media as such. Only rarely did one find self-descriptions like the one presented by a 25-year old male, software engineer (WP4) who said, 'I'm a typical man on the phone ... "Yeah ... ok ... see you there ... bye."' [laughs].

Euh ... yes, this especially concerns chat programmes, I have to say that you will notice differences there. Euh, ... a guy immediately gets rid of all his lack of self-confidence and begins to force himself upon people, he starts to act up. A woman, on the other hand, she stays herself online. That is sometimes strange to watch. (WD11, male, 21, works for Telenet – a Belgian cable company.)

Gender thus played a role both when sitting in front of the screens as well as online, on the screens. These differences have been described by other users, by marketing specialists, by the programmers and the social norms. When interviewees were asked about it, they tended to overstate the differences. Usually, however, the respondents did not think about the issue of gender themselves. The lack of explicit awareness of these differences reinforced the problem of those differences that remain problematic (for example, females who get harassed online).

Real or Virtual?

One of the more surprising outcomes of the research was the fairly clear distinction (and especially evaluation) between the 'real' and the 'virtual', between the face-to-face and the online, between wrong and right ICT uses, among the interviewees. In contrast to many early theorisations of cyberspace and to the web-generation discourse, there was no particular articulation of virtuality (or of the blurring of boundaries between the virtual and the real) as desirable. Instead, mistrust towards anything virtual tended to dominate. 'And also I don't see anything, for me personally, in online-friendship. You can't trust it, it is more superficial, it is usually not "the real thing" ...' (J1, female, 22, student).

The most important differentiation here was between the real and the 'not real', that is, the virtual. This differentiation came with a whole set of values attached. There was a differentiation between real life, real emotions, real friendships that prohibited any prolonged engagements with unknown people or other online phenomena. Clear-cut differentiations between 'real' and 'not real', between unmediated and mediated communication, between truth and lies, were repeatedly made in many interviews. The real was mostly seen as inherently better than the other, the supposedly 'not real'. Real was considered to be anything known, physically accessible, local. The condemnation was partly based on the perception of dishonesty. 'I did come in contact with people online, but I don't regard them as my friends, because it always remains superficial. And, pff, yes, here and there people lie' (D6, female, 20, student).

No, I might be small-minded but no, I don't have an awful lot of interest in going into a chat room with a bunch of people I don't know ... yeah, it's great to meet new people but I have no idea who those people are, what their backgrounds are, what their motivations are for being in this particular chat room, whether they are who they say they are, and I don't feel I need a forum where I can express my opinions in a situation of anonymity, I'm quite happy to do it with the people I know, or people I meet through work, whatever. (WP1, female, 24, trainee solicitor.)

It was not a lack of technology or technological knowledge that led to a refusal to embrace virtual encounters. Most of the respondents actually knew chat and instant messaging programs and the latter was used often: but not with strangers. They were used to staying in contact with existing friends (and family) networks. Sometimes strangers that the interviewee had seen face-to-face were allowed into the circle of friends.[18] Not all the interviewees made this distinction but it is interesting to note that a high proportion of respondents did with a great degree of clarity. These opinions were also a continuation of the moral stance referred to earlier.

Mobility or Belonging?

'But it has happened that I knew people from seeing them around and that I then got to know them better via the internet, yes, that has happened. ... But to get to know someone online who I didn't know at all, that hasn't happened' (D5, female, 20, student).

The overall idea of getting to know someone new was described as a possibility that might actually be interesting, but usually for other people. An unknown 'other' was used to describe this distinction and how it was evaluated.

> I can imagine people who like to chat, that it is quite nice to get to know people this way, that it may be very pleasant to chat with people all over the world and via a certain network ... I prefer personal contact, I don't think I will get to know someone through the internet ... well, I know people who got to know their boyfriend/girlfriend through chat, but I don't think that that will happen in my case. (D7, male, 21, student.)

Discourses such as these about what is and is not permissible have consequences. They sometimes lead to the denial of possibilities for online encounters by those people who have actually experienced them:

> A.: I actually met my girlfriend on the internet, too ... I hate to admit this. [laughs]
> Q.: Why do you hate to admit it?
> A.: Well, it's got this whole stigma attached to it, you know. I think we only emailed each other a couple of times, it turned out we lived very close ... (WP4, male, 25, software engineer).[19]

Despite his positive experience of establishing a 'real' relationship with the help of the machine, this interviewee immediately justified his own experience and proclaimed it to be limited (they met face-to-face soon after the initial online contact, that is, the online contact was soon replaced with 'real' contact). Even the combination of 'real' and 'virtual' encounters – as exemplified here – was rarely mentioned as an option. Instead, most of the interviewees placed a great stress on their social life offline. Social meant personal, which again was supposed to be based on face-to-face contact (if not regularly at this moment in time, at least in the past). As Berker (Chapter 8) states in reference to Koku et al. (2001), ICTs are often used to initiate and organise corporeal co-presence. In order to protect this secure haven, the technology and its 'extreme' users have to be defined as a danger for the good social life and thus condemned: '... but these are always people I already know. ... but even then, I don't really like to do this ... Thus, not that it is really useful for friendship or so. ... I really like, well, I actually prefer face-to-face.' (WD2, female, 23, personnel assistant in the local community.)

In the following differentiation, the possibility of playing with identity was indirectly acknowledged. However, this aspect of playfulness was not seen as just another aspect of one's personality or as a useful space for trying out other identities, but simply as 'not the right thing'. '[About online friendship] Well, pff, why it should be impossible? ... [because] as I said: you present yourself differently from who you actually are.' (WV2, female, 21, works as bank teller.)

The same respondent even went so far as to proclaim that ICTs enabled a new form of (mis-)communication, that is, that they were used to hide behind. 'I think that more and more people will use their mobiles to hide themselves behind them. So, well, so they don't see the person and then the confrontation is less hard or actually less' (WV2, female, 21, works as bank teller).

Rather than as an extension of the self, ICTs were seen as limitations of the self – as screens (literally and metaphorically) to hide behind. In the above quote, quite a radical shift in communicative behaviour, thanks to ICTs, was predicted for the near future. Thus, while these possibilities for playing with one's identity and one's communicative abilities were acknowledged as a potential part of ICT use, they were not considered by this – and many other – respondent(s) as desirable for themselves or as permissible for others.

Few interviewees saw radical change or increased mobility resulting from their engagement with ICTs. Instead, they envisaged the possibilities of protecting their existing communicative structures against such possible or perceived threats. Proclaiming the 'real' to be more important (and truthful and desirable) than the 'virtual' was one such coping mechanism, one strategy to defeat the changes, to express belonging that was expressed by interviewees. Just as 'when knowledge is domesticated, when it is locally embedded and embodied, it is made relative to local culture and practice' (Sørensen et al., 2000, p. 253), the same applies to media technologies. In the study detailed in this chapter, such local embedded-ness and embodiment was taken quite far.

Home or Not Home?

The idea of belonging was also communicated in the actual, physical expression of the households that the interviewees frequent and live in. In this study, households were questioned and made permeable in several ways, but they did not disappear. Rather, belonging remained important at this domestic level as well. The households they lived in were, for many of the young people, manifold: their parents' home (sometimes more than one); their own home (student 'kot' or other);[20] in some cases their partner's home. The patterns of movement between these households was often seen as significant for the way the routines were structured – they were often also most significant in the context of the reasons given for the first acquisition of the mobile phone. Thanks to this physical dispersal, the term 'home' was often used to signify the most stable of the households: that of the parents. At the same time, much emphasis was placed on the young adults' own status of near grown-ups. ICT use was part of these complex narratives of growing up, of defining one's own life and establishing one's own everyday routines.

Last, but not least, the local and familiar also influenced what content was allowed to be accessed online and what kind of engagement was required:

Q.: What internet applications, apart from MSN, do you also use?
A.: ... not much actually. So far, I have not had to search much on the internet and ... maybe that will still come, but not until now. But what I do is to access sites from my friends. People who made their own site – there I go and have a look once in a while to see what has changed and what they've done with their site. ... And yes, hey, the world is a big village – [that's] an advantage of the internet. (WO1, male, 22, accountant.)

The Middle Ground

What happens there: you used to visit friends and began to talk. Now you see mostly that a PC is on, or they are playing a game. And this stops everything a bit. In the past, we usually sat together and had a chat and now there is always a third medium present. (WR1, female, 21, works in a photography shop.)

I have chosen this last quote to underline that changes are indeed taking place and were sometimes also perceived as changes by the interviewees. Most uses that had been talked about in the interviews, however, actually provided a middle ground. Uses were kept in check through rules of use – for oneself, but also for an abstract 'other'. This contradicts the normative expectation of ICT use within this age group, the web-generation discourse, since this discourse points to change – and only change. The interviews have primarily shown, however, that existing structures and patterns within everyday life (and the social) are often strengthened, while new ones are rejected. The real, the local, the already known, are those factors that are reinforced through much of the new media uses that I have described. A much more considered approach than anticipated by these popular and policy discourses is needed to highlight both the hesitation of users while at the same time noting that innovation is indeed taking place – but at a slower pace and more differentiated. What is happening is that identities are being protected. This protection partly includes a wilful ignorance concerning some of the possibilities that ICTs have to offer.

Generally, one can detect widespread use and acceptance. These young people clearly knew what they were talking about; they had no problem referring to the technologies and their content. All of them comfortably talked about these media and most used them widely in their everyday lives, not only for work or education but also for the organisation of their everyday lives and equally for pleasure.[21] At first sight, then, use seems to take place according to what the web-generation discourse and similar understandings have repeatedly proclaimed. That is, that young people take the new technologies on board and will then use them extensively.

This is only one part of the story, though. In many smaller ways, the technologies and their applications were rejected as well – or at least regulated. There were, for example, several mechanisms to stop using the technologies 'too much'. This could mean that the computer was only used at work (this is both a time-and-place restriction on use) or that certain uses were declared as wrong (as when games are not allowed to interfere with more serious uses). The declaration of 'wrong behaviour' was the clearest indication of the need to draw boundaries around use. This was primarily done by condemning other people's uses, but the interviewees' own fears, values and ideas were clearly visible underneath. The most dominant underlying argument repeated what I have temporarily labelled the education-entertainment divide. It was the extent of use that was partly portrayed as problematic. Here, the danger of becoming dependent on certain technologies, the danger of spending too much money, the danger of being introduced too early to these media was mentioned. The primary focus of this negative portrayal was, however, the actual content of use. The two main topics here were extensive use of entertainment on the one hand and chatting online with strangers (and indirectly any identity shifts taking place online) on the other hand. The 'other' was feared – the unknown person with whom one could come in contact online and be betrayed. In order to show that this danger did not apply to them, the young adults stressed how good their own offline lives were. In contrast to the virtual worlds (and what they thought these were), the value of the local and the familiar were stressed. Technologies were widely used to reinforce this, to strengthen existing networks rather than to attempt to build new ones. Similarly, information was not accessed randomly, but with often clear limitations ('I always look at the same websites').

These findings lead me to argue against the divide between the use of information, education and entertainment. The normative judgements that were visible in these reservations by the young adults at least partly stemmed from the public discourses around new media and around new media use by young people. These moral panics that clearly suggest the dangers of encountering the unknown and of the extensive use (especially of entertainment applications) only served to weaken the engagements with new technologies. Most of the interviewees did not let themselves be led by curiosity and experimentation, but by clear-cut rules. In this way, new uses were rarely discovered. This is one reason why the discourses have to change. Here, the web-generation discourse in all its optimistic extremity actually provided a useful outlook: the web-generation is portrayed as creative and playful, as using all the applications with ease. The differentiation between information, education and entertainment is simply not made anymore.

My argument is not that there is no difference between education, information and entertainment applications. There clearly is. And they often serve very different functions. For the general attitude towards ICTs to change, however, the differentiation needs to be less rigid and value-laden. This applies to critical engagement as much as it does to the embrace of the new. Exactly for that reason those responsible for education have more consciously to introduce entertainment applications in their teaching. So, the discourses (and practices) need to change for a conscious application of all the different possibilities of the new technologies. The playful furthers confidence and openness. Thus, the values attached to the different applications are wrong.

These kinds of differentiations can only take place in detailed qualitative research. Thus, the final point to stress is that such research on young people and new media should be continued in the future. Media use statistics provide very important overviews of developments and often provide a good first impression of what is happening. Quantitative research can equally provide a good overview of opinions and behaviour patterns. But it rarely provides the 'reading between the lines', the more differentiated part of the story of what young adults think about and do with new technologies. And this story shows resistances and fears that are otherwise lost.

Notes

1 Here I side with Murdock and McCron that a 'comprehensive analysis of youth … must necessarily be capable of accommodating and explaining not only deviancy and refusal but also convention and compliance (2000 [1976], p.206).

2 David Buckingham, writing about children online, points to the continuities in the separation of education and entertainment in this history of media technologies, from television onwards, and at the same time challenges the appropriateness and usefulness of seeing them as unrelated (Buckingham, 2002, pp.78–79).

3 Playful stands here for curious and striving for experimentation.

4 The signifiers of adulthood were – not necessarily in this order – a) finishing education, b) leaving the parental home, c) starting a job, d) financial independence from the parental home, e) the formation of a (heterosexual) couple, f) the subsequent formation of a family.

5 The latter also implies that some young people might be under threat from the others, that is, victimisation is part of this framework.

6 They have also been named after more specific technologies, like the Atari-generation, the Nintendo-generation or even the 486-generation. These differentiations are, however, only marginal to a wider debate. Despite the differing terminology, these authors are all talking about nearly the same age group, that is, current teenagers with a possible extension into the mid-twenties and/or childhood.

7 Obviously, these kinds of claims have to be seen in context. First of all, authors that support the claims stated above only represent a small number of authors. But they have been heard widely. Most of these authors address a wider audience than the usual academic one and thus tend to simplify the actual complexity. Secondly, these discourses appear at specific times (mostly when the technologies are still new and not widely used).

8 Students at the Free University of Brussels (VUB), where I worked at the time, conducted the interviews. This allowed for a larger sample and a good knowledge of the local language as well as of the age group. The interviewing process was part of their overall course requirements, that is, a taught programme ran in parallel to the interviewing process. Each student had to do one self-interview, in which they interviewed themselves, and six other interviews. More specific questions were added to the thematic interview guide by every interviewer. All interviews were recorded and later transcribed.

9 The selection resulted in 81 self-interviews and 117 non-student interviews (198 interviews in total). To further reduce that number (in order to provide an adequate analysis), 50 of these 198 interviews were randomly chosen for a detailed analysis.

10 Overall trends were initially derived from an analysis of some quantitative material. Some of this material additionally offered illuminative qualitative insights (for example, Deutsche Shell, 2000 and 2002; Oksman and Rautiainen, 2001).

11 The information given about the interviewees consists of the following: a) a code to identify the interviewee (which helps both the researcher and the reader to differentiate between different actors), b) their gender, c) their age and d) their occupation. All quotes have been translated from Dutch.

12 The Shell study shows that while 68 per cent of German youth between 15 and 17 years old play computer games very often, only 41 per cent of 22 to 24-year-olds still do so (Deutsche Shell, 2000:202). The Belgian study states that the *playful* aspects of ICTs are very important for teenagers. More *communicative* aspects are also important. The relationship between the two aspects changes substantially from teenagers to young adults (InSites, 2000).

13 As one interviewee (one of the only ones to have used MUDs) stated: 'There was a time when I MUD-ed real intensely, maybe six or seven hours a day or sometimes even throughout a whole night. … you have a feeling of belonging. … When there is no one to

chat to, you simply begin to research the world of the MUD' (P1, male, 23, student). The intense engagement had eventually eased off.

14 For Livingstone the engagement, potentially challenging traditional notions of literacy practices and other readings of media texts, is more important than the content as such. I would see this general engagement as applicable to children, but would want to hold on to the importance of specific content for the young adults, since the interviews seem to show that the general engagement can still lead to a very limited form of new media use.

15 The EU, however, suggests a traditional view of digital literacy: 'It's also obvious that young people are very interested in ICTs. Most of them think that "digital literacy" is nowadays (…) one of the keys to having a good job. Unfortunately between expectation and reality, there is a gap. … Technology in itself is not a panacea' (eEurope, 2000). The move away from technological determinism is laudable, but this openness needs to be extended to a general 'experimentality'.

16 Some research suggests that computers are used to play around, but not to create directly. Instead, a passive creativity emerges, which Sefton-Green calls '… "lego-creativity": it was possible for them to make things, but the building blocks were factory made' (Sefton-Green, 1998, p.71).

17 Many games can be used in social ways. Quite in contrast to the idea that games replace friendships, they often become shared spare-time entertainment: 'it was also more social with the Playstation, it meant making arrangements to meet people at home so that we were playing with four, five or sometimes six people. And we did our own competitions …' (WP3, male, 23, worker – shelf stocking).

18 One interviewee stated that she chatted with someone who she had only once met offline before she met him online for a chat, which continued regularly. Since then, she interacts with him offline much more frequently. This initial face-to-face contact seems to have made a crucial difference.

19 The same interviewee also showed a more differentiated (albeit less common) view concerning the advantages of online encounters: '… it kind of divorces the physical world from … you know, what you look like or who you are to how your mind works and how your personality is. So I think a lot more people have a lot more confidence on the internet and as such it allows them to develop themselves and their friendships in a way it couldn't in real life' (WP4, male, 25, software engineer).

20 The 'kot' is the Flemish expression for student housing. Characteristically, student kots in Belgium are single rooms in larger houses that consist entirely of such student rooms (plus some shared facilities). Students do not register these kots as their homes, but remain registered at their parents' address. Due to the smallness of the country, most students, especially the younger ones, commute back to their parents' house most weekends.

21 One particularity of the here-presented identities is that they are on the move anyhow – these young people are in a phase of transition in every sense of the word. This transition phase leads to more rigid reactions to the challenges posed by ICTs.

References

ARD-Forschungsdienst (2003), 'Jugendliche und neue Medien', *Media Perspektiven*, No.4/2003, pp.194–200.

Aufenanger, S. (2003) *Media literacy as a task for school development*. URL (consulted April 2003): http://www.elearningeuropa.info/.

Bingham, N. et al. (1999) 'Bodies in the midst of things: re-locating children's use of the internet', in S. Ralph et al. (eds) *Youth and the global media*, Luton: University of Luton Press.

Buckingham, D. (2002) 'The electronic generation? Children and new media', in L. Lievrouw and S. Livingstone (eds) *The handbook of new media*, London, Thousand Oaks, New Delhi: Sage.

Deutsche Shell (eds) (2000) *Jugend 2000*, Opladen: Leske and Budrich.

Deutsche Shell (eds) (2002) *Jugend 2002. Zwischen pragmatischem Idealismus und robustem Materialismus*, Frankfurt a.M.: Fischer Taschenbuch Verlag.

eEurope (2000) *eEurope 2002: an information society for all*, Brussels: CEC Action Plan.

Eurobarometer (2001) *Young Europeans in 2001. Results of a European opinion poll*. URL (consulted May 2002): http://europa.eu.int/comm/education/youth/studies/ eurobarometer/ eurobarometer.html.

Eurostat (1997) *Youth in the European Union – from education to working life*, Luxembourg: Office for Official Publications of the European Communities.

Haddon, L. (2001) *Domestication and mobile telephony*, Unpublished paper presented at the 'Machines that become us' conference at Rutgers University, NJ, 18-19 April.

Hartmann, M. (2004) 'Young people = "young" uses? Questioning the "Key Generation", in N. Carpentier et al. (eds) *Het on(be)grijpbare publiek: een communicatiewetenschappelijke exploratie van publiekonderzoek*, Brussels: VUB Press.

Hebecker, E. (2001) *Die Netzgeneration. Jugend in der Informationsgesellschaft*, Frankfurt a.M. and New York: Campus.

Hörisch, J. (ed) (1997) *Mediengenerationen*, Frankfurt a.M.: Suhrkamp.

Howard, S. (ed) (1997) *Wired up: young people and the electronic media*, London: UCL Press.

IARD (2001) *Study on the state of young people and youth policy in Europe*, URL (consulted June 2003): http://www.europa.eu.int/comm/education/youth/studies/ iard/iard.html.

InSites (2000) *'An expanding Belgian web-generation' – Youth Online Survey 2000*. URL (consulted May 2002): http://www.insites.be/Freeff/press/yol2_eng_051200.asp.

ITU (2003) *ICT – Free Statistics Home Page* (consulted June 2003) http://www.itu.int/ITU-D/ ict/statistics/.

Kellner, D. (1997), 'Die erste Cyber-Generation', in SpoKK (eds) *Kursbuch JjugendKultur* URL (consulted May 2002): http://www.uni-giessen.de/fb03/vinci/labore/gen/kellner.htm.

Kellner, D. (2002), 'New media and new literacies: reconstructing education for the new millennium', in L. Lievrouw and S. Livingstone (eds) *The handbook of new media*, London, Thousand Oaks, New Delhi: Sage.

Koku, E., N. Nazer and B. Wellman (2001) 'Netting scholars: online and off-line', *American Behavioural Scientist*, 44 (10), pp.1752–74.

Lie, M. and K.H. Sørensen (1996) 'Making technology our own? Domesticating technology into everyday life', in M. Lie and K.H. Sørensen (eds) *Making technology our own? Domesticating technology into everyday life*, Oslo: Scandinavian University Press.

Liebert, R.M. and J. Sprafkin (1988) *The early window – effects of television on children and youth*, third edition, New York: Pergamon Press.

Ling, R. (2001) *Adolescent girls and young adult men: two sub-cultures of the mobile telephone*, Telenor R & D Rapport 34/2001.

Livingstone, S. (2002) *Young people and new media*, London, Thousand Oaks, New Delhi: Sage.

Montgomery, K. C. (2001) 'Digital kids – the new online children's consumer culture', in D. Singer and J. Singer (eds) *Handbook of children and the media*, London, Thousand Oaks, New Delhi: Sage.

Murdock, G. and R. McCron (2000 [1976]) 'Consciousness of class and consciousness of generation', in S. Hall and T. Jefferson (eds) *Resistance through rituals. Youth subcultures in post-war Britain*, London: Hutchinson & Co.

OECD (2002) *Measuring the information economy 2002*, Paris: OECD.

Oksman, V. and P. Rautiainen (2001) *'Perhaps it is a body part' – How the mobile phone* became an organic part of the everyday lives of children and adolescents. A case study of* *Finland*, unpublished paper, the 15th Nordic conference on media and communication research, Reykjavik, 11-13 August 2001.

Opaschowski, H.W. (1999) *Generation@ – die Medienrevolution entläßt ihre Kinder: Leben im Informationszeitalter*, Hamburg: British American Tobacco.

Sefton-Green, J. (ed.) (1998) *Digital diversions: youth culture in the age of multimedia*, London and Bristol: UCL Press.

Silverstone, R. and E. Hirsch (eds) (1992) *Consuming technologies: media and information in domestic spaces*, London: Routledge.

Sørensen, K.H. (1994) *Technology in sse. Two essays on the domestication of artefacts*, Trondheim: Senter for Teknologi og Samfunn.

Sørensen, Knut H., Aune, Margrethe and Hatling, Morten (2000) 'Against linearity: on the cultural appropriation of science and technology', in Meinolf Dierkes and Claudia von Grote (eds) *Between understanding and trust: the public, science and technology*, Amsterdam: OPA, pp.204–22.

Tapscott, D. (1998) *Growing up digital: the rise of the net generation*, New York: McGraw-Hill.

Chapter 10

The Future of Ambient Intelligence in Europe – The Need for More Everyday Life

Yves Punie[1]

Introduction

Ambient intelligence (AmI) refers to a vision of the future information society where intelligent interfaces enable people and devices to interact with each other and with the environment.[2] Technology operates in the background while computing capabilities are everywhere, connected and always available. This intelligent environment is aware of the specific characteristics of human presence and preferences, takes care of needs and is capable of responding intelligently to spoken or gestured indications of desire. It can even engage in intelligent dialogue. AmI is all about 'human-centred computing', user-friendliness, user empowerment and the support of human interaction (ISTAG, 2001; Aarts et al., 2002).

Many implicit shifts underscore this vision. The first is whereby computing systems move from mainframe computing (1960 onwards) to personal computing (1980 onwards), and from multiple computing devices (2000 onwards) towards invisible computing (2010 onwards). The second is the expectation that communication processes will change, from people talking to people, to people interacting with machines, to machines/devices/software agents talking to each other and to people. A third important shift is the one which presumes that interfacing with computing capabilities will become natural and intuitive, in contrast with current Graphical User Interfaces (GUI). In short, AmI promises to transform the role of information and communication technologies (ICTs) in society and ultimately, to transform the way people live, work, relax and enjoy them. According to Miles et al. (2002, pp.4–9), this is probably one occasion where the overused phrase 'paradigm change' is appropriate.

Such a compelling vision is reflected in a variety of terms that have emerged in recent years: ubiquitous computing, pervasive computing, disappearing computing, proactive computing, sentient computing, affective computing, wearable computing and ambient intelligence. The different terms may imply a different focus and a geographical preference. Hence the term AmI is more prevalent in Europe and ubiquitous computing more so in the US and Japan. What is specific to AmI is that it is based on the convergence and seamless inter-operability between three key technologies: ubiquitous computing, ubiquitous communication and intelligent user-friendly interfaces. Other projects might focus, for instance, on just one or two key technology domains.

The objective of this article is not only to situate and discuss the AmI vision, but also to identify and detail major challenges and bottlenecks for its realisation. This is relevant since the EU has based the principal focus for its FP6 Information Society Technologies (IST) programme on the creation of this AmI world, bearing in mind that these are next-generation technologies not (yet) on the market. As a result, this article also raises questions about IST innovation policy on advancing AmI. It will do so by arguing the need for, and significance of, an everyday life perspective that confronts (potential) users with future visions and technologies. It will provide insights on what can be learnt from existing user research for advancing the AmI vision and its implications and applications in everyday life.

Visions of the future of technology in society tend to be shaped by what the technologies have to offer. They often suffer from technological determinism. The ambient intelligence vision has the potential to be different, however, not only because it claims to be different but also because it proposes to embed IST RTD (Research and Technology Development) in its socio-economic and user context. In the second part of this chapter, the AmI vision is extensively analysed. But first, it will outline insights on the context and the origins of the AmI vision: where did it come from and who promotes it? This will be followed by the argument that the origins of the AmI vision are not only technological ones, as is usually assumed, but are also social and economic. The chapter then takes this point one step further and discusses how AmI initially addressed the tendency of technology vision building to be technology deterministic. And more recently, Experience and Application Research Centres are promoted by ISTAG to address the challenges of human-centred technology development

I will then develop further the notion of user involvement by looking at what ethnographic, qualitative research can reveal. It introduces the domestication approach as illustrative for such research. Such an approach would recognise that power relations in everyday life need to be taken into account for advancing AmI. It also suggests that there is a need to understand the difference between the physical and mental disappearance of computing and that a future challenge is to find a balance between adaptability and rigidity of AmI systems and services. Other socio-economic and policy-related issues are related to the risk of an ambient intelligence divide and the need for tackling privacy, security and dependability as bottlenecks for the acceptance of AmI. Lastly, I will seek to wrap up the plea in this chapter for radical everyday life perspectives on developing and implementing ambient intelligence in everyday life.

The Ambient Intelligence Vision

The objective of this section is to understand the AmI vision. Therefore, its context and origins will be discussed. It is argued that the vision is potentially different from earlier technology visions because of its explicit human/user-oriented claims. But to realise the potential, AmI technologies need to be designed and prototyped by taking (potential) users seriously, meaning that the micro-context of their everyday life needs to be taken into account.

Context of the AmI Vision

A major step in developing the vision of ambient intelligence in Europe has come from the IST Advisory Group (ISTAG), a group of experts from industry and academia advising the IST RTD Programme of the European Commission.[3] ISTAG envisages a higher level of focus and a higher pace of development of ICTs in Europe. In 1999, it published a vision statement for the Fifth EC Framework Programme (FP5) that laid down a challenge to 'start creating the ambient intelligence landscape for seamless delivery of services and applications in Europe relying also upon test-beds and open source software, develop user-friendliness, and develop and converge the networking infrastructure in Europe to world-class'. Following this vision statement, AmI became broadly embedded in the FP5 IST work programme for 2000 and 2001. At the same time, a scenario exercise was launched with over 35 experts to develop a better understanding of the implications of an AmI landscape. This scenario report (ISTAG 2001) is one of the reference documents in the field. It also identified major key technologies, socio-political issues and a research agenda for AmI.[4]

ISTAG continued to develop the vision of AmI in preparation for the sixth RTD Framework Programme (FP6). Its report was published at a time when confidence in the ICT sector had been shaken by the burst of the dot-com bubble, by the September 11 events and by a more general slow-down of the economy. Therefore ISTAG argued for an urgent need for targeted and far-sighted investments in ICTs. FP6 needed to be a-cyclical: 'Those who will come out strongly during the next "upturn" will be those who have maintained their investment in innovation during the present phase of the cycle' (ISTAG, 2002, pp.3–4).

Following the work of ISTAG and of other consultative procedures organised by the European Commission, AmI became the key concept in the FP6 IST programme for the period 2002–2006. The overall vision was that the IST thematic priority would contribute directly to realising European policies for the knowledge society as agreed at the Lisbon Council of 2000 and as reflected in the e-Europe Action Plan.[5] The strategic goal for Europe in the next decade was 'to become the most competitive and dynamic knowledge-based economy in the world capable of sustainable economic growth with more and better jobs and greater social cohesion'. This required wider adoption, broader availability and an extension of IST applications and services in all economic and public sectors and in the society as a whole:

> The objectives of IST in FP6 are therefore to ensure European leadership in the generic and applied technologies at the heart of the knowledge economy. It aims to increase innovation and competitiveness in European businesses and industry and to contribute to greater benefits for all European citizens (EC, 2002: pp.4–6).

AmI is seen as a key concept in making this possible. With ISTAG and the EU IST RTD funding programme (€3.6 billion for four years against €16 billion for FP6 as a whole)[6] considerable efforts have been made in the EU to mobilise researchers and companies towards realising the building blocks for an AmI landscape. The goals are to support and stimulate innovation and the Science and Technology (S&T) knowledge base for growth, competitiveness and well-being in the future information society. Other pan-European and national R&D programmes on AmI exist as well, such as the ITEA consortium and the UK EQUATOR Interdisciplinary Research Collaboration.[7] As a result, the AmI vision is gaining momentum, and in its focusing of resources on a common project will possibly lead to greater economies of scale while at the same time avoiding fragmentation and duplication of efforts. It might, however, exclude alternative visions.

The Origins of the AmI Vision in Social and Technological Factors

AmI is usually seen as the product of an exclusively technological evolution, but it will be argued in this subsection that it is rather a specific constellation of social – defined in its broadest sense – and technological factors that have enabled AmI to become an effective vision of the future rather than being pure science fiction.

At the level of technologies, progress in three domains – that is, microelectronics, communication and networking technologies and intelligent agents/user interfaces – has given rise to the idea of AmI. Microelectronics has been driven during the last decades by Moores' law on the increasing capacity of computing power and storage at fixed costs. Cheaper, smaller and faster computing capabilities make it possible for computing functionalities to be embedded in potentially every object or device. Progress in communication and networking technologies has given rise to the idea that these widely distributed computing devices could become networked or connected to one another. Breakthroughs in mobile, wireless and fixed (broadband) communication networks have increased the capacity (bandwidth), speed and availability of communication networks. Computing devices have also become user-friendlier with the introduction of the GUI. First-generation intelligent agents, that is, personal software assistants with a certain degree of autonomy have been developed as well. Examples of existing agents are (personalised) email alert agents informing the user about news, offers, events or changes (for example, My Yahoo!).

Technological progress in all these fields has contributed to the shaping of the AmI vision, but progress in the diffusion and acceptance of past and current ICTs was equally important. In the last ten years, mobile telephony has grown in Europe to more than 300 million users. In many European countries, penetration rates of mobile phones are above 70 per cent of households. And SMS has given a considerable boost to the mobile services market during recent years. Internet access from home has increased in the EU15 to 40 per cent in June 2002 (against 28 per cent in October 2000) (Eurobarometer, 2002). If the increased diffusion and usage of computer, internet, mobile phone and PDA had not happened, technological progress in the fields of microelectronics, communication technologies and intelligent agents/user interfaces would certainly have slowed down.

And acceptance of these technologies is enabled by demographic and social trends such as individualism, diversity, mobility and the choice of personal life styles, affecting the structure of groups and communities and the ways we live and work. Mobile phones, for instance, are enablers of lifestyles that are increasingly individual and mobile. Household structures (family size and composition) are changing too, with a decline of traditional nuclear families and an increase of dual income households and single parent/single person households (Ducatel et al., 2000; Gavigan et al., 1999). ICTs are envisaged as being able to help to cope with the effects of these changes.

The point is that although technological progress has made the idea of AmI possible, it would probably not have existed at all if many of the existing ICTs had not been taken up by the consumer market, the latter being driven by demographic and social trends. Moreover, many of the so-called technological advances are only made possible by the specific socio-economic context in which they are developed. Take the example of Moores' law. It is typically seen as a technological prophecy but as Tuomi (2002) argues, the prophecy could only hold because of the unique economic and social conditions under which the semiconductor industry operated during the last decades. Moores' law alone was not responsible for that. Another example is the European success of GSM. Technological progress has enabled this but the European efforts to agree on a common standard, the Global System for Mobile communications, undoubtedly have contributed to its success. As these cases illustrate, the AmI vision needs to make the socio-economic context of its development more explicit. The AmI vision is not only about technological progress. For a full understanding of AmI, such non-technological, or rather socio-economic, issues need to be made more explicit.

The ISTAG Focus on Human-centred Development of AmI

AmI is more a vision of the future than a reality. In common with the earlier vision of the role of technology in society, it promises a better, faster and happier world (see also Punie et al. in this volume). This was also the case for discourses surrounding the introduction of the telegraph, telephone, radio, television and mechanical household appliances (for their histories, see Flichy, 1995; Marvin, 1988; Forty, 1986). Every time a new technology pops up, revolutionary social changes are promised and promoted. The problem with these visions is that they are, for the most part, technologically deterministic. Technologies are supposed to impact directly on society by causing social change (for the better). They only look at what is technologically feasible and ignore the socio-economic context and user dynamics that are shaping the innovation process as well. The present question is whether the AmI vision is able to escape technological determinism and thereby avoid one-sided promises of a better world.

Right from the start, the AmI vision focuses on people, not technologies. The visions of people benefiting from services and applications supported by new technologies in the background, and of people interacting via intelligent user interfaces were essential to ISTAG, according to its report. The experts involved in constructing the scenarios emphasised that people, potential users, were to be given the lead in the way systems, services and interfaces are implemented (ISTAG, 2001 pp.3, 11–12). At the level of discourse, this is probably what makes AmI different from earlier visions of technology.

The four scenarios that were developed in the 2001 ISTAG report underscored this view. They contrasted applications that served to optimise efficiency (whether in business or in society) against those that emphasised human relationships, sociability or just having 'fun'. They also underlined the place of AmI in serving society and supporting the community as well as individuals. The scenarios sketched out different pathways towards AmI but with the common ground that they are all situated at the human interface. This emphasised a key feature of AmI, which is that the technologies should be fully adapted to human needs and cognitions. It could be argued that AmI, consequently, represents a step beyond the current concept of a 'User Friendly Information Society' (ISTAG, 2001, pp.16–17).

The observation that the scenarios were to focus on the human should not be understood to mean that AmI is only about individuals. It is intended to be also about IST support to manufacturing and the production of goods and services through, for instance, virtual enterprises. To elaborate that point, in 2002, ISTAG introduced the notion of Ambient Intelligent Space, that is, the seamless connection and interoperability between different AmI environments such as home, work, school and car. The individual is expected to move through these environments expecting seamless services. AmI Space interacts with the user, knows how to model user behaviour, controls the privacy and security of the transferred personal data and deals with authorisation, key and rights management. It should also ensure the quality of services as perceived by the user. ISTAG has realised that all of this is not trivial, and certainly not only technical. There is perceived to be a need for a combination of applications, services and infrastructure to realise AmI: 'More is needed than more technology' (ISTAG, 2002, pp.15–22).

This is confirmed in the 2003 revision and updating of the AmI vision. In 2003, ISTAG still believed that AmI can only be fully developed by a holistic approach encompassing technical, economic and social research. It should not just consider the technology, but the complete innovation supply-chain from science to end-users, and should take into account the various features of the academic, industrial and administrative environment facilitating or hindering the realisation of the AmI vision. Moreover, it is not seen to be necessary to define the term AmI more tightly. It should be regarded and promoted as an 'emerging property' rather than as a set of specified requirements (ISTAG, 2003a, pp.12–13).

In short, the ISTAG vision strongly emphasises the need for AmI to be driven by humanistic concerns, in contrast to the technologically deterministic tendency of mainstream vision building. But given its *raison d'être*, ISTAG argues that neither ISTAG nor the IST research community should shrink from the exciting possibilities. AmI does, it insists, represent a new paradigm for citizens, administrations, governance and business. Radical social transformations are expected from its implementation. Although AmI is not a panacea for social problems, it could offer innovative ways to address the fundamental socio-economic challenges that Europe will be facing during the coming years, such as the increase of its customers and citizens, the aging population and increased mobility (ISTAG, 2003a). As such, the ISTAG vision positions itself carefully in between technological determinism and societal reductionism.

It remains to be seen however if and how the vision will further influence research, development and design of AmI applications. This issue is tackled in the next section.

User-oriented Design

There are many different approaches to user-oriented design, that is, to designing new technologies by taking into account, in one way or another, users, user requirements and user behaviour. The design guidelines proposed by ISTAG (2001) in its scenario exercise are situated at the generic socio-cultural, economic and political level. They provide some guiding principles for how technologies 'should' be designed. AmI should, for instance, facilitate human contact, be oriented towards community and cultural enhancement and should inspire trust and confidence.

Usability research is situated at the more concrete human-machine interaction level, as it looks at applying some of the above mentioned design guidelines. The ISO 13407 'Human-centred design for interactive systems' standard requires human-centred design to involve users actively; to clearly understand and use task requirements; to appropriate the allocation of functions; to use the iteration of design solutions; and to set up a multidisciplinary design team. Another design standard that is promoted by the European Commission is 'Design for All' which aims at increasing the accessibility of information technology products. This concept is mainly applied in the disability field.[8] Most of these activities are primarily based on functional descriptions of how to involve users in the design process. They are mainly routed within the traditions of behavioural science and engineering, but increasingly, efforts are undertaken to bridge both worlds and to take users seriously, especially within the fields of Human Computer Interaction (HCI), Computer Mediated Communication (CMC) and Computer Supported Cooperative Work (CSCW).

This constitutes a first logical step, but the real challenge is to involve users in a sociological sense, that is, by taking into account the micro-context of their everyday lives (Punie, 2003). In its latest reports, ISTAG (2003a, 2003b) also acknowledges this challenge, and proposes the concept of EARCs as a possible way to address it. Experience and Application Research Centres (EARCs) are considered as a new approach to prototyping necessary for the successful development of AmI products and services (see also ISTAG 2004). Functional, technical, social, economic and cultural requirements that are gathered from users and stakeholders need to be put at the centre of the development process, revisited through design, implementation, checking and testing. Experience prototyping can be used to understand user experiences and their contexts, explore and evaluate new designs, and communicate ideas to designers and stakeholders. This should 'allow people to live in their own future' and should bring AmI research closer to the needs of citizens and businesses (ISTAG, 2003a, p.5).

The EARC approach is extremely challenging and extends well beyond current engineering and design approaches. It provides multi-dimensional strategies for involving users in the design process by responding to the growing recognition that acceptance of ICTs is not only shaped by their technological possibilities or by their functionality, but also by the micro-social context of the household or of other social settings (ISTAG, 2003a, p.29). The EARC approach seems to favour more in-depth studies of users, but it also recognises that user studies vary according to when users are consulted in the innovation process. Therefore, a distinction is made between:

(i)   Science and Technology Centres for basic research on component technologies for AmI (with little user input);
(ii) Feasibility and Usability Centres for basic (small-scale) user research on the integration of AmI technologies and systems into real user environments (e.g. living labs);

(iii) Demonstration and Evaluation Centres for (large-scale) user research whereby prototypes are integrated into large-scale demonstration facilities (e.g. smart home demonstrators);

(iv) Field trials for small and large-scale longer-term studies of technologies and systems undertaken with users in their real life environments (for example, home, work, airport, hospitals, etc.) (ISTAG 2004, p.14).

The way user research is conducted, and the kind of results that can be expected, depend on where user research is located in the innovation process. More research is needed to map user studies and to highlight the pros and cons of each of these stages of user research. But it may already be argued that even within each stage a good deal of variation is to be expected. Ethnographic research on ICTs in the home environment, for instance, may be oriented towards design or can have more broadly based sociological objectives.

Small-scale ethnographic work has been undertaken for instance on domestic routines and the way such practical routines can influence the design of new ICT technologies in the home (Crabtree and Rodden, 2004; Crabtree, 2003). The research focused on the specific case of the way incoming and outgoing mail is organised in the home. Mail is purposefully placed in the household at different locations depending on what needs to be done. This is described as an 'ecological network of displays' constructed by household members to co-ordinate the actions occasioned by the arrival of mail. The introduction of digital media to support the handling of mail would need to be very flexible and would need to take into account these complicated patterns of displaying and moving of mail objects around the home.

This study also confirms that human-machine interaction is not just about a simple relation between an individual user and an individual artefact. User research needs to go beyond the usual focus on individual users, especially when taking into account that AmI products and services will be intelligent, adaptable and networked, in contrast with stand-alone products. As Tuomi (2003) argues, machines are to be seen as media that connect systems of social activity. This means that designing a product actually means designing the structures for social interaction. The problem of design cannot be reduced to abstract functionality (engineering) nor to aesthetic considerations (design) or to usability design. There is a gap to be filled by refining design methodologies that take the social foundations of product use into account.

These social foundations are also shaped by socio-cultural routines and habits. The ethnographic approach that will be presented in the next sections focuses on these routines. As will be demonstrated, the orientation of this ethnographic research is, however, more sociological than design-oriented.

Ambient Intelligence and Everyday Life

Domestication is an approach for studying the information society from the users' point of view by focusing on the acceptance of, or resistance to, ICTs within the context of everyday life (Lie and Sørensen, 1996; Silverstone and Haddon, 1996; Silverstone, 1994). Domestication studies are field trials of users in their natural environment. Domestication refers to the capacity of individuals, families, households and other institutions to bring new technologies and services into their culture, to make them their own. In this approach, the users take part in the process of shaping ICTs through making meaning of/with them, and integrating them into their everyday lives, their social networks, their ideas about themselves and their value-systems (see also the articles of Hartmann, Ward and Punie et al. in this volume).

Domestication finds its origins in social-constructivist approaches to science and technology, in audience and user research in media studies and in the sociology and anthropology of everyday life. Qualitative research methodologies are usually applied within a domestication approach, while other approaches such as diffusionism tend to prefer quantitative methods (for example, Rogers, 1995).

It is the objective of this section to take insights from domestication studies on existing and past technologies as a basis for reflecting on how they can be used to advance thinking on future technologies. Such an everyday life approach is especially relevant for looking at ambient intelligence since one of its central claims is indeed to place the user, in its context, at the centre of development.

Power Relations and Everyday Life at Home

By taking an everyday life perspective on acceptance and use of ICTs, domestication studies look at how technologies are negotiated within the household or within the more general structures and patterns of our everyday life. Such a perspective implies that the enactment of structural power relations of class, gender, age, ethnicity and others should be taken into account, based on sociological theories of social stratification. Domestication would argue that social activities are neither completely determined by these power relations (structural determination), nor that they are completely absent (individual freedom) but rather that these power relations are negotiated within the regularities and irregularities of everyday life (Punie, 2004).

Gender studies, for instance, illustrate how socially and culturally prescribed roles of masculinity and femininity shape differences in attitudes, acceptance and use of ICTs. A typical example is the remote control (TV, VCR) that is handled – in many households – primarily and sometimes exclusively by men (the father and/or the son). It is seen as a visible symbol of ICT-related masculine power in the household where the men determine and/or decide over possible family viewer conflicts (Lull, 1988). Gender also shapes ICT competences and skills. Gray (1992) provides empirical accounts of woman using very sophisticated pieces of domestic technology, that is, the so-called white goods (for example, microwave, washing machine) while at the same time not being able to operate electronic brown goods (for example, VCR). This is sometimes the result of a deliberate, strategic choice not to be able to use ICTs, labelled by Gray 'calculated ignorance' as a strategy of division of labour in the household.

These examples may now seem a bit outdated but they do indicate that use and acceptance of ICTs are negotiated within power relations of the household, be it gender, age, class, ethnicity and combinations of these. With future ambient intelligence systems and services in everyday life, these structural relations will persist, although most likely in different forms. Let me explore this argument through two examples: the absence of housework in the notion of everyday computing and the notion of intelligent agents as social actors.

Everyday Computing and Housework

'Human centred computing' and 'everyday computing' is exactly about supporting and enhancing everyday tasks, the informal and unstructured activities typical of much of our everyday lives. Familiar examples are orchestrating tasks, communicating with family and friends and managing information. Designing for everyday computing requires addressing these features of informal, daily activities (Abowd and Mynatt, 2000, pp.30–31).

A particular type of everyday activity in the home however, namely housework, is rarely considered. This is surprising since housework (for example, cleaning, washing, ironing) is still one of the most repetitive and time-consuming tasks to be executed in the home. There are exceptions. The 'intelligent vacuum cleaner' for instance is already for sale.[9] Also, scenarios describing an intelligent washing machine communicating with the intelligent clothes it is washing exist, but in general, housework seems to be relatively absent in visions and projects about the future of computing. Feminist research on smart homes in Norway at the beginning of the 1990s observed a similar trend (Berg, 1996, pp.87–9). Ethnographic research on the everyday thus highlights that housework occupies a central place in the everyday and that power relations are exercised around it. But within the concept of everyday computing, it seems to be invisible.

Intelligent Agents as Social Actors

The cross-cutting idea for many of the AmI projects and applications is context awareness, currently based primarily on the identification of the user and his/her location. Context awareness renders AmI applications, to a certain extent, smart since they adapt their behaviour based on information sensed from the physical and computational environment. Intelligent agents are central to context-aware services and to AmI in general.

Current descriptions of both context awareness and intelligent agents tend to present them as neutral, that is, not taking a position within social relations. This will be difficult to sustain when confronted with users and non-users in their everyday life, since the latter is not at all neutral. As argued above, the everyday is shaped by an individual's socio-economic position (class, gender, and ethnicity), his or her history (parents, education, etc.) and symbolic position in society. Social capital also plays a role here (van Bavel et al., 2004). Since intelligent services are proactive, they have to present certain choices and/or take some decisions for users, therefore preferring certain options above others. This runs the risk of causing problems and even conflicts in everyday life. Preliminary results of a living lab experiment called 'Ambient Intelligence Homelab' confirmed this.[10] The intelligent agent dealing with entertainment schedules was criticised by the son because it favoured the preferences of his father. Can intelligent agents take a fair or egalitarian position within family relations? Who will be blamed for unequal access within the family?

Rieder (2003) argues that intelligent agents should not only be regarded as software programs, but also as 'social actors' since they inevitably take a position. Agents present a certain view on the world. Making the machine more subjective and thus bringing it closer to everyday life is exactly the objective of the new generations of agents under development. There is a risk however, that agents' functioning becomes a new 'black box', since it is not obvious for users to understand how algorithms yield certain results. How will users be informed about this process? And what is the position of authority of agents' results? Are they exclusive or better than other sources of information? It is clear that social and user-oriented research is needed to better understand the position of intelligent agents in everyday life. They cannot be neutral since it is precisely because they are not neutral that they will be intelligent.

The Disappearance of Computing

At the core of ambient intelligence is the idea that computing becomes invisible by embedding it in the environment and in everyday objects. Computing should be in the background, in the periphery of our attention and should only move to the centre if necessary, hence the existence of EU RTD programmes such as 'the disappearing computer'.[11] At first sight, there is a striking parallel with the domestication approach. Ultimately, technologies are domesticated when they are 'taken for granted', when they reach a state of mind of being a 'natural' part of everyday life. As such, they are not perceived anymore as technologies, as machines, but rather as an almost natural extension of the self. By claiming to move technologies to the background and people to the foreground, ambient intelligence promises a disappearance of the technical artefact and its underlying technologies. As a result, it can be seen as the ultimate stage of domestication.

However, domestication also highlights that the process of acceptance and use of ICTs is not necessarily harmonious, linear or complete. Rather it is presented as a struggle between the user and technology where the user aims to tame, gain control, shape or ascribe meaning to the technological artefact. It is not a sign of resistance to a specific technology but rather of an active acceptance process. The material invisibility of technological artefacts – aimed at through miniaturisation and/or embedding – may well harm rather than facilitate their acceptance. Exactly because they are invisible, they become uncontrollable. Making technologies disappear, while reducing tensions, could on the contrary make them insoluble. There is a difference between the physical and mental disappearance of computing, and it is incorrect to assume that physical disappearance will lead automatically to acceptance and use, and thus to mental invisibility.

Adaptive Computing

Studies of technological innovations have indicated an important difference between the intended use of ICTs by its designers and their real, effective use by users. Users and uses are pre-configured in the design of ICTs. This pre-configuration shapes, to a certain extent, the way ICTs will be used. One cannot leave this frame, as a user, but there is freedom for users to experiment with ICTs, to invent new uses and to make them their own (Flichy, 1995). Users take up this activity. This can lead to surprises, such as the recent success of SMS, which was not expected by the technology designers. Another typical example is the French Minitel of the 1980s. This videotext system was set up to be used as an informational service but the French users 'invented' another, more successful use, that is, communication and erotic services

(Bouwman and Christofferson, 1992). And also the telephone answering machine is used in a way not originally foreseen, that is, for screening incoming calls, and thus actually for increasing inaccessibility instead of accessibility (Frissen and Punie, 2001).

These studies highlight that for ICTs to become accepted, there needs to be some degree of flexibility for users to experiment and find their own uses. With AmI this degree of flexibility can be increased significantly because new services will be driven by software and thus be programmable. Re-programming might become possible both for developers and for users. This is partly incorporated in the idea of adaptive computing whereby devices and services will have a high degree of heterogeneity. Their functions and possibilities are changeable based on user preferences. Truly personal devices will become possible (for example, Islam and Fayad, 2003). Philips calls such an approach 'open tools' (Aarts and Marzano, 2003, pp.338–9).

Also, multimodal appliances are envisaged. A cellular phone can be used as a remote control, for instance. This does not mean one device will do everything but rather that there will be different devices that can handle multiple media related to their specific task. Standards for interoperability will be essential in this context (ITEA, 2001, p.59).

Devices and services that are completely open to users or that are completely adaptable may face the risk, however, of becoming unusable or unappealing for users. Certain degrees of flexibility are necessary but pre-configured uses and users are needed for potential users as guiding forces. They reduce the complexity and uncertainty that typically emerge when users are confronted with innovations. They also help users understand what is new about innovations. A challenge for adaptive computing and for AmI in general is to find an acceptable balance between openness and adaptability versus user guidance and rigidity.

The Ambient Intelligence Divide

According to the Lisbon European Council of 2000 and the e-Europe 2005 Action Plan, the EU is committed to developing, amongst others, 'an information society for all' and to enable all European citizens to benefit from the knowledge society. The Lisbon process clearly stated that the European knowledge-based society should also be a socially inclusive one. This places notions of the digital divide on the policy agenda. It is of concern to policy makers that (new) technologies should not become a (new) source of exclusion in society.

The term 'digital divide' is used and defined in many different ways. It can be observed between regions (for example, North and South), nations, companies, households and individuals (within nations and across nations; with or without disabilities). Research also suggests that the digital divide is not just a question of access to telecommunications and ICT services (for example, the internet) but also of skills, competencies, appropriate content, access to the necessary resources (for example, time and money) and different ways of using ICTs. Voluntary exclusion is also to be taken into account (see for an overview: Cammaerts et al., 2004).

Although the diffusion and penetration of ICTs in Europe, especially of the internet and mobile phones, have increased substantially during the last years, recent empirical data confirm the persistence of digital divides at different levels (for example, Corrocher, 2002; Eurobarometer, 2002; de Haan et al., 2002). At the individual and household level, differences in ownership and usage of ICTs still seem to exist, for instance, between the younger and the older, and between the higher educated, financially well-off families and the lower educated, poorer families. Socio-economic criteria (age, sex, education, income, family composition) do influence not only user acceptance but also users' attitudes towards, and knowledge of, new technologies, and their availability of resources (time and money) as well (for example, Punie, 2004; Frissen and Punie, 2001). And although women are catching up, gender differences persist in ICT usage, both in terms of quantity (for example, time spent on the internet) and in terms of quality (for example, the way ICTs are used).

Ambient intelligence, however, promises to remove some of the existing barriers for the acceptance of new technologies. It challenges current thinking on use and acceptance of ICTs. AmI, indeed, addresses certain issues that are at the core of the digital divide debate, that is, user-friendliness, relevant (context-aware) services and natural interfaces. The latter for instance envisage human-machine interactions that will become more like the way humans interact with each other in the real world (via speech, gesture, touch, senses). It is thought that this evolution away from desktop graphical interfaces would make it easier and faster for everyone to learn to use ambient devices and services (for example, ISTAG, 2002, p.29). Therefore, they would also attract the non-users who today lack the skills and competences to use ICTs.

Even if AmI is adapted to people and even if AmI-facilitated interaction will consequently be relaxing and enjoyable for individual citizens and consumers, it is difficult to believe that AmI will be able to appeal to all groups in society, certainly not in a similar way and at the same time. Given socio-economic differences and individual preferences, there will probably always be 'early adopters' and 'late adopters', and even people who will resist AmI. Although AmI puts a huge emphasis on its user orientation, there are no guarantees that users will indeed embrace AmI in the way it is proposed or developed today.

Moreover, new and other concerns, possibly affecting universal access to, and use of, AmI services and devices, are likely to emerge. New skills, competences and types of literacy could emerge. They could include content selection, content interpretation and creative and innovative thinking (Bogdanowicz and Leyten, 2001). ISTAG (2001) sees new skills arising in relation to social know-how and information manipulation. As AmI increases the means of personal expression and interaction, users will need to learn how to deal with digital identities and intelligent agents. This also raises concerns over the protection of privacy. The question is 'whether people will be able to adapt to the feeling that their environments are monitoring their every move, waiting for the right moment to take care of them' (Aarts et al., 2002, p.249). The threat of the invasion of one's privacy might indeed be one the barriers to AmI's social acceptance.

Privacy, Security, Surveillance and Dependability

As our lives, homes, cars, neighbourhoods, cities and other environments become increasingly digitised and connected, more and more personal information will be digitally gathered, stored and possibly disclosed to other sources, services, institutions and/or persons. Such intrusion concerns not only basic personal identification data such as age, sex and location but also information and communication content such as events information (past, current and future), working documents, family albums (pictures, video, chat) and other medical and financial records (Beslay and Punie, 2002).

With ambient intelligence, the monitoring and surveillance capabilities of new technologies can be massively extended beyond the current credit card and shopping records (for example, consumer loyalty cards), internet logs (for example, email, news postings, discussion forums) and detailed phone invoices. This is possible not only because this intelligent environment is able to detect and monitor constantly what people are doing in their everyday lives, both offline and online, but also because of the possibility of connecting and searching isolated databases containing personal information. Some argue it might even mean the end of privacy (Garfinkel, 2001). It will be very difficult for people to find a place where they can hide themselves, where they will have 'the right to be left alone', the latter being one of the first (liberal) definitions of privacy developed by Samuel Warren and Louis Brandeis (1890).

Monitoring and surveillance techniques create new opportunities for so-called 'border crossings' between what is public and what is private. The problem is that with new AmI technologies, the crossing of these borders becomes easier and possibly more likely. Also, AmI 'needs' to contain historical and current data about individuals' preferences and activities (user profiles) in order to deliver context-dependent, value added, proactive services. A crucial but inevitable trade-off between having privacy of certain personal information and receiving convenient, efficient services will have to be made (for example, SRI, 2003).

But without effective privacy protection measures, this brave new world of smart environments and interconnected objects could become an Orwellian nightmare (Mattern, 2004; Bohn et al., 2003; ISTAG, 2001). Addressing the balance between privacy and security will be a core challenge for the future of ambient intelligence. For people to feel at home within AmI, it needs to be able to represent their multiple identities, respect their privacy and establish an acceptable level of security (Beslay and Punie, 2002).

Technology can do a lot to protect privacy, but in reality, 'it can only safeguard privacy. Figuring out what the safeguards ought to be, and where our zone of privacy actually lies, is a matter of policy, law, and ultimately, social norms' (Waldrop, 2003). Legal and social questions have to be dealt with in relation to the control and management of the information that is collected about an individual and how that information is going to be used. Concerns about privacy are part of larger concerns about control, about people having control over their own lives

Ambient Intelligence and the Need for More Everyday Life

This chapter has identified major challenges and bottlenecks for ambient intelligence in everyday life. It has explored key questions for advancing AmI from a qualitative and critical everyday life perspective. The way ambient intelligence in Europe is being developed holds a lot of promise. The AmI vision explicitly aims to avoid two pitfalls that are common to technology vision building, that is, technology determinism and rhetorical claims of promising a better world. It recognises the need for AmI to be driven by human rather than technological concerns, and it proposes human-centred design and development guidelines together with other social concerns in order to advance this process.

Experience and Application Research Centres (EARCs) are a new approach promoted by ISTAG to take into account functional, technical, social, economic and cultural requirements via prototyping. This should 'allow people to live in their own future' and should bring AmI research closer to the needs of citizens and business. EARCs seem to provide a promising way forward by embedding IST RTD in its socio-economic and user context. It remains to be seen though how EARCs will be implemented and how different levels of user research will reveal different results depending on their location in the innovation process. There are many differences, even within ethnographic approaches to the home, some being more oriented towards design and others more towards a critical sociological underpinning of technology development.

Taking the micro-social context of everyday life seriously would mean that power relations such as class, gender, age and ethnicity are taken into account in the ICT innovation process, and in future studies and vision building. Such an approach would reveal for instance that although the home of the future may bring a good many advantages, it also is the place where power relations and inequalities are fought out. Even if home is a place where people can enjoy being disconnected from over-intrusive AmI, it is not either necessarily, nor indeed often, a place where they can hide from the tensions, struggles and inequalities which are the bane of everyday life. Such an approach also highlights that certain ideas have yet to be included within the framing of AmI, such as housework. This particular type of continuous and time consuming everyday work at home is rarely touched upon in claims about human centred and/or everyday computing, nor does it seem to be prevalent in RTD projects.

Intelligent agents will also need to be seen as social actors that inevitably take a position in social relations; current descriptions of both context awareness and intelligent agents tend to present them as neutral. This will be difficult to sustain when confronted with users and non-users in their everyday life. Therefore, social and user-oriented research needs to better understand the position of intelligent agents in everyday life in order to avoid their agents becoming a new 'black box in society'.

Ambient intelligence promises the 'disappearance' of computing as an object by embedding computing intelligence in the environment and in everyday objects. Ethnographic research suggests that technologies and technological artefacts are domesticated when they are 'taken for granted'. There is a substantial difference between these two perspectives, however. AmI assumes the material or physical disappearance of computing while domestication refers to the mental invisibility of the technology. The two might exist together but not *per se*: physical disappearance will thus not lead automatically to mental disappearance and hence to smooth acceptance and use of AmI. The former may even harm rather than facilitate acceptance, precisely because AmI is invisible, and thus difficult to control.

Another challenge for AmI is to find an acceptable balance between adaptability and rigidity. Devices and services that are completely open or that are completely adaptable may face the risk of becoming unusable or unappealing to users. Certain degrees of flexibility are necessary but pre-configured uses and users are also needed to guide potential users. They reduce the complexity and uncertainty that typically emerge when users are confronted with innovations. They also help users understand what is new about innovations, while completely open tools risk leaving them without direction.

The risk of a digital, or rather an AmI divide, is also an important issue. It is of course difficult to anticipate or predict the possible acceptance of AmI, and although AmI promises to remove some of the current barriers to the acceptance of new technologies, it is unlikely that AmI will appeal to all groups of society. Socio-economic and cultural resources are unequally distributed in society and personal preferences differ as well. Moreover, new skills and competencies are likely to emerge which will result in different degrees of acceptance and even, possibly, rejection of AmI.

There are also strong concerns over the protection of privacy. The invasive potential of AmI might indeed be one of the barriers to its social acceptance. The dilemma is that AmI cannot deliver context-dependent, value added, proactive services without containing historical and current data about an individual's preferences and activities (user profiles). A crucial but inevitable trade-off between having the privacy of certain personal information and receiving convenient, efficient services will have to be made.

Notes

1 The views expressed in this article are the author's and do not necessarily reflect those of the European Commission.
2 Thanks to Jean-Claude Burgelman (IPTS), Marc Bogdanowicz (IPTS) and Rene van Bavel (IPTS) for their comments on earlier versions of this paper.
3 See www.cordis.lu/ist/istag.htm.
4 For an overview of different scenarios on the future of IST, see Popper, R. and Miles, I. with Green L. and Flanagan, K. (2004) Information Society Technologies Futures Forum: Overview of selected European IST scenario reports, PREST for the FISTERA project D1.1, http://fistera.jrc.es.
5 See for respective documents: www.europa.eu.int.
6 Official Journal of the European Communities, 29.8.2002, Decision No 1513/2002/EC of the European Parliament and of the Council of 27 June 2002 concerning the sixth framework programme of the European Community for research, technological develop-ment and demonstration activities, contributing to the creation of the European Research Area and to innovation (2002 to 2006).
7 See http://www.itea-office.org; www.equator.ac.uk.
8 http://www.iso.org; http://www.usabilitynet.org/tools/13407stds.htm; http://www.ucc.ie/hfrg/emmus/methods/iso.html; http://www.e-accessibility.org/.
9 http://www.roombavac.com.
10 Aerts, E. (ed.) (2002) Ambient Intelligence in HomeLab, Published by Philips Research for the occasion of the opening of the HomeLab on 24 April 2002, Philips Research, Eindhoven. http://www.newscenter.philips.com.
11 http://www.disappearing-computer.net.

References

Aarts, E., R. Harwig and M. Schuurmans (2002) 'Ambient intelligence', in P. Denning (ed.) *The invisible future. The seamless integration of technology in everyday life*, New York: McGraw-Hill.

Aarts, E. and S. Marzano (eds) (2003) *The new everyday. Views on ambient intelligence*, Rotterdam: 010 Publishers.

Abowd, G. and E. Mynatt (2000) 'Charting past, present, and future research in ubiquitous computing', *ACM Transactions on Computer-Human Interaction*, 7 (1), March, pp.29–58.

Beigl, M., H-W. Gellersen, and A. Schmidt (2001) 'Mediacups: experience with design and use of computer-augmented everyday artefacts', *Computer Networks*, 35 (4), March. http://www.comp.lancs.ac.uk/~hwg/.

Berg, A-J. (1996) *Digital feminism*, Rapport Nr. 28, Centre for Technology and Society, Norwegian University of Science and Technology, Trondheim.

Beslay, L. and Y. Punie (2002) 'The virtual residence: identity, privacy and security', *The IPTS Report, Special Issue on Identity and Privacy*, No. 67, September, pp.17–23.

Bogdanowicz, M. and J. Leyten (2001), 'Sympathy for the cyborg: research visions in the information society', *Foresight*, 3 (4), pp.273–83.

Bohn, J., V. Coroamã, M. Langheinrich, F. Mattern and M. Rohs (2003) 'Disappearing computers everywhere. Living in a world of smart everyday objects', Paper for the EMTEL Conference, London 23–26 April 2003. www.inf.ethz.ch.

Bouwman, H. and M. Christofferson (eds) (1992) *Relaunching videotex*, Dordrecht/Boston/London: Kluwer Academic Publishers.

Cammaerts, B., L.Van Oudenhove, G. Nulens, and C. Pauwels (eds) (2004) *Beyond the digital divide. Reducing exclusion, fostering inclusion*, Brussels: VUB Press.

Corrocher, N. (2002) 'Internet diffusion dynamics in Europe: demand scenarios and the digital divide', STAR Issue Report No. 29, Databank Consulting. www.databank.it/star.

Crabtree, A. (2003) *Designing collaborative systems: A practical guide to ethnography*, London: Springer-Verlag.

Crabtree, A. and T. Rodden (2004) 'Domestic routines and design for the home', *Computer Supported Cooperative Work: The Journal of Collaborative Computing*, Pre-print article: www.kluweronline.com/issn/0925-9724.

de Haan, J. and F. Huysmans, in collaboration with J. Becker, K. Breedveld, J. de Hart and M. van Rooijen (2002) *E-cultuur: een empirische verkenning*, Den Haag: SCP.

Dewsbury, G., B. Taylor and M. Edge (2001) 'The process of designing appropriate smart homes: including the user in the design', Paper presented at the 1st Equator IRC Workshop on Ubiquitous Computing in Domestic Environments, University of Nottingham, 13–14th September 2001. http://www.equator.ac.uk.

Ducatel, K., J-C. Burgelman, F. Scapolo and M. Bogdanowicz (2000) 'Baseline scenarios for ambient intelligence in 2010', IPTS Working paper, Sevilla, EC DG JRC.

Eurobarometer (2002) 'Internet and the public at large', *Flash Eurobarometer 125*, Eos Gallup upon request of the EC, DG Information Society, July 2002, Brussels: European Commission.

European Commission (2002) 'Information society technologies. A thematic priority for research and development under the specific programme, *Integrating and strengthening the European Research Area* in the Community Sixth Framework Programme, IST Priority, WP 2003–2004', EC: Luxembourg. http://www.cordis.lu/ist.

Flichy, P. (1995) *L'innovation technique. Récents développements en sciences sociales. Vers une nouvelle théorie de l'innovation*, Paris: Editions La Découverte.

Forty, A. (1986) *Objects of desire. Design and society 1750-1980*, London: Thames & Hudson.

Freed, K. (2002), 'American cable adopts Europe's iTV standard', www.media-visions.com/itv-openmhp.html.

Frissen, V. and Y. Punie (2001) 'Present users, future homes. A theoretical perspective on acceptance and use of ICT in the home environment', Delft: TNO-STB Paper, May 2001.

Garfinkel, S. (2001) *Database nation. The death of privacy in the 21st Century*, Sebastopol, California: OReilly Publishers.

Gavigan, J., M. Ottish and C. Greaves (1999) 'Demographic and social trends, panel report', Futures Report Series 02, IPTS, JRC, European Commission.

Gray, A. (1992) *Video playtime: the gendering of a leisure technology*, London & New York: Routledge.

Islam, N. and M. Fayad (2003) 'Towards ubiquitous acceptance of ubiquitous computing', *Communications of the ACM*, February 2003, 46 (2), pp.89–91.

ISTAG (2001) 'Scenarios for ambient intelligence in 2010', K. Ducatel, M. Bogdanowicz, F. Scapolo, J. Leijten, J. and J-C. Burgelman (eds), IPTS-ISTAG, EC: Luxembourg www.cordis.lu/ist/istag.

ISTAG (2002) *Strategic orientations and priorities for IST in FP 6*, Report of the IST Advisory Group, EC: Luxembourg. www.cordis.lu/ist/istag.

ISTAG (2003a) *Ambient intelligence: from vision to reality: For participation in society & business*, ISTAG Consolidated Document, September 2003. www.cordis.lu/ist/istag.

ISTAG (2003b) ISTAG in FP6: Working Group 1 on *IST Research Content*, Final Report, September 2003. www.cordis.lu/ist/istag.

ISTAG (2003c) ISTAG in FP6: Working Group WG3 on *Research results exploitation*, Final Report, September 2003. www.cordis.lu/ist/istag.

ISTAG (2004) *Experience and application research: involving users in the development of ambient intelligence*, ISTAG Working Group Final Report Version 1, June 2004. www.cordis.lu/ist/istag.

ITEA (2001) *Technology roadmap on software intensive systems, information technology for European advancement (ITEA)*, ITEA Office Association, Eindhoven. www.itea-office.org/index.htm.

Lie, M. & K. Sørensen. (eds) (1996) *Making technology our own. Domesticating technology into everyday life*, Oslo/Stockholm/Copenhagen/Oxford/Boston: Scandinavian University Press.

Lull, J. (ed.) (1988) *World families watch television*, Newbury Park, CA: Sage Publications.

Marvin, C. (1988) *When old technologies were new. Thinking about electric communication in the late nineteenth century*, Oxford: Oxford University Press.

Mattern, F. (2004) *Ubiquitous computing: scenarios for an informatized world*, ETH Zurich, Paper to be published. http://www.inf.ethz.ch/vs/publ/index.html.

Miles, I., K. Flanagan and D.K. Cox (2002) *Ubiquitous computing: toward understanding European strengths and weaknesses*, European Science and Technology Observatory Report for IPTS (EC DG JRC), PREST: Manchester, March 2002.

Punie, Y. (2003), 'A social and technological view on ambient intelligence in everyday life: What bends the trend?', European Media, Technology and Everyday Life Research Network, *EMTEL2 Key Deliverable* Work Package 2, September 2003, EC DG-JRC, IPTS, Sevilla. [EUR 20975].

Punie, Y. (2004), 'Een theoretische en empirische benadering van adoptie, gebruik en betekenis van Informatie-en Communicatietechnologie in het dagelijkse leven', in N. Carpentier, C.Pauwels and O. Van Oost (eds) *Het on(be)grijpbare publiek: Een communicatiewetenschappelijke exploratie van publieksonderzoek*, Brussels: VUB Press.

Rieder, B. (2003) 'Agent technology and the delegation-paradigm in a networked society', *Paper for the EMTEL Conference*, London 23–26 April 2003. www.emtelconference.org.

Riva, G., P. Loreti, M. Lunghi, F. Vatalaro and F. Davide (2003) 'Presence 2010: the emergence of ambient intelligence', in G. Riva, F. Davide and W.A IJsselsteijn (eds) *Being There: Concepts, effects and measurement of user presence in synthetic environments*, Amsterdam: Ios Press.

Rogers, E. M. (1995) *The Diffusion of innovations*, New York: The Free Press (Fourth Edition).

Silverstone, R. (1994) 'Domesticating the revolution. Information and communication technologies and everyday life', in R. Mansell (ed.), *Management of information and communication technologies. Emerging patterns of control*, London: Aslib.

Silverstone, R. and L. Haddon (1996), 'Design and domestication of information and communication technologies: technical change and everyday life', in R. Mansell and R. Silverstone (eds), *Communication by design. The politics of information and communication technologies*, Oxford: Oxford University Press.

SRI (2003) 'Distributed identities: managing privacy in pervasive computing', *Explorer Viewpoints*, SRI Consulting Business Intelligence, May 2003.

Tuomi, I. (2002) 'The lives and death of Moore's Law', First Monday, 7(11), November. http://firstmonday.org/issues/issue7_11/tuomi/index.html.

Tuomi, I. (2003) 'Beyond user-centric models of product creation', Paper presented at the *COST A269 Conference: the good, the bad and the irrelevant*, Helsinki, 3–5 September 2003.

van Bavel, R., Y. Punie, J-C. Burgelman, I. Tuomi and B. Clements (2004) 'ICT and social capital in the knowledge society'. Report on a Joint DG JRC-DG Employment Workshop, Sevilla, 3–4 November 2003', *Technical Report EUR 21064 EN*, January 2004.

Waldrop, M. (2003) 'Pervasive computing. An overview of the concept and an exploration of the public policy implications', Paper for the *Future of computing project, foresight and governance project*. www.thefutureofcomputing.org.

Warren, S. and L. Brandeis (1890) 'The right to privacy', *Harvard Law Review*, IV (5). http://www.lawrence.edu/fac/boardmaw/Privacy_brand_warr2.html.

Weiser, M. (1991) 'The computer of the 21st century', *Scientific American*, September 1991, pp.94–101. http://www.ubiq.com/hypertext/weiser/SciAmDraft3.html.

Weiser, M. (1993) 'Some computer science issues in ubiquitous computing', *Communications of the ACM*, July 1993, 36 (7), pp.75–84. http://www.ubiq.com/hypertext/weiser/UbiCACM.html.

Part 3
Methodology and Policy

Chapter 11

The Information Society in Europe: Methods and Methodologies

François Pichault, Dorothée Durieux and Roger Silverstone

Introduction

The empirical research reported in this book has resulted from a principled commitment to a range of qualitative methodologies of social investigation. The claim is not that such methodologies are sufficient for an understanding of the place and significance of new media and technology in everyday life in Europe, but that arguably they are necessary. They are necessary because without them the fine grain of social interaction around, and the social consequences following, the introduction of new media and communication technologies will be forever out of reach. And they are also necessary insofar as that fine grain, in its capacity to illuminate these actions, values and beliefs, might go some way to disturb the presuppositions of those who are involved with, and also maybe of those technologically and politically responsible for, the innovation and diffusion of ICTs across Europe.[1]

This chapter intends to highlight the key components of methodologies employed within the EMTEL network, and to provide a critical summary and analysis of the approaches taken and their possible significance both for future research in this field, and in the formation of ICT policy. It is structured in the following way:

(i)   It analyses the various methodological approaches taken by the EMTEL researchers from a perspective that recognises that they occupy a converging space between research pursued within the social studies of science and technology, and that pursued in the study of users and audiences within media and communications research.
(ii) It discusses the methods used for collecting and analysing the data, as well as the methodological themes and debates that emerge.
(iii) It identifies some of the implications of these research methods for European innovation policy.

Methodological Positions of EMTEL

Three methodological overlapping approaches emerge in the EMTEL research taken as a whole. The first is that derived from user-centred research in media and communications; the second from an approach in the social construction of science and technology, which similarly focuses on the capacity of users to influence, if not define, the trajectory of innovation; and the third brings a more critical approach into the frame; one which takes the analysis of the information society beyond the usual, mostly national, boundaries.

Everyday Life and the User

The everyday life perspective is present in the various EMTEL projects through their investigations of everyday and informal processes related to ICT use. The choice of a 'user-centred' approach is more specific to the contributions of Hartmann, Berker, Ward and Durieux, which explore ICT use and users in everyday contexts. This perspective on ICT in everyday life follows research on domestication (Lie and Sørensen, 1996; Silverstone, 1994), the social construction of technology (Bijker and Law, 1992; Chambat, 1994) and research on 'human agency' (Loader, 1998; Wyatt et al., 2000), where the research focus is the user and not the technology.

Maren Hartmann (Chapter 9), for example, bases her methodological approach on the notion of *domestication*. Domestication describes and analyses the capacity of families, individuals and households, but also other institutions, to make new technologies (and services) their own, to integrate them into their everyday lives. Skills and practices have to be learned in order to deal with ICTs, while meanings are constructed in the same – dialectical – process. The aim of her project, given such a perspective, is to understand what 'user-friendly' might mean in the context of an information or network society. Katie Ward's research (Chapter 7) also addresses everyday processes and follows research directions focusing on the interplay between the local/global and the public/private spheres in understanding the shaping of internet media (Castells, 1996, 2001). Since the domestic environment, or household, has emerged as a fruitful area of study, in terms of the internet's imposition and negotiated position in this private environment (Silverstone, 1994, 1996, 1999; Lie and Sørensen, 1996), this research concentrates on users and the way in which they shape the internet in their everyday life. It also investigates the way in which the construction of meaning does or does not extend into public fora, rendering the boundaries between public and private difficult to distinguish. Similar approaches have been used by Smith and Bakardjieva (2001) where research concerning internet consumption and the domestic environment sought to explore 'behaviour genres' that were established in relation to the internet media and their meaning within the domestic context.

Dorothée Durieux's contribution (Chapter 5), on the other hand, directly challenges the conventional methods of assessing success or failure in the innovation of ICT, and through qualitative empirical involvement with both managers and clients in an innovation setting, it seeks to avoid the temptation to investigate activity in virtual space alone, preferring to examine the interface, both substantively and methodologically, between work online and offline in the negotiation of everyday life (see Jones, 1999, and Mann and Stewart, 2000). It tries to explore experiences and motivations that lead ICT users to develop, or not, different forms of social behaviour or 'virtual togetherness' (Bakardjieva, 2003) in their everyday life. This everyday perspective targets ICT users, who appropriate a PC and/or the internet in various ways in specific contexts of training and work.

Myria Georgiou (Chapter 3) and Bart Cammaerts (Chapter 4) also participate in this everyday life perspective, though they take a more expansive orientation. The latter explores the role of the internet in the organisation of transnational social movements, in their attempts to mediate (online) civic engagement and to influence the (offline) political process. Based on an acknowledgement of what is increasingly seen as a crisis of democracy, the project explores the relationship between ICTs and these alternative or sub-politics and seeks a deeper comprehension of the impact of ICTs on informal and/or formal political processes and participation. Georgiou's project also aims to highlight a number of areas where everyday and informal processes relating to media cultures and ICT appropriation serve to challenge exclusion and further inclusion of those populations in the local, the national and the transnational spheres.

Punie's study (Chapter 10), with its foundations in desk research but also using expert groups, owes its framing and conceptualisation to the same commitments as are found elsewhere in EMTEL research. But his challenge is to use the insights gained to challenge the received wisdom in the management of technological futures and in particular to point to the huge importance of user-oriented research in the context of the emergence of Ambient Intelligent technologies (AmI), whose particular future will depend entirely on the ways in which such intelligence 'disappears' into the experience and environment of the private and public spaces of everyday life. It therefore envisages bringing together technology trends and social/user trends. Punie argues for the need to study new technologies in their social and economic context, and, drawing on the theoretical approach of the social shaping of technology, (Bijker et al., 1987; Bijker and Law, 1992), he suggests a critical perspective on the vision building and technology foresight processes of AmI.

Beyond Boundaries, Towards Critical Research

At one level Punie's approach has already signalled the way forward and indicated one of the many ways in which qualitative research of the kind being pursued here leads almost inevitably to a challenge to the preconceived notions of what constitute appropriate tools and indeed respectable findings in this field. What the research does, at best, and most significantly, is refuse to recognise the etically[2] derived boundaries between domains, for example that between the individual and the social, in order more precisely to link the analysis of technology use to their construction in the patterns of everyday life. So, a number of the EMTEL projects suggest a range of more critical approaches and in particular find themselves questioning references to the usual boundaries and categories in the study of the information society. Several of them clearly involve a more critical approach towards, perhaps above all, the boundaries between work and home, between public and private spheres and spaces, between the relationship between the human and the non-human (the technological), and in relation to the shifts between the local, national and transnational spheres.

First, Berker problematises the boundary between work and home, seeing it not as a starting, but as an end point in the work undertaken by his respondents in managing their own particular boundary between public and private space and their technologies' mediation of those spaces. This of course relativises such a boundary and invites its interrogation elsewhere. Berker is particularly concerned with situations where the heavier use of ICTs involves access both from the home and the workplace. Indeed, it is appropriate to point out that during the course of his study the main instrument, the thematic interview guide, had to be adjusted because it still assumed too clear a line between home and work. Of course, the whole of everyday life can be considered as being divisible between work and non-work. Yet, even in cases of a clear separation between both domains, which are the exception rather than the rule (Nippert-Eng, 1996), the exact location of the boundary may change over time or be in constant dispute. Therefore, the common expectations of studying ICT exclusively in one area or the other become vulnerable.

This project also explores the re-territorialising and de-territorialising practices of individuals in their everyday lives and their mutual inter-relationship. In so doing, the methodology requires an interrogation not just of media or technology use, but of the full range of social and technological relations within which such uses are implicated and on which they make an impression.

Finally, Berker is inspired by the 'agnosticism' of actor-network theory (Latour, 1993 [1991]) in its refusal of an *a priori* division between technology and non-technology. The shaping and embedding of technologies in social practice is a common theme, of course in much research in this area. However, the existence and whereabouts of the boundary between social and cultural 'interpretations of technology' (Bijker et al., 1987) and its materiality as technology *sui generis* is still disputed. Actor-network theory draws the most radical conclusion in declaring this boundary as non-existent, treating objects, institutions and humans as equals. Although one need not to subscribe completely to this 'principle of symmetry' between humans and non-humans in order to harvest its virtues for an exploration of technologies in everyday life, the openness gained by the adaptation of this kind of agnosticism enables the systematic search for the meaning of the otherwise clear-cut boundaries between the social and the material in everyday life.

The exploration of boundaries is also a specific focus of Katie Ward's project, though in her case the boundaries are the already more diffuse ones between the private and public spheres. Ward's project seeks to examine not only perceptions and constructions of meaning relating to internet media within the home, but also the ways in which domestic internet use facilitates participation in public fora. The ethnographic approach to the research allowed an in-depth exploration of the way in which users in a specific locality use the internet to facilitate communication within, but also outside, public fora. The ethnographic approach provided a clear picture of the way in which domestic internet users balanced the relationship between management of the internet within the home with movement into the public sphere.

Finally, both Cammaerts and Georgiou pursued methodologies addressing the transnational. In the first case, the focus was on transnational organisations, in the second on transnational migrant cultures. In both cases, the concern was the relationship between online and offline activity, once again indicating its problematic status but also its importance in addressing the significance of ICT in everyday life. In both cases the sphere of action, both political and in its widest sense cultural, depends on the capacity to translate meaningful mediated communication, both online and in more conventional and monological media environments, into the frameworks of action in the real world. The two cases, of course, present this problematical differently and find different consequences in the analysis of their data.

Methods and Emerging Debates Within EMTEL

Qualitative research requires a strong articulation between data collection and analysis, as well as a close interaction between the researcher and the data. While not in any strict sense being ethnographic, much of the research conducted within the network drew on ethnographic approaches to the study of everyday life. The individual studies depended, albeit in varying degrees, on close engagement with the subjects of the research and a clear commitment not to abstract immediately derived data from the social context in which it was generated, and within which it was to be understood. Clearly some studies were able to devote more time to this kind of detailed questioning and observation than others. But all pursued the kind of interpretative work which such an approach requires and which in turn places considerable responsibility on the analyst to respect, and to respond to, both the words and the settings within the research. The first section below describes the different methods used within the network. The second discusses a series of themes or debates, which may be seen to have emerged from the different projects.

Methods Used Within the EMTEL Network

We can start with Yves Punie's study of AmI innovation, for while it does not depend on the kind of detailed interrogation of everyday life settings that defines the remainder of the research for the most part, it uses the same methodological principles. It takes everyday life and its dynamics as both its start and end. His study of ambient intelligence, in so far as it was directed principally to the future, relied significantly on desk research. His approach worked with the social and user trends, and it inevitably involved reflections and educated guesses rather than observed qualitative or quantitative data. The specific methodological focus of the study consists, therefore, in a critical engagement with the discourses and claims that are developed in the AmI vision-building process and in AmI research and development projects and policies. The discourses, scenarios and AmI road-mapping activities provide the 'texts' to be read and analysed. These 'thick descriptions' are the main empirical material for this research. The analytic method is a version of discourse analysis, which aims at decoding the kind of society that is envisaged within technological visions and textual versions of AmI and the underlying visions of users. In this study, desk research was a primary, but not an exclusive, method. Elsewhere (Hartmann and Cammaerts), it was a significant secondary. It is unlikely to have been absent, however, in any of the studies conducted here.

The second type of method used within the network involves semi-structured or in-depth interviews processed through discourse analysis. Two projects used individual interviews as a main approach to the research focus (Hartmann and Berker), while Durieux conducted individual interviews as a main approach to one of its targeted groups and as a secondary approach to other groups within her two case studies. Hartmann undertook a qualitative study of individual young adult (18–25) users of new media based on semi-structured interviews conducted with students. Each student interviewer undertook one self-interview and six others. All interviews, which together represented nearly 550 semi-structured interviews, were recorded and later transcribed by the students. From these, 198 interviews were selected for more detailed analysis.

The projects led by Berker and Durieux were able to work with smaller numbers: the first based on 20 and the second on 41 in-depth interviews. Berker's interviews were carried out in Trondheim, Norway (twelve interviews) and Darmstadt, Germany (eight interviews). Methodologically one central aspect of this study was the proximity of the researcher to his subjects, since the EMTEL network is one of the numerous efforts undertaken within the European Union to encourage mobility among its citizens, more particularly among academics and researchers. Participants in Trondheim were recruited through emails sent to all participants of the language summer school in 2001 and to non-Norwegian employees of a large Norwegian research institution, as well as through snowballing. In Germany snowballing, personal contact through the University Dean's office and emails sent to ERASMUS students were used to recruit participants. The interviews, where possible, were conducted in the office of the respondent, which provided additional observational data recorded right after the interview. The main researcher carried out preparation and analysis of the data.

Durieux conducted her interviews among the unemployed and the physically disabled in the context of two specific case studies.[3] The aim was to reconstruct their experience of ICT and inclusion through their individual trajectories and their own meanings. The content of those individual interviews was processed through an analysis based on a thematic re-transcription of their discourses, structured around the main topics emerging from the interviews themselves. This analysis focused on usages and representations related to their appropriation of ICT in various spheres of everyday life and their inclusion or exclusion experiences. On the basis of this thematic analysis, interviews among the two groups of interviewees were analysed comparatively in order to identify the different ways in which ICTs were appropriated and the significance of those differences for their subjects' inclusion or exclusion.

Beside individual interviews, interactive workshops were also used in the research. These were undertaken by Punie as supplements to his desk research and as a primary data input to enhance the interpretation of the data as a whole. This method, based on a technique called Science and Technology Road-mapping (S&TRM) was developed under the auspices of the EU project, *Ambient Intelligence in Everyday Life* (*AmI@Life*). S&TRM is one of the methods used in prospective studies and consists of the mapping, in a graphical way, of current and future technological developments in the display and synthesis of past, present and future stages of science and technology developments. During those workshops, experts discussed the issues, functions, technologies and roadmaps for *AmI@Life*, and their discussions and findings were fed into the EMTEL research.

The third type of method was the more self-consciously ethnographic, such as participant observation, semi-structured interviews and local media analysis. Katie Ward used these together with a mix of online research tools such as web-based content analysis, online survey and interviews to develop her project of the local use of ICTs in Loughrock. This project was based on offline and online ethnographic data and interviews with domestic internet users carried out between January 2001 and January 2002. This ethnographic approach involved participant observation in organisations and groups, 23 semi-structured interviews with households, a survey of 250 houses in Loughrock, an examination of local newspapers and the analysis of community-related information. The overall analysis provided details of the patterns of participants' ICT use and an analysis of the ways they chose to appropriate the internet into the home.

This combination of online and offline methods was also used by Cammaerts as a way to produce his case studies. This project conducted online surveys, hermeneutic web-analysis, content analysis of web-forums, discussion mailing lists and general web-presence, and combined these in one analytical framework. Instead of looking at a single issue in depth, this project explored the triadic relationship between transnational social movements, ICT use and civic engagement. The techniques used comprised a mix of a documentary desk-study, online methods and in-depth interviews of key people involved in the civil society organisations. For instance, the degree of transnationalisation and virtualisation was determined through an analysis of the web-presence of the different organisations, and of its different functions, in terms of informing, mobilising, providing space for discussion, and networking.

The case study became a core component of the EMTEL research as a whole. Both Durieux and Georgiou used it as a method to compare ICT translation processes, in the first, and diasporic media cultures throughout Europe, in the second. The first project used the case study as a main approach to the fieldwork, while the second used it as a part of a wider methodological frame based on a more catholic transnational approach.

The fieldwork conducted by Durieux consisted of two main cases selected among European-funded initiatives in Belgium. Following other studies in this field (Akrich, Callon and Latour, 1988, 1991), cases were analysed through a retrospective content analysis of documents provided by both organisations; interviews among key-actors and *in situ* observations. The content of individual interviews with participants was processed through a comprehensive analysis focusing on the uses and representations relating to the appropriation of ICT. They were also processed through an analytical thematic framework, which helped to identify, in the different cases, the influences and inter-relationships between the individual experiences and collective experience of participants in both initiatives. In this way the single interview, through its location and contextualisation, became the raw material of two case studies that, in turn, enabled a degree of comparison.

Georgiou's transnational fieldwork was explored through cross-national research, principally using mapping, and through comparative research based on data from national reports and case studies. In deciding to try to map European media cultures, the research concentrated on the width of the cultural experience of exclusion/ inclusion rather than on its depth. This mapping was based on a combination of different methods. The first involved 13 national reports from across the EU. All EU member states were represented, apart from France and Luxembourg: though there were differently oriented case studies from France, as well as an extensive map of minority publications. As those reports were conducted by researchers living (or who had lived) in each of those countries as well as being native speakers, they offered an insider's perspective, an obvious advantage in comparative research (Livingstone,

2001). In order to gain additional understanding of the diverse spatial positioning of diasporic groups and a qualitative comprehension of the specificities of diasporic experience and media cultures, the study also drew on a series of case studies either produced for this project or from compatible secondary sources.

Georgiou had two objectives in analysing this wide-ranging data. The first was to map the diverse diasporic presence and patterns of communication across the EU, and the second was to develop a more thematic framework exploring different aspects of inclusion and exclusion. The combination of the national reports and the case studies enabled a modest spatial triangulation within the study – that between the local, the national and the transnational.

The use of case studies raises, of course, the familiar question: how can the results obtained be generalised to other concrete situations? Several authors (Yin, 1994) argue that the multiple dimensions of a case study may help to understand the complexity of real life much better than quantitative studies, undertaken on a large sample but forced to select some specific dimensions and to abandon some others. And case studies are capable of apprehending the interconnection of multiple temporalities – a critical factor in the formation of ICT uses – via longitudinal investigations, which are not limited to a simple snapshot. Ultimately, one must keep in mind that a recourse to a case study does not aim at covering all possible situations: even an accumulation of multiple case studies could not lead to exhaustiveness. It rather looks for a 'reasoned' diversity of situations (according to such explanatory variables as cultural contexts, organisational settings, etc.), which allow the testing of different hypotheses linked to ICT uses.

Emerging Themes and Methodological Debates

The different projects reflect the diversity of the methodological debates that have been raised within EMTEL. Different concerns and choices are inevitably expressed in the design of each of these studies. Discussions during the course of their development equally inevitably emerged as to their viability, their coherence, and the clarity and rigour with which they could be pursued. It would be fair to say that most, if not all, of these debates were never finally resolved. But it would also be fair to say that any methodological discourse should not be a singular one: in areas such as those investigated here, there are substantial challenges in a field which is still developing its own methodological priorities and values.

The first issue that was on the table was that of the relationship between quantitative and qualitative research. Maren Hartmann's project, for example, generated nearly 550 semi-structured interviews. These were conducted as part of a teaching exercise and involved students as interviewers. It was clearly impossible to analyse all of these as qualitative data and therefore a selection was made based on identifying two distinct sub-populations. The first of these were the interviews conducted by the students 'on themselves'. These self-interviews produced rich material on the individual use of new media enhanced by a high degree of reflexivity, since the students were able to engage more thoroughly with the data they themselves could generate and compare it (explicitly or implicitly) with that collected from others as part of the classroom exercise. The second sub-population comprised non-students, chosen as a distinct group in order to provide a clear basis for comparison and to cover a wider range of experience. These two groups included 198 interviews (81 self-interviews and 117 non-student interviews) all of which were read for an overall impression and 50 were thereafter randomly selected to perform this basis for the detailed analysis (with the help of the qualitative research software NUD*IST). Overall, the fact that the students interviewed their own age group helped to reduce potential barriers between interviewer and interviewee and produced some interesting research questions.

The second issue concerned the acceptability of imposed boundaries and categories of analysis. Thomas Berker, for example, quickly accepted that the crucial determinations of difference between the core categories of experience in everyday life, those for example between the material and the social, work and home, work and non-work, co-presence and distance were impossible to impose *a priori*, without predetermining and undermining the status of the results. To avoid the risk, as far as possible, Berker followed Donna Haraway (1991), in advocating a 'perspective from the margins' and a focus on the actual construction of boundaries by those who were subjects in the research. Given this perspective the task was to describe categories in terms of a dialectics of stability and change.

A third concern emerging from the research of the network as a whole was the relationship between the real and the virtual. Ward not only examined the construction of the public and private spheres, but she also investigated the way in which users inhabit and traverse the real and virtual realms in an attempt to organise and manage domestic and public life. This approach follows that of Miller and Slater (2000), whose ethnographic study of the internet in Trinidad generated a rich account of the way in which 'Trini' people had not only used the internet to supplement their existing behaviour patterns and routines, but had also challenged the notion that the online and offline or real and virtual spheres can be separated and perceived as independent entities. Georgiou's research also contributes to this debate, in its challenge of the false dichotomy between the virtual and the real. Her research, as well as that of others in the EMTEL network, can be related to many studies on virtual and real life communities, for example that of Bakardjieva's (2003). Bakardjieva criticises the distinction between the two kinds of community and argues that 'so called "real life" communities are in fact virtual in the sense that they are mediated and imagined' (Bakardjieva, 2003, p.4). Following such studies, EMTEL projects also suggest that virtual life 'cannot be studied and characterized exclusively by what is produced online as the cultures enacted online have their roots in forms of life existing in the "real" world' (Bakardjieva, 2003, p.5).

A fourth and final theme of the EMTEL research concerns the comparative, both as transnational (in Georgiou and Cammaerts) and transorganisational (in Durieux).

Georgiou's contribution is principally based on what might be called, if somewhat loosely, mapping: a methodology that learns from the strengths and weaknesses of cross-national comparative research. On the one hand, it aims at recognising themes and significant relations across geographical areas aimed at expanding our understanding of social phenomena (Blumler et al., 1992) and on the other, it attempts to overcome the limitations of many cross-national comparative research projects that consider the nation-state as the most significant unit of analysis (Livingstone, 2001). The project proposes a cross-European analysis, which takes into consideration the national context, but also the local and the transnational. The analysis of the data offers a descriptive mapping of cultural and media diversity, as well as a qualitative/ interpretative analysis of media and cultural practices.

Durieux and Cammaerts suggest a further approach, which is also based on comparative contextualisation of users and everyday experiences, where the context is the organisation rather than the transnational (although Cammaerts takes a broadly cross-national perspective). In the first contribution, different types of contextualised results – the descriptions of political aims and their translation, the evaluation of success/failure within individual projects, the comprehensive presentation of individual discourses – are compared in two different ways. Firstly, the analysis of each case is compared to individual stories of their participants in terms of convergence/divergence of interests and social impacts on the less abled in their everyday life. Secondly, both cases and individual results are compared to each other in order to identify convergence and divergence between the two initiatives, specifically in relation to their success or failure in generating social inclusion.

Cammaerts follows a similar approach, as his case studies are analysed comparatively with regard to organisation, civic engagement and political process. Different issues are addressed in each of these three areas and this required the adoption and use of different methodological approaches for each topic, though for the most part each of them depends principally on web discourse analysis.

The two types of comparisons – firstly, within each fieldwork setting between the collective and the individual and, secondly, between fieldwork settings – are attempts to integrate individual, organisational and contextual factors in a transverse analysis of ICT's social implications and to overcome the limitations of a single study. Perhaps it would be fairer to say that strictly speaking this research is cross-sectional rather than comparative.

Conclusion: Methodological Challenges for EU Innovation Policy

It is perfectly understandable that policy makers in this field, as in most others, are concerned to plan for macro-social change and as such they need the indicators that large-scale quantitative studies provide. It would be foolhardy to pretend or suggest otherwise. Our argument is not that quantitative methodologies do not deliver, or that the kind of micro-social qualitative research projects that we have been discussing are sufficient for their replacement. Nor indeed are we saying that they merely offer a kind of gloss, a nuance, on the supposedly more rigorous and the more powerful methodological tools. In this area, as in many others, the research reported does both more and less than is commonly assumed. It does less, obviously, because it cannot provide a generalisable account of a large slice of the social world. It does more because, in its attention to detail and in its equivalent attention to the interaction, indeed the dialectic, between the social or the technical and between the minute patterns of belief and action in the everyday and the large scale structures of policy and markets, it offers a material and a materially different account of the way innovation can, and should, be understood. The methodological choices are therefore not innocent of theory and indeed both emerge from, and lead to, a kind of theory which requires a different way of seeing and understanding the world (all good theory should do that). We think more of this research should be done and more of its power should be recognised, as indeed it is beginning to be, in commercial and market research settings where the details of decision making, valuation and the actual practice of individuals (rather than their fantasies or the aggregation of their individual decontextualised choices) is now being seen as crucial to an understanding of behaviour in the social world, and to its better management and prediction.

It is of course reasonable to expect that global observations and quantitative trends of, for instance, IT development stages, ICT penetration rates within households, individual access to ICT, number of public e-services, or the security of system infrastructures, will be a first step in the development of a structured knowledge about the information society. But we would contend that the kind of research discussed in this book, based as it is on predominantly qualitative indicators of well-being, inclusion/exclusion, citizens' participation and domestication, will enable the generation of in-depth knowledge about everyday and informal processes which should, when combined with existing indicators, help policy makers avoid misinterpretations of social processes and restrain their tendency to exaggerate the potential of ICT for social, cultural or economic development. In this effort to overcome the use of bounded categories or fixed boundaries, the EMTEL research suggests a specific approach that claims a better understanding of the place of ICT in the everyday life of European citizens.

The EMTEL project, as a whole, has orientated much of its efforts towards generating a significant degree of reliability in its approach to qualitative research, and in this way, it hopes to make an equally significant contribution to social analysis and the development of policy. The combination of offline and online methods, the investigation of so-called cyberspace in relation to the lived and experienced social contexts of the everyday, together offer new approaches to the way in which we might think about, and manage, the information society in Europe. The distinction between the real and the virtual should not be taken for granted but used instead as a challenge to our understanding of social and everyday processes around ICT. This everyday perspective also leads to a re-conceptualisation of comparative research and the development of new comparative methodologies, moving from studies based on a juxtaposition of national observations to cross-national and cross-sectional analysis of individuals, groups and organisations in various European contexts.

Those various constructions of methods and methodologies in the investigation of the information society also reflect the 'user friendly' orientation of the EMTEL network. This is, one might suggest, perhaps its most important contribution. In developing its agenda it has sought to go beyond the familiar rhetoric of the information society in order to ensure a more sensitive, and therefore a more accurate, account of the varieties of experience and meaning in relation to information and communication technologies in the everyday lives of the citizens of present-day Europe.

Notes

1 More detailed accounts of the methodologies employed in each of the studies can be found in their authors' final reports; for a full list of these see p.xiii.

2 Etically derived categories emerge from outside the research domain, as opposed to those which are called emic, and which derive for the practices and values of those being studied, that is from the subjects of the research.

3 A third group, the elderly, were included in the main study, but have not been reported in the chapter presented in this volume.

References

Akrich, M., M. Callon and B. Latour (1988) 'A quoi tient le succès des innovations? 1. L'art de l'intéressement', *Gérer et comprendre*, 11, pp.4–17.

Akrich, M., M. Callon and B. Latour (1991) 'A quoi tient le succès des innovations? 2. L'art de choisir les bons porte-parole', *Gérer et comprendre*, 12, pp.14–29.

Anderson, B. and K. Tracey (2001) 'Digital living. The impact (or otherwise) of the internet on everyday life', *American Behavioural Scientist*, 45 (3), pp.456–75.

Bakardjieva, M. (2003) 'Virtual togetherness: an everyday life perspective', *Media, culture and Society*, 25 (3), pp.291–313.

Bijker, W.E., T.J. Pinch and T.P. Hughes (1987) *The social construction of technological systems: new directions in the sociology and history of technology*, Cambridge, Mass.: MIT Press.

Bijker, W.E. and J. Law (eds) (1992) *Shaping technology/building society. Studies in sociotechnical change*, Cambridge: MIT Press.

Blumler, J.G., J.M. McLeod and K.E. Rosengren (eds) (1992) *Comparatively speaking: communication and culture across space and time*, Newbury Park, London, New Delhi: Sage.

Castells, M. (1996) *The rise of the network society. The information age: economy, society, and culture Vol. I*, Cambridge, Oxford: Blackwell.

Castells, M. (2001) *The internet galaxy: reflections on the internet, business, and society*, Oxford: Oxford University Press.

Chambat, P. (1994) 'Usages des technologies de l'information et de la communication: évolution des problématiques', *Technologies de l'Information et Société*, 6 (3), pp.249–70.

Haraway, D. (1991) 'A cyborg manifesto: science, technology and socialist-feminism in the late twentieth century', in D. Haraway *Simians, cyborgs and women: the reinvention of nature*, New York: Routledge.

Jones, S. (ed.) (1999) *Doing internet research. Critical issues and methods for examining the net*, London: Sage.

Latour, B. (1993 [1991]) *We have never been modern*, New York, London: Harvester Wheatsheaf.

Lie, M. and K.H. Sørensen (eds) (1996) *Making technology our own? Domesticating technology into everyday life*, Oslo: Scandinavian University Press.

Livingstone, S. (2001) 'On the challenges of cross-national comparative media research', Unpublished paper.

Loader, B.D. (ed.) (1998) *Cyberspace divide*, London: Routledge.

Mann, C. and Stewart (2000) *Internet communication and qualitative research. A handbook for researching online*, London: Sage.

Miller, D and D. Slater (2000) *The internet: an ethnographic approach*, Oxford: Berg.

Nippert-Eng, C.E. (1996) *Home and work: negotiating boundaries through everyday life*, Chicago: University of Chicago Press.

Silverstone, R. (1994) *Television and everyday life*, London: Routledge.

Silverstone, R. (1999) *Why study the media?*, London: Sage.

Silverstone, R. and L. Haddon (1996) 'Design and the domestication of information and communication technologies: technical change and everyday life', in R. Mansell and R. Silverstone (eds) *Communication by design. The politics of information and communication technologies*, Oxford: Oxford University Press.

Smith, R. and M. Bakardjieva (2001) 'The internet in everyday life: computer networking from the standpoint of the domestic user', *New Media and Society*, 3 (1), pp.67–83.

Wyatt, S., F. Henwood, N. Miller and P. Senker (eds) (2000) *Technology and in/equality. questioning the information society*, London: Routledge.

Yin, R. (1994) *Case study research: design and methods*, (2nd ed.), Beverly Hills, CA: Sage.

Chapter 12

ICTs in Everyday Life: Public Policy Implications for 'Europe's Way to the Information Society'

Paschal Preston[1]

The new knowledge-based society must be an inclusive society ... [and] in emphasising digital inclusion, the European Commission aims to distinguish the European approach to the information society from other regions of the world (EC, 2002c, p.4).

Introduction: Social Science Research and the Policy Dimension

Over the past decade, a succession of national and EU level public policies have played a major role in shaping the diffusion of new ICTs and 'information society' developments more generally. Despite a fundamental emphasis on a 'market-driven' approach (EC, 1994a), the influence of such national or supra-national state policies should not be underestimated (Preston, 2001). Quite apart from explicit 'information society' initiatives, such influences range from the establishment or extension of property rights, new forms of competition and privatisation policies, the protection of minors, to research and development and educational policies. They also include public procurement or purchasing policies, as the public sector has been a very significant customer for new ICT-related products and services.

In this context, we may simply note that the public sector has been a key force in shaping the design and supply-side aspects of new ICT-related developments in Europe and beyond. Alongside private corporations based in the ICT-related sectors, the public sector has played a significant 'top down' role in shaping 'Europe's way to the information society' over the past decade. Indeed, a number of studies in the European Media Technology and Everyday Life Network reveal how national and EU policy discourses have played an important ideological role in changing users' perceptions and in stimulating their purchase of ICT equipment and services quite separately from the marketing operations of corporations involved in the supply of such products.

Clearly, such top down or supply-side factors are important objects of study in terms of advancing our understanding of the socio-economic dimensions of an evolving information society. Indeed, they have been the direct concern of many other projects funded under successive EU Framework programmes. However, the research from the network and reported in this book has adopted an alternative, but complementary, 'bottom up' approach to the research agenda. EMTEL has been concerned to address the sphere of everyday life and so it has conducted detailed empirical studies addressing the interfaces between new ICT and social change. In essence, our research has set out to explore 'the nature, direction and speed of technological change, and the significance of the everyday as a context for the acceptance of, or resistance to, new communication and information technologies' (Silverstone, this volume). It has investigated the ways in which users (defined as both consumers and citizens) incorporate or fail to incorporate the new and the technological into their everyday life.

Thus, the EMTEL studies afford distinctive and challenging insights into the role and meaning of new ICTs in the everyday life of citizens and consumers in contemporary Europe. In particular, the project's perspective and methodology affords a very different view of the European information society (or knowledge society) compared to that which informs most research and policy discourse in this field, whether at the European or national levels.

This particular chapter will identify some of the key *implications for public policies* and strategy emerging from the final reports of the EMTEL project. In particular, it will focus on policies related to the European information society. We use the term 'policy *implications*' here quite deliberately as it is neither within our competence nor is it our intention to produce detailed or specific recommendations for policy practitioners. As researchers, our optimal contribution to the policy process is not to presume to tell policy specialists what to do or decide. Rather, our optimal engagement with the policy process is more modest and limited. Yet it is one that is perfectly in keeping with a reflexive understanding of the context of the ever-deepening division of labour so characteristic of the contemporary 'knowledge-based society'. It is to draw on our research to identify key findings that may serve to challenge or enhance the kinds of thinking and considerations that currently inform policy decision making or practices.

This chapter will draw on this research to focus on some of the key implications for public policy. Here, we may note that the work aims to achieve its distinctive contribution precisely because its empirically-grounded research strategy does *not* start from a portfolio of ideas, issues or concerns directly driven by the current 'top down' policy agenda of the EU or of national governments. Indeed, for the most part, the researchers paid relatively little explicit attention to the official policy discourses and documents related to new ICT or 'the information society' until the final stages of their work. Indeed, in 'reflexive' mode, the very fact that many of those involved were little motivated to address directly the content of such documents may itself be regarded as an important 'finding' concerning the perceived role and impact of such political initiatives and policies in contemporary Europe. This, in turn, may well be related precisely to the new kinds of political cultures, lived subjectivities and identities that have been discussed in the preceding, empirically based chapters of this book.

Inclusion and Exclusion: Key Policy Implications

Dimensions of 'Inclusion' and 'Exclusion' Related to ICT and the 'Information Society'

Much of the ICT policy discourse surrounding 'the digital divide' has focused on measures of access to computers and/or connection to the internet and related network services. But as the more nuanced policy approaches have well recognised, measures of access or indeed of frequency of use comprise only a part of the problem of exclusion and inequality.

The EMTEL studies illustrate the benefits of adopting a wider view of the role and significance of new ICTs in the evolving patterns of exclusion and inequality in the everyday life of contemporary European society. For example, Myria Georgiou has explored the evolving cultural and media-related dimensions of inclusion and exclusion among increasingly important diasporic minority groups in contemporary Europe. This research reveals not only the growing role of minority media in the European information environment but also addresses the significance of media cultures for a wider understanding of social inclusion and exclusion. The study addresses how technological as well as other material and symbolic resources are very unequally distributed between and within minority groups in Europe.

Like many other EMTEL studies, Georgiou indicates that many of the 1990s information society policies have been very highly focused on technology-led visions. The argument serves to highlight the central importance for policy makers of transcending the narrow confines of (technical) access and connectivity in order to address more fully new digital and other media-based cultures and content. This is deemed necessary if policy is to serve the goal of creating a more inclusive (diverse and tolerant) 'information society' in the face of new multicultural communities in contemporary Europe.

In turn, other studies presented here reaffirm the point that the major forms and sources of social exclusion are not primarily ICT-related and that they are often far from technological in character. Rather, many key forms of exclusion reflect the growth of inequalities in the contours socio-economic power, new barriers to participation arising from increasing globalisation and unemployment levels, or the sheer fact of being less abled (Durieux, Chapter 5). The resulting implication is that policies predominantly focused on ICT access and use, however well framed or well-intentioned, are unlikely to have much impact in alleviating such forms of social exclusion. In the case of the less abled, for example, there are significant questions raised concerning the realism and viability of ICT-focused projects compared to alternative strategies addressing other kinds of structural or socio-economic barriers to participation in the jobs market and other spheres of everyday life.

The Limits of Singular Quantitative Standards (Measures) of ICT Access/Use

The overriding objective of European and national IST and information society policies since the mid-1990s has been to maximise the production and (perhaps, especially) the use of new ICTs. To that end, policy makers have been heavily concerned to develop, fund and compare standardised quantitative measures (or universal 'barometers') of such ICT use, both within nations and across Europe or more globally.

Clearly, such quantitative data can certainly play an important and valid role in informing policy. But I want to suggest that the detailed qualitative research reported in this book provides more nuanced understandings of the social (or socio-technical) significance of the processes of ICT use and adoption. Our work thus serves to complement the relevant knowledge base available to policy makers in this field. It also poses certain important questions concerning the limitations or validity of some of the ways in which such quantitative studies have been interpreted and used in policy discourse and practice.

For example, the findings suggest that the apparent 'facts' or data emerging from such quantitative studies may not be as solid or as self-evidently informative as often assumed. The bald fact that a certain percentage (say 30 per cent or 70 per cent) of persons are regular users of the internet tells us very little about the social (or socio-technical) significance of such patterns in isolation from an explicit consideration of the everyday life practices and contexts of the user group(s) under study. The social significance of a particular quantitative score (for example, percentage of internet users) is not universal, but varies significantly from group to group. For example, it may be the case that a particular quantitative measure, such as that 70 per cent of professional workers (for example, academics and lawyers) in Norway are active internet users, may be much less significant than one indicating that 'only' 20 per cent of farmers in southern Spain are active users. Such apparent facts do not 'speak for themselves'. Rather, from a socio-technical change perspective, the latter datum (lower percentage of users) may well prove to be a much more significant development than the former.

One of the key insights provided by this approach is that it is important to recognise the limitations of any 'universal' measures of internet or other ICT use, especially if the concern is to understand the co-evolution or extent of social and technical development or change. Both the (quantitative) extent and social significance of technology-enabled change is highly context-sensitive as well as being dependent on its relevance to the everyday life activities, values and meanings of different social groups. This applies even in the case of emerging new kinds of 'ambient', invisible and apparently very much more user-friendly technologies (Punie, Chapter 10).

Other studies reported here raise very similar policy relevant implications concerning the limits of one-dimensional quantitative measures or singular 'universal' barometers of ICT access, use and associated targets and assumptions. In different ways, our work has highlighted how current and future uses of new ICTs are often highly context-dependent. The differential uses and appropriations are not determined by the technical features and functions of new ICTs but closely linked to their relevance and meaning as shaped by socially prescribed roles and identities in the everyday life activities of different groups of users. Besides, such conditioning social factors are not fixed with respect to time and place but are themselves changing or co-evolving. For example, some of our studies indicate that long-documented evidence and images of gender differences in ICT access and use may have become less significant by the late 1990s (Ward, 2003).

Thomas Berker (Chapter 8) examines migrant researchers as a relatively privileged group of potential users (in terms of ready access to all kinds of new ICTs at low cost).

These may be generally typified as comparatively high/heavy users of new ICTs compared to most other social groups. But Berker also suggests significant difference in the patterns of ICT use amongst such migrant researchers. He suggests that existing social networks (rather than technical networks) play a major role in determining the nature of ICT use. Even in this relatively small and privileged group of migrant users, there are significant variations in terms of the types and intensity of ICT use.

One key and pertinent policy implication arising from such research findings concerns the need for more sophisticated measures or 'barometers' of ICT use and consumption across different countries or social categories if these are to prove of real relevance to public policies. Any new and more nuanced measures or 'barometers' of ICT use and consumption would have to combine relevant inputs from both quantitative research methods as well as the kinds of qualitative methods adopted in our approach.

Overload: An Excess of Inclusion

Recent ICT policy debates and practices have usually been framed around the core assumptions that ICT access or inclusion is 'good', and that 'non-use or exclusion is bad'. They have also tended to assume the more inclusion, the better, and to highlight the universal benefits of maximising the use of new ICT-based connectivity networks and communication services.

In many respects, such ICT policies have tended to focus almost exclusively on the perceived benefits of new ICT for the production and distribution of information and (the initial 'sender' stages of) its communication. Our research has indicated that ICT policies have tended to neglect some important demand-side issues, user and consumption aspects of such developments. Indeed, we suggest ways in which policy making may be enhanced if the relevant actors were to pay more attention to the consumption and user aspects of new ICT-based networks and communication services.

Berker's work also raises some relevant issues in this context – some of which have been neglected in recent policy discourses and practices. He provides examples of how high levels of ICT-based flexible connectivity may become a problem rather than an automatic benefit for some users. He finds that some users complain about the problems arising from universal accessibility, such as being interrupted too often or drowning in too much information. The study indicates how these individuals develop their own practices to restrict accessibility or to filter information by means of comparison with other sources. But this does not always provide an adequate solution: the cases where this is not working are, without exception, exposed to forces which are not mentioned by most EU or other relevant policy papers.

According to Berker, one important variable here is the *individual's workload*. To a large degree, this determines whether access and flexibility bring about 'benign or malign consequences' for the user. This is particularly the case for users exposed to flexible connectivity whose everyday life is characterised by the highest degree of spatial and temporal flexibility, such as the lack of embeddedness in familial structures or very short-term work contracts. Berker consistently draws our attention to the possible dysfunctionalities of flexibility.

These and other findings suggest that future policy making and research should pay much more attention to such consumption and user aspects of new ICT-based connectivity and communication services – not least the much-neglected impacts of the expanding forms of information 'excess' or overload. This includes the issue of time as an increasingly scarce or 'precious resource', as recognised in the growing literature surrounding work-life balance issues and as long flagged in academic models of the information society (Preston, 2001).

Limitations of Privileging Certain New ICTs and Their Uses Over Others

We may note also that in policy discourses that emphasise the maximum adoption of new technologies, the dominant orientation privileges certain types of new ICT at the expense of others. There is a marked tendency to assume, and highlight, the use and benefits of the computer and the internet with a relative neglect of other kinds of ICT use (for example, mobile telephony).

Some of our studies suggest that such policy assumptions do not well match the use and benefits of new ICTs as experienced or performed by users in the domain of everyday life. For example, even for the so-called 'web-generation', the uses and benefits of the computer and the internet may be somewhat less important in the domain of everyday life than other facets of new ICTs. Hartmann's study of young people's engagement with new ICT suggests that mobile telephony may well play an equal if not greater role in shaping change in the everyday social patterns of communication. Similarly, among migrant researchers, a relatively privileged group of potential users (in terms of ready access to all kinds of new ICTs), there are those who prefer interpersonal communication (be it mediated or not) to information seeking.

Taking Play Seriously: Instrumental vs. Ludic Applications/Aspects of New ICT and the Information Society

The thrust of 'top down' policies, at both the national and European levels, has been firmly focused on the instrumental uses and benefits of new ICT and/or the information society, highlighting, for example, the economic benefits, including enhanced productivity and better paid jobs.

In contrast, some of our studies suggest that policy making might usefully pay more attention to the more playful, ludic or entertainment-oriented applications of new ICT in everyday life (see especially, Hartmann, this volume). Indeed, it may be the case here that middle-aged policymakers, no less than senior researchers, have some lessons to learn from children's and young adults' engagement with new ICTs. It is possible to suggest that for many children and young adults, new media and ICTs are beginning to reach a state of 'naturalness' in their everyday lives. But more importantly in the present context, perhaps, it should be noted that for such users, ICTs are not primarily associated with instrumental applications such as those related to education and work. Furthermore, as Hartmann suggests, young adults who had the opportunity to 'play around' with computers in their childhood years were much more inclined to simply adopt them – partly playfully – into their later lives without much trouble (Hartmann, 2003).

Close Inter-connections Between Online and Offline Activity and Forms of Exclusion/Inclusion in Everyday Life

Our general finding that there are dense and complex interconnections between the processes of online and offline exclusion (or inclusion) within the sphere of everyday life poses another important implication for policy thinking and practice.

These studies underline the fact that access to, and use of, new ICT and related online services does not mean that users become inhabitants of some discrete new social realm of 'cyberspace' essentially separate from their everyday life in an 'offline world'. This has been a common theme in the speculative constructions and images of the internet (and new ICTs), which proved so popular in the late 1990s. The empirically grounded research emerging from the EMTEL studies tells us a somewhat different story. It highlights how the users' appropriation of the internet and related new ICTs tends to be not only highly selective but also very closely intertwined with their everyday interests, activities and needs in the offline realm. Katie Ward, for example, argues that much of the everyday use of the internet involves its personalisation, in which the technology is constructed to supplement the enactment of existing habits and routines (Ward, this volume).

From the outset, our project's approach and qualitative methodology has been very attentive to the potentially creative and active role of users in adapting, using or appropriating new ICTs in unforeseen ways. This includes the internet's capacity to expand and enhance participation in the political public sphere (as, indeed, do many current e-Government initiatives).

Here, some of our work suggests that this potential may have been somewhat exaggerated or reflect misplaced or mistaken conceptions of public communication processes. Ward clearly finds that the residents of 'Loughrock' had very little engagement with these publicly oriented uses of the internet. Rather, the predominant use was centred round highly personalised and private concerns. The majority of surveyed residents adopted and adapted the internet for email purposes (to maintain contact with friends and family) and for the consumption of health and educational content as well as that provided by the websites of older/mature media organisations. Others within the network, and in this volume, however, suggest that new ICTs may be creatively harnessed by minority, less powerful or excluded groups to expand the range and quality of the performance of their public communication processes.

But, contrary to the claims of techno-centric analyses and gurus of the 1990s, in no case was there evidence of an autonomous new ICT or specific 'new media effect', particularly one that disturbed the fundamental patterns of unequal power or access to material and symbolic resources. As proved to be the case in prior debates about the role of communication technology in socio-economic development and change, there is no 'magic multiplier' effect. Indeed, in this regard, our overall findings tend to emphasise the dense and deep interplay between exclusion/inclusion processes and other social practices across both the online (or ICT-based) domains and the offline domains of everyday life.

Dorothée Durieux's study also illustrates well the potential and limitations of ICT/technology-centred inclusion policies and initiatives directed at the less abled and their interplay with the socio-economic dimensions of unequal life opportunities (Durieux, Chapter 5). Her research indicates how well-structured ICT-centred training initiatives may well produce a virtuous convergence of interests between diverse actors in the construction of effective 'inclusion' efforts, specifically to enable previously less-skilled and otherwise disadvantaged groups improve their opportunities in the labour market. In sharper contrast, however, the research on the call-centre initiative illustrates that ICTs cannot act as a significant factor, alone, in reducing the exclusions of the less abled.

New Media (Internet/the Web) and Public Communication

'They've Not Gone Away, Y'Know': Mature Media and Everyday Life

Our research points to the important limitations of technology-led or techno-centric approaches to policy making when it comes to questions of digital media and content developments. For example, despite the claims of popular techno-centric analyses and digital beings in the 1990s, and of those policy reports and discourses influenced by them, the 'old' or established media have not been displaced, or substituted, in any significant way by new media.

Some of the work examines how the role and use of new/digital media has increased in recent years. But at the same time, it also affirms that the established media continue to play a dominant role within the increasingly complex media environment in which everyday life is now embedded in contemporary Europe. Furthermore, when it comes to accessing and use of so-called new media, a number of our studies clearly indicate that the content and other services offered by the 'old media' play a major role in the online activities of many users.

'Alternative' Communication: Minority Media and Transnational Social Movements

As noted earlier, Katie Ward's study of Loughrock found that the residents of this small urban community in Ireland tended to use the internet predominantly for private and personal communication affairs. The internet was not considered or used as an important mechanism to participate in or contribute to public debate and this was especially the case when it came to a number of key local policy and community planning issues. Indeed, the majority of participants in this study considered publicness or public affairs to be best symbolised and most appropriately conducted via the mature media such as newspapers or even leaflets, and by face-to-face communication. Residents of Loughrock indicated that they did not consider, or use, the internet as an important mechanism to participate in or contribute to public debate. Indeed few residents ever made use of the websites containing information related to local community or political affairs.

Other EMTEL studies focused on the transnational level rather than the local community level of ICT-based communication networks and services, and these provide some interesting contrasts to Ward's study.

Myria Georgiou provides a rich description of minority media initiatives, cultures and practices in a dozen European countries whilst also raising a number of important implications for media-related aspects of ICT and information society policy. Her work suggests that there has been a significant increase in the quantity and diversity of media projects originating among the ethnic and cultural minorities residing in EU member states. However, the level of inclusion in the mainstream media may have declined (marked, for example, by decreases in subsidies, cuts to policy supports for multicultural media projects, lower or stable levels of employment of minorities in mainstream media). This contradiction can enforce not only exclusion, but also the sense of exclusion amongst minorities (Georgiou, this volume; Georgiou, 2003).

She describes how new ICTs do not merely support the expanded potential for communication within and across diasporic groups and/or between diasporic groups and their country of origin but she also suggests that the qualities and meanings of such communication processes are also being altered. Her work indicates how the old myths of return to the original *homeland* are now taking a new form, as instead of a physical return, there is a *virtual return* taking place via the networks and communication activities supported by new ICTs (Georgiou, 2003).

One of the key findings emerging from her work concerns the major inequalities that exist with respect to the quantity and quality of digital media content and services now available between and within different ethnic minority groups. Some well-established groups, and those with more ready access to material resources than others, clearly produce and control much more communication flows and outputs than others. Once again, we are reminded that the levels and forms of 'exclusion' online or otherwise associated with new ICT are not 'stand-alone' but closely linked to prevailing material and cultural inequalities in the social realm. Such findings are directly linked to questions about the responsibility of states and the EU for promoting differentiated rights (for example, Walby, 2001).

The implications for policy point to the potentially egalitarian role of subsidies to support the most excluded minorities and the minorities within minorities. European information society policies should go beyond the functional and linear technology-centred views of the significance of ICTs for inclusion to embrace content and other downstream application services which may expand the communication potentials of excluded populations and their cultural inclusion and empowerment. Georgiou finds that although internet access has increased and become cheaper in recent years, significant inequalities exist. This supports the need for national and EU policies directed at increasing the levels of access of underprivileged groups.

This research also indicates that there is an inevitably complex interaction between the general political discourse and the policies about immigration, minorities and communication within both EU-level bodies and those of member states. Even if these have emerged and grown with relevant independence, some level of integration in these policies is increasingly necessary.

Lastly, this study also suggests that European transnational media policies should not only think within the nation-state frame, but also address transnational media flows, some of which are those of diasporic populations. Initiatives such as *Television without Frontiers* cannot be a 'privileged' area of interest of major national broadcasting corporations. The present approach of top down cross-border co-operation must be complemented by considerations of parallel bottom up processes. These reflect the significance of transnational cross-European flows, which have resisted the constraints of national boundaries. The major top down policies could even learn how decentralised, transnational networks become successful and inclusive (Georgiou, 2003).

Somewhat similar points emerge from Cammaerts' research (Chapter 4), which emphasises the growth of political engagement in less formal civil society organisations in more recent years and the need to value this shift in a positive light 'not as a threat to the present order, but as a democratic enrichment' (Cammaerts and Van Audenhove, 2003). This particular study also stresses the importance of policy approaches which maximise the scope for expression of diverse views and opinions in digital media domains and expressly warns against policy approaches or regulations which might serve to diminish an 'open network philosophy'. Cammaerts and Van Audenhove suggest that effective inclusion policies must be broadened beyond current technology-centred views of the digital divide, especially to address the extent to which contacts between the citizen and state become increasingly digitised. It suggests the need for new kinds of socially-centred 'universal service' policies, embracing the barriers to inclusion imposed not merely by inequalities in education and training, but also addressing the role played by structural inequalities on a global and local scale.

The Relative Absence of 'Radically New' Content and Content Use

As noted earlier, the development and use of new ICTs has not changed the fundamental inequalities of material and symbolic power, nor 'cured' other aspects of socio-economic and political exclusion in contemporary Europe. At the same time some of the EMTEL studies do indicate the manner in which new ICTs, with appropriate policy supports, may be creatively harnessed by minority, less wealthy or other less powerful ('excluded') groups to expand the range and quality of the public communication profile and activities. They can be used to enable, as Cammaerts and Van Audenhove (2003) argue, civil society actors to organize themselves more efficiently, to network and to mobilize and may serve to facilitate the attempts to reinvigorate civil society and social movement participation.

At the same time, some of the other EMTEL studies confirm, on the one hand, a significant gap between actual levels of new media developments thus far and, on the other hand, the common expectations of policy makers (and many of their related consultancy and research reports) in the 1990s. In essence, there is a major gap between earlier expectations and the actual delivery with respect to the extensive 'potential' of new ICT to support radically new content forms or modes of public communication (for example, EC 1994b, 2002c).

For example, Hartmann's study suggests that among the so-called 'web-generation', the lives of young people may now be widely touched by new ICT use and their practices fairly radically – yet their content use is mostly not radical at all. Rather their content use largely comprises the reinforcing of existing communicative networks and informational patterns. This kind of finding echoes those emerging from Ward's study of Loughrock residents' use of online content.

Our research suggests a significant 'gap' or lag between the potential of new-ICT enabled communication and content developments and those actually realised so far, which poses some interesting challenges and implications for approaches to policy making. At the very least, they seem to point to the far-from-new question of whether approaches to policy making have thus far paid adequate attention to the 'I' (information and content) and 'C' (communication) as opposed to the 'T' (technological) dimensions of new ICTs.

Ever since the seminal Bangemann Report, *Europe's way to the information society*, EU policy has been defined as fundamentally 'market driven'. At the same time, public policies have involved the mobilisation of considerable material and symbolic resources towards the development of new technological artefacts and networks, and have encouraged or even 'pressurised' users towards maximising their purchase and use of new ICTs. In comparison, the amount of public policy supports directed at supporting the development of novel and innovative ICT-based content and communication forms has been very low in comparative terms (Preston, 2003). At the same time, the design, authoring and publication of novel content forms, especially those appealing to minority, local or otherwise diverse audiences, may be deemed high-risk and subject to 'market failure' as they are relatively costly (Preston, 2001).

In this context, our work, echoing earlier research, points to the high value that users place on diverse forms of content – directed at specifically local or minority cultures. The Irish study, for example, points out that locality continues to remain important to people, suggesting that European and national policy must incorporate the significance of the local; that national and European policies on public communication and participation must be tailored to meet local needs; and that print and other older media must be acknowledged as continuing to play a key role in facilitating public communication, implying that the role of all media must be considered when thinking about and formulating policy relating to public communication (Ward, 2003).

Issues of New Media Regulation and 'Trust'

One of the policy implications highlighted by Cammaerts (Chapter 4; Cammaerts and Van Audenhove, 2003) is that regulation of the new media arena should be minimalist in scope. They suggest that the 'open network philosophy ... is doing fine' and that there is little reason for content regulation on the internet (Cammaerts and Van Audenhove, 2003). In contrast, Ward reports significant concerns among users in Loughrock about the lack of safety and trust associated with the new media, particularly in the case of children as internet users (and their parents). She recommends a stronger role for the established media and for official task forces (at national and European levels) to provide reliable information and guides concerning potential dangers, methods to protect children and steps to create a safer domestic environment (Ward, 2003).

Conclusions: Diverse 'Exclusions' and 'Inclusions'

'Exclusion' from What?: Definitions of the Information Society

As I have indicated so far, our research has revealed a considerable degree of diversity when it comes to users' adoption of, engagement with and attitudes towards new ICTs in the sphere of everyday life in contemporary Europe. These range from 'intensive users' such as mobile professionals (and some young persons to some very infrequent or low-level users).

But this diversity in use may not necessarily or always constitute 'a problem' as so often assumed in current policy discourses. This, as indicated, is especially the case with conceptualisations and analyses of 'the digital divide' focused on singular quantitative differences between different regional or social collectivities.

In part at least, the meaning and appropriate policy responses to such diversities may be related to competing definitions of the role and importance of new ICTs, and in particular to different conceptualisations of that core concept of 'the information society'.

Quite simply, the issues here revolve around a number of basic, if often neglected, questions: what kind of social entity or space, precisely, is this information society that engenders so much attention from researchers and policy makers?; what kind of 'exclusion' is involved when it comes to considerations of 'the information society'?; what is meant, exactly, when researchers write (or talk) of 'an information society', wherein the 'exclusion' or 'inclusion' of particular groups of people is deemed to be a significant political issue?; what kind of 'exclusion' (or 'inclusion') in relation to what kind of social setting?

Significant tensions between competing definitions or conceptualisations of the information society and the role of new ICTs as drivers or markers of socio-economic change, have been identified throughout our empirical work. Even if such differences or tensions are often implicit rather than explicit, especially in the arena of policy discourses and practices, it may be useful to make them explicit in the present context. Quite simply, they have significant implications when it comes to identifying and addressing the spectrum of ideas as well as the actual and potential ambitions, objectives, goals and practices underpinning public policies related to 'the information society'.

Not surprisingly, perhaps, there are multiple examples of different definitions and meanings attached to the notion of 'the information society' since it first began circulating more than 30 years ago now (Preston, 2001). For present purposes, however, it is useful to summarise some of the key differences along a simplified typology (Table 12.1), while acknowledging the limitations of all such simplifying schema, including the tendency to highlighted distinctions, which may often be blurred in practice.

Firstly, we find European policy making and practices usually operate with a definition which privileges or highlights selected new ICTs and their adoption or use as the key or sole indicators of 'the information society'. Implicitly at least, in such definitions, the key policy goal and objective is to maximise access to, and use of, such new ICTs. Secondly, we find alternative policy usages of the term, which focus more on changes in the info-structure (as opposed to ICT infrastructure or 'techno-structure'), including the changing role and character of knowledge or information capabilities. Thirdly, we may note that both of the above-mentioned definitions differ from the more influential and robust academic definitions of the information society idea. The latter focuses attention on changes in both the technical infrastructures and info-structures. But these are complemented by equal if not greater attention to socio-political and even cultural changes.

Table 12.1   Simple Typology of Competing Definitions of the 'Information Society'

Three competing definitions or conceptualisations of the 'information society'	The key 'changes' which define the 'information society' (explicit or implied)	Assumed key benefits for users	Key goals of public policies
Type-1: The dominant policy-related discourses/ definitions (in the late 1990s)	The new technical devices and infrastructures; (production and use/ diffusion of new ICT, especially computers and the internet)	Enhanced 'competitiveness', productivity and socio-economic 'welfare'	Maximise the production and use or diffusion of new ICT. Minimise the 'digital divide'
Type-2: Subsidiary (secondary) policy-related definition	The info-structure (the socio-economic and cultural role of knowledge functions)	Wider diffusion of power (knowledge = power)	Maximise access to formal education and expand the role of 'knowledge work' or functions (not simply ICT related)
Type-3: Seminal or classical academic definitions	(i) ICT infrastructures (ii) Info/knowledge structures/functions (iii) Increased social regulation, planning and meritocracy	A more inter-dependent and egalitarian (just or 'good') society	Expanded role of social planning and reducing role of 'market forces'

Source: Adapted from Preston, (2002)

Furthermore, as indicated in Table 12.1, proponents of all three positions may embrace a wider definition or view of the information society as a distinct new kind of social formation, one that is frequently assumed or deemed to equate with a better (the 'good' or a more just) society. Yet, it should be noted that the precise drivers and direction of such socio-economic transformations might differ in significant respects across these quite distinct definitions of the 'information society'.

Key Conclusions and Implications: ICT and Socio-economic Change

1 will now turn to some of the practical benefits and main implications for policy makers that emerge from such differences in definitions of the 'information society' and from the findings of the EMTEL studies.

One fundamental policy implication is that whilst the widespread use and adoption of new ICT may well be an increasingly necessary condition for instrumental goals (related to economic performance of firms, regions/countries and even individuals) that is not the end of the story by any means – at least in three respects:

(1) The first definition of the information society tends to place a heavy, if not predominant, emphasis on the quantitative distribution of new ICT use. Our studies suggest that this, somewhat inevitably, leads to unwarranted expectations of patterns of diffusion and misleading understandings of the significance and sources of differential use of new ICTs in everyday life in contemporary Europe.

In many cases, the low or non-use of new ICTs may have very little to do with enforced exclusion due to the lack of technical skills or other resources as often assumed in contemporary policy discourse. In other words, such practices may well be perfectly rational and in keeping with users' informed calculus of the optimal disposition of their, always finite, time and money budgets and resources, which in turn will be conditioned by their location in different kinds of professional, socio-economic or cultural settings (within the now expanding 'EU region').

For example, respondents in our studies reported a reflexive awareness of 'pressures' to acquire and use new ICT products and services arising from Type-1 policy discourses. While many users respond to such pressures, others must be viewed as opting out. In some cases at least, this must be treated as a legitimate option rather than being automatically deemed a policy 'problem'. Indeed, 'non-use' should be seen as a valid choice (not least as the people concerned may not have the necessary time, energy, desire or need to engage in such processes).

As noted earlier, one key and pertinent policy implication arising from such research findings concerns the need for measures that are more sophisticated or 'barometers' of ICT use and consumption across different countries or social categories if these are to prove of real relevance to public policies. Any new and more nuanced measures or 'barometers' of ICT use and consumption would have to combine relevant inputs from the kinds of qualitative methods adopted by EMTEL, as well as those derived from quantitative research.

(2) The Type-2 definition of the information society implies a much greater attention to the overall spectrum of knowledge(s) and information structures, not merely those directly related to ICT production and use. Indeed, it furthermore suggests that users' actual and potential (or 'appropriate') engagement with new ICTs may well be highly dependent upon:

(i) The differential distribution of knowledge, capabilities/resources and related 'dispositions'.

(ii) The degree of relevant investment in and policy support for novel and accessible forms of content.

This implies that policy making must take a much less technology-centred approach to the issues of ICT exclusion and inclusion. It means revising the predominant tendency to focus on ICT devices and infrastructures and allocating proportionately more policy attention and material resources towards 'downstream' applications in the areas of digital content and communication services that are relevant to the diverse needs of marginalised groups.

(3) The third definition serves to remind us that everyday social life or the 'good society' (whether in an 'information' or other society) involves much more than instrumental rationality or economic efficiency – and certainly much more than simply 'maximum use of ICT' as the goal and end of social development in Europe or elsewhere. This kind of consideration poses important issues for the appropriate approach to future policy making at the European, national levels and indeed international levels of policy making. Berker highlights the problems associated with information overload or what we might term 'an excess of inclusion' in an information society. Such findings point attention to the issues of a 'communication' as well as an 'information' society and the fact that the work of consumption of such new services is increasingly time-intensive. Indeed, they serve to underline the fact that time is an increasingly scarce and precious resource in the contemporary experience of everyday life.

One further implication is that more nuanced and broader approaches to ICT policy may be more useful, if not desirable in themselves. For example, Hartmann suggests a more integrated approach to ICT and ICT use and youth policies in general as this would be more demand-driven than policy-pushed (this volume).

Another is that more attention may be paid to the prevailing 'images of participation' in the network or information society. Policy approaches may have much to gain by looking beyond ICT access issues or ICT instruction at school or in workplaces. For example, policy makers may need to acknowledge and support, if not indeed learn from, the innovative modes of networking, participation and organisational forms being pioneered in the transnational communication spaces of civil society.

Cammaerts further suggests that policy makers may also benefit from greater attention to non-utilitarian applications of new ICT, including playful/ludic applications and new modes of media literacy, as well as supporting the new forms of communication enabled by ICT networks. This also implies more sustained attention and policy supports for 'content' related issues, both on the input/creative side as well as the capacity to critically engage with new content and new ways of accessing information (Cammaerts and Van Audenhove, 2003).

Note

1 The author gratefully acknowledges the work and contributions of Katie Ward (the EMTEL post-doctoral researcher based in COMTEC) in helping to stimulate and inform the ideas and analysis advanced in this chapter.

References

Bell, D. (1973) *The coming of post-industrial society*, New York: Basic Books.
Berker, T. (2003a) *Boundaries in a space of flows: the case of migrant researchers' use of ICTs*, NTNU, University of Trondheim.
Berker, T. (2003b) *Conceptions of ICTs in European policy* [mimeo, NTNU-STS, Internal EMTEL research note, May 2003].

Cammaerts, B. and L. Van Audenhove (2003) *ICT usage among transnational social movements in the networked society*, ASCoR/TNO, University of Amsterdam.

Castells, M. (1996) *The rise of the network society*, Oxford: Blackwell.

Durieux, D. (2003) *ICT and social inclusion in the everyday life of less-abled people*, LENTIC, University of Liège and ASCoR, University of Amsterdam.

European Commission (1993) *Growth, competitiveness and employment – challenges for entering in the 21st century*, White Paper, colloquially called 'the Délors Report', Luxembourg: European Commission.

European Commission (1994a) *Europe and the global information society: recommendations to the European Council* ['Bangemann Report'] Brussels: CEC.

European Commission (1994b) *Strategy options to strengthen the European programme industry in the context of the audiovisual policy of the European Union*, Green Paper, Brussels: EC [Com(94) 96 final].

European Commission (2000) *Five year assessment report related to the specific programme: user-friendly information society, 1995–99*, Brussels: EC. Accessed from EC website, 13 December 2002.

European Commission (2002a) *Science, technology and innovation key figures, 2002: towards a European research area*, Brussels: EC Research Directorate General.

European Commission (2002b) *eEurope 2005: an information society for all: an action plan to be presented in view of the Seville European Council*, Brussels: CEC COM(2002) 263 Final. 21-22 June, 2002.

European Commission (2002c) *Towards a knowledge-based eEurope: the European Union and the information society*, [EC, DG for Press and Communication; Accessed from 'Europa' website, November 2002].

European Commission (2002d) *eEurope Benchmarking Report*, [COM(2002)62 Final].

Freeman, C. and F. Louça (2001) *As time goes by: from the industrial revolution to the information revolution*, Oxford University Press, Oxford.

Georgiou, M. (2003) *Mapping diasporic media across the EU; addressing cultural exclusion*, Media@lse, London School of Economics and Political Science.

Hartmann, M. (2003) *The web-generation: the (de)construction of users, morals and consumption*, SMIT-VUB, Free University of Brussels.

Heap, N., R. Thomas, G. Einon, R. Mason and H. Mackay (eds) (1995) *Info technology and society: a reader*, London and Thousand Oaks: Sage.

IT Advisory Panel (1982) *Making a business of info*, London: HMSO.

van Langenhove, L. (2001) 'Rethinking the social sciences: initiatives from multilateral organisations', in K. Verlaeckt and V. Virginia Vitorino (eds) *Unity and diversity: the contribution of the social sciences and the humanities to the European Research Area*, EC: DG Research.

Mansell, R (ed.) (1994) *Management of information and communication technologies: emerging patterns of control*, Oxford: Oxford University Press.

Mansell, R. and R. Silverstone (eds) (1996) *Communication by design*, Oxford: Oxford University Press.

Masuda, Y. (1980) *Managing in the information society: releasing synergy Japanese style*, Oxford: Blackwell.

Mills, C.W. (1956) *White collar: the American middle classes*, New York: Oxford University Press.

Preston, P. (2001) *Reshaping communications: technology, information and social change*, London and Thousand Oaks: Sage.

Preston, P. (2002) 'The diverted "coming" of the information society', paper presented at EMTEL2 workshop, Seville, March 2002.

Preston, P. (2003) 'The European Union's ICT policies: neglected social and cultural dimensions', in J. Servaes, (ed.) *The European information society*, Bristol, UK: Intellect Books.

Punie, Y. (2003) *A social and technological view of ambient intelligence in everyday life*, IPTS, Seville.

Silverstone, R. (June, 2003) *Media and technology in the everyday life of European societies*, Draft EMTEL Final Deliverable. [June 2003].

Walby, S. (2001) 'From community to coalition: the politics of recognition as the handmaiden of the politics of equality in an era of globalization' in *Theory, Culture and Society*, 18 (2–3), pp.113–35.

Ward, K. (2003) *An ethnographic study of internet consumption in Ireland: between domesticity and public participation*, COMTEC, Dublin City University.

Webster, F. (1995) *Theories of the information society*, London: Routledge.

Chapter 13

Towards the 'Communication Society'

Roger Silverstone and Knut H. Sørensen

From IT to ICT

In the academic and policy discourses on the emergence of the information society and the characterisation of the technologies that were driving, and would continue to drive it, the presence of the word *communication* has for the most part been overlooked. The society was to be an *information* society and the technologies were *information* technologies; the 'C' in ICT was given short shrift. EMTEL research, as reported in these pages, has, if nothing else, brought the 'C' back into ICT. And insofar as it has done this persuasively, we would argue that it represents a significant shift both in the nature of everyday life in European society and in our understanding of it. It signifies a turn to communication. This, at least, is what we want to argue in this brief conclusion.

When the acronym IT still dominated, the dominant technological image was that of the computer as a machine with awesome abilities to collect and process information. These abilities could also be used for artistic and even entertainment purposes, but the computer was either related to the workplace or seen as belonging to an everyday life space mainly populated by enthusiastic boys and young men: hackers, geeks or nerds.

This is no longer the case. In popular discourses about new electronic technologies, the image of the calculating, information processing and graphical computer seems to be giving way to those of the internet and the mobile phone, technologies that signify communication in its broadest form. In turn, this implies a very different set of practices when such systems and relevance of such systems and artefacts are incorporated into the fabric of everyday life. The widespread use of the add-on letter 'e' – e-shopping, e-education, e-life – is another symbolic representation of this impact. As more and more everyday life activities go e, when people increasingly utilise electronic mediations, this is in a very basic sense related to communication. The contributions in this book underline the importance of this move and how this should change our perception of the information society and its analytic and normative status.

Within this context, EMTEL research has begun to suggest that the information society is too imperial a notion, defining, expecting and valuing a new social order without sufficient sensitivity or understanding of the realities of everyday life within Europe. It also suggests that we might need to rethink the fundamental presuppositions, at the level of practice and of value, which arise when the co-production of technological and social change in these domains is on the agenda.

Access to information is, by itself, a necessary but an insufficient condition for participation in late modern societies, and European society is no exception.

Communication and connection, which are not of course necessarily the same thing, are, as Cees Hamelink (2002) has noted, curiously missing from the core rhetoric of the information society debates. EMTEL research suggests that this can no longer be sustained if we are both to understand and better manage the socio-technical changes underway in Europe as elsewhere in the world today. So, what is at stake when we inquire into this 'communication turn'?

Perspectives on the Information Society

There is a large and still growing literature that in quite diverse ways tries to account for the socio-technical changes that are occurring in relation to ICT, under the headline of the information society. One strand of research has been concerned with the transcendence of the previously dominant industrial culture of Western societies, focusing on changes in work and employment and increasing levels of education. The emerging view of a post-industrial society, argued quite early by Daniel Bell (1973), has been taken further by invoking the character of the knowledge worker (see, for example, Kumar, 1995). From this point of view, the main feature of new ICTs is their ability to replace repetitive, manual labour in the industrial and the service sectors by machinery. In addition, new ICTs provide the kind of supportive technological infrastructure needed by a growing number of what Peter F. Drucker (1993) has called knowledge workers.

While this approach provides strategic insights into the co-production of a new set of technologies, a new economy and a new working life, the emphasis has remained on the information-processing capabilities of computers, their uncanny capacity to calculate and control. However, there are other strands within the information society discourse that for a long period of time have been concerned with the potential of computers to facilitate human communication and the implications of trying to realise such features, in particular related to everyday life (for example, McLuhan, 1964; Toffler, 1970).

The communication aspects of the information society have been analysed in quite diverse ways, the scope of which may be illustrated by reference to the following quite different catchwords that may be observed in this discourse:

- New media
- Network
- Community
- Anarchy

As new media, ICTs may be considered as technologies of mediation where communication needs to be understood as an economic, political, social and material contingency (Liewrouw and Livingstone, 2002). ICT-mediated communication, from this perspective, invites a focus on issues related to interactivity, access, and the potentially ubiquitous character of such communication.

Thinking in terms of networks provides a different emphasis. The network as a concept has been invoked particularly forcefully by Castells (1996, 2001) in his argument that computer-related technologies facilitate a process of globalisation where the importance of place is reduced by the power of ICT-mediated networks. These networks gain economic and political significance through their ability to access and manage information. Communication both glues and fuels the network, but in an instrumental context where it is evaluated through its capacity to produce economic and political results.

This is in contrast to the mainly expressive character of so-called online or virtual communities that has been highlighted in many studies (for example, Rheingold, 1993; Turkle, 1996; Jones, 1998; Baym, 2000; Howard and Jones, 2004). These communities, like Castells' networks, emerge from interactive, ICT-mediated communication, but they tend to have a more singular social purpose in the sense that communication seems to become an end in itself. Discussion lists, e-rooms, for example, may start from stated political aims, but frequently become more social in their orientation and functioning.

The internet has also been characterised as anarchistic, to emphasise the freedom of speech, communal property and as a weak structure of governance claimed by many of the pioneers that helped to develop this medium (Grossman, 2001). The present controversy related to the Open Source movement suggests that some such anarchist features of online communication provide a productive environment for social as well as technological development (Castells, 2001; Himanen, 2001).

The diversity of ideas related to catchwords such as new media, networks, communities, and online anarchy suggests the need to analyse 'the communication turn' in an extensive way, emphasising that communication is an inclusive concept that covers a diversity of social phenomena. They also allow us to make the point about the fundamental and constitutive significance of human communication at the core of social life. This is to suggest, then, that a movement towards a communication society, both conceptually and empirically, is primarily meaningful in a context of other, similar scenarios like 'information society', 'post-industrial society' or 'knowledge society'. The EMTEL research reported in this volume provides an opportunity to reflect particularly on technologically mediated communication in relation to everyday life. Arguably, this focus on everyday life generates a view of ongoing change that is overlapping with, but also supersedes, those provided through the lenses of 'new media', 'network', 'community' and 'anarchy'. In particular, it allows us to observe some of the normative work that is involved in 'the communication turn'.

This is evident from Thomas Berker's contribution in Chapter 8. His study of migrant knowledge workers was intended as a study of a group of people assumed to be at the front end in the use of ICT, due to their position as migrants as well as knowledge workers. We can observe how Berker's informants build networks, participate in communities and utilise ICTs as new media. However, we can also see how they become highly dependent on ICT-mediated access to various forms of communication in their everyday life, professionally and socially, in public as well as private. In fact, this dependence is seemingly reinforced by the ubiquitous character of new communication technologies like the internet and the mobile phone. Consequently, communication is always an option in the sense that it is becoming increasingly possible to engage in mediated contact with other people everywhere and at all times. To Berker's informants, this poses a difficult challenge. How to manage such opportunities?

This challenge needs to be understood from the fact that interactivity and engagement with other people, mediated or non-mediated, holds a seductive power that for most people is much stronger than the one related to the metaphors emerging from the information society – 'gathering', 'searching' or 'surfing'. From this point of view, a shift from thinking in terms of an information society to a communication society provides a clue to understanding why ownership and use of information *and* communication technologies has become so much more widespread and popular than that of information technology only. Moreover, it strongly suggests that we need to explore further the social and moral foundation of such communication, since 'the communication turn' seems to involve changes that cannot be considered to be unequivocal.

Access, Presence or Performance?

One set of moral concerns is related to the importance given to the risk of an emerging digital divide and the related exclusion processes in the EU discourse on the information society. This discourse defines as a main challenge the development of policies that support inclusion and thus facilitate citizenship in this emerging society of technological interaction. How, it asks, is it possible to achieve membership in the information society for everyone?

In their chapter, Kees Brants and Valerie Frissen remind us that the set of concerns that underlies the concept of the digital divide are diverse. Moreover, the concept itself is problematic, analytically as well as politically. An important weakness, they argue, is the singular focus on one aspect of inclusion and exclusion, namely access to ICTs. Another problem that they identify is the strong tendency in the policy discourses to overlook the highly ambiguous nature of inclusion and exclusion processes, for example the possibility that access to ICT may facilitate the production of exclusive communities.

Still, the digital divide discourse signifies an important moral concern that lack of access to ICT may mean that one becomes marginalised in a society where such access is increasingly vital to participation in many kinds of economic, political and social activities. Probably, this concern is fuelled by a widespread belief that IT, as well as ICT, holds considerable potential as an equalising power, manifesting technological features that could help transcend social inequalities be they regional, based on gender or ethnic differences, or on physical abilities. Thus, a digital divide would be a two-edged problem; it would reinforce existing inequalities while stifling ICT's potential to reduce unwanted differences.

However, as Wyatt et al. (2002) have pointed out, there are good reasons why people may choose not to use ICT. To surf the internet to gather information may not be that interesting in the long run. The information society discourse, with its emphasis on economic growth and the instrumental usefulness of information, may, as Maren Hartmann shows in her chapter, be recognised as a norm and an expectation that one should use ICTs. Yet at the same time it generates its own resistance, and may, at the same time, make the use of ICTs less attractive.

Statistical measures show that ownership of mobile phones, access to computers and access to the internet have grown particularly rapidly during the last five to six years (see, for example, Stewart, 2002). Phenomena like the widespread use of SMS, chatting and email suggest strongly that it is the possibilities related to new or enhanced abilities to communicate that form the main attraction of ICT in everyday life for most people. As suggested in the previous section, the communication turn may provide a remedy for the digital divide worry embodied in the scenario of the information society. This does not mean to suggest that the social inequalities related to access and use of ICT will disappear, but current developments suggest that they at least are becoming less pronounced. Recent Norwegian research suggests strongly that the communication turn has been instrumental in making many more girls and women enthusiastically engage with computers, and with ICT more generally (Nordli, 2003; Gansmo, 2004).

It is of course an open question whether this increased engagement in various forms of communication represents progress or not. Many promises have been made on behalf of ICT development, like improved democracy, the reduced importance of physical disabilities, or time-space compression, which will do away with the significance of physical location. Such promises are at the backbone of what Mosco (2004) with reference to Nye (1994) calls the 'digital sublime'. ICT is a sublime set of technologies because it expresses a mythology, a belief in what could take place, rather than realised achievements. From this perspective, when we make general references to the information society or the communication society, we invoke such an understanding of ICT as sublime, as a potentially guiding image of social and technological designs.

The EMTEL research reported in this book has looked critically into some of the promises made on behalf of ICT, which in turn may qualify the argument of an emerging communication society. Bart Cammaerts (Chapter 4) has studied the use of ICTs by transnational social movements, which is one way to explore how the presumed democratic potential of this technology has been practised. The analysis focuses on three forms of political communication, related to the efforts of transnational social movements to organise, mobilise and debate. The findings are ambiguous. On the one hand, Cammaerts shows that the use of ICT facilitates the communication efforts of these movements in a substantial way, helping to link local, national and transnational conversations. On the other hand, the achievements are mainly successful in the Western context. The communication turn is embedded in a world system of unequal distribution of access and competence, where one's country of residence is quite decisive.

Georgiou's investigation of European diasporic media cultures in Chapter 3 finds, in a way similar to Cammaerts, that both old and new media technologies facilitate the interweaving of the local, the national and the transnational arenas. This may destabilise mainstream mediascapes that otherwise tend to exclude minorities. Diasporic media, says Georgiou, provide more space for tense and intense dialogue across European cultural spaces. Again, this may be regarded as a positive achievement with regard to the democratic potential of ICT-mediated communication, even if the achievement runs the risk of (re)creating conflicting cultural differences that work in an exclusionary fashion. As Georgiou reminds us, ICT-mediated communication should be conceived of as an area of contest and conflict, not just as a space for harmony and cosiness. In such ways, everyday life is intersected by communication efforts that may not be appreciated by everyone.

In a way, this contrasts with the findings reported by Katie Ward in Chapter 7, looking into the way households in small, Irish seaside towns make use of the internet. While the communication activities transcend the physical boundaries of the town, the content remains solidly entrenched in very local, very personal social spaces. This results from the way online and offline communication is mixed, to the extent that online and offline conversations become seamless continuations of each other. People communicate through a manifold of different channels, but in a way that renders their communication unremitting. The idea of a life on the screen, of autonomous virtual existences, so eloquently proposed by Turkle (1996), is shown to be sublime, a beautiful but erroneous mirage. The reality of communication is basically mundane; it is performed in relation to place rather than space.

Moral Limits to Ambient Communication? The Normative Protection of Everyday Life

One of the emerging digital sublimes of the EU is the idea of ambient intelligence, of access to advanced ICT everywhere and at any time. Of course, ambient intelligence is equivalent to ambient communication with other people as well as with assumed caring computers. As Yves Punie shows in Chapter 10, we are promised a computer-supported life as well as perpetual communication. Whether this is a dream or a nightmare is definitely an issue.

Punie argues that ambient intelligence may be considered a peril to everyday life because it represents an invasion of private spaces and threatens the protection of privacy. However, ambient communication also raises additional concerns about the options that will be provided for the management of presence and absence, availability and non-availability. In this way, the potential fear of ubiquitous accessibility involves and proposes an important limitation to the communication society. In a way, this suggests that we may become too included as users of ICT. Thus, regulation of some sort is needed.

The ambiguity of the situation may be emphasised through reference to Dorothée Durieux's contribution in Chapter 5. Her findings clearly indicate that the potential of ICT to integrate less-abled people into working life and everyday life communication has not in any full or consistent way been realised. This suggests that it might be preferable to support more initiatives to ease access to technologies that mediate communication, regardless of competence and abilities. Ambient intelligence could be a response to such demands. However, as Durieux shows, the difficulties are rather more social than technological. The ambiguity juxtaposed in the fear of too many as well as too few possibilities of mediated communication cannot be resolved by technology alone.

Technologically mediated communication is, as previously noted, critical to the performance of everyday life. The development and diffusion of ICT across Europe has meant that human interaction in mediated form has been facilitated in a remarkable way. Not everybody has such technologies at their fingertips, and the digital divide discourse serves as a reminder of the – primarily social – challenges that are involved in bridging such gaps. However, in the light of the initiatives presented by Punie, we also need to emphasise the obvious point that everyday life cannot be about communication only. In addition to issues related to the protection of privacy and the individuals' rights to be offline, we face the banal problem that time is limited.

The latter predicament is made clear by Thomas Berker when he describes how the migrant knowledge workers – like any group of heavy users of ICT – need to limit the time spent on communication. We may inhabit the communication society, but we are also supposed to be citizens of the information society, the knowledge society, and so on. Thus, there is an emerging moral agenda that is expressed through the normative work done by Berker's informants when they invent rules and routines to help themselves to limit their use of their mobile phone or the internet. What emerges are a set of autochthonous practices designed to manage and regulate the social space which otherwise would be overrun by these technologies, and to justify those defences and boundaries by a code, a set of private rules and values, that in turn legitimate both their own practice and allow them to reflect, sometimes critically, on the practices of others.

Maren Hartmann (Chapter 9) encountered a similar moral regulation of the use of ICT among young Belgians. They knew that they should use ICTs, but they also manifested awareness that they should not use these technologies too much. Thus, both Hartmann and Berker observed an established morality of moderation with regard to the use of ICT and the engagement in ICT-mediated communication. What was considered to be the healthy middle-road varied, but there is no doubt that the extent of communication is the site and indeed source of moral regulation in the communication society. Communication may be perpetual, but not round-the-clock!

The End of Computing?

As suggested previously, we may consider the computer as the root technology of the traditional information society discourse. The well-known promises of the information society emerging from this discourse are, as we also noted, based on the ever-growing capacity of computers to calculate and otherwise process more and more information from increasingly diverse sources. Moreover, they are basically addressing issues of economic growth and supposedly increased welfare. But, as suggested by EMTEL research, the computer's discursive power to define the agenda of technological development and diffusion seems to be vulnerable, perhaps even fading. Is the communication turn of the information society, which we have emphasised, also an indication of the end of computing?

The turn of the millennium appears to have brought forward many 'end-of' stories: the end of history, the end of science, or the end of politics. To claim the end of computing obviously runs the risk of being accused of running this sort of bandwagon. But what could such an assertion mean?

Already, the scenarios related to ambient intelligence seem to transcend the understanding of computers and computing as defining ingredients of the information society. The computer disappears: it shifts from a distillation of technology, boxed and machined, to a dispersed functionality, both wired and wireless. If ambient intelligence holds any attraction, it is because it represents access to diverse, but quite concrete services and options. This is also what we are told by the informants in Berker's, Hartmann's and Ward's research. They do not tell us about generic use of computers; nor do they invoke the concept of computing to describe their activities with the computer. Instead, they tell about reading newspapers on the net, playing computer games, sending emails, chatting, and so on.

Clearly, the computer has become a 'natural' part of everyday life, more or less in line with TV, radio, washing machines and toasters. This suggests that the computer has been trivialised (Weingart, 1989) to the extent that its presence and usefulness is taken for granted. To use it is seen no longer to require special skills or insights into the way computers work. Such competence is increasingly perceived to be basic to the performance of everyday life activities. Everyone is supposed to know how to turn on and tune into the socio-technical activities that ICT offers.

Instead, what is required is the possession of particular skills related to particular tasks that are performed with computers as a backstage ingredient, not least the kind of social competence needed to perform all the different kinds of communication people do in everyday life, mediated and non-mediated. In this sense, access is becoming less interesting as a key to citizenship in the information society. The pertinent issue is increasingly knowledge and competence. And above all, the issue is that of literacy.

Policy makers in the EU, and elsewhere, perhaps in acknowledging the same limitations, have seen that what is at stake in their benevolent move into social engineering is not so much an information society as a *knowledge society*, for knowledge is meaningful information: information that can be applied and used, and which mobilises in creative ways the intellectual and experiential products of contemporary culture and society for the benefit, at least in principle, of all. Furthermore it does this in inclusive rather than exclusive ways. Knowledge is participative. And indeed access to knowledge is not so much a matter of access to technology as access to the skills and cultural resources which allow it to be used constructively. As we have just suggested, a key term and a key ambition at the heart of the knowledge society needs to be literacy: the skills and capabilities which all citizens will need fully to participate in it, and fully to take advantage of the resources released by the internet, mobile telephony and broadband delivery. Yet it is not always fully recognised and operationalised, since for the most part participation still seems to mean, predominantly, access, and the information society is defined, even in the most recent public pronouncements, principally as a market for new technologies (EC, 2002).

Our research suggests that there may be yet another step to be taken. Such a step follows from our observations of the centrality of multiple mobilities in the everyday life of the citizens of Europe, and the consequent centrality of media and technologies of communication to those who are, individually and collectively, geographically and socially, culturally and psychologically, materially and virtually, on the move.

Such an observation reinforces the role of communication, and the need to take communication seriously. It is a truism to suggest that society is not possible without communication, and that communication must, morally and sociologically, precede knowledge which in turn presumes information. Without the capacity to communicate, neither knowledge nor information have much meaning. In the sphere of the everyday, and in the everyday lives of individuals within Europe, the drivers of the so-called information society have, in fact, consistently been those addressing the need for, and management of, communication rather more than the need for information. This is evidenced above all in our research in the cases of minorities, the young and the cosmopolitan in their use of the mobile phone, satellite television and email. But it is also a significant dimension of the internet culture of the otherwise sedentary population of the town in Ireland and of the networking possibilities of online political activism.

To cope with the challenges that face us in the wake of continued technological developments, be they framed in the context of the information society or the knowledge society, we need to understand better the social and moral underpinnings of the performances implied in this sort of techno-cultural imagery. Without such insights, we may come to misunderstand the claimed emergence of the end of computing and the trivialisation of the now widely diffused information and communication technologies, claimed to belong to the information society. Of course, the end of computing does not mean that computers have become unimportant. Rather, it heralds their final breakthrough as 'natural' constituents of everyday life. However, since everyday life is a moral order where diverse norms are juggled into liveable practices, this breakthrough should not be interpreted as an invitation to just increase the influx of new ICTs. Rather, the normative regulation that both facilitates and limits the appropriation and use of ICTs suggests that techno-cultural imageries should be more restrained.

References

Baym, N.K. (2000) *Tune in, log on. Soaps, fandom, and online community*, Thousand Oaks, CA: Sage.

Bell, D. (1973) *The coming of post-industrial society*, New York: Basic Books.

Castells, M. (1996) *The rise of the network society*, Oxford: Blackwell.

Castells, M. (2001) *The internet galaxy. Reflections on the internet, business and society*, Oxford: Oxford University Press.

Drucker, P.F. (1993) *Post-capitalist society*, Oxford: Butterworth-Heinemann.

European Commission (2002) *Towards a knowledge-based Europe: the European Union and the information society*, Europa.eu.int/information_society/newsroom/documents/catalogue-en.pdf (downloaded 5/08/03).

Gansmo, H.J. (2004) *Towards a happy ending for girls and computing*, PhD dissertation, report 67, Trondheim, NTNU: Department of Interdisciplinary Studies of Culture.

Grossman, W.M. (2001) *From anarchy to power. The net comes of age*, New York: New York University Press.

Hamelink, C. (2002) *Keynote at the opening session of the civil society meeting at the Prepcom 1 for the World Summit on the Information Society*, July 1 2002, Geneva, https://ss.cpsr.org/pipemail/wsis-prep/2002-July/00199.html (downloaded 5/08/03).

Himanen, P. (2001) *The hacker ethic and the spirit of the information age*, London: Secker & Warburg.

Howard, P.N. and S. Jones (eds) (2004) *Society online. The internet in context*, Thousand Oaks, CA: Sage.

Jones, S.G. (ed.) (1998) *Cybersociety 2.0. Revisiting computer-mediated communication and community*, Thousand Oaks, CA: Sage.

Kumar, K. (1995) *From post-industrial to post-modern society. New theories of the contemporary world*, Oxford: Blackwell.

Liewrouw, L.A. and S. Livingstone (2002) 'Introduction. The Social Shaping and Consequences of ICTs', in L.A. Liewrouw and S. Livingstone (eds), *Handbook of new media*, London: Sage.

McLuhan, M. (1964) *Understanding media: the extensions of man*, London: Routledge & Kegan Paul.

Mosco, V. (2004) *The digital sublime. Myth, power and cyberspace*, Cambridge, MA: The MIT Press.

Nordli, H. (2003) *The net is not enough. Searching for the female hacker*, PhD dissertation, report 61, Trondheim, NTNU: Department of Interdisciplinary Studies of Culture.

Nye, D. (1994) *American technological sublime*, Cambridge, MA: The MIT Press.

Rheingold, H. (1993) *The virtual community. Homesteading on the electronic frontier*, Reading, MA: Addison-Wesley.

Stewart, J. (2002) 'Information society, the internet and gender. A summary of pan-European statistical data', in K.H. Sørensen and J. Stewart (eds) *Digital divides and inclusion measures. a review of literature and statistical trends on gender and ICT*, report 59, Trondheim, NTNU: Department of Interdisciplinary Studies of Culture, pp.37–56.

Toffler, A. (1970) *Future shock*, London: Pan.

Turkle, S. (1996) *Life on the screen: identity in the age of the internet*, New York: Simon & Schuster.

Weingart, P. (1989) 'Grosstechnische systeme – ein paradigma der verknüpfung von technikentwicklung und sozialem wandel', in P. Weingart (ed.) *Technik als sozialer prozess*, Franfurt aM: Suhrkamp.

Wyatt, S. et al. (2002) 'They came, they surfed, they went back to the beach: conceptualizing use and non-use of the internet', in S. Woolgar (ed.) *Virtual society? Technology, cyberbole, reality*, Oxford: Oxford University Press.

Glossary

Prepared by Anita Howarth

Ambient intelligence (AmI) is a vision of the future information society where intelligent interfaces enable people and devices to interact with each other and with the environment. Technology operates in the background while computing capabilities are everywhere, connected and always available. This intelligent environment is aware of the specific characteristics of human presence and preferences, takes care of needs and is capable of responding intelligently to spoken or gestured indications of desire. It can even engage in intelligent dialogue. Different terms have been used to reflect this vision including ubiquitous computing, pervasive computing, disappearing computing, proactive computing, sentient computing, affective computing, wearable computing and ambient intelligence. The differences between these terms imply a different focus and a geographical preference. So, the term 'AmI' is more common in Europe and 'ubiquitous computing' more common in the US and Japan. What is specific to AmI is that it is based on the convergence and seamless inter-operability between three key technologies: ubiquitous computing, ubiquitous communication and intelligent user-friendly interfaces. Other projects might focus, for instance, on just one or two key technology domains.

Access is rarely well defined in debates on the 'digital divide'. Sometimes it is used to refer to availability or opportunity, but such physical access does not necessarily mean that people feel able to make use of these opportunities. It may be more useful to describe 'access' in terms of a hierarchy that reflects connectivity, capability and distribution of access.

Appropriation is concerned with the dialectical relationship between technological and social change as well as the way technologies and cultures change in the process. The relationship is essentially a struggle over control and over capacity.

Diasporic has been used in preference to *diaspora* for two main reasons. Firstly, the latter implies long settlement in the host country, but this does not apply to many of the recent migrations. Secondly, the concept of *diasporic* rather than *diaspora* challenges the assumption that the populations in question are by definition and forever attached to a homeland and to a certain identity. The *diasporic condition* has been defined here as transnationality, a sense of ethnic commonality, myth and memory of a common original homeland as well as experiences of exclusion because of ethnicity. It also implies the possibility of change.

The digital divide is heavily critiqued in this book as theoretically vague and ambiguous, defined and operationalised in a multiplicity of ways. These include: (i) a global divide (between industrialised and developing societies in terms of internet access) (ii) a social divide (between the information rich and poor in each nation; as well as referring to the social exclusion mechanisms of individuals) (iii) a democratic divide (those who do and those who do not use the digital resources to access and participate in public life as well as the political exclusion of NGOs (iv) an economic divide (between large enterprises that experience inclusion and smaller enterprises that experience exclusion of small enterprises; as well as between individuals who have the basic skills and access and those who do not).

Domestication describes and analyses the capacity of families, individuals and households, as well as other institutions, to make new technologies (and services) their own, to integrate them into their everyday lives. Domestication is not necessarily harmonious, linear or complete. Rather, it is perceived as a process born of, and producing, conflict where the outcomes are heterogeneous and sometimes irresolvable. It is also noted that needs and changes in the household, through ageing, break-up or children leaving the home, have implications for the domestication process. Domestication is presented as a struggle between the user and technology, where the user aims to tame, gain control, shape or ascribe meaning to the artefact.

Etically-derived categories emerge from outside the research domain, as opposed to those which are called *emic*, and which derive from the practices and values of those being studied, that is from the subjects of the research.

Exclusion in ICT terms is often discussed in one-dimensional ways, that is, participation in economic life. But it can take place in many other dimensions of everyday life as well: the political, cultural, social as well as the economic. And inequality and exclusion can also take place in other areas like civic engagement and political rights such as voting; elections to a representative function or to demonstrate cultural citizenship; or the right to express and enhance one's own identity; as well as ordinary processes that take place in everyday life, social welfare and well-being. Some studies stress the capabilities that are needed fully to function in society. Others also refer to cultural qualities, mutual acceptance and well-being as factors that correlate with social inclusion and social exclusion. This involves not so much lack of food, money or work, but rather a deprivation of value, meaning and self-respect, which leads to stigmatisation impeding full social acceptance.

Mobilities are plural and they manifest themselves at many levels. These include: (i) movement of populations in the form of migrations (geographical mobilities) (ii) the movement of individuals and groups of individuals between public and private spaces, between roles and identities, and between the spheres of work and leisure (social mobilities) (iii) between online and offline communication and interaction, and between personal and social spaces (technological and cultural mobilities) (iv) between individual and collective identities, and in the instabilities of belonging and identification (cultural mobilities).

Index